SIGN of the CROSS

A MYSTERY

ANNE EMERY

ECW Press

Published by ECW PRESS
2120 Queen Street East, Suite 200, Toronto, Ontario, Canada M4E 1E2
416.694.3348 / info@ecwpress.com

LIBRARY AND ARCHIVES CANADA CATALOGUING IN PUBLICATION

Emery, Anne
Sign of the cross : a mystery / Anne Emery.

ISBN 978-1-55022-819-9

I. Title.

PS8609.M47S53 2008   C813'.6   C2007-906559-7

Cover and Text Design: Tania Craan
Cover Image: Chris Amaral/Nonstock/Firstlight
Typesetting: Mary Bowness
Production: Rachel Brooks
Printing: Victor Graphics   2   3   4   5

This book is set in AGaramond.

The publication of *Sign of the Cross* has been generously
supported by the Ontario Arts Council; by the OMDC Book Fund,
an initiative of the Ontario Media Development Corporation; by the Canada Council for the
Arts, which last year invested $20.1 million in writing and publishing throughout Canada; and by
the Government of Canada through the Book Publishing Industry Development Program (BPIDP).

 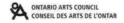

PRINTED AND BOUND IN THE UNITED STATES

ECW PRESS
ecwpress.com

for J and P

Acknowledgements

I would like to thank the following people for their invaluable assistance: Joe A. Cameron and Patrick Duncan, Q.C., for their expertise in criminal law; Dr. Laurette Geldenhuys for the details only a pathologist can provide; Heather MacDonald for advice on forensics; Kevin Robins and Katie Cottreau-Robins for their knowledge of Halifax history and architecture; my troika of first readers: Rhea McGarva, Helen MacDonnell, and Joan Butcher; Jane Buss and the Writers' Federation of Nova Scotia; my editors, Edna Barker and Gil Adamson; and, for many reasons, PJEC.

All characters in the story are fictional. Most locations are real; a few are made up. Any liberties taken in the interests of fiction, or errors committed, are mine alone.

I am grateful for permission to reprint extracts from the following:

Part One

Chapter 1

He looked into her eyes when she stopped him to ask
If he wanted to dance; he had a face like a mask.
Somebody said from the bible he'd quote.
There was dust on the man in the long black coat.
— Bob Dylan, "The Man in the Long Black Coat"

I

Gargoyles. I hardly notice them anymore. Gargoyles are a part of your life when you've spent your entire career in the criminal courts. The creatures you see leering out at you from the Halifax Courthouse on Spring Garden Road are technically known as grotesques, fang-baring faces that were set in stone when the building was constructed in 1863. A plaque on the building describes the "vermiculated" stonework; it looks as if worms tunnelled through it. I'm not surprised.

Thursday, March 1, 1990 was a typical day at the courthouse. I had managed to get my client off unexpectedly at the conclusion of a three-day trial on charges of assault, extortion and uttering threats against his old girlfriend's new boyfriend. His gratitude lay unspoken between us. He swaggered from the building, trailed by three teenage girls in leggings and stiletto heels.

"Congratulations on the acquittal, Monty!" I turned at the sound of a voice as I was leaving the courthouse and saw our articled clerk coming out behind me. Petite, sharp-faced and keen, Robin Reid wore a lawyerly black suit that looked too big on her. I nodded absently in response. "Though I have to say," she went on, "I didn't think much of the judge's remarks about our client. 'Well, Mr. Brophy, you're free to go. The system worked. If I see you in my courtroom again you may not find the system so benign.' What kind of attitude is that to take to a man he just declared not guilty?"

"It's the attitude of a judge who knows I outlawyered the prosecution and knows he'd be overturned on appeal if he convicted my client."

Robin and I left the courthouse and crossed Spring Garden Road to the city library, where someone had built a snow fort around the statue of a striding, heavily masculine Winston Churchill. I was on a hopeless quest for a children's book with a character named Normie. My wife and I, in the afterglow of a magnificent performance of *Norma* at La Scala, had named our baby Norma after the noble druid at the centre of the opera. With sober second thought, neither of us liked the name for anyone under forty. The best we could do was "Normie" after that. Now seven and wondering why she wasn't named Megan like everybody else, she had looked askance at my brave assertion that there were lots of Normies in the world. She issued a demand: "Find me a book with somebody named Normie in it. It can be an animal; it can even be a bug. But," she warned darkly, "it better not be a boy!" I was met with a sympathetic shake of the head yet again at the children's desk.

As we left the library, Robin returned to the acquittal of our client, Corey Brophy. "But Corey didn't do it, Monty! You demolished the Crown witnesses on cross-examination; their stories fell apart."

I looked at her with surprise. "Of course he did it. You haven't seen the file and you've never met the client. But that's over and done. Now, tomorrow we have — Well! I spoke too soon. Looks as if you're going to meet Corey after all."

Robin turned to follow my gaze across the street and saw my newly released client being manhandled by two police officers in the driveway of the courthouse. He twisted around and caught sight of me. "Are you just going to stand there, Collins? You're my lawyer, for fuck's sake. Get over here!"

I sighed and crossed the street. Short, skinny, and scabious with a patchy goatee, Corey was the picture of belligerence.

"What's going on, Frank?" I asked one of the cops.

"Mr. Brophy is under arrest for assaulting his ex-girlfriend."

"Corey, give me a call after you're processed," I told him. "In the meantime, keep your mouth shut. No statements." The other cop bundled him into the cruiser for the trip to the station.

"This must be a record for you, Monty," Frank remarked. "Your client reoffending —"

"Allegedly reoffending!"

"— What is it, twenty-five minutes after he was released?"

I didn't tell him my record was a guy reoffending twenty-five *seconds* after his release; he had been overheard threatening one of the witnesses before he even left the courtroom.

I glanced at Robin as we started back to the office, and was about to speak when she said: "You've got that 'Robin, you're such a bleeding heart' expression on your face again. You think all our clients are guilty."

"And yet I defend them. Year after year after year." I looked into her eyes. "So come on now. Who's the bleeding heart?"

Yes, criminal practice had its aggravations. But at least with the usual run of petty criminals, I could forget their existence as soon as I was out of sight of the gargoyles. In the kind of case I dealt with, there was no mystery involved; you knew all too well what went on at the crime scene. You knew your client was there. Your only hope was that he had kept his mouth shut when the police showed up. Soon, although I didn't know it yet, I would be involved in a case I would not be able to shake when I left the building. Or even when I closed my eyes to sleep. For the first time in my career I would be flying blind, unable to fathom what was behind the brutal murder of a young woman whose body had been carved with a religious sign and dumped beneath a bridge. And the client? My mother had a saying: "Be careful what you wish for." For years — decades! — I had been longing for a client a cut above the poor, uneducated, hopeless, heedless, unstable individuals I usually represented. A client more like . . . more like *me*. Well, I was about to have one. Be careful what you wish for.

The next day my firm's senior partner, Rowan Stratton, slipped me an envelope containing newspaper clippings about the murder and said we'd speak about it on the weekend.

The victim was Leeza Rae and she was twenty years old when she was killed. On February fifteenth, a Department of Public Works crew spotted her body on scrubby, rocky ground beside a service road under the A. Murray MacKay Bridge, still known, twenty years after its construction, as the "new bridge." It is one of two bridges joining the cities of Halifax and Dartmouth, Nova Scotia. The crew radioed the information to the Halifax Police Department just after three in the afternoon. Leeza was wearing an oversize black plastic raincoat with a hood. This had not been her attire when she was last seen alive, leaving a dance at St. Bernadette's Youth Centre in downtown Halifax. News stories gave the cause of death as a fractured skull, believed to have been caused by a heavy, blunt instrument. The police stated that the victim had not been killed in the spot where she was found; the body had been dumped there after death. One report quoted an unnamed source as saying the body had been "tampered with."

I skimmed the clippings and put them aside. Rowan had asked me not to discuss the murder with anyone until we spoke. Why the secrecy, I wondered.

II

Saturday morning was bright and crisp, a beautiful day for a family outing. I picked up the phone.

"What?" came her answer.

"Well, I see today is starting off like all your other days."

"And I see you are still in need of a remedial class in, one, when to call and, two, when not to call. It is eight-thirty in the morning. We are, or were, sleeping in today because the children don't have school. It's Saturday. Far be it from me to encourage mindless consumerism, but I think it's time to acknowledge the invention of an item known as the fridge magnet. I have invested in four of those for you and have utilized them to stick a calendar on your refrigerator. That calendar, had you consulted it, would have told you that this is the weekend, and you might then have surmised that we would be catching up on our sleep."

"For once I have to agree with you. You should catch up on your sleep. What do you do, by the way? Keep your tongue in a jar of acid beside your bed at night?"

"Why not? It would be more attractive than what I used to see when I opened my eyes in the morning."

"All right, all right, enough pillow talk. I was calling to see whether the kids might like to come with me this afternoon for a drive."

"They're with me this afternoon. Now let me go so I can get back to sleep and forget about this interruption." Click.

That of course was my wife. A failed social worker. Think for a moment about social workers. My perception of them is that they tend to be very accepting of human error, very non-judgmental, as they say. My wife, Maura MacNeil, had been in her last year of the Bachelor of Social Work program when it was decided that her "particular set of skills and abilities could be best directed to other challenges." That was one version of events. Maura's version was more succinct: "They turfed me out." She had directed her abilities to the law and was now a professor, teaching poverty law. Scourge of the right, she was hardly more popular with the left, owing to her stubborn refusal to accommodate herself to the emerging sensitivities of the nineties. Politically correct she would never be. She and I had been living apart for years.

So. No children for me today. I wrestled briefly with the temptation to go back to sleep myself, then spend the afternoon with cronies in the Midtown Tavern. Instead, I passed the day doing household chores that were months overdue.

That evening found me in the library of Rowan and Sylvia Stratton, who lived in an elegant house overlooking the sparkling waters of Halifax's Northwest Arm. The Strattons had come to Halifax from England at the end of World War II. My brother Stephen had married their daughter Janet. I considered Rowan an in-law once removed, especially since I was *persona non grata* with my own father-in-law. We had just had dinner, and Rowan was going to join me in the library. While I waited, I had another look at the news clippings about the murder.

Leeza Rae had grown up in a low-income suburb of Halifax. Her mother was in her teens when she gave birth to Leeza, and the father did not stick around. Leeza had had two stepfathers, and a succession of other men had drifted in and out of her mother's life. There were half-brothers and stepsisters on, the scene from time to time. Leeza had not done well academically and had been suspended from high school on a couple of occasions. She stopped attending in grade eleven. Leeza spent all her free time, which was considerable, hanging out at various malls and convenience stores with people of similar background. She had a minor criminal record and a sporadic history of low-paying employment. At the time of her death she was working part-time at the St. Bernadette's Youth Centre.

In 1988, Leeza's boyfriend, Vic Stillman, was sentenced to seven years' imprisonment for his part in the gang rape of a fifteen-year-old girl. He was in Dorchester Penitentiary when Leeza was killed. Two other boys had been incarcerated but had been released before the murder. A source close to the investigation was quoted as saying there was no known connection between the murder and the rape. Police were following several leads and were optimistic about making an arrest in the near future.

Rowan came in and made a stop at the sideboard to pour us each a glass of scotch, which he said went into the cask around the time I was admitted to the bar. He sank into a green leather club chair and pushed his greying blonde hair off his forehead. Rowan had the rosy complexion I often associate, probably wrongly, with the English. It gave him a deceptive air of benign goodwill. He got right to the point.

"I told you I had a rather delicate matter to discuss with you, Monty. Our partners can remain in the dark. For now, at least." He took a sip of his drink. "You have seen the press cuttings?"

"Yes. They haven't picked anybody up for it yet, have they?"

"No." Rowan was gazing out to the garden, which led down to the water. "There may be a religious angle to it. At least this man Walker seems to think so. A retired police sergeant."

"That would be Emerson Walker. They call him Moody. But why is he thinking anything? He should be playing golf, or opening a Tim Hortons, whatever retired cops do."

"One would think so. But he's taken quite an interest in this girl's death."

"Sounds like Moody, refusing to let go. I remember him from a few cases of mine. Once he got on to something, he bored into it with everything he had. He could get a bit obsessive, but he was usually proved right in the end."

"I haven't spoken to him directly. I have it on good authority, though, that he considers it some kind of religious killing."

There had not been a word of this in the newspapers. If there was something religious or ritualistic about this murder, the police were keeping it quiet. Then I remembered one report said the body had been tampered with.

"So, Rowan, how does this concern us?"

He looked at me intently as he spoke. "Walker has it in his head that the killer is a priest."

"No!"

"I don't know what evidence he purports to have but something has led him, in error, to our client."

I leaned forward in my chair. "Who is it?"

"A clergyman of my acquaintance. A Roman Catholic priest by the name of Burke. He's from New York but he worked here in Halifax in the past. He is here again, at St. Bernadette's parish. Directs a choir school. These suspicions must be put to rest before they become widespread. So far, there hasn't been a whisper of this in public. And it is up to us to keep it that way. But we are not helped by the fact that this ex-policeman, Walker, is thick as thieves with the other priest at St. Bernadette's, an older chap by the name of O'Flaherty. Fine fellow, from what I hear, but not what one would call discreet. He, Walker and a couple of other gentlemen of a certain age often meet at one of the local doughnut shops and gossip over their coffee. I shouldn't think an old cleric's gift of gab is of much use to the police in normal times. But Walker will be all ears now, waiting for our client's name to come up. And we can assume it will, rectory life being what it is." Stratton looked at his watch. "There is no question of guilt here, at least on the part of our client."

"Tell me about him."

"He is the priest who started up the first choir school here back in 1968. Do you remember it?"

"Vaguely."

"He had been involved in something similar in New York City. He was familiar with this area, having spent some time in Chester during the summers when he was younger. That is where Sylvia and I first met him, in fact. Our summer place is close to where he used to visit. Some of the local choir aficionados discovered the New York operation and enticed him to come up and create a similar school in Halifax. It carried on successfully for a few years, I understand, but the effort petered out after Father Burke returned to the U.S. A group of us from the Anglican and RC dioceses formed a committee to get the choir school going again. St. Bernadette's had an available building, so that is where the school is now. Its real name is the Halifax Christian Academy of Sacred Music but everyone, including its principal and its music director, calls it St. Bernadette's. We Anglicans lost the battle of the names, but everyone is pleased to have the school up and running; there has been no internecine conflict.

"Anyway. The school admits children from grades four to eight; they do their other years in the regular system. The curriculum is top-of-the-line and the fees are quite high, as you might expect. But there is financial assistance available for a few talented students who are unable to pay the tuition. The children have only been at it for six months but they really are quite splendid."

"I'll have to check out the choir. And its director. This priest —" As I was speaking, Sylvia Stratton glided into the library.

"Priest? I assume you're referring to Father Burke. You should meet him, Monty. What was the story we heard about him years ago, Rowan? A cross and a fire? Something ghastly and mystical." She gave a delicate shudder.

"There was a fire when he was young, in New York. He must have got too close. I never heard the whole story but, supposedly, the image of his crucifix was burned into his skin. Great fodder for the parish bulletin, I gather. Not generally known up here, though, and that's the way he wants it."

III

Short, chubby, balding with a fringe of fluffy white hair, a twinkle in the eyes behind his smudged spectacles, and an air of scholarly distraction. That's what I was expecting when I heard the choirmaster was coming in to see me. But that is not what walked in the door. This man was tall with a full head of cropped black hair rimed with silver, and his hooded eyes were so dark they looked black. Stern and hawk-featured, he was someone you'd address as "Colonel" before you'd say "Father." There was no Roman collar in sight under his leather jacket. He smelled faintly of smoke.

"Mr. Collins. I'm Father Burke." We shook hands.

"Have a seat, Father. Rowan told me you were coming in but he didn't tell me much about your case."

"There is no case."

"Why don't you tell me how I can help you."

"I can't imagine why I need help. And there's nothing I can tell you."

I couldn't hear New York, but there was a not-so-distant echo of Ireland in his voice: the kind of curt, clipped voice you heard just before you lost your kneecap. Burke struck me as a man of great intensity, his strength held in check by sheer effort of will. A very self-contained individual.

"Would I be right in thinking our appointment today was not your idea?"

Burke gave a terse nod. He reached into a pocket and brought out a pack of cigarettes, stuck one between his lips, then looked to me for permission. All I could give him in return was a wry "I don't make the rules" shake of the head, and he reluctantly put them away before speaking again. "Rowan has heard somewhere that there is a religious connection to the murder of a young girl. For some reason the police think a churchman killed her."

"Not the police at this point, as far as we know. A retired detective by the name of Emerson Walker."

"So it is. I know Rowan has my best interests at heart. But what can I say? The idea that I would be out there sending people to meet their maker is absurd."

"Did you know the girl who was killed?"

"She was connected with the youth centre at St. Bernadette's. I may have spoken to her half a dozen times. That's all."

"Do you know anything about her? Other people in her life, who may have —"

"No."

"Here's what I'm going to do, Father. I'll meet with Moody Walker — the retired sergeant — and try to find out what the hell is going on. How about that?" Silence. "We're better off knowing than not knowing, wouldn't you agree?" I didn't tell him Rowan had commanded me to find out what was going on and keep the priest informed.

"Won't meeting him reinforce these daft suspicions of his?"

"Oh, I won't mention any connection with you. We'll keep that to ourselves as long as we can. I'll bump into him accidentally. He's a regular at Tim Hortons. I'll be in touch when I have something to tell you. And I hope it won't be much."

His black eyes bored into mine. "It won't be." He nodded goodbye and left the office.

Choirmaster? I couldn't picture it. The sharps had better be sharp in that choir. I went out to reception to see whether Rowan was in. He wasn't. As I turned to go back to my office I heard our receptionist, who insists she is with us only until her first romance novel finds the right publisher, whisper to one of the secretaries: "As handsome and cruel as a Spaniard!"

"Get over me, Darlene, I'll only break your heart."

"I'm not talking about you, Monty. I'm talking about the tall dark client who just strode through here. Without giving me the time of day."

"Hold your tongue! He's a man of God."

"I'll say."

IV

I did not yet have a file titled *R. v. Burke*, the "R" of course standing for Regina, in reference to Her Majesty the Queen. In Canada, all criminal proceedings are conducted in the name of the Crown. Rowan wanted me to keep the Burke matter to myself, but it was never too soon to find out what we might be facing.

It took a few coffee and doughnut runs at the Robie and Young Street Tim Hortons before I spotted my quarry. Sergeant Walker did not notice me as I slipped into a seat behind him. He had coffee and a blueberry fritter, and was sitting with two other men. One of them, I was interested to note, was a priest, who looked about seventy. He was short, slight and of cheerful countenance. This was obviously Father O'Flaherty, the pastor of St. Bernadette's. Now that I was seeing them together, I had the feeling I had seen them in each other's company before. I did not recognize the other man at the table, but I heard them call him Larry. Moody Walker could not have been more than fifty-five but he looked much older. Must have been the job that had worn him out; I'd probably be the same when my time came. He was heavy-set, his brown hair now almost entirely white. He had small, dark brown eyes that fixed on you in a most disconcerting way. I settled in to eavesdrop on the conversation, in the age-old spy posture, with my paper and a coffee in front of me.

"You boys spend too much time at the track," Larry was saying. "I wouldn't put two bucks on a horse, let alone the amount you guys piss away. Cards, now, that's another thing. Poker's my game. Ever play, either of you?"

"I used to play. Not as much now," Moody replied. "I hear you have a card sharp over your way, though, Mike. Maybe Larry here could get in a game some night at the rectory."

"Father Burke, that would be," O'Flaherty replied in a soft Irish brogue. "A real poker face. I'd invite you over, Larry, but I wouldn't want to be settin' you up."

"I may get into a game myself some night. Give me a call." This from Moody Walker.

O'Flaherty leaned towards the detective. "Moody, were you involved with that huge boatload of drugs that came ashore at the mouth of the harbour? I'm thinking they couldn't read their charts, to land where they did. That's coming up for trial next week."

"You didn't just ask if that was my case, did you, Mike? Huge boatloads of drugs are the Mounties' problem, not mine. If a big Baptist revival tent came to town, I wouldn't go out there expecting to see you."

Larry added: "Father, go back to your tabloids and those dog-eared true crime books you keep under your pillow. You'll get more from them than you ever will from this guy. Everything you bring up, Walker says he wasn't involved. Guy shot down on the steps of the police station? Doesn't know a thing about it. To hear him tell it, he didn't do any work the whole time he was on the HPD payroll. They found him out and that's why he's sitting here, too cheap to pick up the tab for us today."

I had the feeling this was a well-worn routine around the table.

"So tell us, Padre," Walker said, "what's the latest at the rectory these days? Housekeeper nipping into the communion wine? Using one tea bag instead of two, and sending the other bag back to the old country? Anything of that nature we should know about?"

"Secrets of the confessional, lads, secrets of the confessional," the old priest carolled. "There is one bit of news from our patch. Sad, though," confided Father O'Flaherty. "You know old Tom Lacey?" His cronies shook their heads no. "Well, they rushed him to hospital night before last. Pain in his side. They opened him up. And just closed him right back up again. Nothing they can do but wait for the end." Both men roared in protest. "Death and dying. It never stops, does it? Speaking of which, I must be off. Time to make the rounds at the infirmary." The priest went off with a little salute. The other two men crushed their coffee cups and left the building.

I finished my coffee and headed to the office, none the wiser about the young woman's death. But I knew for certain that Walker was interested in Burke. Moody was keen to get into a card game at the rectory, all in the interests of putting the new priest under his own personal surveillance.

V

The next sighting of my new client took place a few days later, during an event I had not attended since I was young enough to be tugged along by my mother's hand. A church fair. Prodded none too subtly by Rowan Stratton to stop in and spend some money at the choir school, I grudgingly gave up my Saturday morning and headed out to the fair. It would have been better with the kids, but I wanted to get in, and out, early, and I had no intention of being reamed out for waking the family up. So I went alone.

St. Bernadette's was located at the corner of Byrne and Morris streets in the southeast part of the city, not far from the waterfront. The building that housed the youth centre and choir school was on the west side of Byrne across from the church and rectory. It was a stone structure in the Second Empire style, with a mansard roof, dormers, and a cupola topped with a cross. A brick extension had been added later. I climbed the stone steps to the heavy double doors and walked into a room festooned with green crepe paper and cardboard cut-outs of shamrocks and harps. St. Patrick's Day already. Coming towards me was Father O'Flaherty, a kelly green scarf wound round his neck, and a big welcoming smile on his pink-cheeked face. He held out his hand. "I'm Michael O'Flaherty. Welcome to St. Bernadette's. Have I made your acquaintance before?"

"I know we've seen each other around, Father. I'm Montague Collins. Monty."

"Do come in, Monty, and put down your money at one of our tables. Or several tables. But first, let me show you around." The priest led me through the building, which had offices, a gymnasium, classrooms, meeting rooms, and a large auditorium with a piano. There were brightly coloured posters on the walls, along with group photos of children, nuns, priests and dignitaries. In one classroom there was a bingo game, the numbers being called by a genial red-faced man with a booming voice. Other rooms had crafts and bake tables, games and face-painting for children; my little girl would have loved it. Father O'Flaherty encouraged me to watch the video presentation of a variety show put on by the church and youth centre at Christmas.

"And much of the work for the show was done by this fine lady, Eileen Darragh." A big, capable-looking woman was steaming towards us, and O'Flaherty made the introductions. Ms. Darragh was in her late thirties or early forties, plain of face and stocky of build. She wore her straight brown hair in a no-nonsense bob that just covered her ears. Her clothing did not look expensive but it gave her an efficient appearance. I could well believe it when the priest said: "Eileen is the woman who runs this place! We won't tell Sister Dunne I said so, eh Eileen? Sister Dunne is our executive director and principal of the school, and Eileen is her assistant."

Eileen greeted me warmly, then told us there were three other places she was supposed to be. She took large strides down the corridor, stopping briefly to ruffle the hair of a small child who stood behind a huge puff of cotton candy, which completely hid his face. Or hers.

Father O'Flaherty left to greet more visitors, and I moved quickly through the fair, picking up some cookies, a pie, and a couple of novelty items for the kids. I was looking at a display set up by one of the religion classes when I noticed a group of elderly women sporting lapel pins that identified them as members of the CWL, the Catholic Women's League. Two of the women wore top hats of moulded green plastic. They fluttered around a tall man in black.

"Oh Father, you missed our last meeting, and the one before. We're not going to let you get away from us again! But I can't promise you the girls will be well-behaved. Millie will be serving her sherry!"

Another woman said: "A man alone with all those women! You may be too shy to come, Father!"

The man turned slightly and I recognized the unyielding features of Father Burke. He was an impressive-looking cleric, standing ramrod straight in his black suit and Roman collar. There wasn't a touch of green on his person. He put me in mind of the old-school priests of my childhood. They would bawl at you from the pulpit if you shuffled in late for Mass and cuff your ears if you took the Lord's name in vain. Then, on a good day, they'd join you in a game of touch football in the school yard. Father Burke disengaged himself from his admirers and moved towards the door. He came to a halt when he saw me and regarded me impassively with his hooded black eyes. "Mr. Collins. I would not have expected to see you here." The Irish was more clipped than ever. Either he didn't like the look on my face or he saw me as the harbinger of a painful ordeal in his future.

"Hello, Father Burke," I responded as I would have to a courteous greeting. "The boss gave me a nudge in this direction. Some of the funds will be going to the choir school, he said. Has he been here today?"

"Ah. I see. And no, I haven't seen anyone here from the House of Stratton."

"Well, I'd better put down enough money on the Crown and Anchor for both of us."

"You do that, then." He gave me a curt nod of dismissal.

I moved on to a casino table where I dutifully lost a few dollars, then bolted for the exit. But I wasn't fast enough. Father O'Flaherty came by at that moment and smiled at me. "Good, Monty. You're still in time to catch some of the variety show. They're running the video now. After you, sir." He ushered me into the conference room. The place was filled with people who, I suspected, were there to watch their own or a family member's performance. On the screen, two middle-aged men were hamming it up on the subject of fundraising from the pulpit. Then a young girl read a poem she had written about the youth centre. The scene switched, with an amateur-looking segue, to a group of children shuffling onto the stage in choristers' robes. "Our junior children's choir," O'Flaherty whispered to me, "with a few young adult choristers to help out with the lower voices."

A priest joined the choir on stage and said in a broad Irish brogue: "And now we'll be singing 'Faith of Our Fathers.' Here, let me play the first few bars for you." At this, the children covered their ears as if in pain. The priest played two bars on the piano and then hit a comically sour note. "Sure, we'll be doing it *a cappella*, I'm thinking." This brought knowing chuckles from the people around me. The skit was mildly amusing from my point of view but it was more than that to these people, so I assumed an in-joke was in progress. The priest turned to the choir and I saw that it was in fact an attractive young woman in her late teens. The clerical uniform was a black suit jacket with its lapels pinned around a small square of white at the throat. Her short dark hair was sprinkled with white powder at the temples. This was meant to be Father Burke.

Another figure came on stage then. Dressed in an early nineteenth-century coat and wearing a wig, the figure was immediately recognizable as Beethoven. The choir children made exaggerated gestures of delight and beckoned Beethoven closer to the piano. They pointed to the Burke character and Beethoven nodded. Like a magician, he put his hands over the head of the Father Burke character, who then played the music correctly. The children sang the piece, and sang it quite well. Beethoven turned from the piano to the audience and shrugged as if to say: "See? It's easy." Laughter again. I was stunned to see that the man in the Beethoven wig was Burke himself.

17

Father O'Flaherty whispered in my ear again. "Father Burke. He works magic with the children; he's a brilliant choir director. And he's God's gift as a singer himself. But on the pipe organ? He's Paddy from Cork, I'm afraid. Just plays enough to pick out the melody line and accompanying chords."

"And he agreed to take part in this little vignette?" I couldn't picture it, from what I had seen of the man.

"Oh sure. It's pretty well known about his playing. He'll tell it on himself. 'The only musical instrument I can play well,' he says, 'is myself.' Most of what he does with the children is unaccompanied, *a cappella*. If not, he brings someone in to play the organ. He was good-humoured about the skit."

When I turned to the screen again, the Burke character stood and Beethoven moved back. The children shuffled into a new order and picked up pieces of music from their seats. Then Beethoven spoke in a German accent: "Zere is a little heiliger Engel who hass not got her music. Get your music, Fräulein." Beethoven put his hands on the shoulders of a gorgeous little black girl with long braids, who was peering out at the audience and waving. She jerked around, startled, and the audience on the videotape laughed affectionately. When she had her music in place, Beethoven moved out of view, leaving the "choir director" in charge. The Burke character lifted his hands and amateurishly waved them in front of the children as they sang Franck's *Panis Angelicus*. Every once in a while Beethoven's hands came into view at the edge of the screen, and a finger pointed heavenward to keep the pitch up. The singing was heartbreakingly sweet. When the last chord faded, both audiences burst into applause. The Burke character bowed deeply and Beethoven waved a hand in acknowledgement.

"They are wonderful," I said to O'Flaherty.

He beamed back at me. "Do you know Father Burke?"

"I've met him. I'm a little surprised to see him taking part."

"Sure, I can see your point, not knowing him well at all."

"He seems pretty tightly wrapped. He doesn't really strike me as a guy who's open to the redeeming love of Christ."

Michael O'Flaherty smiled. "Maybe he's got his own private stock bottled up inside."

Chapter 2

Locus iste a Deo factus est, inaestimabile sacramentum.
Irreprehensibilis est.
(This place was made by God, a priceless sacrament.
It is beyond reproach.)
— *The Mass,* Graduale

I

I made a pass by Tim Hortons the next Monday morning hoping to
see Sergeant Moody Walker, but there was no sign of him. I had better luck in the afternoon. I was just about to give up when I spied
him lumbering in from the parking lot. When he had his coffee, I
raised my cup and he came over to join me.

"How have you been, Moody? I hear you've retired."

"Bored. Dull. After all the long nights on surveillance, you'd think
I'd be glad of the spare time. But I'm not much of a man for spare
time."

"Don't tell me you miss work. The rest of us live for the day we
don't have to pick up a pen or take a call ever again."

"I do miss it."

"I wish I had a job I loved that much," I said to him.

"Didn't say I loved it. Said I miss it."

"Did they see you off properly? Big piss-up at the Police Club?"

"My lips are sealed." Walker's eyes narrowed as the door to the
shop opened wide. Two young people jostled each other in the door-

way. They had pieces of metal sticking out of the bits of flesh we could see, and every item of clothing was ripped and frayed. "Will you look at that," the policeman groused. "Ever notice that about nonconformists, Collins? They all look alike."

"I guess I'd have to go along with you on that, Moody. So, how are they making out in your absence? Police business shut down, or what?"

"Right," he grumbled.

"You didn't leave anything on your desk, did you?" I persisted. "Somebody about to be collared when your last shift ended?"

"Nah, not really." He bit into a powdery lemon doughnut. "There are a couple of unsolveds that are pissing me off. But not much I can do about that."

"Unsolved what?" I asked as I toyed with the rim of my cup. Maybe this time I'd roll it up and find I'd won a prize. A free cup of coffee, for instance.

"Unsolved murders, what else? I don't much care about unsolved car stereo thefts. Those could be seen as a service to the public."

"What killings have been eating away at you? They never got whoever gunned down that crack dealer in the park, did they?"

Walker snorted. "Everybody knows who did that one. He'll make a mistake. They always do. And we'll — the department will nail him." I waited, taking a leisurely look around the coffee shop. "The guy I want is the guy who bashed in the skull of that young girl and left her under the bridge. Leeza Rae. Happened after I left the shop but it pisses me off. The department hasn't got its head around that one, but I think they're just not looking in the right place." Moody patted his pockets and brought out a cigarette and lighter. He offered me a smoke but I shook my head. I had embarked on a long painful withdrawal from nicotine when my son was born.

"I have my own ideas about what happened there." He drew in a lungful of smoke and blew it towards the empty table to his right.

"What's the story?"

"I have my eye on somebody I think is a bad, bad actor. A fine, upstanding citizen by day, a twisto by night."

Oh, God. "What do we have here, Moody?" I tried to keep it light. "The mayor using his chain of office for grisly deeds?"

"Not a politician, no." Moody took a sip of coffee, and leaned forward. "A priest."

I nodded as if this was something I heard every day. "Why do you say that?"

"Forensic evidence on the body." Moody took a quick look around him. "Some ritualistic, uh, aspects . . ." His voice trailed off.

"Like what? Don't leave me hanging off the cliff here, Moody."

"Hmph. You know better than that, Collins." I did. There are things about a murder scene that are known only to the police and the killer, and the police want to keep it that way. A member of the defence bar would be the last person Walker would confide in. I tried again anyway.

"Okay, but why this priest in particular?"

"Things I know about him. And things I've heard. Product of bad cream. His old man has a history . . . But back to this girl. I'm not telling you anything you didn't read in the papers. She worked at the youth centre they have over there at St. Bernadette's. Attended a dance there the night she was killed. Probably thought she was safe as houses, all the kids dancing and drinking unleaded punch, with a bunch of priests and nuns scowling at them from the sidelines. She left the dance alone." He shook his head and took another sip. I resisted the urge to push for more. Then Walker spoke again.

"Ever wonder about religious people, Collins? I don't mean your church-on-Sunday types, but the professional God-botherers. Especially, between me and you, the RCs." I had served my time as an altar boy, but I was a typical lapsed Catholic and rarely went near a church. Walker went on: "But I'll say this much for them — at least they don't dunk pubescent girls in tanks of water like they did in my church. We were Baptists. *Were.* You can ask my sister about that! Anyway, back to the Catholics. The priests, the bishops, this vow of no nookie. What do you think that does to —" He broke off. I looked up and saw Father Michael O'Flaherty glowering at Walker. He looked like a different man. Gone was his customary cheerfulness.

"Oh, Mike, sit down for Chrissake. This isn't the first time you've heard me fretting about your sexual wellbeing."

"Indeed it is not, and I'm none too pleased to be hearin' it again. It's like I said before, you're wasting your time fretting about me. It's well documented that people in religious life tend to live longer than laymen!"

Moody lifted his cup in the priest's direction, and I got up. "Coffee, Father?"

O'Flaherty looked at me. "Ah. Mr. Collins. Much obliged. Small double cream double sugar."

I went to the counter to get the old fellow his small double double, and to give the two of them a moment to patch things up. When I started back to the table, I heard O'Flaherty say: "Repressed this and repressed that. Bollocks! And you know what I think of this murder theory you're propounding. If you'd only tell me what information you think you have, then —" He fell silent as I approached, but I noticed he had been looking intently at the retired detective as he spoke.

"Father Mike here is trying to find me a hobby," Walker said lightly as I returned.

I made an effort to get into the spirit of things. "Moody was just telling me, Father, that he hopes to take up folk art as a pastime."

"Ha!" the cop bellowed. "I can't do art, so I don't. Why can't everybody stick to what they know?"

"Whyever don't you join me in my hobby, Moody?" The priest had recovered his good humour.

"What? Carting a bunch of old farts halfway around the world on specialized bus tours? No thank you."

"What is it you do, Father? Organize trips of some kind?" I asked.

Walker answered for him. "Michael O'Flaherty is a professional Irishman. Born and raised in Saint John, New Brunswick, he is more Irish than Saint Patrick."

"I am indeed," the priest agreed, not in the least stung by the jibes of his crony. "Saint Patrick was not blessed with the Irish parentage that I was privileged to enjoy. A four-cornered Irishman, and proud of it . . . that means all my grandparents, by the way, Mr. Collins. And you too may be proud. I'm sure you don't need any lessons from me —"

"But he'll instruct you anyway, as long as the subject is Ireland," Walker butted in.

"— about the great Michael Collins, 'the Big Fellow' as he was known. Put the run to the Brits, but then was gunned down by his own —"

"A violent death. Why doesn't that surprise me?" Walker muttered.

"The first time I saw my colleague Father Burke I thought I was having a vision. He looked enough like Mick Collins to be the Big Fellow reincarnated. Or at least he did back then. Not so much now that he's older, except for the Irish mouth on him. I must inquire whether there's a family connection."

"Oh, so Father Burke is someone you've known for a long time?" I asked.

"No," O'Flaherty said quickly, "I never met him until he arrived here in the fall. I've seen photographs of him when he was young, that's all. Now, you were asking about me, so —"

"We were?" Walker interrupted.

"I spend as much time as I can on the old turf." O'Flaherty warmed to his subject. "Tours, religious retreats: Knock, Lough Derg. I'd be happy to have you along. We could put on a Speeches from the Dock tour for you and fellow members of the bar. Nobody can do a speech from the dock like a condemned Irishman!"

There was a shrewdness evident in the mild blue eyes, and I got the impression that the old boy did not miss much in spite of his jovial facade. After all, he had found out what I did to earn my daily bread. He now had a plan for Walker: "Moody, I'll help you set it up. Sergeant Walker's Police Tour of —"

"You want me to lug a busload of gawks around famous crime scenes across the pond? You old ghoul. You're awfully interested in blood and guts, for a man of the cloth."

"Not blood and guts, my dear Walker, not at all." The priest's expression grew sombre. "I am interested, in spite of myself — or is it because of my vocation? — in examining the depths to which man will sink when he turns from God and gives himself over to temptation. You both see it in your everyday lives, the evil perpetrated by men. And — I beg our Blessed Mother's forgiveness — perpetrated by women as well. Does it come from within, or is there a cause that resides beyond human ken? The *fons et origo mali.*" Walker, for once, was without a rejoinder.

"But the source of evil is not my concern at the moment,"

O'Flaherty announced, slapping both hands on the table and pushing himself upright. "'There's husbandry in Heaven; their candles are all out.'" We looked at him blankly. "Votive candles. Need replacements. Shakespeare. Don't you two know anything?" He walked out with a spring in his step.

I raised my eyebrows at Walker across the table. He just shrugged. "Like I said, Collins, you have to wonder." The policeman got up heavily from the table. "Great guy, though, Mike." We waved to each other and he was off. I drove back downtown, to the Stratton Sommers office on Barrington Street.

I was uneasy with the little I had heard from Walker, particularly his comment about a twisted element to the murder. Especially unnerving was his conviction that the killer was able to pass himself off as a good citizen while keeping a dangerous or deranged persona hidden from view. And what was this forensic evidence? Did they have threads from vestments or other clerical garb? Was there a lab report already? Possibly. And what were the ritualistic elements at the scene? It would be difficult to learn anything concrete about the evidence without tipping my hand to the police and drawing attention to my client. If Moody was alone on this, and the department was not looking seriously at Burke, I wanted to keep it that way. It was not part of my job description as a lawyer to investigate crimes, but I would have to do some detective work on this one. First I would have to persuade Father Burke to open up.

II

I called the choir school and was told that Father Burke was over at the rectory. I decided to go see him on my way home, not that I had anything more than vague suspicions to report after my conversation with Moody Walker. And from what I had seen of the priest, it was not likely that he would be forthcoming with any information of his own. The telephone conversation was brief.

"Father Burke?"

"Yes."

"Monty Collins here. I had a word with Moody Walker. I could stop by the rectory on my way home this afternoon."

"Very well." Click. And I thought my regular clientele was aggravating? I made a mental note to ask Rowan who was paying the shot here. If Burke was paying my fees personally, I would bill him for the time it took me to travel the few blocks to the rectory. Didn't they take an oath of poverty? He'd be a saint in rags by the time he faced his Lord on Judgment Day.

When I arrived I was greeted by a middle-aged woman in a washed-out print dress and bedroom slippers. She had faded blonde hair and the face of one descended, perhaps through some mitotic process, from a long line of Irish aunts. I introduced myself and she told me her name was Mrs. Kelly. I followed her to a closed door.

"Someone to see you, Father!"

"Who is it?" The abrupt tone was instantly recognizable.

"Mr. Collins, Father."

"Send him in."

I entered a small parlour with an Oriental carpet, a dark wood desk and several chairs. The walls were lined with books. Father Burke was at the desk looking crisp and efficient in clerical black and Roman collar. "Thank you, Mrs. Kelly." She shuffled out.

"Mr. Collins." He stood and gestured to a couple of chairs near the window.

Dispensing with pleasantries, I started right in: "I was able to speak briefly with Sergeant Walker. He —"

We were interrupted by the ringing of the telephone. The priest snatched up the receiver. "Yes?" he barked. "Yes, Michael. Where is he? The VG. No, I'll get the room number. I'll run right over. Fine, Mike." He hung up and rapped out an apology to me. "I'm sorry. That was Father O'Flaherty. A parishioner is at death's door over at the hospital. O'Flaherty can't get there and he asked me to go over and give the last rites. I'll call your office and make an appointment with you. Not that I think this man Walker could possibly have anything to say."

I watched as he donned his leather jacket, muttered "Christ," and stuffed a few items in the pockets.

"Would you like a lift? That way, you won't have to park."

"All right. Thank you."

We hurried to my car. I pulled out of the parking lot, turned left

25

on Byrne and right on Morris. The Victoria General Hospital was several blocks up the street. "Flat!" Burke exclaimed in disgust, as he reached over and snapped off my car radio, arresting a female pop singer in mid-howl.

Other than that there was no conversation until we were within a block of the hospital, when I couldn't help but remark: "So your cheery smile is the last thing this poor devil is going to see before he leaves this world?"

Father Burke had his foot out the door before I'd come to a stop: "What do you mean by that, Collins? You don't see me as a great comfort to the sick and dying?" Was this more of his overweening self-confidence, or was I getting a glimpse of a dry sense of humour?

We missed each other again Tuesday morning, and then I was bogged down at the office. When I was finally free I picked up the phone and called the rectory. Mrs. Kelly informed me Father Burke had taken the junior choir over to the church for practice.

Rehearsal was under way when I arrived. I had been in St. Bernadette's the odd time for weddings and funerals. I had never until now appreciated the acoustics. It was a modest-sized stone church built in imitation gothic style with ribbed vaulting, pointed arches and gorgeous stained-glass windows glowing like jewels. The bisque-coloured walls could have used a coat of paint, but it hardly mattered at this time of the afternoon — in true gothic fashion, the interior space was ablaze with heavenly light.

As I started up the stairs to the choir loft I heard a skidding noise behind me, followed by a crash. I turned to see a small girl with a huge mass of long, curly black hair. I recognized her from the video-taped variety show. Now, she collided with the wall, righted herself and pushed past me on the stairs. "I'm late — Father Burke is going to kill me again!" Above me, I heard another crash as a chair was knocked over.

"Alvin!" The choirmaster spoke, *subito fortissimo*.

"Father Burke, why you always calling me Alvin? My name is Janeece."

"Once upon a time," said Burke, "there were three chipmunks: Simon, Theodore, and Alvin. Alvin was never where he was supposed to be, when he was supposed to be there. That was before your time, when my brothers and sisters were small. But to me you'll always be Alvin. So, Alvin. *Locus Iste*, setting by Bruckner. Recite it to me and tell me what it means."

The young voice began: *"Locus iste a Deo factus est, Inaestima — aestima —"*

"Een - es - tee - ma - bee - leh," Burke corrected.

"Inaestimabile sacramentum." She took a deep breath, and soldiered on. *"Irreprehensibilis est.* There!"

"And what does it mean?"

This time she had it by heart and rattled it off like machine gun fire: "This place was made by God, a priceless sacrament, it is beyond reproach."

"Thank you. Now sing the alto part, all the way through from bar twenty-two. The others have already sung it and are ready to move on. But let's hold everything up and hear you."

I was in the loft by this time and tried to be unobtrusive. The choristers ranged from around nine right up to university age. Obviously, the junior kids were getting some support from their senior counterparts for today's repertoire. There were three basses and two tenors, the rest altos and sopranos. The little girl known as Alvin, dressed in a denim jumper with a bright pink cardigan buttoned unevenly over it, had enormous chocolate brown eyes and her hair fanned out in a riot of curls beside her face and down her back. Her flawless skin was the colour of mocha. This was the closest I was ever going to come to looking upon an angel. My angel hawked and made a series of other unseemly noises to clear her throat, then proceeded to sing in a clear, low voice.

"Wrong," Burke interrupted, and I wanted to clout him on the head. "Wrong page. Once again, you're not singing from the same hymn book." The priest was wearing jeans and an old grey T-shirt that said "Fordham." He glared at Janeece over the top of a pair of half glasses. The child scowled back at him. "But what you sang was beautiful. I have a piece you might like to sing by yourself. We'll talk about it next practice, if you deign to show up on time.

"All right, ladies and gentlemen. The *Agnus Dei* from Byrd's *Mass for Four Voices*. Red book, Alvin. Sopranos, you'll be singing some of the most beautiful lines of music ever written, so don't belt it out the way you did last time. It's the *lamb* of God, not the *ram* of God. Keep that in mind. Quiet, reverential, hopeful. You're imploring God to grant you peace. Bring out those *dona nobis pacems* near the end. Crescendo over the bar line. Let's hear it the way it's meant to be sung."

Father Burke lifted muscular arms and the children sang to the Lamb of God. Occasionally he raised his left index finger to keep the sopranos from losing pitch. "Sharpen the tone," the finger was saying. He brought out the crescendoes he wanted in the *dona nobis* lines. In a clear, straight, English style, the choir gave life to a Mass that was written four hundred years ago. The last chord echoed from the altar, and filled the acoustically blessed space. A smile spread across the priest's stony face, and seeing it was like witnessing the Transfiguration.

When the sound faded, Alvin piped up: "Can we do something easy now?"

"What is it you'd like to sing, Alvin?"

"You know," she said, the way a child would to a parent dense enough to ask whether anyone wanted a bedtime story.

"*Mass of the Angels,* could it be?"

"Yes." She drew the word out with exaggerated patience.

"All right. *Missa de Angelis.* People have been singing this for a thousand years. But remember: it's not 'easy' to sing chant. You can hear every mistake. Sing it as if you people really were — I can hardly bring myself to say it — angels. If you do a good job, we'll sing it at Mass soon. Ready?"

He raised his arms and favoured them with a smile. And was I imagining it, or did I see a little wink directed at Alvin? What they sang was a Gregorian Mass, a melody of ageless beauty, which I recalled hearing as a child when the Mass was still in Latin. To my ears, they sang it to perfection. But he wanted more.

"Back to page one. Diction. I want to hear every k, every t."

"Yeah but we, like, sound fruity when we do that," whined a thin-haired boy of about twelve.

Burke peered over the tops of his half glasses. "It won't, *like,* sound 'fruity' down there, Ronald." He gestured with his head to the body of the church. "You'll sound like a choir that knows the words as well as the tune. Once more."

They sang the piece again from start to finish, every consonant sharp as the crack of a rifle. When they finished Alvin dropped to her seat with a loud thunk. She gripped her head with both hands.

"What's the trouble there, Alvin?"

"All these k's and t's being spitted out, Father. I have to stop. I have nothing left!"

"Ah. Then my work is done," Burke replied.

After the choristers had stomped their way down the stairs and left the church, Father Burke straddled a chair and faced me.

"What have you got to tell me?"

"Not much, I'm afraid. But that may be good." Burke was my client — if a reluctant one — and I had to be as forthright with him as I could be, but I chose my words carefully. The "twisto" angle would antagonize him and make him even more difficult to deal with. There was also, simmering on the back burner of my mind, the healthy *soupçon* of doubt I carried with me into any criminal case. Notwithstanding his ability to coax the music of the spheres from a rabble of mortal children, my client might well be guilty, might well be a twisto, and I did not want to do anything to set him off.

"Well, what the hell evidence does he think he has, that could possibly link me with this girl's death?"

"He says there was forensic evidence found on the body —" Burke started to interrupt but I held up a restraining hand. "He wouldn't say what the evidence was. The police aren't going to show their hand. But forensics are usually hairs, fibres, bodily fluids, things like that. And —" again I fended off an interruption "— there was something ritualistic done to the body or the scene. He didn't provide details. Nor is he likely to."

"If there were body fluids on that girl, they didn't come from me. That should go without saying," declared Burke in his curt Irish voice. "Hair? Maybe or maybe not."

"What are you saying?"

"I gave the police a sample of my hair when —"

"You did *what?*" I yelped, lurching forward in my chair.

"When the police came around interviewing us all as witnesses," Burke stated placidly, "they asked who had had any kind of contact with the young girl. I couldn't remember if I had done a turn around the dance floor with her or not. There were so many people. I think she danced with O'Flaherty and, of course, with the young fellows who were there. Anyway, they took samples of my hair. With my consent, of course."

"Obviously. So. They took samples from where?"

He pointed to the top of his head, then to the temples. "Black ones from here, white from here. Though I didn't have as many grey hairs before this torment —" He caught something in my expression. "What?"

"Just from your head, then?"

"What exactly do you mean?"

"Did they ask . . ."

"For something below the — neck? No."

"Good."

"I wouldn't have been so cooperative if they had. Do you think I'm daft?"

I didn't respond. If there was a common thread running through the great majority of my criminal clients, it was that they could not keep their mouths shut in the presence of the police. Oh, the hard cases, the professionals, knew better. But most of my clients believed the officer when he said he just wanted to get things cleared up, and would appreciate hearing from the client what really happened. They all thought they were clever enough to outwit the police (wrong), and that whatever they were saying would help exonerate them (wrong again, because they had no idea how their words would fit in with, or confirm, other evidence the police were keeping to themselves). Even the most innocent-sounding (to the clients) admissions often served to nail into place the cases against them. Now here was a worldly, highly educated, very intelligent man, one of the most self-contained, tight-lipped individuals I had ever met, and he had turned out to be just as gabby and naive as all the rest of the sad, hopeless parade of humanity I had seen shuffling through the justice system over the years. Burke was sitting there unperturbed.

I started again. "The police told you they wanted hair samples from you, if you were willing, so they could 'eliminate you from consideration, of course Father.' Maybe a little laugh from the officer

— they were only trying to find the source of the evidence found on the body. And you rolled over for them. So now they have their evidence, and Moody Walker thinks you did it."

"Mr. Collins, if my hairs were on her clothes, then they were on her clothes."

"And now there's no room for doubt on that point, thanks to you."

"On her clothes from whatever contact she had with me at the dance. I would have given them whatever they asked for. I was a witness, not a suspect. I didn't kill her."

If only life were that simple. "Why didn't you tell me this when we met in my office?" I asked, thinking: If he says because I didn't ask, I'll go for his throat.

"That appointment wasn't my idea, as you know. I found it hard to take any of this seriously. Now it seems I have no choice." Burke leaned over and reached for his jacket, then stopped. Going for a cigarette, I guessed, before he remembered where he was.

I sighed and moved on. "Tell me then, if you will — or would you rather go down and phone it in to the police? — tell me about the dance."

He gave me a cool look and said: "The youth centre — does anyone use the word 'youth' in normal conversation? Nobody under forty says it, you can be sure. The centre puts on these dances a couple of times a year. This was for Valentine's. Not a big day on my calendar, but I'm a good sport as I'm sure you can tell, Mr. Collins. They draw a good crowd. Kids from sixteen to their early twenties. They serve soft drinks and some kind of sugary punch." He made a face. "This was the first one I had been to. Father O'Flaherty supervised, along with the centre's director, Sister Dunne. In the past, apparently, they've hired an off-duty policeman for security, but they didn't this time."

This time they had you, I thought. "How late did the dance go on?"

"Started at nine, ended at one. It wasn't bad as dances go. Recorded music, of course. We couldn't spring for a band. There were no fights or anything. A strict no booze policy helps there, I'm thinking."

"Do the grown-ups abide by the no liquor rule, or is it just for the kids?"

"Nobody drinks."

"Is there a lot of mixing at these dances? I mean, does everyone make it to the dance floor or is it just boyfriend and girlfriend sticking together for the night?"

"They mixed it up pretty well, I thought. One of the girls, I can't remember who, initiated a couple of games to encourage people to change partners."

"All right. Now who did you say was in charge, and who all worked at the dance?"

"Sister Dunne, Marguerite, is the centre's director as well as being principal of the school, so she'd have been the woman in charge. She and Eileen Darragh, her assistant. But it was actually run by two of the college students who volunteer at the centre, Erin Christie and Tyler MacDonald. Tyler also played the music. A couple of fellows from the parish council helped out. Bertie O'Halloran ran the bar, such as it was. Rudi Martini was on the door, taking tickets and keeping an eye on things. Mike O'Flaherty and I were inside as well."

I would try to speak with all these people, keeping my questioning as low-key as possible. I decided to consult Rowan and see whether we could pass off my involvement as an investigation on the part of the choir school. Protecting its interests without saying as much.

"Now. Do the priests and nuns dance with the kids on these occasions?"

"There was only one nun, and she didn't have her dancing shoes on. But my understanding is yes, it's considered something in the way of a friendly gesture for the priests to dance with the girls for a bit."

"And did you? Dance with the girls for a bit?"

"Yes, I had short dances with a number of the young girls. It's a bit of a lark, that's all. Mike O'Flaherty is the man for dancing with the ladies. He was on his feet all night."

"Did you dance with Leeza Rae?"

"I probably did. I'm assuming I did . . . But I just cannot remember for sure." Let us hope so, I said to myself, given the hair samples he had handed over.

"If you danced with her, or when you were dancing with any of the girls, would these have been close waltzes, or what?"

"Hardly. I'm thirty years older than these girls. I don't try to get them in a clinch."

"How well did you know Leeza Rae?"

"Not very well. I had spoken to her a few times. She came to the centre as a part-time staff person some months before, I believe. She seemed to be a troubled young girl. Not surprising, I suppose, with the boyfriend in jail."

I knew the answer but I asked anyway. "In prison for what?"

"Rape." He practically spat out the word.

"And this guy was still locked up at the time of the murder?"

"Yes. That was my understanding."

"And what did you do after the dance?"

He raised an eyebrow at me. "Looking for my alibi, are you then? I helped clean up afterwards, stacked chairs, took some items to the basement. Made a couple of trips back to the rectory with borrowed trays and things. Nothing much else."

"And how long did this go on, the cleaning up?"

"I don't know. An hour would it be? Not sure," he answered.

"You were seen doing all this good work, I assume?"

"Ah. Your tone betrays a bit of exasperation with your client, Mr. Collins. But yes, of course I was seen. We were all pitching in. I wasn't under anybody's eye constantly, but I was in and out." He leaned forwards with an amused look on his face. "The police were satisfied that I was where I was supposed to be."

"And after the ball was over, what did you do then?"

"Mike O'Flaherty and I went back to the rectory, had a shot of whiskey each, and I went to bed. I assume Mike did the same."

"Is there anything else I should know, that you haven't seen fit to tell me?" I asked as I got up and made ready to leave.

"Not that I can think of."

"Do something for me, Father. Write up your version of events at the dance and any contact you ever had with Leeza Rae. Don't leave anything out, no matter how insignificant it may seem. Just drop it at my office in an envelope with my name on it."

He nodded.

I started for the stairs, then turned around. "Beautiful sound, your choir."

"Thank you. Keep that foremost in your mind, Mr. Collins. I'm a choirboy."

Chapter 3

*Way back in history three thousand years, in fact ever since
the world began,
There's been a whole lot of good women sheddin' tears over a
brown-eyed handsome man.*
— Chuck Berry, "Brown-Eyed Handsome Man"

I

The day after my choir loft summit with Burke, I went to the St. Bernadette's Youth Centre to see what I could glean from staff members who had attended the dance on the night Leeza Rae was killed. I decided not to phone first. Sometimes a cold call is more effective, and I wanted this probe to be as low-key and casual as possible. I started with the executive director, Sister Marguerite Dunne. She was a tall, distinguished-looking woman in her early sixties, with short iron-grey hair and shrewd green eyes. Sister Dunne was in civilian clothes — maybe all sisters are these days — but she wore a large silver cross around her neck. The nun had an aura of unshakeable confidence and authority. She seemed amused by my explanation that Rowan Stratton and other board members had asked me to gather some information about the night of the killing, in case parents of the students voiced any concerns. But she did agree to talk.

Leeza Rae had come to St. Bernadette's in January of 1989. One of the staffers met Leeza somewhere, after the boyfriend had been packed off to jail, and invited her to the centre. She volunteered for a few weeks, then was taken on as a part-time staff member. She got along fairly well with the others but, perhaps understandably given her history with an abusive partner, she tended to be easily upset and angered. There were no serious personality clashes, the nun hastened to say.

"Now, on the night of the dance, Leeza was there how long? Did she stay till the dance was over?"

"Yes, I'm fairly sure she did."

"Did she leave by herself?"

"I didn't see her leave."

"Who did she dance with, do you remember?"

"I saw her dancing for part of the night. She also spent some time chatting with people and discussing the music with Ty MacDonald. But she danced, yes. I couldn't tell you the names of her partners."

"Did she dance with any staff members? Or priests?"

"Staff members, I don't think so. They were quite busy, though they may have had a dance or two. Priests, yes. Father O'Flaherty anyway. She danced with him a couple of times."

"And Father Burke?"

"I believe so, but I couldn't say for sure."

I asked Sister Dunne who was around the building after the dance. She said all the organizers stayed to clear up. Among the people she saw lugging things in and out was Burke. Eileen Darragh was there the whole time afterwards and would be the best person to say who had been doing what.

The other staff interviews were much the same. There had been nothing unusual in Leeza Rae's demeanour. She was not a bubbly person, but she had been "on an even keel," in the words of Rudi Martini, the man on the door.

Eileen Darragh had a bit more to offer about the dance. She seemed to be the powerhouse, running the youth centre while Sister Dunne carried out her duties as a teaching principal of the choir school. I finally found Eileen becalmed when a scheduled meeting fell through. She remembered our hurried introduction at the church fair, and we shook hands. Eileen worked in the outer area of the director's office, where she had a desk, a typewriter, computer, filing cabinets, and other accoutrements of office life. A black-and-white photograph of the centre hung on the wall beside her. There were several photos on the opposite wall, some in black and white, some in colour, showing groups of children staring into the camera.

"Thanks for seeing me, Ms. Darragh."

She smiled. "I'm glad you managed to find me at my desk. And it's Eileen."

"I'm Monty. What can you tell me about Leeza Rae?"

"Leeza Rae." Eileen shook her head as she remembered. "Oh, Monty, there was a girl with problems. Some of them she brought on herself. That boyfriend. The gang rape of a young girl, fifteen years old. Thank God, the law made quick work of him. Serving time in Dorchester now." Eileen sighed. "I should be more Christian about him, shouldn't I? But there are certain things a woman cannot bring herself to do. Like take the side of a rapist. But don't let me get off the subject. You were asking about poor Leeza. I met her a few months after the boyfriend was sent up the river. She was working as a cashier at the Windsor Street Sobeys, where I buy my groceries, and I started to chat with her. She was only a temporary replacement and was at loose ends. Of course I started going on about the centre and what we offer. She told me, not in any great detail, thank the Lord, about the boyfriend, Vic. And how she had taken the bus up to Dorchester to visit him! Imagine that. Well, the poor thing. Anyway I invited her to drop in any time. Hoping of course she would meet somebody better than Vic. She started coming in, volunteering on the desk, and later applied for a part-time staff position."

"How did she fit in?" I asked.

"Not too badly, really. We had to tone her down a bit, smooth out some rough edges. But that's what we're here for, to help young people."

"Was there anyone in particular she was close to here?"

"Me, to an extent," Eileen answered, "which makes me ask myself, over and over, whether I should have seen warning signs. But it's too late for that, isn't it?"

"Now, Eileen, the night of the dance. Did you notice anything unusual about Leeza? Anything different in her mood or behaviour?"

She looked thoughtful. "Nothing I can put my finger on."

I heard footsteps outside the office. Eileen looked up and blushed a bright pink. "Oh, hello, Father." The footsteps halted momentarily, then continued on. Eileen turned away to burrow in her handbag. When she surfaced her face was still pink but this could have been from bending over the bag. She had a tissue in her hand.

"Who was that?" I asked innocently. "Am I taking up somebody's time?"

"No. It was just Father Burke." She blew air into the tissue and tossed it into her waste basket. "Now, where was I? Leeza Rae. She may have had something on her mind, but I could be imagining it. When tragedy strikes, I think we tend to look back and find significance in things we would have forgotten otherwise. But Leeza chatted with people, had a few dances. I can't really say there was anything unusual."

"Who did she dance with, can you recall?"

"Several of the young men. She had a couple of dances with Tyler MacDonald. Other than that, I don't know."

"Did she dance with any of the priests?" Either of the priests, I meant.

"No. I don't think so."

"No?" I asked.

"Well, maybe with Father O'Flaherty. That man never gets tired of dancing. But I didn't see them together myself."

"And Father Burke?"

"No, I'm pretty sure about that. He hardly knew Leeza." Protecting him, I wondered, or trying to blot out the image of the priest in the arms of the younger woman?

"Did you see her leave, Eileen?"

"I've tried to remember that. I think I saw her leave alone. If only I could remember more clearly."

"I appreciate this, Eileen. I'll let you get back to work."

She saw me looking at the pictures on the wall as I got up to leave. "St. Bernie's in the olden days," she explained. "We were an orphanage, you know." Yes, I remembered that now. The St. Bernadette's Home for Children. "The orphanage ceased operations in, what was it, 1979? By then there weren't as many orphans, or abandoned children to be more accurate, so the archdiocese closed the orphanage. The building sat empty for a long time, then it was resurrected as the youth centre. And choir school, of course."

"How long have you been here, Eileen?"

"I've been here all my life. Do you believe that?"

"You mean —" I gestured towards the group photos "— you were here as a child?"

"Yep. That's me. In 1968. I was eight years old then." A plain, slightly overweight child, with a round face and lank dark hair, stared morosely at the camera. I had been estimating her age at around forty. She was in fact ten years younger. "I look a bit like a lost soul there but I wasn't really." She gazed intently at her former self.

"What was it like for you, being brought up in an orphanage? I can't imagine it, I'm sorry."

"Few people can imagine it, I know, those who grew up in families. But it wasn't all that bad. They did their best. You hear horror stories about places like this, but nobody was treated badly here. At least not by the standards of the time. People sometimes forget that what is not acceptable now was the norm back then. Some of the nuns were strict, and some were a little too free with the strap, but others were kind." She swallowed, clasped her hands together and went on. "It wasn't like being in a family of your own, but they did their best for us, God love them. And I'm still here! No wonder I tend to — well, some people say I'm a bit bossy here, Monty. They may be right. St. Bernie's has been my whole life, and sometimes I forget I don't own the place!"

II

I wasn't getting a lot of useful information about the last hours of Leeza's life. And I knew virtually nothing about her death. What had been done to her body to convince the police, or Moody Walker at least, that this was a religious killing? The details would not be available from the police unless, well, unless my client was charged with the murder. But the police were not the only ones who had seen the victim's body. The technicians at the morgue would have seen it, as would the pathologist who performed the autopsy, and the people at the funeral home. Stratton Sommers often used a private investigator for surveillance and matters that required clandestine activity. But the

Burke file was not being circulated around the office and I suspected Rowan would not want to bring in a private eye. I decided to handle this my own way.

If there was one person in the world I could rely on to do something right and keep quiet afterwards, it was my wife. Estranged wife. She may have been the one person in the world I did not want to be in the same room with for more than five minutes, but I had faith in her abilities and her discretion. Maura knew a number of people who toil away at the kinds of tasks the rest of us take for granted, necessary but unpleasant work that we may not want to hear about. She was frequently at the side of underpaid workers in their struggles for better conditions and job security. Did she perhaps know some of the people who had handled Leeza Rae's body once the police and the crime scene people had finished with it?

To maintain solicitor-client privilege, I would retain Maura as a lawyer working as part of a team for Burke. That way, nobody could say we had waived his right to confidentiality by revealing something to an outsider. I called the rectory but Burke was out. I heard from him an hour or so later.

"Hello, Father Burke."

"What can I do for you, Mr. Collins?"

"I'm not comfortable operating with so little information about the murder scene. If there were religious or ritualistic aspects to the killing or to the scene, I want to know what they were."

There was silence at the other end of the line. Burke eventually spoke. "Yes?"

"I do not want to stir anything up when I go looking for this information. Nor do I want your file going outside a very limited orbit."

"Right."

"So what I would like to do, with your permission, is retain someone I can trust to be very discreet. My wife."

"Some class of husband-wife confidentiality, you mean?"

"No, that's not what I mean. She is a lawyer and a law professor."

"Ah."

"She would be one of your solicitors, so there would be no breach of confidentiality. And she has ways of getting information out of people without them realizing what she's doing. Finally, and this is crucial, she keeps her mouth shut. Except when she's tearing strips off me."

He laughed, in a rather unpriestly manner. "Sounds like my kind of woman."

"I meant she can be very, well, assertive. Verbally."

"Yes, I get the picture. She gives you a tuning now and then, does she, Montague? More women should be like that. The world would be a finer place. Do what you think is best, counsellor. And if you ever want to get information out of me, send her over." Click.

I took that as my authorization to retain Maura on his behalf and I wrote an ass-covering memo to that effect for the file. Now it was time to endure the sort of verbal abuse that a lawyer expects to receive from a judge, or opposing counsel, but that he hopes he will not have to suffer from the person he once pledged to love and honour until death. I dropped in at my wife's office at the law school.

Maura MacNeil was admittedly an attractive woman. She was probably twenty-five pounds over her ideal weight and, to give credit where credit is due, she didn't give a damn. She had dusky brown hair to her shoulders, grey, slightly almond-shaped eyes, a generous mouth, and a deceptively sweet face: the "pretty face" that people are apparently not supposed to mention — for reasons I have never understood — in connection with a zaftig figure.

It had been a while since I'd been in her office but the place never changed, except for the addition of more and more books to the piles on the table and floor. The wall to my left was covered with banners exhorting people to wake up to poverty, injustice and exploitation; wickedly funny cartoons lampooned the exploiters and their lackeys in government. The wall opposite contained gorgeous photos of her native Cape Breton, and a poster of the Men of the Deeps, the coal miners' choir, of which her dad was a member. The men wore their helmets and their lights were shining. Alec "the Trot" MacNeil's daughter was writing furiously at her desk.

"Good morning, Professor," I began. "What's the rule against perpetuities? I've forgotten, and I need it for a case I'm working on."

She looked up. "Oh, it's you, Collins. We've all forgotten the rule against perpetuities. Nobody needs it. So move on to your next point."

"I need you."

"Well, I don't need you. But your children do, so I guess you're going to be a part of my life into perpetuity, aren't you?"

"Looks that way."

She got up from her desk and cleared an armload of journals from one of the chairs. "Well? You don't have to stand there. Have a seat."

Emboldened by what I perceived almost as kindness, I ventured a compliment. "You look bright-eyed and rosy-cheeked today."

"I have a fever of a hundred and four!" she retorted.

Shit. I decided not to waste any more time. "Listen, Maura. I'd like to retain you on a murder file I'm working on."

"Murder? You don't get many of those at Stratton Sommers."

"I'll explain. Can we get together? Maybe you could bring the kids over for dinner tonight."

"Is your place still all torn up? How long does it take to get some floors refinished? I don't relish sitting there and getting dust all over my arse, just for the privilege of eating overcooked spaghetti and listening to you."

"So," I sought clarification, "you're inviting me to your place then."

She sighed. It never ended. "Six-thirty. The kids will be hungry."

Maura lived downtown on Dresden Row, in the place we had shared as a family. The house was a typical Halifax variation of the Georgian style, grey with double-hung windows trimmed in white, and distinctive five-sided Scottish dormers. I was there on time, with a bottle of Australian wine and all the fixings for ice cream sundaes for my children. They, at least, were happy to see me. My wife and I were able to agree on one thing, our kids.

Tommy Douglas was shorter and thinner than I was, but he had my dark blonde hair and blue eyes. A fine-looking lad of sixteen. We had named him after T. C. (Tommy) Douglas, the eloquent and witty Baptist minister who, as premier of Saskatchewan, had faced down the doctors to become the father of universal free health care in Canada. Normie was a little girl who made her way through the world by crashing against it at full speed. She had big, near-sighted hazel eyes, and I cannot count the pairs of eyeglasses we bought and she lost. Her nose was spangled with freckles and she had fat curls in a rich shade of auburn. Her hair was a big part of our mornings because she tended to twirl it in bed; you could tell whose week it was to have the children by the size and complexity of the tangles still in place on Normie's head. My wife, out of the mainstream in many ways, was an old-fashioned mother who believed a child's hair and nails spoke volumes about the quality of the home. "You look like a motherless child" meant face, hands, and hair were not suitable for public viewing. If it weren't for Tommy Douglas and Normie, Maura MacNeil and I would have been rid of each other a long, long time ago.

We were civil in the presence of the children and sometimes it was easy to forget for a few minutes that we were not a family anymore. When the young ones went off by themselves after dinner, I got down to business. "I'm hoping you know somebody at the morgue."

"I won't say who I'd like to see in the morgue, because I wouldn't really mean it, but don't tempt me like that again, Collins." She smiled and sipped her wine. I waited. "I could probably drop in and see how things are going for some of the people I know over there. If I just happened to be visiting a sick friend at the hospital, angel of mercy that I am, what could be more natural than to pop over to the morgue and say hello? What is it you want to know?"

"You heard about the body found under the bridge a few weeks ago."

"Yes, I heard."

"Apparently, the body was desecrated in some way, and the police suspect a religious angle to the murder."

"Really!" She put down her glass. I had her full attention.

"Moody Walker — you know who I mean — he's retired now, but he thinks the girl was killed by a priest."

"Whoa!"

"I think the police are looking further afield than Walker is. They may be more open to thinking it was an impostor, or someone pretending to be a priest. But Walker has his sights set on —" I nodded in her direction "— our client."

"Our client is who?"

"A Catholic priest by the name of Burke. He's from New York. Ever hear of him?"

Maura shook her head. She was brought up Catholic, although, like her Trotskyite father in Cape Breton, she had numberless grievances against the church, and enjoyed nothing more than airing them when offered the slightest encouragement. She did, however, find much to like in the social gospel. I could see the pros and cons of Holy Mother Church warring within her as we spoke, but she knew how to stick to the matter at hand.

"Why Burke?"

"The victim, Leeza Rae, was a part-time staffer at St. Bernadette's Youth Centre. She knew Burke casually as a result. She also would have known the other priest there, Father O'Flaherty. She was last seen alive at a dance at the centre. Valentine's Day. She may or may not have danced with Burke —"

"Wouldn't that be a hot time? Hubba hubba," Maura put in.

"You may want to reserve judgment on that. Anyway, he gave a statement to the police."

"Wasn't that good of him."

"Oh yeah. If you knew Burke, you'd think he would be the last person on the planet to give anything up. Very acerbic and difficult to talk to. I can barely get a civil word out of him. But there he was, offering himself up to the police."

"The layman might take that as a sign he is innocent." We shared a laugh, and I poured us both another glass of the Shiraz.

"And yet, this priest works with children at the choir school several days a week. He's fairly brusque with them, but not brutal. The only time I ever saw him lighten up was when the children were singing. And they were singing beautifully. You really ought to hear them. He obviously knows what he's doing. The beatific smile on his face, he looked like a different man."

"That's what the cops did then. Softened him up with Mozart. I'm told they carry small cassette tapes in their night sticks, for the hardened choirmasters among us, and he rolled over for them. So why isn't Father O'Flaherty a suspect?"

"I'm not sure. He's older, for one thing. Not ancient, but seventy anyway. He's short and slight, and I think a young girl could easily fend him off."

"Which is not the case with Burke, I take it."

I shook my head. "Burke is in his late forties, maybe fifty. Tall, muscular, in good shape. I'm not sure I could fend him off myself." I paused. "I got the impression Moody Walker was predisposed to suspecting Burke. Maybe he knows something we don't know. He was quite prepared to regard the priest as a sicko. Which brings us to your mission. Something was done to the girl, or to the body. Perhaps the killer left a signature. I'm hoping you'll be able to ferret out exactly what this was. The people at the morgue, and at the funeral home, would have seen it. We have to know what we're dealing with here."

"Time to get chatty with the body snatchers. I'll try to bury my inquiries in a string of other bullshit, so they won't know what I'm after." She was thinking ahead.

"And Maura, I don't have to tell you —"

"No, you don't. I shall maintain my silence even in the face of the most exquisite . . . music in the world." She drained her glass. "Grab a cab. I'm going to bed. Pick your car up in the morning."

III

The next morning was Friday and I was in the Spring Garden Road courthouse for the sentencing of a client named Ricky Wellner. Our articled clerk, Robin Reid, came along with me. Wellner had been convicted of assault causing bodily harm to his common-law wife, Crystal Green; she had two fractured ribs and needed stitches in her lip. This was far from Wellner's first violent offence. The case had been adjourned so a pre-sentence report could be prepared. I had set up a meeting with the Crown prosecutor, Blaine Melvin. He was looking for five years; I suggested nine months. He wasn't buying that.

"Keep Ms. Green off the stand," I urged him, "and we'll take two years. Wellner is better off with federal time anyway. He'll be able to tap in to some programs and get the help he needs."

"I'm not surprised you want her kept from the stand, considering the picture she'll paint of your client," the Crown replied, "but Crystal is going to get up there and read her statement."

"I'll have no choice but to go after her on cross-examination, and it won't go well for her." I rarely cross-examine someone on a victim impact statement but I couldn't let this testimony pass unchallenged. "Save her, and her family, the grief. Take the two years."

"Oh, I don't think we have anything to fear from your cross, Montague."

Another sentencing was wrapping up as we entered the courtroom. The upper part of the room was painted a light cream, with dark wainscoting below and wooden beams criss-crossing the ceiling. The bench, and the tables used by the clerks and counsel, were in the same sombre shade. Her Majesty Queen Elizabeth II gazed coolly at all who entered, an incentive perhaps to the males to doff their caps before the judge bellowed at them to do so. His Honour Judge Ivan Thomas was slumped on the bench, his white head barely visible; he glowered at the stunned-looking young man whose fate was in his hands. The judge's voice boomed from the bench: "Break, enter, and *leave*, Mr. Willis, break, enter, and *leave*. Don't dally at the liquor cabinet and pass out in the victim's house. We'll have to amend the Criminal Code so you'll know what to do next time. Do you have anything to say? No? Six months. Next!"

Crystal Green was a heavy, tired-looking woman with long, dun-coloured hair scraped back tightly from her round face. I made a motion for exclusion of the public. I wanted the courtroom cleared of the media and all spectators, including the victim's supporters. Melvin objected, and the judge denied my motion. Crystal read her statement, describing in detail the effect the assault had, and continued to have, on her life. She said she feared men, was afraid of emotional attachment, and was destined to be alone as a result. She broke down several times, and Melvin was solicitous with a newly opened box of tissues.

I rose and asked whether the victim would like a short break before cross-examination. She gave me a tentative smile and shook her head.

"Ms. Green, you have stated that you've been unable to form a new relationship in the year or so since you were assaulted by your common-law husband, is that correct?"

"Yes."

"Do you know a man by the name of Darnell Johnson?"

Crystal's eyes darted towards the Crown attorney. She didn't speak.

"Ms. Green? I asked you if you know Darnell Johnson."

"I know him."

"How do you know him?"

"He . . . he lives in the neighbourhood."

"Does he live with you?"

"He has his own place."

"His own place. Is that also your place?"

Silence again. "Ms. Green, do you have a relationship with Mr. Johnson?"

"What do you mean, a relationship?"

"What did *you* mean when you testified that you have been unable to form a relationship?" I brought out a story involving her and a group of friends in a bar; Johnson showed up and physically dragged her from the building.

"Did you ask for assistance? Call out for help?"

"No. I knew he'd settle down once we got home. He don't like me out with my friends."

"I see. So you went home with him. Home being where?"

Silence. Then: "My place." I waited. "Our place," she conceded, in a small voice.

I paused for a drink of water. "Ms. Green, do you know a man named Clifford Trites?"

The woman gave a little cry and put a hand up to her mouth.

"Clifford Trites. Did you have a relationship with him in the past?"

Blaine Melvin was on his feet. "Not relevant, Your Honour."

The judge roused himself and asked: "Relevance, Mr. Collins?"

"Your Honour, Ms. Green has testified about the impact this attack has had on her life. I am trying to explore her life a bit, in order to help the court assess the true magnitude of that impact."

"Very good of you, Mr. Collins. But try to get to the point."

"Yes, Your Honour. Ms. Green, you lived with Clifford Trites some years ago, correct?"

Her answer was barely audible. "Yes."

"Did you have children living at home at the time?"

She looked at her supporters in the gallery, then lowered her head. "My girl. Tiffany."

"Was Tiffany living with you the whole time you and Mr. Trites were together?"

Crystal Green's chin was trembling and she looked down at her clenched hands. I waited.

"No, she went to live with relatives for a couple of years."

"How old was Tiffany when you sent her to live with relatives?"

Crystal turned to face the judge, but he could barely be seen behind the slab of oak. "Why is he askin' me all this? What's this got to do with anything?"

The judge's voice came gently from somewhere on the bench. "Just answer the questions, Miss Green."

When she looked at me I could see the pleading in her eyes, but I continued to stare at her, waiting for her answer. "She was nine. She came back when she was eleven."

"And you stayed with Mr. Trites during this whole time?"

I saw a blaze of hatred and, possibly, shame in her eyes. "Yes! I stayed with him. You don't understand."

"Mr. Trites sexually assaulted your little girl, didn't he, Ms. Green? Repeatedly, over a period of nearly two years." The courtroom erupted: howls from the witness, shouts of disbelief from her stricken family, outraged objections from Crown counsel. The judge was sitting bolt upright, trying to control the court. I overrode the noise: "The man molested your child. You got rid of *her*, and stayed with *him*. This latest assault is not responsible for destroying your life, as you would have us believe. My client assaulted you, and he'll do time. I'm hopeful that he'll get the help he needs while he's in prison, and I hope you get the help you need. But he is not responsible for all the other pain you've endured in your life. That started long ago. I ask the court for the minimum federal time, two years. Thank you, Your Honour."

Over the ruckus, the Crown was asking for a publication ban on all the evidence, on the grounds that it would identify a victim of sexual assault, a child victim at that.

"I have no objection to a ban, Your Honour. It was never my intention that this should be public."

My client got two and a half years. When I turned away from the bench, I noticed that Robin Reid had fled the scene. Disillusioned no doubt, but with whom?

My clerk was gone. But Father Burke was there. Sitting at the edge of the public gallery, in civilian clothes, his face as pale as the envelope he gripped in his hand. He rose and came towards me with the envelope. His write-up of the Leeza Rae affair. I took it. His black eyes looked into mine and I was unable to turn away. His face was without expression but I knew he was spooked. Whether by me, or by something he saw in his own future, I could not have said. I was jostled by someone behind me and twisted to let the person pass. When I turned back, Burke had vanished.

Chapter 4

So taunt me and hurt me, Deceive me, desert me.
I'm yours till I die, So in love with you am I.
— Cole Porter, "So in Love"

I

The following Monday I reached Tyler MacDonald on the phone, and we agreed to meet that afternoon in the St. Bernadette's gymnasium. I arrived soaked from a cold, wind-driven rain. Eileen Darragh caught sight of me and handed me a paper towel. She was dusting her photos.

"Cleaning house in your spare time, Eileen?" I asked her. She struck me as a woman whose spare time was limited. But it might well be filled with fits of tidying up.

"You should see the dust on the tops of these old frames. Would you watch the phone for me for two seconds, Monty? I'm going to run down the hall to find a proper cleaning rag."

"Go ahead." She smiled and bustled away. I studied the photos, dated between 1953 and 1979. It was hard to picture all these children — many of them my contemporaries — living in an orphanage while I was growing up a short distance away, rolling my eyes at the absurdities of my parents and never giving a thought to what my life would have been without them. Some children smiled, some looked solemn, some forlorn. One boy was giving the photographer a particularly dark scowl. Eileen returned, short of breath, brandishing a rag and a jar filled with water.

"This will do the job," she promised. "Oh, will you look at that? Georgie, making such a face. He was lucky to be alive; he should have been smiling from one little pointy ear to the other." She clucked over the photo as she wiped its frame.

"Had he been ill?"

"No, he nearly drowned one summer. Our annual trip to Queensland Beach. And it was nearly our last, thanks to him."

"There's always one like that, isn't there?" I remarked.

"Oh yes. I remember that day so clearly. I was eight. It was early August. We all had our bathing suits on under our clothes, we had our towels and sun hats, and we piled onto the bus they hired for us. The sisters had prepared a picnic lunch, and the priests hefted these huge picnic baskets onto the bus. I don't know what caused greater anticipation, the swimming or the food! There were thirteen or fourteen of us I think, and the two priests. Father Burke was one of them. He was here for a couple of years, back in the late sixties, to set up the original choir school. It wasn't at St. Bernie's then, but he used to come to the orphanage to help out sometimes. And dear old Father Chisholm. I remember he had on this funny tie. The priests have these summer-weight short-sleeved shirts, black of course, and he wore a tie with a picture of a mermaid on it. A mermaid with cat-eye sunglasses and a cocktail in her hand. Sweet man, Father Chisholm. He died a few years ago.

"So we all headed out to Queensland. Oh, it was hot! Hard to imagine, looking out the window today. We paddled in the waves and made sandcastles, and drank orange pop. And peed in the water! The surf was quite heavy. Then, wouldn't you know, we heard Georgie hollering from way out in the water. How he got out that far without anyone seeing him, I don't know. He had everyone's attention now, though. We'd see his head, then he'd go under. It was really frightening. Father Burke swam out to get him. You know how you hear about drowning people dragging down their rescuers? I can believe it. Georgie was only around twelve, and not all that big, but

Father Burke had quite a time getting hold of him and hauling him in. Georgie choked up a lot of water but he was all right. Naturally, the times being what they were, the priests lit into him and gave him h-e-double-hockey-sticks.

"They let us have the rest of our day, thank the Lord, but it wasn't quite the same after that. Food was delicious, though. The sisters must have dug into their own pockets for it. It was only on the way home on the bus that we started to feel how sunburned we all were. One of the kids jumped on Father Burke's back, fooling around, and the poor man looked as if he wanted to scream. And Georgie threw up in the back of the bus just before we pulled off the highway into Halifax. Father Chisholm shouted at the driver to stop, and he jerked the bus over to the shoulder. What came out of Georgie slopped all the way to the front where I was sitting. I screeched and pulled my feet up and my sandal flew off and into the mess. Father Burke said in a loud whisper: 'You'd better tell Sister you lost your shoes at the beach, Eileen. It's all right. You can come to me for confession. Say a Hail Mary now for the lie and get it over with. Whisper it in my ear.' He lifted me over the back of my seat and sat me down beside him. He said: 'And don't be slurring any of the words together, or it doesn't count.' Then we all got the giggles. You know how kids remember things like that forever. Georgie wasn't the most popular boy in the home, let me tell you. Didn't have the beach trip again till two summers later."

I asked what else Eileen might be able to tell me about Burke. Here was someone who had known him when he must have been in his late twenties. But her response was disappointing.

"Oh, I hardly knew him, really. The kids didn't get to know the priests very well at all. They were quite remote figures to us, even the young ones, except for those rare occasions like the beach trip. Father Burke helped out in the office occasionally, doing what, I don't know. But he did teach us music twice a week, and that was fun." She focused her gaze on the gallery of photos. "I wonder what became of all those children. God love them."

I was silent for a few moments, then said I had to go see Tyler MacDonald.

"Off you go, then."

Off I went with visions of glory, for my client of course, not for me. If I hadn't gleaned much new insight into Father Burke, at least I had a minor story of heroism if I ever needed it. "My Lord, I have one more witness to call, a man who cut short his appearance at a pediatric surgeons' conference in Toronto to speak on behalf of my client, who, as we shall soon hear, is a saver of lives, not a killer. Dr. George McWitness will tell the court how, if it hadn't been for Father Burke, Dr. McWitness would never have grown up to be the country's top —" Sure. I hoped and prayed we would not get to that point. And I thought poor Georgie, if he had survived this long, was more likely known to police than to the Royal College of Physicians and Surgeons.

One thing I noted: Eileen Darragh had managed to get Father Burke's name into the conversation without once blushing. Eileen had been at St. Bernadette's all her life. She had met Burke when she was a child and he a young man. A plain little girl who had been singled out for a few moments of priestly attention on a bus trip. The woman could be forgiven if she felt a bit proprietorial. This could be a godsend if we ever needed a supporting witness.

Tyler MacDonald was a tall, nice-looking kid in jeans and a Dalhousie University sweatshirt. I found him shooting baskets with some younger kids; he signalled that he would be through in a few minutes. I waited. Good thing I did. If not for Tyler, I would still be in the dark about the door-slamming episode involving Leeza and my client. But we began with the dance.

"Did Leeza Rae have a dance with Father Burke?"

"Yeah, I think so."

"What kind of dance was this, do you remember?"

"Waltz. But somebody may have cut in on them."

"What do you mean?"

"You know, somebody tapped her on the shoulder and took over dancing with Burke."

"Who?"

"I can't remember. I'm not absolutely sure it was him they cut in on. Sorry. But if someone did, he must have thought 'oh, shit.' Leeza was quite a babe, between you and me. Even a priest would be bummed out if he blew the chance to get hold of something like that.

But I don't know; I was paying more attention to the girl I wanted to cut in on, at the far end of the dance floor!" He grinned.

"So, Tyler, are the priests well-liked around the centre?"

"Oh, yeah. Old Father O'Flaherty's a hoot. And Burke, well, he's a pretty interesting guy. All that music and Latin . . . but he also played football. Back in his high school and college days. We had a couple of touch football games and he came out and joined us. And he was going to be an architect, until he switched to something priestly and boring. I like Father Burke. It just takes a while to get to know him."

"Do the other staff people like him, do you think?"

"Yeah, I think so. Once they get used to him."

How was I going to approach this? "He's kind of a striking looking guy. Not exactly cute and cuddly —" Tyler laughed in agreement "— but someone a woman might look at. Anybody have a crush on him, do you know?"

"Yeah, well, one of the girls maybe. Erin. When he first got here. She used to talk to him about her problems, whatever they were. But I don't think she's still moony-eyed over him. She has a boyfriend now. Girls probably go through that with any priest who's not too old and doddering. Of course, people joke about the nuns being in love with him. Well, Eileen's not really a nun — but her and Sister Marguerite. I think people would say that, though, about any sister or church lady, and a priest."

"Any signs of it, though? Love?" I made a joke of the word.

"Well, Eileen gets a bit tongue-tied around him, but he's the type that makes some people nervous, you know? Except Marguerite. Nobody makes her nervous. She could command a battle zone. She was stationed in some scary hot spots around the world, before she came here. Practically in the middle of a gun battle, I heard. Marguerite and Burke talk to each other a lot; sometimes they seem to be arguing, but it's about stuff that only, like, one percent of the population would understand. He'll stick his head in her office and announce: 'You were wrong again. It wasn't St. Augustine who said blah, blah whatever it was.' She caught him up in the hall once, I remember, and spouted some Bible verse, Paul's letter to the Fallopians or something. She said: 'If you'd read it and understood it Father, you'd be a better man for it. A humbler man.' And he shot back something like he was already perfect in his humility. I didn't get it, but it's funny because neither of them ever cracks a smile at the other one. That's not hearts-and-flowers stuff, though. I don't really see much of that around here."

"Just a couple more questions, about Leeza Rae. What was she like?"

"Screwed up. I'm sorry to say that about a dead person and all, but that's it. Screwed up. She had this boyfriend, in prison somewhere. I think he even raped a girl. And Leeza talked about him as if he was a regular guy. He was going to marry her when he got out, and all this bullshit. He wouldn't be getting out for years, so what was she going to do? Wait around for this creep, all through her twenties? I couldn't figure her out. She used to crap on the other girls here, putting them down, how they looked, what they wore, all that. I steered clear of her, to tell you the truth. She used to flirt with me in a really gross way. Not just me, but the other guys too. In one way, you wanted to take her up on it. But you just knew something would go wrong. Some violent boyfriend would come out of the woodwork. And I guess one did."

"How did she act around the bosses here, the nuns, Eileen, the priests?"

"Oh, she behaved a lot better in front of them. Didn't want to lose her meal ticket. She was nice as pie to Eileen and Sister, and Father O'Flaherty too."

"And with Father Burke?"

"I only saw her with him once. They had some kind of a fight. An argument. I don't know what it was about."

Oh, what now? "Tell me."

"I was cleaning the windows in the conference room. The door to the next room opened and I could hear Leeza say 'Fuck you.' Then: 'Let me go, you broke my fucking watch.' Next thing I heard was Father Burke saying: 'Don't do anything stupid.' He sounded really pissed off. The door slammed and she ran off. I went into the hall and watched her go. Burke yanked the door open, and looked as if he was going to go after her. But he saw me and went back inside the classroom. I didn't know what to do, so I got on with cleaning the windows. You know, like the bartender who keeps wiping the bar, pretending he didn't hear anything. I looked out and there was Leeza giving the finger to somebody in the building and it wasn't me. Father Burke must have been in the window too." Tyler shifted in his seat. "I thought . . . I thought she had a couple of buttons of her blouse unfastened." He turned slightly red. "But maybe I just imagined that. I wouldn't be the first guy to picture her with her clothes undone. Sorry if I'm coming off as an asshole."

What the hell was going on? "No, Tyler, you're doing great. I appreciate anything you remember. Honestly."

"It's just that I feel, you know, as if I'm crapping all over someone who's dead. Saying she was stripping off in front of a priest. It all happened so fast."

I was not sure I wanted to ask the next question, but it would be better if it came out now rather than in a courtroom. "So, your take on it was that it was her doing, if any clothing was undone, and not something the priest did?"

"Oh God, no. Father Burke wouldn't do anything like that. Or if he did, he wouldn't be dumb enough to try it in a classroom where anyone could walk in. There are no locks on those doors. And Leeza was so, well, unpredictable, she might have done anything. Screamed the house down, who knows?" Tyler looked miserable. "Maybe I should have kept this to myself."

"Did the police discuss any of this with you, Tyler?" I asked, dreading the answer.

"No, I didn't get into it. I didn't even think of it then. Everybody was just trying to remember what happened during the dance and afterwards. And Leeza was always flying off the handle at somebody. It just went out of my mind." He looked at me. "I hope I don't get in shit for not telling them."

"You won't. I'm sure if they want to talk to you again, they'll call. One last thing, and I'll let you get back to your life. When did this happen, this disagreement between Leeza and the priest?"

"It must have been February because I remember thinking I was going to have to finish the windows early so I could do some ordering for the dance during office hours."

So, it had happened at most a couple of weeks before the murder. I thanked Tyler, tried to reassure him, and left the gym. Seething.

II

Defence lawyers must be the most patient, self-controlled people in the world. How else to explain the fact that the tabloids are not filled with story after story of lawyers murdering their clients in a fit of rage and frustration? Burke had been forced on me by my dear friend Rowan Stratton, who had succeeded in luring me away from my former job with Legal Aid, with all its lying, unreliable clients. Like Burke. An altercation with the victim, an eruption of strong feelings between them, seen and overheard by a reliable witness. The girl running away from Burke, who had obviously been gripping her wrist, and her with her shirt undone. This was textbook Criminal Law 101. Here's the kind of thing you have to watch when you get out there practising law, kids. It's hard to believe now, but clients think you're the enemy. So they don't tell you what you most need to know. But they'll squawk to the police.

I was barely coherent as I made my way down the corridor towards the choir school, where the good priest no doubt sat, smirking and self-satisfied — No sign of him. I headed outdoors in the lashing rain, which did nothing to lighten my mood, and made for the rectory.

I was nearly out of breath, not from the short walk but from tension. Mrs. Kelly met me at the door. I hardly recognized my own voice. "Is Father Burke in, Mrs. Kelly?"

"Oh, no, not today." She gave a doleful shake of her faded head.

"Where is he, do you know?"

"Jail."

"What?"

"It's his day for ministering to the prisoners, Mr. Collins. Wouldn't you be terrified of those animals out there? Not him, though. Well, as the good Lord said: 'Verily I say unto you, inasmuch as ye have done it unto one of the least of these my brethren, ye have done it unto me.' Father Burke sure lives up to the Lord's holy word. I'll tell him you called."

"Will he be in tomorrow?"

"Oh, yes. He'll be back by then. God willing." She looked around. "I'm alone here today. It makes me jumpy. Lord knows who is going to come in."

"What are you afraid of, Mrs. Kelly?"

"We had a break-in," she confided.

"Oh? When was this?"

"New Year's Day. The office was closed and everyone was over at the archbishop's levee. That's when it happened."

"What were they after? Was anything taken?"

"Oh, I don't know. They wouldn't tell me that."

"Well, did you notice anything missing? The silverware? The teapot?"

"Oh, it wasn't here at the rectory. It was over at the archdiocesan office."

"Then maybe you have nothing to worry about. Don't forget to ask Father Burke to call me. It's important. Goodbye now." She nodded and swiftly shut the door. I heard a bolt click into place.

That night, Monday, was blues night. I was supposed to have my children with me that week, but they had been at Maura's most of the past month. That was only because I had finally made the effort to hire someone to replaster some walls and sand the old wood floors, and the work still wasn't finished. There was no point in having the kids shoved into the only room that had not been torn apart. I hadn't wanted to leave our old place on Dresden Row, but, when Maura and I split up, I found a house I liked just off Purcell's Cove Road on the other, much more affordable, side of the Northwest Arm. Its waters were a feature of my front yard. I had a dock and, for a while, a sailboat. But sailing left little time for my main avocational interest, music, so I sold the boat.

That way, even on a clear day with a brisk breeze and the sun dancing on the water, I could sit in a dingy room and jam with the little blues band I had started up two decades before. We called ourselves Functus. There were three guys and a woman I had gone to law school with, veterans of many a night spent listening to our local blues hero, Dutchie Mason, in a variety of never-to-be-yuppified bars where the smoke was so thick it seemed to be part of the bass line. When I formed the band I was single and lived like a single guy. Now, even though my marriage was in the bin, I did not want to become an *habitué* of the local pick-up joints. That's not to say I wouldn't have enjoyed it once in a while but, as an over-forty father of two, I tried to preserve some dignity. Blues night, though, kept me from going raving, barking mad.

We were at my place this week. My forte was harmonica and slide guitar, although I sang from time to time. This was one of those times. I knew what I was talkin' about when I wailed "Stormy Monday Blues."

III

Blues night went a long way to calming me down and I slept well. But as I drove to the office the next morning, late, my blood began to boil again over that perfidious client I had taken on. I'm not much of a coffee drinker, unless I'm in spying mode, but I went to a Tim's drive-through and ordered a medium double double and two big, fat doughnuts. At least the rain had stopped. When I walked in, Darlene was on the phone.

"Oh, just one second. He's walking in the door. I'll put you on hold." She gestured to me with the phone. I went to my office, sat down at my desk, took a big gulp of hot coffee and picked up the receiver.

"Yes?" I growled.

"Father Burke here. You sound a little brusque this morning. Have a bad night? Mrs. Kelly left me a message —"

"How fast can you get over here?" I hissed into the phone.

"Well, I —"

"I'll expect you in ten minutes." Slam.

He arrived right on time, wearing his leather jacket over a black clerical shirt but no white collar. "Morning, counsellor."

"Shut the door."

He closed the door and sat down, never taking his dark eyes off my face.

"Two weeks before the murder, you and the victim had a little set-to at the youth centre. You were grasping her arm, she told you to fuck yourself, and she ran from the room with her shirt half off. Strong feelings, strong words, physical contact, and the whiff of sex.

When I hear something like this, Burke, I hear a bell tolling the death of your defence. And you didn't see fit to tell me about it?"

For the first time ever in my presence, Burke looked less than supremely confident. He put his head back and closed his eyes.

"Do the police know about this?" I asked.

"I don't think so," he answered quietly.

"Then you didn't tell them."

"Right." His eyes were still closed and he began massaging his temples.

I leaned forward and said into his face: "You told me you hardly knew her. Now, what's the story? Were you, or were you not, having it off with Leeza Rae?"

His eyes flew open and he sat upright. "No. I was not."

"Well then, how do you explain what happened? Why do I get the feeling that, if I stay on this case, I'm going to spend all my time running after you for explanations of things I should have heard about on day one? Now, tell me the truth. What was going on?"

"There was nothing going on between me and the young girl," he began in a quiet voice. "It's true we had an argument that day about that boyfriend of hers. A real piece of work. Sitting up there in Dorchester Penitentiary for the rape of a little teenaged girl. Leeza wanted me to go up to see the boyfriend. What is it? Two, three hours away? She knew I do prison visits once a week. He needed help, she said. What she really meant was she wanted me to start paying this clown regular visits, so when parole time came round, I'd be there to support a recommendation for release."

This sounded plausible. But it would. Burke had had a month and a half to think it up.

There was a knock at the door and my client looked as annoyed as I felt. "What is it?" I snapped, and Tina, my secretary, poked her elaborately styled head in the door.

"I'm sorry to interrupt, but what response did you want me to give Mr. Gillis on his offer to settle? You told me you're turning it down but what do you want to say in the letter?"

"Just tell him no. We'll be a while here, Tina, and I don't want to be disturbed." She apologized and backed out.

Burke was looking at me with a glint of amusement in his eyes. "You were saying?" I prodded him.

"Aside from the parole assistance the girl envisioned down the road, what she was really after was a regular ride up to Dorchester to see this gobshite. I would drive and pay the expenses, and she'd save herself a bus trip." He seemed genuinely angry. "Can you figure that out, Collins? A girl still wanting to cozy up to a boyfriend who'd not only had sex with another girl, but had committed rape?"

"Why did she think you would even consider this?"

"Out of the goodness of my heart, I'm thinking. But if not that . . ."

"There was something in it for you."

"Right. She started to unbutton her shirt, telling me that all this would be mine, if we could take off together the next week for Dorchester."

"So what was your reaction to that?"

He glared at me and peppered me with some unsacerdotal language: "You mean, did I try to get a leg up over her? I'm a little more self-disciplined than that. Besides, I was too pissed off. I grabbed her wrist to stop her taking her clothes off. To prevent her from demeaning herself any further. Then she said she was quitting the youth centre and moving to Dorchester to be close to this arsehole. She'd get some kind of work up there, or sell herself if she had to. I told her not to do anything so idiotic. Christ. This girl would do anything for that woman-hater of a boyfriend!"

"We're guys, Father. We both know what assholes men can be. But I have yet to see a male so vicious or so ugly that he does not have a woman waiting faithfully in the wings. You witnessed a prime example that day you were in the courtroom. Mother of an abused child. And I'm sure you'll remember it was the woman's boyfriend who abused —"

Burke was shaking his head. "Don't be telling me that again."

"And in order to do what I had to do for my client, I took her apart on the stand."

He didn't need me to tell him this was what the Crown prosecutor would do to him if his case went to trial.

He gave me a long look, then returned to the encounter with Leeza Rae. "Anyway. I grabbed her wrist, she told me to fuck off, and she ran out of the building. You can be sure I didn't mention this to the police when they didn't seem to know about it."

"We can't assume they don't know about it."

"Oh God," he muttered, "somebody killed this girl, and, considering the company she kept —"

"Moody Walker thinks it was you."

"It wasn't."

"And I would like to convince him of that. Or at least find something I can toss his way to make him look elsewhere and stop dropping your name to his old cronies on the force. I can't do it directly. I don't want him to know you've retained counsel. But listen to me, Father. I cannot represent you if you continue to withhold evidence from me." The priest nodded, taking it in at last. "Now, I'm going to ask you once more. Is there anything else that happened between you and this girl? Anything. Any time. Anywhere."

"Just one thing. After that row we had in the classroom, she came in and apologized. It may have been the next day. She said she had been out of line, she was sorry, and could we be friends again? I have no doubt that she just wanted to butter me up, so she could work on me again. But I said I was sorry too, for getting angry with her. After that, we just said hello in the corridors. No tension, but no more chats. I saw her at the dance the night she was killed. I think I danced with her but if I did, it wasn't for long, or she probably would have started up a conversation and I'd remember it. It may have been one of those dance games where everyone cuts in. I simply don't know."

Father Burke looked exhausted. My fury had dissipated and my heart went out to him, as aggravating as he could be. After all, I had spent my adult life defending people accused of doing the most wretched things to other people. Some innocent, most guilty. So I must have been a softie, deep deep down. "Why don't you go home now, put on a set of headphones and listen to some music? Or make your own. If there's nothing more you can tell me, we'll just have to wait this out."

"I'm not a wait-it-out kind of man."

"I can see that, Father. But we can't make any moves, apart from some discreet investigating on the side. But that's not you, it's me. I'll be in touch."

He stood and put out his hand. I reached for it and we shook.

"Montague," the clipped tone had softened somewhat, "I know you're doing your best for me, and I appreciate it. I'm a little tense these days."

I smiled. "Little wonder. Talk to you soon."

Chapter 5

Always with true faith my prayer rose to the holy shrines.
Always with true faith I gave flowers to adorn the altar.
In my hour of sorrow why, why, o Lord,
why do you reward me this way?
— Puccini, Giacosa/Illica, "Vissi d'arte," *Tosca*

I

The circus had come to town and I brought Tommy Douglas and Normie to the Metro Centre for the show. Normie was bouncing with excitement, as much because it was a school night as because this was her first time at a circus. I had her umpteenth pair of eyeglasses stored safely in my pocket, to be handed out when the show began. With any luck, they would emerge unbroken at the end of the evening. All three of us got caught up in the show. It was not until intermission that the evening lost its lustre. The kids joined a long line at the canteen and I stood around waiting, enjoying the crowd. Then I spied Moody Walker, dressed in a tweed sports jacket over a St. Mary's University sweatshirt, in the company of two young boys. Nephews, or possibly grandsons. Walker saw me at the same time, and I went over to be civil. We chatted about the show and upcoming sports events.

"How's retirement suiting you these days, Sergeant? Settling in to it any better?"

"Not quite yet. I'm helping the police with their inquiries, you know, the way civilians are supposed to do." His lugubrious features brightened into a smile. "That murder we discussed a while back."

"Oh, yes?" I held my breath.

"Vern Doucette, who's in charge of the case, is setting aside some time for me day after next. I'm going to lay it all out for him, the case I think we have against this priest. These guys think they can get away with anything, wearing that collar. I'll show him a collar!" He peered at me. "You don't look so good, Collins. You're not an altar boy or anything, are you? If you're a friend of this Burke, better find yourself another confessor. Hey, Phil!" Walker spotted a pal and gave me a farewell salute. I waited for the kids to get their snacks. Tommy came towards me with an enormous bag of buttered popcorn, and offered it to me. I couldn't even look at it.

"You guys go back to your seats. I'll be with you in a second. And Tom, make sure she goes to her seat and stays in it. And keeps her glasses on."

"Sure, Dad. You all right?"

"Mmm." I turned and went into the nearest washroom, where I splashed my face with cold water and stood for a minute to calm down. The mirror told me I looked the way I always did, as if I did-n't have a care in the world. Then I headed for a phone and dialed the Strattons' number.

"Hello." Sylvia's plummy voice.

"Hello Sylvia. It's Monty."

"Oh, yes, how are you Monty? You must pay us a visit soon. We haven't seen you."

"Thanks, Sylvia. I'll do that. Is Rowan around?"

Rowan came on the line. "My dear Collins. Good of you to call. You've just saved me from a very bad hand at whist. I shall be eternally grateful."

"Rowan, I'm at the Metro Centre. Just ran into Moody Walker. He says he has a meeting set up with Sergeant Doucette the day after tomorrow. He's going to lay out his case against our friend."

"Does he know we're on for Burke?" Rowan asked quickly.

"I don't think so. But he noticed I looked a little distressed when I heard the news. Wondered if I'm a friend of our man."

"Well, I have a few chips to call in over at the police department. A certain senior officer — my source for the Moody Walker information in the first place. He'll tell me yes or no when the decision comes down. Won't pass along anything about the evidence though, blast him. We'll have to wait till disclosure time for that. If it goes that far, I should say. Of course we shan't know how long Doucette will take to mull things over. Do you want to give our friend the heads up, or shall I?"

"I'll speak to him tomorrow. Thanks, Rowan."

II

I called the rectory first thing in the morning, but Mrs. Kelly told me Father Burke was out for choir practice and would not be back until late afternoon. I found it hard to concentrate on my other files. I was supposed to conduct a discovery examination of the plaintiff's expert in a complex construction suit, but I turned that over to one of the associates, someone whose mind would be on the job. I was half-heartedly proofreading draft one of an appeal factum when my phone rang.

"Montague. Brennan Burke here. You called."

"Yes, I did. Brennan, could we —"

I heard a child's voice. "Who you talkin' to, Father?"

"Just a minute, Montague. What did I ask you to do there, Alvin? Not pester me, was it?"

I remembered the little dark-skinned angel I had seen clambering up to her place in the choir loft. And the sweet voice that emerged once she had cleared her throat.

"Who's that on the phone?" she wanted to know.

"Someone very important," Burke replied.

"Who? That white guy?"

There was a moment's hesitation. "He's a white guy, yes."

"No, I mean that guy in the white dress and hat."

"Ah. That's a picture of the Pope, Alvin. Is he on the phone with me, you're asking?"

"Where am I s'posed to start singing?" she demanded.

"As I said, you start the second line, there, after I sing *Deo*. Right there. *Gloria in excelsis Deo,*" the priest intoned, beautifully, and then I heard the child's voice join in: *"Et in terra . . ."* She sang directly into the phone, to me, the guy in white.

"Get thee behind me, Satan!" This from Burke. "Go over by the window, Alvin, start your part again, and let me make my call." The child began to sing again, farther from the phone. "Sorry." Burke lowered his voice. "Her father, or stepmother, or whoever it is this week, forgot to come pick her up. Again. Usually I leave her with one of the volunteers at the centre, or Eileen. We've all had our turn. But nobody's free today. Imagine the parents forgetting their child. So, what's on your mind?"

"I'm just on my way out now," I hedged. "Is there somewhere we could get together this evening?"

If my client was worried, he didn't let on. "You could always come up to my room. You'd be even more welcome if you brought with you, say, a Tomaso pizza."

The *Gloria* stopped and the little voice said: *"Pizza?* I love pizza, but it makes me burp."

"Are you hungry, Al? Maybe we could walk up the street and find something for you to eat. You've done enough work for today."

"Go for something to eat, with *you?*" she squealed.

"Why not? You don't want to walk up the street with an old fellow? I didn't have a grey hair on my head till I met the likes of you, Alvin."

"What are we gonna eat?"

"Have to go, Montague. You know how it is when you have kids. How about eight o'clock?"

"Fine."

I stayed on at the office and did some other work. Then I ordered a pizza and drove to the north end of the city to pick it up. The pizzeria was in the Hydrostones, so named for the type of concrete block used in the houses that were rebuilt following the catastrophic Halifax Explosion of 1917.

I arrived at the rectory a few minutes early, still in my business suit, pizza in hand. Mrs. Kelly directed me to a dark-varnished staircase to the second floor. Just as the first step creaked under the weight of my foot, Sister Marguerite Dunne charged through the rectory door and pointed her finger upward. Mrs. Kelly nodded and we went up together.

"Moonlighting, are you, Mr. Collins? Not enough skullduggery to pay the bills?" Sister Dunne clearly found my situation amusing.

"Actually this is my real job, Sister. The work I do by day is just something to tide me over when there's a lull in the pizza business, like weekdays nine to five. With the pizza job I provide a useful service, and I meet a nicer class of people."

We walked to the end of an east-west corridor, which intersected with a hallway running north. The priest's was the last room on the right before the turn. The door was ajar and I pushed it open. He was flaked out across an armchair, dressed in a thin white T-shirt tucked into a pair of faded denim shorts, and his feet were bare. His eyes were closed and he was conducting the music coming from the stereo. A woman with a glorious voice was singing *misericordia* something, and the melody was splendid enough to be Mozart. Father Burke heard the door but didn't open his eyes. He waved a hand at me to be quiet.

"Her voice is like cream. Do you suppose she'd move in with me, Montague? If I spruced this place up a bit? Let her choose the curtains? Kiri Te Kanawa and Brennan Burke, together at last. All he asks of her is that she sing to him every night. She desires more of him, of course. But Brennan, his vows intact, merely plants a chaste kiss on her —"

I cleared my throat. "Uh, Father Burke . . ." I tried to impart a warning in my tone.

He reluctantly opened his eyes, which fell, not on me, but on Sister Dunne, and his eyelids flew open like sprung window shades. Until that instant, I could not have imagined such a look on his face, normally so composed. Surprise, embarrassment, and a complete inability to formulate an appropriate response. A rare experience for him, I expected.

"Marguerite!" he croaked, bolting from his chair and reaching out to snap off the stereo.

The nun's habitual air of restrained amusement had blossomed into undisguised triumph. "Well, Brennan! If I'd known you were sitting here in your underclothes, communing with a woman in New Zealand, I would not have intruded." She smiled in joyful malice.

"I'm not in my underclothes!" Burke protested.

"Good thing she wasn't singing the 'Habanera' from *Carmen*. We don't know whether the vows would have remained intact in that case. Well, I won't keep you. I just wanted to drop this off. I'll get your comments later, if you're still interested in 'Christology in the Patristic Age: Development and Synthesis.' Oh, and Brennan, the pizza man is here. The least you can do is come out of yourself and give him a tip. And do eat up." She looked him up and down. "You look as if you're losing weight. Must be love." She smiled widely at me and clacked out of the room, her day complete.

"Shit!" Burke exclaimed, hands running through his hair.

"I have to admit, Brennan, that little scene did a hell of a lot to brighten up my day."

"Glad I could be of service," he replied with something of his usual tartness. "What's on the pizza?"

"The works."

"Good. I have a couple of very nice Italian wines a friend brought over for me. Unless you'd prefer whiskey."

"Wine would be perfect," I told him.

"We'll open the Barolo and let it breathe for a bit; it's been bottled up for ten years. Let's start swigging the Chianti with our pizza." He went to a cupboard and brought out the bottles and a corkscrew. His room was filled with books, ancient and new, musical scores, albums and compact discs, on the shelves and on the floor. But his bed was made up tight as a drum, and his clothes could be seen through the open door of his wardrobe, all hanging neatly with plastic over them to keep off the dust. There was a street scene that must have been Rome tacked on the wall, a calendar that obviously came from Ireland, and a couple of Renaissance reproductions in frames. No religious kitsch. I was especially taken with one of the prints and went over for a closer look.

Madonna della Melagrana," he explained. "It sounds better in Italian so I won't translate. It's Botticelli. Have you ever seen anything more beautiful than the face of this Child? It's in the Uffizi. The first time I saw it I stood in front of it so long I missed out on all the other rooms of the gallery." He handed me a wine glass brimming with dark red liquid. He raised his glass and touched it lightly to mine. "Whatever it is you have to tell me, keep it till after we eat."

He produced some plates and silverware and cleared a table near one of the windows, gestured for me to sit, and we fell upon the pizza as if it was our first meal ever, or our last.

"This wine isn't for swigging," I remarked, holding it up to the light.

"There's Chianti, and there's Chianti," he agreed. "But, if you like this, wait till we get to the next bottle."

"I just hope we'll be able to appreciate it."

"We will."

"What was that piece of music you were playing when Sister Dunne and I walked in on you?" I couldn't wipe the grin from my face. "I'm a product of Catholic schools and I can tell you that was the most ecstatic expression I have ever seen on the face of a nun."

"Oh, that little scene will sustain the good sister like the bread of life. That was Mozart's 'Laudate Dominum.' Sung to perfection by —" he looked over at me and raised his glass in her honour "— my beloved Kiri Te Kanawa. Did you hear those long lines? She doesn't seem to breathe when she sings. And a beautiful woman to look at, incidentally. Well, you probably know that." He sighed, and forked another bite of pizza into his mouth. We ate in silence for a few moments.

"So you went to Catholic schools, did you?" Burke said. "I thought as much." He made a show of looking at my hands. "Though I don't see the scars. But judging by that boyish face, I'd guess you were everybody's favourite altar boy."

"Yeah, I was an altar boy. I've since been defrocked."

"Nah, you still have the look. Must be an advantage in the courtroom. The poor wretched woman you had on the stand the other day didn't know what hit her."

I had no desire to dwell on that episode so I went back to the cosh-wielding nuns. "I got slammed a few times, like everybody else," I recalled.

"I suppose you did," he replied. "The only thing that saved me from getting pounded even more often was the fact that I was singing in the choir. I was no angel, but I sure as hell sounded like one."

"So, what made you decide to be a priest? With your voice, even if you had nothing else going for you, you could be married to Kiri and have a houseful of little choristers."

"Houseful of little hellions, probably." He took a sip of wine. "Why a priest? I got the call, Montague, that's all I can say. I had other plans. I started university in the sciences. I was going to be an architect. But there are things I was meant to do, and I'm doing them. What's your excuse? Why put yourself in the way of so much aggravation, being a lawyer?"

And so it went. We exchanged stories from our university days, his time playing football at the home of the Seven Blocks of Granite, Fordham University. Mine playing hockey. I regaled him with some of the typical war stories any lawyer accumulates. He spoke about teaching at this or that university or seminary. Then he decided he wanted to teach children at an earlier stage of their development. I said I'd always thought priests were under orders to obey and go wherever they were sent. He said that was usually the case, but every few years he wore the authorities down with a request to go somewhere of his own choosing. I asked whether he had any ambitions to rise in the hierarchy. It wasn't hard to picture him lording it over others as a bishop. I got the impression that the opportunities were there for him if he wanted them. But it was apparent that he, like many people satisfied with their lives and impatient with others, had no desire to lead.

We talked about music, without which, we agreed, life would not be worth living. He clearly saw it as his role to introduce children to the world's great sacred music, hence his involvement with various choir schools. He was composing his first Mass, for four voices. On a theological note, he observed that some people had been inspired to believe in God by the simple fact that Mozart had been in the world. And he was convinced that Van Morrison was in direct communication ("unmediated communion") with the divine. Like me, he enjoyed all forms of music with few exceptions, disco, country twang, and soft rock being among the exceptions. "If it's rock, it ought to rock," we agreed as we neared the midpoint of the second bottle of wine. The Irish intonation in his voice had become much more pronounced over the course of the evening. God knows what I sounded like.

I leaned closer to the window and looked out at the street below us. Dark and still. "Is that Father O'Flaherty down there?"

Burke looked down. "Yeah, that's Mike."

"Where would he be going at this time of night? Sick call?"

"I doubt it." Burke craned his neck to watch as the old priest rounded a corner below us. "We don't see a sprightly gait on the man, *ergo* no sick call. Besides, Mike reports all those to me before he trots off, every blessed one of them, forgetting that I wouldn't know the person from Finn McCool. I've only been in the parish since the fall. I'm long past reminding him." Burke glanced at the window again. "Maybe he's bringing the Word of God to the street trade. Mike wants to save everybody: boozers, hookers, accountants, lawyers. He leaves the jailbirds to me. Wise man. I suppose I'm ministering to some of your clients. Taking up where you left off."

"You're suggesting my clients do jail time, Brennan? Oh ye of little faith."

Even with the second bottle of wine, the subject I most wanted to hear about never came up. Whenever we got close to speaking of the women in our lives, he deftly steered the conversation in other directions. I did tell him that my wife and I were separated, that we shared custody of our two children, and that it took a superhuman effort for us to handle this with civility. He asked about Normie and Tommy Douglas, and enjoyed hearing about their antics.

It was getting late, the pizza had been annihilated hours before, and the wine was down to the dregs. I could no longer avoid the topic I had come to discuss: Moody Walker's planned meeting with the officer in charge of the Leeza Rae murder investigation. I was about to broach the subject when Burke left the table and returned with two big Havana cigars. I shook my head and he lit up, then regarded me with steady eyes as black as coal behind the pall of smoke.

"Am I going to be charged with this, Monty?" he asked abruptly.

"Not yet, if at all. But Sergeant Walker is meeting with the officer in charge tomorrow, to lay out his case against you. Whatever it is."

"Of all the things I've faced in my life — and it hasn't all been sweetness and light — I could never have imagined being under suspicion of murder." There was sadness and bewilderment in his voice.

"Rowan has an in with the department, and he'll know in advance if anything is going to happen. I wish I could tell you more. It sounds inane to say we'll have to wait and see. But that's what we're faced with. If the worst happens and charges are laid, then we get to work demolishing their case. We get their evidence, and we proceed to explain it away."

"You won't have to explain anything away. There cannot be any evidence against me. I didn't do it," he said, and drew heavily on his cigar. "Monty, go home and get some sleep so you can do good works for those of us in need. I'll call a taxi. You're not fit to be driving." He got up and stabbed some numbers into his phone.

"Will you be able to sleep, Brennan?"

"In heavenly peace," he replied, smiling ironically, and he put a consoling arm around my shoulder.

III

I had not attempted to push my wife along in her assignment at the city morgue. One got nowhere with Maura by being pushy and I knew she was busy with the children and with work. She would get to the morgue as soon as she could. The call finally came the morning after my session with Burke at the rectory.

"I got it. Can you talk?"

"Tell me."

"A small cross was carved above the victim's left breast." Oh, God. "And initials over the right one. The initials were 'IBR.' Mean anything to you?"

"No." I thought for a moment. "And I don't for a minute think it stands for 'I, Brennan.'"

"Who's Brennan?"

"Burke's first name."

"Oh. And, Monty, I do mean above the breasts, not on them."

I paused. "I don't like that."

"No."

"So now we know what the police are looking at this week. I wish I could make sense of it."

"What's this about the police? I thought we were dealing with an overly zealous retired sergeant."

"We were." I filled her in on Walker. "Now we have to wait."

"What are you going to do about the initials? Are you going to mention them to Burke?" she asked.

"I don't know what to do. Obviously, if he's guilty, he's going to send me to Mars for the answers. If he's innocent, of course, he could be a help. This may have some religious significance, but somehow I suspect it's more obscure than that. More personal. I'm going to sit on it for a while. If I can't come up with an interpretation myself, I'll bring it up with Burke. The first thing we have to do is wait to see if anything organic hits the fan as the result of Moody's presentation to the Major Crime Unit. God knows what he's telling them about our client."

Chapter 6

Now MacHeath spends just like a sailor.
Could it be our boy's done something rash?
Now Jennie Diver, yeah Sukey Tawdry,
Miss Lotte Lenya and old Lucy Brown
Oh that line forms on the right, babe,
now that Macky's back in town
— Kurt Weill, Bertolt Brecht, Marc Blitzstein, "Mack the Knife"

I

I had not yet got around to interviewing Father O'Flaherty about the February 14 dance, and I was anxious to talk to him now. I called and was told he was doing his hospital rounds, but was expected back by four-thirty. That was good timing for me because it coincided with a partners' meeting at the office. I was way behind in the time sheets we all had to fill in, recording our entire work day in tenths of an hour. Making a phone call or dictating a short memo might take "point 1," or six minutes of billable time. You don't want a day full of tasks like that. Attending a trial for five hours was a lot less of a pain to record. Typically, I had not kept track and now would have to estimate how much time I had spent on each file. But there was no point in troubling myself with time sheets if I couldn't make the afternoon meeting.

I had started my career as a Legal Aid lawyer, doing defence work on a government salary. In some jurisdictions I would have been called a public defender. Over the years I became increasingly burnt out by the aggravating horde of clients and exhausting court schedule. Rowan Stratton lured me away after a string of acquittals I achieved, in some cases against considerable odds. I found private law gratifying at first. The court schedule was manageable and my earnings were higher. Of course not everyone in the firm appreciated the criminal clients slouching in the waiting room with the corporate clientele. I did other kinds of work as well, but I was generally pegged as the firm's criminal lawyer.

It was not long before I understood why so many Legal Aid lawyers make a career of it. They like the court work, they know they are providing a crucial service, they have a good shot at a judgeship, and they can do without the seventy-hour weeks that many private lawyers feel compelled to put in, with the billable hours quota hanging over their heads. When I made the move, I did not foresee — though perhaps I should have — that my new career would be the *coup de grâce* for my failing marriage. My wife gave up on me when I told her I could not make a long-planned vacation with the family. The day before we were to leave, a corporate client demanded that I fly to his headquarters in Toronto, a thousand miles away, to hold his hand during negotiations that could just as well have been handled by the company's in-house counsel. When I told him I was about to embark on a family vacation, he said: "Welcome to my world." He advised me that I had better get my wife trained early; she would be spending a lot of vacations with the kids and no Monty.

Well, my wife is not trainable. But he was right about one thing: I no longer featured in her holiday plans. Of course work wasn't the only thing we clashed over, far from it. But what could I say when she reminded me of the way we had planned our future together? We had wanted a houseful of kids, and intended to devote our lives to them and to each other. Yet, here I was, a partner in a private firm and a week-on, week-off dad to our two children. Ironically, after the separation, I made an arrangement with the firm that I would forgo much of the night and weekend work. (The corresponding reduction in compensation was only fair to my partners.) It came too late for my wife, but it salvaged my relationship with the kids.

I looked at my watch. Four-fifteen. Time to clear out before the partners' meeting.

Father O'Flaherty met me in an old-fashioned parlour furnished

75

in a vaguely Victorian style with a worn Aubusson carpet, and some large, ornately framed portraits of former bishops.

"Good day to you, Montague," Michael O'Flaherty said cheerfully. "Tea?"

"Not for me thanks, Father." He poked his head out and asked Mrs. Kelly for one cup of tea and a plate of sweets to go with it.

"How can I help you this fine day, sir?"

"I'd just like to get your recollections of the dance, if I could."

"Certainly, certainly. What would you like to know?"

"What time did you get there, do you remember?"

He paused to think, then said: "I got there early and helped the youngsters set up the bar. Well, not what you and I would think of as a bar. Soft drinks only. I looked through the selection of music, but once again there was nothing from my era! That's only to be expected. The dance was for young people of the nineties, not for those of us who were young in the thirties and forties. But the music was tuneful enough for me to carry on as a dancing fool." Mrs. Kelly arrived with tea for the priest, and a tray of sweets.

"What time did Leeza Rae arrive, did you notice?"

"Yes, I noticed, because she was supposed to help out like the rest of the young people who worked at the centre. But she got there just as the dance was about to start. Young Erin made a remark to her, and Leeza must have sassed her back because Erin just walked away from her. A minor little spat, though. It happens."

"Did you notice whether Leeza arrived alone?"

"I didn't see her till she was inside the gym, so how she got there I can't say. She didn't live on the peninsula, though, so she must have had a ride or taken a bus."

"Was there anything different about her that night, that you were aware of?" I plucked a brownie from the plate.

"She seemed just the same to me, but then I didn't know her very well. So I'm obviously not the priest she claimed had taken such an interest in her." He put his teacup down and looked at me with a sombre expression. "In retrospect, I wish I had shown more of an interest, found out what was going on in her life. Maybe I could have made a difference, prevented this tragedy." He sat back and took a deep breath.

"What did you mean just now, Father, when you said a priest had shown an interest in Leeza?"

"I'm not sure, to tell you the truth. That was something I heard from certain acquaintances of mine in the police department. You're aware that I have friends in those quarters?"

"Yes. So what is it you heard?"

"Just that this girl had been telling people — friends, family, I don't know who — that there was a priest she had 'wrapped.' Around her little finger, I take it. My police informant tried to say this priest had the Rae girl 'wrapped' around his, em, well, a crude suggestion. I was having none of it. And I told him so!" Father O'Flaherty was offended all over again at the insinuation.

"Who did you think he was talking about?" As if I didn't know.

"Well, it wasn't me. You can rest assured of that," he said with finality.

"So, unless she made a practice of attending religious activities around the city — and I don't think you and I believe that — we're talking about Father Burke."

The old priest reddened. "That was the implication. But I said flat out that the idea was preposterous. Brennan is no fool. There was nothing going on." I thought back over my heated conversation with Burke about Leeza and her attempts to seduce him into helping the boyfriend. His explanation had sounded convincing, but I recalled thinking he had had time to fabricate a story to explain the tawdry scene.

"How did Leeza behave towards Father Burke at the dance?"

"Honestly, Monty, I didn't even see them together. Whenever I stopped to have a word with him, she wasn't anywhere near him. That much I can remember."

"Do you know whether he danced with her?"

"I don't know. I didn't see them dancing together."

"Did you dance with her yourself, Father?"

"Yes, I did. For one number at least. I can tell you proudly that, as a man of seventy, I danced with every female in the gym that night. Well, with the exception of Marguerite Dunne. Marguerite doesn't dance. A bit of a relief, to tell you the truth."

"Did you see Leeza when she left?"

"No, Monty, I didn't. I'm sorry I can't help you there."

"Can you tell me anything about her time at the centre?" He shook his head sadly, as if admitting failure. "Father, what went through your mind when you heard about a religious angle to this killing?"

"It didn't make any sense to me at all!" He was emphatic. "I don't believe for one minute a priest, or anyone else in religious life, committed this murder. Moody wouldn't . . . nobody I know in law enforcement circles would tell me what kind of religious signs or signals were left at the murder scene." The priest looked at me shrewdly. "Do you know?"

I shook my head and he went on. "It has to have been someone with a grudge against the Church. But why take that out on her? Unless somebody was jealous of the time she spent around here. Which seems unlikely, doesn't it? Or somebody was jealous of this priest she was supposedly spending time with. Perhaps she told these stories to provoke some other man in her life. Provoked him beyond endurance." It was as good a guess as any I had come up with.

As I walked back to the office, I remembered something I had neglected to ask, so I dialed the rectory and got Father O'Flaherty on the phone.

"Just one more thing Father. Did the police question you after the murder?"

"Yes, they did." I thought I detected a trace of excitement in his voice.

"Did they ask you for samples of threads or anything like that, for elimination purposes?"

"No. They didn't." Excitement had turned to puzzlement and perhaps disappointment. I thanked him and hung up.

II

It was the first week of April and the weather was balmy. Maura had agreed to drop the kids off before she headed out for the evening. They greeted their dad and went off in their own directions, Tommy Douglas to my collection of guitars and harmonicas, Normie to the boathouse. Later we had a pleasant dinner of poached salmon, which of course must be eaten with boiled potatoes, peas and strawberry shortcake.

"Let's take a walk around the park and see if anyone has a boat out," I suggested.

Normie asked: "Can we go up to the top of the tower? Please!"

It's a long climb up the steps of the Dingle Tower but the view from the top of the stone structure is magnificent. You can see the city, the waters of the Arm, and farther out the blue of the Atlantic Ocean. The three of us went off and had a brisk walk around Fleming Park, donated to the city by Sir Sandford Fleming, the man who devised the system of Universal Standard Time. Normie, as she always did, nearly had a stroke trying to choose among the playground, the beach, and the tower. But we managed, as we always did, to enjoy all of them. It was cool and breezy, not yet prime sailing season, but one hardy mariner had his sails up. We peered across the water at the houses, some of them grand, on the other side, and waved at the Strattons' place just in case they were gazing over the water in our direction. They were not, as it turned out. At least Rowan wasn't. He had gone to the office, which I found out when we got back to my house and I listened to my answering machine.

I dialed the office number and Rowan answered on the second ring. "Rowan. You called."

"Splendid news, Monty," came the British voice over the phone. "There will be no charges laid against Brennan Burke in the Leeza Rae case. My man tells me the police were satisfied with our client's alibi. There were 'indications of physical contact' between Brennan and the victim, as my source put it with great delicacy, but whatever traces they found could have been transferred if he danced with her. So at this point they are not looking at him as a suspect. It was suggested to me that this chap Walker is a little intense on the subject of religion. Sounds as if there was a spot of bother with his sister when she was young, something about a preacher. Walker may have a motive of his own."

"Motive?"

"His own agenda, going after Burke the way he did. But as far as I am concerned, Brennan is clear."

III

Now that Father Burke was not going to be charged with murder, a low-key celebration was in order. Or so the Strattons believed. They invited Burke to join a few people at their house on Friday night. I wondered whether this sort of thing was, as the Strattons would otherwise have put it, good form. Rowan had to use all his powers of persuasion to get Burke to come, and people were warned not to breathe a word about the murder.

Maura and the kids had been invited, as they always were when there was an extended family gathering at the Strattons', and they would be coming a little later. My brother Stephen and Janet Stratton were there with their children. A couple of lawyers from our office were in attendance. The others were people I did not know.

Burke, dressed in a dark blue suit, tie, and crisp white shirt, was perched on the edge of a chesterfield next to the fireplace, the tension of the past weeks still evident in his face. He was clutching a glass of whiskey like a relic of the true cross. Sylvia and a younger woman were chatting to him and he nodded absently in time with the cadence of their speech.

"I'm fascinated to meet you, Father Burke," the young woman said. "I don't know any priests."

"I'm a bit of exotica for you then," he said, and downed his whiskey.

"No, no, not at all. I just haven't had much contact with people of your persuasion, your religion."

"Ah." His eyes followed the drinks tray as it sailed past without stopping in port.

"But I'm very accepting of all religions and faiths." She smiled and put a hand lightly on his left arm. "My idea is that we're all God."

"Speak for yourself," he retorted, giving her a look that would curdle mother's milk.

Clearly, he had not yet unwound. Or, more likely, he found such theological twaddle offensive at the best of times.

"Hey Dad!" We all looked up, whether we had a sixteen-year-old son or not.

"Tommy! Come on in. Hello, Tanglyhead!" I put one arm around my boy and hoisted my little girl up in my other arm. "Are you all set for a party?"

Maura swept in and made a beeline for Rowan, who was lifting a glass in greeting.

"Is the revolution here at last?" Rowan greeted my wife.

"The revolution is imminent, Rowan, and you and I are the vanguard. So pack up some of these baubles and choose a room for yourselves. Nothing too big. I'm moving six families into this house tomorrow. In the meantime let's fortify ourselves with drink. What have you got?" Rowan had everything, and Maura accepted a large tumbler of it. She took a long swig and turned in my direction. She caught sight of Father Burke and gave him an appraising look.

"So you're the demon priest." She held out her hand to Burke, who eyed her coolly as he rose to shake her hand. "I'm Maura MacNeil. Did you find him to be of any use at all?" She jerked her head in my direction as she spoke.

"He has been an enormous help to me, Professor MacNeil. Even an innocent man needs wise counsel."

"Bit of an arsehole personally, though, eh? But that needn't put you off. You're not going to marry him. I'm pleased to meet you, Father. Now, do I hear music being played, badly?" Maura tilted her head towards the sound.

"The children, I'm thinking," answered Burke.

"Well then, we'll let it pass."

"Sounds like a magnificent piano, whoever is playing," Father Burke remarked. He got up to have a look. Someone called to Maura, and she went over to chat.

Normie looked vexed with boredom, so I took her downstairs to a playroom the Strattons had set up for their grandchildren. My son joined us. We played games and laughed and lost track of time. Eventually they remembered there were treats upstairs so we trooped back up to the party. My watch told me I had missed more than an hour of the soiree. I could hear snatches of conversation from the piano room. As Tommy helped himself and his sister to an assortment of sandwiches and sweets, I headed for the piano.

At the far end of the glassed-in conservatory was Burke, his tie off and his crisp white shirt unbuttoned at the neck. His head was thrown back as he laughed and he was enjoying himself immensely. With, of all people, my wife. I attributed this to Rowan's top-of-the-line whiskey, the mind-altering properties of which I had yet to sample. I picked up a music book and thumbed through it. When I looked up again, Burke and Maura were in deep conversation. He reached out and lifted an errant strand of hair from her face and patted it back where it belonged. He appeared to have done this without thinking. Could anyone be that comfortable in the presence of my wife?

Somebody called to Burke from across the room. I could not make out the question but his response was that he would be saying a Latin Mass early the next morning.

"I thought the Latin Mass was *verboten* these days," Maura said.

"*Non licet,* you mean? Not at all. A common misunderstanding. But if I told you it was forbidden and had to be celebrated clandestinely in the hedgerows, you'd be the first one there, now wouldn't you?"

"You got me there. But I just may show up anyway. I grew up with the Latin Mass."

"Well, this is the new version, but I'm planning to set up a high altar and start saying the old Tridentine Mass as soon as I can."

"I saw a very clever cartoon once," Maura said. "It showed a really depraved party going on, people in masks, performing all kinds of bizarre antics, and the caption read: 'I prefer the old Latin Mass myself.'"

"Yes!" Burke smiled in appreciation. "It was in *Punch*, a contest. That was the winning caption. I have it tacked up on the wall in my room. I can't, of course, invite you up to see it." He paused. "Because it's in New York." She laughed. "Yes, another whiskey would be just the thing," he said to someone going by with a tray of drinks. "Thank you."

"What time is it on?" asked Maura. He gave her a quizzical look.

"The Mass," she said.

"It's *on* at nine a.m."

"Could be worse."

I heard Burke asking Maura about her job, and she told him about the various Charter of Rights cases she had launched on behalf of the poor and disenfranchised. Some challenges — and some challengers

— had more merit than others, as she freely acknowledged. She was also big enough to admit that she had recently been named in a discrimination suit herself, after she refused to hire a certain applicant as a research assistant. Her defence consisted of one sentence: "She can't spell." Maura told him about the poverty law course she taught at Dalhousie Law School. Burke obviously liked what he heard, because he favoured her with a most charming quotation: "The wise shall shine brightly like the splendor of the firmament. And those who lead the many to justice shall be like the stars forever."

"Sweet of you to say so," Maura responded with surprised pleasure.

"Once a sweet-talking guy, always a sweet-talking guy. And not above stealing a line from the prophets, in or out of context. That's Daniel, by the way, chapter 12, verse 3. I'll write it out for you. If anyone challenges your efforts, you can point to a higher authority."

Just then, Normie barrelled into the room and made for the piano. I saw Burke snatch her up by the back of her overalls. A fellow lawyer started to regale me with a long story before charging after a tray of profiteroles. Then it was Maura at my side.

"Did you see that?" she demanded.

"What?"

"Normie and Brennan?"

"No."

"She careened past us and he caught her by the overalls. I growled at her for running around blind without her glasses. Anyway, Brennan picked her up. She looked at his face, then started staring at the front of his shirt. Where his heart would be. Or *is*, I should say. Then she pressed her hand over it, drew her hand back and looked at the palm, pressed it and looked again. As if expecting to find something there. They exchanged a long look and he said to her, speaking quietly and sounding very Celtic: 'Oh, you can see just fine, can't you, you little Druid?' She just nodded, never taking her eyes off him. What do you make of that?"

I shook my head. Whatever it was, I did not want to get into it at the party. "Right now, she should be in bed. I'll take her."

I got Normie settled in a spare room, poured myself a large glass of whiskey, and returned to the conservatory to find my brother Stephen at the piano. The guests joined in, and old tunes were sung badly with great enthusiasm. It was not until the good father picked up a beer bottle for a microphone and began belting out "Mack the Knife" that I realized he was hammered. Burke had a magnificent voice and, in full party mode, was not above milking the song for all it was worth. A drunken but effective rendition. I looked around and found everybody spellbound. Even Sylvia Stratton was gaping in a most undignified manner, delicate fingers toying with a strand of lustrous pearls at her neck. My wife seemed to have been frozen in place, a glass halfway to her lips.

It went on from there. Every once in a while Burke would look around and say: "What the hell time is it? I have to say Mass." Then he'd go back to singing, dancing, or drinking. Till around five in the morning. It looked to me, although I was not a very astute judge by then, as if he gave up the whiskey at that time and switched to water. He eased off the vocal pyrotechnics, and his cigarette consumption seemed to tail off as well.

Then, somehow, I found myself sitting in the Strattons' Range Rover with half a dozen other people, including my wife and brother. It was a tight fit. Brennan, now silent, sat in the front, his head resting on the window. Rowan pulled up at St. Bernadette's Church and parked the car. *"Domine, non sum dignus,"* Burke muttered, "and I'm sure I speak for all of us when I say that."

"What'd he say?" came a boozy voice from the back of the vehicle.

"Lord, I am not worthy," my wife explained.

It was three minutes to nine when our raggle-taggle group shuffled up the aisle. The church was about one-third full. I had not gone to Mass just for the sake of going to Mass in years. Burke sprinted up a side aisle, still in his suit and leather jacket; his tie had long since disappeared. He was surprisingly agile given the amount of whiskey that must still have been coursing through his veins. Before disappearing into the sacristy, he jerked his head towards the empty second row. That's where we were to sit. We stumbled into place. When Father Burke appeared on the altar two minutes later, his hair was wet and his face had a pinky, scrubbed look.

In nomine Patris, et Filii, et Spiritus Sancti, Amen. The priest, in Lenten vestments matching the amethyst in the church's stained-glass windows, made the sign of the cross over the old, the young, the hung-over and the still-drunk, and began saying Mass in the ancient tongue. He recited the *Confiteor* and those who knew it joined in the public confession, with its abject admission of sinfulness: *"Mea culpa, mea culpa, mea maxima culpa."* For the first time in hours, I thought of the murder charge. I made a conscious effort to dispel any suspicion still lingering in my mind about Father Burke's culpability. He spoke in a clear voice and sang parts of the liturgy in an unaffected baritone, which was only occasionally rough around the edges. The Latin responses came back to me from my days as an altar boy, thirty-odd years before.

Although I thought the sermon might be a good time to close my eyes and drift off, I soon found myself listening to a lawyerly dissertation on the meaning of the triune God. He must have been working his way through the *Credo* over the past few weeks.

"Later in the *Credo* we find: *Genitum, non factum, consubstantialem Patri.* The meaning of these words was hammered out in the midst of an unholy row in the fourth century. From Judaism we inherited the doctrine of the one God. But in the third century, theologians were already wrestling with the unity of God and His threefold manifestation in creation, redemption, and reconciliation. The Council of Nicea was called together by the Emperor Constantine in the year 325, and from it we have the Nicene Creed, which we still recite today. The council established the meaning of the words: *genitum, non factum*, begotten, not made. The Son is not a 'creature.' Rather, He is generated out of the *substance* of the Father . . ." Burke lost me somewhere during an ancient debate over whether the Holy Spirit proceeds from the Father *and* the Son, or *through* the Son. This was likely not everyone's cup of tea, but if I hadn't been so exhausted, I would have enjoyed the interpretive gymnastics that are so dear to the legal mind. I had never realized how much of this went on in the higher realms of theology. When I was a boy, they told you what it meant and that was that. I wondered how the priest was able to think so clearly; my brain was barely functioning.

I had a brief lucid moment at the consecration. Father Burke spread his hands and held them over the bread and wine. The ritual proceeded until he held the bread in his hands, bowed, and spoke the words *"Hoc est enim Corpus meum."* We were centuries away from the raunchiness of the Strattons' party; each gesture was done with reverence and grace.

I was not aware of anything again until I felt a sharp pain in the toes of my right foot. I jerked awake to find that Father Burke had stamped on my foot, hard, and was standing above me with the Body of Christ in his hands. The priest smelled faintly of whiskey, smoke, and minty toothpaste. He looked at me benignly as he said *"Corpus Christi,"* and I responded "Amen," and took the Host. All the Catholics, however lapsed, snapped into line and took Communion. Was it the long reach of the ancient faith, or the magnetism of its enigmatic priest?

Chapter 7

Bless me father — have I sinned. You know what I'm talking about.
For too long I've held it in. Now it's time to let the truth out.
Your silhouette behind this screen. I know what you hide in there.
I know where your soul has been. Darkness hiding in a prayer.
— Lennie Gallant, "16 Angels"

I

I was no longer dealing with Brennan as a client, but I had taken up his invitation to join him and his cronies on their Wednesday poker nights. First, though, there was a bit of business to take care of; he asked me to come by early and bring my bill. He wanted to pay my fees without delay.

"Now there's an offer I don't get every day, Brennan. You're the kind of client I'd like to keep on the hook, so let me know if anything else comes up." I would have occasion to look back on those words with a shudder, much the way Duncan would have reconsidered his remark about the pleasant seat he found waiting for him at the Macbeth residence in Inverness, had he lived to reflect upon it. But for now, I was content to accept payment and move on.

"Wait a minute, Brennan," I said when he handed me the cheque. "Kind of you to round it up, but it's supposed to be written out to me, or to Stratton Sommers. I have to deposit it in the law firm account." He had made it out to Montague Collins and Maura MacNeil.

"What I have written, I have written." He flipped his pen in the air, caught it, smiled, and turned away.

This was Burke's opening salvo in a campaign to get the Collins-MacNeil family back together. But that was not on the table tonight.

I was not an expert card player by any means, but neither was Father O'Flaherty, who beamed with every good hand he received and lost his money every poker night. There were three more men in the regular group, and a couple of others who showed up on occasion. The regulars were a heart surgeon, Dr. Russell Shaw, a contractor named Rick Judd, and a rough-hewn priest, Gerald Brady, from one of the parishes outside the city. The amount of liquor consumed varied from week to week, Judd and Shaw being scotch drinkers, Brennan and O'Flaherty having one or two shots of whiskey, and the rest of us having a couple of beers. There was usually a pall of cigarette smoke, but I noticed Brennan limited himself to one or two cigarettes a night. "The voice, you know," he said, grasping his throat, when he turned down a proffered smoke.

These were enjoyable evenings, even when Brennan and a couple of the others directed most of their attention to their poker hands. Which was the idea, of course, but I had never been able to get very intense about cards. Even the dedicated card sharps contributed to the general conversation, however, and I heard quite contrasting accounts of Brennan's and Gerry Brady's visits to Head Office. Brennan had spent four years in Rome, in the 1970s, studying at the Angelicum and the Pontifical Gregorian University, where he earned degrees in some arcane field of theology. He felt right at home in the eternal city, learned to speak Italian fluently, and lived the good life by the sound of things. Brady's experiences were different, and he kept us in stitches recounting his frequent gaffes in language, etiquette, and mores.

The three priests expressed concern about a spree of vandalism at Catholic churches in and around the city, including St. Bernadette's. The perpetrator broke candles and sprayed the usual foul words on the property.

"Wasn't there a break-in?" I asked. "Mrs. Kelly was nervous."

"Mrs. Kelly is nervous if she hears me strike a match," Brennan replied.

"Our vandal is nothing but a bush-league Satanist," Father Brady declared.

"Satanic stuff, is it?" I asked.

"It's not the real thing," Brady replied. "St. Luke was painted over with 'St. Lucifer.' The number 666 was sprayed on the forehead of St. Joseph. Then there's 'you-know-what the bishop and all his minions' — spelled *minyans*. Not the work of a true Satanic cult, by any means. What did he do here at St. Bernie's?"

"We're the House of Evil and Priests of the Devil," Burke replied. "That just about describes us, eh, Mike?"

But Father O'Flaherty looked more apprehensive than amused.

Nobody had been around when the vandal had struck some months before. And there were no incidents during my evenings round the card table — until late in April.

The six of us were sitting there, playing the hands that had been dealt us, Brennan and Dr. Shaw puffing clouds of smoke from the enormous Cuban cigars they had clamped between their teeth. The doctor had a "Heart Health" T-shirt on; Brennan's said "Roma" and something in Italian that I couldn't read; Brady and Judd wore sport shirts; Father O'Flaherty was ready for bed in an emerald green dressing gown and slippers. Shortly after we sat down, the phone rang. O'Flaherty, who was closest, leapt up to get it. Brennan whispered: "I let it slip that I'm expecting a call from my sister in Dublin tonight. She works over in London, university prof, teaches Irish history to the Brits. The nosy gaffer wants to chat her up." But it was a wrong number. O'Flaherty returned to the fold.

Brady and Shaw were trying to interest the rest of us in a fishing trip to a camp in the interior of the province. "Sounds like great crack, a weekend away like that," O'Flaherty agreed. "What do you say, Brennan?"

Burke just snorted and continued to puff on his cigar.

But O'Flaherty was keen. "We'd get up at sunrise to fish, we'd play cards out on the deck in the evenings, enjoy the silence. Idyllic, I'd say."

Brennan removed the stogie from his mouth and regarded O'Flaherty as if he'd gone simple. "How would you be concentrating on your cards when you've got one hand on the go constantly, swatting flies away from yourself? And fish. They've people to bring fish to you now, Michael. You don't have to go out at the crack of dawn to catch them yourself. Fishmongers, supermarket operators, cordon bleu chefs, Mike. These people are there to be used, when you've a longing for something from the salt seas."

"Fresh water fishing we're talking about here, Brennan," Brady explained. "We're not going to charter a trawler."

"Sorry. My mother never told me where fish come from. You boys go ahead and commune with the wood ticks. Now, are we going to play cards or are you going to treat me to a serenade for banjo —" he looked at O'Flaherty "— and harp?"

"Isn't he insufferable?" Brady remarked to the table at large. "He and my old man would get along famously." The priest launched into a tale about his father, who had taken over the family farm when the grandfather was too enfeebled to do the work. The story of the reluctant and ineffectual farmer could have been tragic, but the storyteller had us in fits of laughter.

"Now tell us about your own da, Brennan," urged Father O'Flaherty, who looked on indifferently as his pile of chips was scooped up by Burke. "A recent immigrant, I understand."

"If 1950 is recent to you, Mike, then my father's still green in the face from the boat trip over."

"Those times get more and more recent to me every day," the old priest replied, to appreciative laughter. "Now, you and your family came over —"

The phone rang again, and Brennan trumped O'Flaherty in a grab for the receiver. "Yes. Hello, darlin! Grand. Ah. Now, are you asking for the wise counsel of kindly Father Burke? Or am I speaking to you as brother Brennan? Thought so. In that case, put the run to him. Oh, you did. Well, between Dublin and London, I know you'll find a man more to your liking. But wait now, Maire. I have just the fellow for you right here. Slight of build, blue of eye, light-coloured hair —" He looked over at the poker table. "Would you gentlemen describe Mike here as cute?"

"Oh, yeah!" we chorused as one.

"Cute as a bug," Brennan said to his sister, "and he loves Irish girls, don't you Michael?" Father O'Flaherty blushed. "Here. I'll put him on, so you can speak to the old sod. *About* the old sod, I mean. To Mike."

O'Flaherty's eyes made the round of the table, then he went for the phone. "Good evening, Maire," he said with hearty good cheer. "You're keeping late hours over there."

Brennan turned his attention to the table. "Let's play a hand without him."

O'Flaherty must have gabbed for half an hour, during which time we played a more serious brand of cards. Then he rejoined us without alluding to the telephone conversation. Ever the gentleman.

It was around eleven-thirty when we heard the sound of breaking glass. We remained stock still for a moment, listening, then jumped from our seats and bolted for the rectory door, Father O'Flaherty shuffling behind. Brennan stopped to get a key from a ring near the entrance, then we went out to the parking lot, and ran to the side door of the church. Burke went through the vestibule into the nave and switched on a light. I was about a dozen feet behind him. Just as he turned to the left, a man leaped from a crouch beside the last pew, jumped on the priest's back, and gripped his throat with one hand. He had something in the other hand, which he raised over Brennan's head. Next thing I knew, Brennan had flipped him off, slammed him facedown on the church floor, and had his arms pinned behind him. This happened so fast I did not have a chance to call out, let alone reach the two combatants. A can of spray paint, full by the sound of it, clattered uselessly to the floor and rolled away. Brennan was on the vandal's back, holding the pinned arms in place; he still had the cigar in his mouth. The phrase "muscular Christianity" came to mind.

"Who the fuck are you?" the man cried in a voice that cracked with pain and anger.

Brennan put his mouth, with the burning cigar in it, close to the man's left ear and whispered: "I'm the Holy Father. And this," he lifted the man's head and twisted it towards the rest of us, "is the College of Cardinals. Prepare to be excommunicated. Right here, right now."

"I'm not even Catholic!"

"Sure you are," said Brennan. "Now be a good lad and tell us what kind of beef you have with the Church of Rome."

"Fuck you!"

Brennan yanked the man to his feet and shoved him into a pew.

His forehead and chin were bleeding, and he rubbed them with a raw-looking wrist. Brennan signalled to the rest of us and we sat around him to block his escape.

"Speak!" Brennan barked at him.

"Now, Brennan," Father O'Flaherty said in his soft brogue, "let's give the lad a chance to get his breath." The man whipped around to look at O'Flaherty, who turned away from the young fellow's blazing eyes.

Brennan continued to smoke and glare malevolently at the culprit, who could have been anywhere from twenty-five to thirty-five years old; it was hard to tell. "Who the fuck are you guys?"

"We'll ask the questions here," Burke snapped. "Who are you?" When there was no reply, Burke leaned towards him and I put a restraining hand on his shoulder. More gently — and anything would have been more gentle — he said: "We all have problems with the Church. What's yours?"

The prisoner looked at each of us, then settled on Father O'Flaherty; he peered closely at the older man before speaking. "You better not be one of them."

O'Flaherty cleared his throat and asked mildly: "One of whom?"

"None of your business, you fucking Irish bog-trotter!"

The Reverend Brennan X. Burke, B.A. (Fordham), S.T.L. (Pontifical Gregorian), Doctor of Sacred Theology (Angelicum), delivered a short homily: "Watch your language, you fecking little gobshite. It's lucky for you Father O'Flaherty's here."

The young man wiped blood from his face and looked belligerently at O'Flaherty in his dressing gown. O'Flaherty reached out a fatherly hand, but the prisoner flinched away. "You have nothing to fear from us, my son. Did somebody hurt you?"

"I'm not hurt!"

"So, what's your problem?" Burke demanded.

O'Flaherty held up a conciliatory hand. "I'm Father O'Flaherty. I'm the rector here. Now let's see if we can get you some help, my lad. What's your name?"

"Yeah, right. Tell you my name. That'd be a genius move on my part."

"We want to help you," repeated O'Flaherty.

The young man's eyes darted nervously to Burke who, in a calmer voice, said: "I'm not going to hurt you."

"Indeed he's not going to do you any harm at all. This is Father Burke."

"*This* guy is a fucking priest?"

"Yeah, yeah, and an Irish bog-trotter too," Burke replied. "Save your breath. Now, why don't you let us take you somewhere you can be safe for the night. This man is a doctor." Brennan turned to Dr. Shaw, who was holding a snow-white handkerchief out to the injured vandal. "He'll have a look at you. And I'm sure he'll be happy to accompany you and Father O'Flaherty to a shelter —"

"I'm not going anywhere with them!"

"— and in the morning we'll set you up with a counsellor, or somebody else who can start to help you."

The captive was escorted to the rectory under guard so that Mike O'Flaherty could get dressed, and he and the doctor could tuck their charge somewhere safe for the night. We followed them to the rectory, Brennan stopping to pick up the paint can and take it with him. The party broke up then.

I called the next evening to see how things had gone and Mike O'Flaherty filled me in. The vandal had taken flight in the small hours of the morning. If Brennan had not been on the scene, and O'Flaherty had got to the guy first, would he have been more inclined to stay and seek help? Then I remembered how the intruder had attacked Burke. Father O'Flaherty would not have had the strength or agility to fight his attacker off. Things could have turned out worse.

O'Flaherty had called a meeting of people from the church and youth centre early that morning. A young man fitting the vandal's description had spent time around the centre a few months before. He had given his name as Jason. One youth centre volunteer said Jason had asked questions about the priests at St. Bernadette's. What kind of questions? The guy wanted to know the priests' names, their ages and where they were from. It was a pity, O'Flaherty observed sadly, that Jason had not stayed till morning.

"Let's hope Brennan is down on his knees somewhere beseeching the Lord to make him a channel of His peace, if the poor lad turns up again."

II

I missed the next poker night, but had made plans for an afternoon of musical theatre at Neptune. It was one of those outings Maura and I were determined to take in together for the children's sake. We had invited Brennan along, and were on our way to pick him up. An argument was in progress about the seats I had reserved.

"If you'd bought tickets for tonight's performance instead of this afternoon, Collins, we'd know for sure that Frank MacKay will be singing the part. If they have an understudy, I won't want to be there . . ."

The kids waited in the car while we went up to Burke's room. "You don't know there's going to be an understudy. Why don't you just wait for twenty minutes until you can read the program? Then you'll know. It's that simple." But it wasn't. Maura came from the kind of family in which everyone, whenever the phone rang, had to speculate and argue about who it was before answering it. If you ever call their house, let it ring ten times.

We knocked on the priest's door. Brennan came to greet us, unshaven, wearing a pair of jeans and an old sweatshirt, with a glass of what looked like chocolate milk in his hand. He stood in the doorway and rubbed his back against the door jamb.

"Sure sign of a bachelor," Maura said, "scratching your back against the door post." She looked him up and down. "I have to tell you, you're the seediest cleric I've ever seen. To think I spent a whole night with you." Brennan looked from her to me in momentary alarm, then obviously remembered the all-night winging at the Strattons'.

He turned to me. "Monty, have you read the papers? About the little girl who died in the car accident?"

"Oh, yes. Very sad."

"And did you hear how she died?" Maura asked. "The news reports glossed over it, but I heard what happened. The child's father is off at a party, all drugged up. He calls in the middle of the night and demands that his common-law wife, the little girl's stepmother, go out and pick up some more drugs or booze or something he wants, and deliver it to him at the party, which is way over in Dartmouth. The stepmother doesn't have the car — *he* has it — but why should he get off his arse when he has her to do his bidding? So the stepmother goes over to another apartment in her building and gets some bozo, who happens to be drunk, to drive her on this errand. A man says 'jump,' she says 'how high and can I kiss your arse on the way up.' She drags the little girl and her brother out of bed and into the car, puts them both in the front seat without seatbelts on, gets into the back seat herself, and reclines for the journey. And away they go to the crack house, or the bootlegger, or wherever they're going. Then they head for the bridge but they don't get there, because the drunk at the wheel loses control of the car and they smash into a power pole. The girl is thrown from the car, and lands on her head." Brennan closed his eyes as if to shut out the picture of the child, still in her pyjamas, broken and dying. "The brother just had scratches. The driver, well, who cares? The stepmother was able to walk away from it. They rushed the girl to the hospital and worked frantically to save her life. This is where I heard the story, from a friend who works for the ambulance service. Anyway, do you know what she said, the stepmother, when the police showed up? 'But he told me to go, he told me to go.' This while the child was lying there losing consciousness! I hope that woman gets —"

"I've heard enough of this! Jesus Christ!" Brennan snapped. He was clearly on the verge of being sick. "Do you know who that was?"

I shook my head.

He took a deep breath and went on in a quieter voice: "It was my little pet from the choir. Alvin. I just can't —" He cleared his throat. "I can't go with you today. I should have called."

"Brennan, I'm so sorry. I didn't recognize her name when I read it. You don't look so good."

"I'm heartscalded, Monty. Heartscalded."

Maura stood there, mortified. Then she turned and ran down the corridor.

We joined the kids and drove to the theatre in silence. Frank was singing the part.

I got a call from Brennan the next day. "I'm sorry I snapped at Maura."

"Brennan, she understands. Believe me. In fact, she felt terrible for spilling the story like that. She gets so worked up when a child is hurt —"

"I want to apologize to her."

"It's up to you." I gave him her number. I thought this was probably as close as he ever came, given his chosen life, to a little imbroglio with a woman; perhaps he'd enjoy calling and trying to straighten it out. As close as he came? How little I knew!

III

Maura and I attended Janeece Tuck's — Alvin's — funeral at St. Bernadette's, arriving separately but sitting together in the middle of the church. She had Normie with her; the child had asked to come. Grieving relatives took their places, father's and mother's contingents studiously ignoring each other. A badly tinted blonde with blotchy pink skin had to be supported up the aisle to a seat a few rows behind Janeece's father. Whispers made it clear that this was the little girl's stepmother, the woman whose heedlessness had led to the fatal car ride. A group of children in uniform filed into the church under the stern guidance of Sister Dunne; these were obviously choir school children who would not be singing today. Overall, the church seemed an empty, lonely place. I remembered Janeece clattering up the stairs to the choir loft. There may have been two dozen people in the building that day, but it had not seemed lonely then.

Father O'Flaherty would be saying the funeral Mass, assisted by Father Burke, who would also be directing the music. An African-Canadian Baptist minister would be saying a few words in remembrance of Janeece, and the minister's sister, a well-known gospel singer, would be doing a solo at the end.

The children of the junior choir, joined by a few young adult choristers, looked angelic in their white robes as they filed in with their music and moved to the chairs that had been set up in front of the altar on the right. When the choir was seated there was one chair left empty, where Janeece — Alvin — would have sat.

As Mike O'Flaherty led the small wooden casket towards the altar, followed by the little girl's family, Burke directed the choir and congregation in the opening hymn. The words promised us that, on some glorious morrow, we would know and understand, we would see the Saviour face to face. But the melody, poignant and moving — it was in fact *Finlandia* by Sibelius — reflected the title of the hymn: "Now Know We Not the Meaning of Life's Sorrow."

Father Burke's face was nearly as white as his vestments. When it was time for the choir to sing the *Kyrie*, he went over and whispered to them, patting a couple of heads, before lifting his arms to direct the music. The space around us filled with the exquisite harmonies of Byrd's *Mass for Four Voices* as the choir asked in song for the Lord's mercy. It seemed to take all of Burke's strength to keep his feelings of grief, and no doubt anger, from showing on his face. Family members wept quietly. The sense of overwhelming grief for the nine-year-old child intensified as the funeral Mass went on. One person in the church, however, was more fascinated than mournful, and that was my daughter. Although she understood that it was a solemn occasion, and that a child not much older than she had died, Normie gazed raptly around the church, at the jewel tones of the stained glass, the dignified statues, the white-robed priests and choristers. Just after the consecration, her eyes seemed to catch those of Father Burke. He made a slight gesture with his hands, almost as if he were inviting her to see, or in some other way experience, what was now present on the altar.

The choir children bore up fairly well until it was time to rise for the last sung part of the Mass, the *Agnus Dei*. I remembered Burke's beatific smile as Janeece and the other choir members sang that day at practice. Now the children stood with their books and Burke waited for their attention. One little red-haired girl in the front row began to sniffle and started to lift her arm as if to wipe her nose on her robe, then she thought better of it and let the arm drop. Another little girl started to cry then, and one after the other, the two girls darted forward and buried their faces in the priest's vestments. He put his arms around them and bent his head towards them. Other choir members looked to be on the verge of losing control. Just then there was a flash and everyone turned, startled, to see a skinny young man in a safari jacket standing beside the altar, a professional-looking camera aimed at the choir. I looked at Father O'Flaherty and saw him shake his head at the photographer, who raised his hand in acquiescence, sat in a pew, and took out a notebook.

Burke, who had ignored the distraction, straightened up and stood for a few moments. Then he motioned with his hands for the children to sit down. He shook his head gently. Taking a deep breath, he turned to face the congregation and began to sing the *Agnus Dei*, not from the Byrd but from the *Mass of the Angels*, the exquisite Gregorian chant that Alvin had requested the day I had listened to the practice. The priest sang with restraint but the timbre of his voice filled the church with the ancient melody. Instead of the usual text he substituted the words from the Mass for the Dead: *"Dona eis requiem."* He gazed into space for a few minutes when he had finished, then returned to Father O'Flaherty's side to assist with the rest of the Mass.

At the end of the service, O'Flaherty incensed the casket and said a prayer for Janeece. Burke followed with a prayer of his own. It was clear that he, like Alvin, did not pray from the same hymn book as the rest of us. Whether he found the old words more worthy of her, or he had reverted to the ancient form the way our regional accents burst forth from us in times of stress, Father Burke prayed quietly in Latin, and then in the vernacular: *"Te decet hymnus Deus in Sion, et tibi reddetur votum in Jerusalem: exaudi orationem meam, ad te omnis caro veniet . . .* O God, Whose property is ever to have mercy and to spare, we humbly entreat Thee on behalf of the soul of Thy servant Janeece, whom Thou hast bidden this day to pass out of this world, that Thou wouldst not deliver her into the hands of the enemy, nor forget her forever, but command her to be taken up by the holy Angels, and to be borne to our home in Paradise." He stood looking down at the picture of a smiling Janeece, her beautiful black hair fanned out beside her face, her huge, dark eyes sparkling. He extended his right hand and made a small sign of the cross over the picture, bowed deeply towards it, turned on his heel, walked back to the altar and out of the church.

As the pallbearers bore the casket slowly towards the doors of St. Bernadette's, the magnificent voice of the gospel singer filled the church. The haunting melody rose until she reached an effortless B flat and then descended again. I realized I had heard this Amen sung by the great soprano Jessye Norman, and it was a reverent and fitting tribute. An Amen to the sacredness of the child's life and spirit.

The Wednesday May 9th edition of the *Daily News* carried a small story on the funeral, accompanied by a photo of Father Burke bending to comfort the choir children. The reporter was someone new, a journalism student perhaps. The story went into detail about the way Janeece died, and described the obvious grief of the choir director, who walked out before the Mass was ended. Sympathetic as it was to the child and to the priest, the story would soon come back to haunt us all.

IV

The funeral was on a Tuesday, and on the Friday, Rowan Stratton and I enjoyed a leisurely lunch in a quiet restaurant on Spring Garden Road, followed by a stroll in the Public Gardens. Magnolias were in bloom around us, and the park benches were full of people soaking up the spring sun.

"For a while there, it looked as though you were going to star in Stratton Sommers's first murder trial," Rowan said as we crossed the stone footbridge near the entrance to the gardens. "But I'm sure you were as relieved as I that the scurrilous accusations against Brennan Burke went nowhere. Good man, Burke. I've known him a long time. I hear he may be asked to direct a segment of an upcoming performance by the Halifax Symphony. I certainly hope so. A talented musician."

"I hope to hear his choir too, on a happier occasion. He's quite a character," I remarked. "Takes a while to get to know him."

"I suppose so, yes. Of course, under a bit of a strain when you met him. Shame, really. And no other suspects in the girl's murder. From what I understand — unfortunate background, nasty connections — the killer could have been any number of people. If only the police had done their job. I should give Brennan a ring. He took it very hard, the little choirgirl's death. Difficult for him. He's not the sort of fellow to put his feelings on display."

"No, he's not." We dodged pigeons, and toddlers feeding them, as we made our way around the duck pond. I smiled when I remembered Normie at eighteen months; she chased a goose across the gardens, right into a wedding party posing for a photograph. That episode, suitably embellished, became her favourite bedtime story.

"Brennan is flying to New York the day after tomorrow to see his family," Rowan said. "The change of scene will do him good." We ambled down Spring Garden Road in the sunshine, greeting people we knew on the way.

The news was waiting for us when we got to the office. At eleven o'clock that morning, the body of Janeece's stepmother had been found wrapped in a black plastic raincoat, in a ravine under the MacKay Bridge, Halifax side. I knew instantly that what we had gone through over the Leeza Rae murder would pale when compared with what lay in the future for Brennan Burke. Same location, same type of raincoat, and a clear connection between Burke and the murdered woman's stepchild, who had died as a result of the woman's negligence. I had to face the obvious: Burke could well be a killer.

I was about to call the rectory when Darlene announced that Father Burke was on the line.

"I just heard," Burke stated without preamble. "What the hell is going on?"

"I just got the news too, Brennan. I don't know whether this killing has the same hallmarks as the other, but —"

"You can be sure it does. Now what?"

"Brennan, all I can say is sit tight. Don't talk to anyone, especially the police. Obviously. And I wouldn't say anything to Mike O'Flaherty either. You know how he is with Sergeant Walker. I'll try to find out more. As soon as I do, I'll let you know."

I entered Rowan's office and looked into his eyes. "Rowan. Did he kill those two women?"

"Steady on, Montague. We mustn't succumb to hysteria."

I persisted. "How well do you really know him? We have to find out what we're dealing with here."

"I have known Brennan since he was what? Sixteen years old. The family he stayed with during those weeks in the summers, the Worthingtons, are lovely people —"

"But Rowan, a boy on summer holiday. How deeply would you have seen into his character?"

"I knew him when he came up here in the late 1960s, as a priest. I know him now. You know him yourself. You and Brennan seem to have become friends of a sort."

"I'm always ready to second-guess my own judgment, Rowan. What do you know of Burke's life in New York? Character forms early. I'm sure we're all agreed on that."

I was of the view, and in the end Rowan could not disagree, that if there was anything in our client's character, or his past, that might rear up and bite us in the event of a murder trial, it would be found in New York. Burke was about to leave for his visit home, so I cobbled together a story about my brother buying airline tickets and having to cancel at the last minute. I now had the tickets. Rowan would be on hand to deal with whatever might happen in Halifax.

I was surprised that Brennan managed to leave the city before any charges were laid against him. I left on a later flight; still no charges.

I brought with me a satchel full of newspapers and I spent the early part of the flight reading about the murder of Tanya Cudmore. She was thirty-four years old. Her first husband had died in a jail cell under mysterious circumstances years ago. Her second had done time for assault; the implication was that Tanya had been the one assaulted. She moved in with the father of Janeece Tuck two years ago. Janeece had a brother, aged seven. Tanya had three children, who lived with her on and off. She had never held a job, and was living on Social Assistance. Photos showed a woman who looked considerably older than thirty-four, her skin pale and her hair lifeless. I remembered the woman being supported into the church at Janeece's funeral.

I put the papers away but could think of nothing else. Brutal images filled my mind. I imagined the violence done to Tanya Cudmore by an unknown killer. And I remembered the violence done to Jason, the church vandal, by Brennan Burke.

Chapter 8

Your mother stands a-crying as to the earth your body is slowly cast.
Your father stands in silence caressing every young dream of the past.
And your troubled young life had made you turn
to the needle of death.
— Bert Jansch, "Needle of Death"

I

Father Burke's old girlfriend was Sandra Worthington. Rowan had given me her address, and here I was on her doorstep in Manhattan's tony Upper East Side. The red brick townhouse was five storeys high with an elegant fan-lighted doorway and eight-over-eight windows.

"We've known Sandra since she was a child," Rowan had said. "Her parents were friends of ours, neighbours at Chester in the summers. We met Brennan there when he was in his teens, visiting Sandy at the cottage. A splendid young couple, really. But, well, he chose another life. There you have it."

Rowan expressed no interest in probing Burke's years as a seminarian and priest in New York. With time running against us, I had to agree: it was the earlier years that were of interest. I would start with the girlfriend.

The woman who met me at the door was nearly as tall as I was, five foot ten or so. Her light brown hair was short and layered; her eyes were almost an aquamarine blue. She appeared to be in her early forties but I knew she was older. There were the inevitable lines around her eyes; I took them to be laugh lines and I was encouraged to think that this was a woman with a sense of humour.

"Rowan tells me you want to hear about Brennan Burke," she said and looked at me for a long moment. "Come in."

I followed Sandra to her second-floor apartment. The living room had twelve-foot ceilings and an intricately carved marble fireplace. I sank into a buttery leather sofa and I had to resist the temptation to stretch out with my hands behind my head and my feet up. Facing me on the wall were three small Impressionist paintings, a framed *Mad* magazine cover, and a page from a musical score. I was curious about the music but I didn't ask.

"Would you like anything? Coffee? A drink?" Her voice was low and cultured.

"No, Sandra, thanks."

"This takes me back a long way. What do you think I can tell you about Brennan? I haven't laid eyes on him in nearly three decades."

"He's a client." I had not been able to decide how to handle this interview, and Sandra's inevitable questions. I would play it by ear. "You may be able to help by telling me what he was like when he was younger."

"A character witness." She looked at me shrewdly. "He must be in a hell of a lot of trouble. Hasn't he been a man of God for a quarter of a century now? Surely you have thousands of character witnesses, or references, or whatever it is you need. So why me?" She leaned forward. "Or are you looking for the bad news, in the hopes that it won't be as bad as you fear, so you can find bottom and look up from there? Tell me. What's he done?"

"Sandra, I can't tell you what he's suspected of. It's not public knowledge, I'm his lawyer, and he has the right to confidentiality. But please understand. The suspicions are absurd. If you can see your way to helping me under these conditions, I'd be most grateful."

"Rowan Stratton is a dear, charming man. An old friend. I couldn't say no. It's something sexual, isn't it?"

"Why would you say that?"

She gave me the kind of look Burke would have given me if I was being an imbecile. "If you think," she said, "that Brennan Burke has been celibate for thirty years, or thirty weeks, I'm not going to give credence to anything else you say." She was shaking her head with a slight smile on her face.

"Tell me about him."

But Sandra got up from her chair and walked over to a demi-lune table covered with photographs in silver frames. "These are my kids." I joined her at the table. "This is Karen. She's in second year law. When your child signs on as a lawyer you think about the clientele she'll have to deal with, but you never really know the worst of it, do you?" I was about to make a polite protest, but I saw a glint of humour in her aqua blue eyes. "My son David is in college out on the west coast. Laura's still in high school." There were other photos. One must have been of her husband. A few years her senior. The distinguished older couple were obviously her parents. Lying flat without a frame was a picture of a bouffanted, kohl-eyed Sandra in the early 1960s; it had the appearance of an album cover.

She stood by the table, seemingly at a loss for the first time since I had arrived. Then she reached over and brought out a picture of a group of children. They appeared to be ten or eleven years old and all were looking at the camera, with the exception of one dark-haired little boy. "That's me," she said, pointing to a pretty smiling girl in the front row, "and that's Bren." The boy who wasn't looking at the camera was looking sideways, at Sandra. "That picture was taken at Mrs. Liebenthal's music school, over on the West Side. That's where we met." She put the picture down gently.

I decided to plunge in again. "Do you think he would hurt anyone?"

"Physically, you mean?"

"In any way."

"In any way, yes. Brennan does whatever he sets out to do, regardless of the effect his actions may have on someone else." I waited and she motioned towards the chesterfield. We sat.

"There was a fire," Sandra said quietly. "A friend of Brennan's died in it. They were all drunk and on drugs. Brennan tried to save his friend but it was too late. That's when he got a sign from God, or whatever he claims happened that propelled him into the priesthood. I never believed a word of it. I think he was planning it all along."

"Planning what?"

"To be a priest. But he didn't let on. That way he could have a girl-friend, or girlfriends I should say, booze it up, dabble in drugs, and cram as much as he could into his life before giving it all up. How does it go? 'Jesus save me, but not yet.'"

"That was either a country singer or St. Augustine. Who could tell me more about the fire?"

"There was a sleazy character Brennan knew in those days, Jake Malone. Grew up to own a string of nightclubs. I read in the paper that he went to prison for a while. For what, I can't recall. If he's still alive and you can track him down, you may be able to learn some-thing."

She sat in silence, looking at her photos. "I went to Bren's ordina-tion, you know. I couldn't decide right up to the last minute whether to go. But I couldn't help myself. I was over the breakup by that time — long past it — but I still felt resentful when I saw him. Too bad. I would like to have enjoyed, without any ambivalence, the sight of that arrogant pr — that arrogant man — lying face down before the altar. Seeing him prostrate himself in front of anything or anyone should have given me the greatest satisfaction. But it was ruined for me by the fact that he looked so handsome, all in white. And he looked so goddamned happy and peaceful. I remember thinking, I need some of that." She looked down at her hands. "He didn't even know I was there."

We were silent for a moment. Then Sandra shrugged, and said: "But I get over things! Sixty percent of my life has been lived since then."

"Tell me something. Was that an album cover I saw on the table?"

She laughed. "I had a brief career in a girl group. Don't ask. Are you interested in music yourself?"

"I like to think of myself as a bluesman. Makes my day job bear-able."

"Bluesman? I don't know, Montague. That hair of yours is border-line blonde and the eyes are a definite sky blue. You've got kind of a boyish look going on there."

"Are you saying I can't pass for an old grizzled black man from the Mississippi delta?"

She made a show of appraising me. "More like a boy soprano, I'd say. I can see you in a chorister's robe and ruffled white collar. Is Brennan your client or your choirmaster?"

"You're killing me here, Sandra."

"Don't feel too bad about yourself, Monty. After all, I had to affect gobs of anguish and heartbreak to make it as a torch singer." The look of amusement on her face intensified as she rose and put out her hand to say goodbye. "I don't know whether to wish you luck or not, with your latest client. After all, I still have no idea what my former heartthrob has done to set you on my trail. But I'll worm it out of Rowan, if I get curious."

"I'd better let you get back to the present. And I'll go somewhere and lick my wounds. I appreciate your giving me some time."

"I didn't mind. Goodbye, Montague."

II

It took most of the morning to find Jake Malone, but I finally reached him and took the subway out to Brooklyn. His establishment was on Flatbush Avenue, a few blocks from the lush Botanic Garden. The dive was marked only by a yellow neon sign that said "Bar," and when I crossed the threshold I was plunged into night. I hoped this wasn't the jewel in the crown of his nightclub empire. Malone was tall and overly muscled. Lots of time in the exercise yard while he served his sentence. His blonde-streaked hair was cut short in front and long in the back.

"Collins?"

"Yes. Mr. Malone, I presume."

"You presume right. Call me Jake. Come sit down." I followed him to a table with a thick and greasy surface, as if the varnish had never set. I had to resist the urge to dig my nails into it. "What can I get you?"

I asked for a beer, and he got something dark in a shot glass for himself.

"So you're here about my long-lost pal Brennan Burke."

"Yes, as I indicated on the phone, I'm representing Father Burke, and I'd appreciate any information you can give me."

"But you can't give me any info about him?"

"Unfortunately, no. We have a delicate matter coming up in court —"

"Yeah, I had a few delicate matters in court myself. Now I'm trying to get back what I lost. This dump is a start. But, anyway, Burke . . . I haven't seen him in thirty years. He dropped all his old pals, just like that." He made a letting-go motion with his fingers. "He's a Holy Joe now. He sure as hell wasn't holy when I knew him."

"You were friends then."

"Friends, pals, whatever you call guys who went out partying together and getting blitzed every night. We knew this guy who could get us all kinds of drugs."

"What drugs are we talking about?"

"Smack, cocaine. None of these designer substances they have now, but there's nothing new under the sun. People were dying of overdoses then just like they are now. So you know, we'd score from this guy, then go to a club. Or somebody's house. A girl whose parents were out of town, that kind of thing. He had a nice piece of ass, Burke did. This Sandy. She had her own girl group for a while. Lucky stiff, that Burke. But he was always like that."

"So, was Brennan hooked on drugs?"

"Brennan wasn't hooked on anything. You know the type? He liked his tail and I can't see him giving it up, but he's not a needy kind of guy, if you know what I mean."

"Do you know anything about this house fire he was in?"

"Well, yeah, I should know. I was there. What a useless dickhead Burke was that night. We were all partying at this girl's place. This guy Stan — Polish guy, friend of Burke's — he had a real oil burner."

He saw the question in my eyes. "Heroin addiction. Smart kid, college boy, really into music. His old man worked two jobs to send him to Juilliard. Burke met him through some music thing. So Stan took up with the wrong crowd, namely yours truly and some other guys. Slumming, Stan was. Same as Burke. Slumming. I could figure that out. Stan started doing drugs and got hooked. Poor fucker, it killed him one way or the other."

Malone gestured to a waitress and she brought us fresh drinks.

"We were all at this party. Some of us were dancing in the living room. There was lots of booze so it wasn't exactly ballet, just some stumbling around and trying to cop a feel. Burke was doing all right for himself as usual. He was in a bedroom banging a couple of strippers. It's not funny the way it turned out, but I gotta laugh: that was the night I decided I was going to get into the club scene. Figured it would be a good way to get laid! Hire my own strippers, offer cheap drinks to chicks. And guess what? I was right. I had three clubs going before I did time on some bogus drug charges. Got out, and bought this place at a discount. I'm looking at another place over in Queens."

"Good luck with it. You were telling me about the fire."

"Yeah. Stan was down in the basement, wasted, doing something with matches. He managed to set the place on fire. He called upstairs for help, and me and this girl tried to put out the flames. We couldn't, so we went up and yelled for Burke. After all, it was his friend. I was hammering at the bedroom door, where Brennan was with these two bimbos. I said his pal Stan was in trouble and there was a fire. Music was blasting from the bedroom. I don't know how much Burke heard, but all he said was 'fuck off.' I went downstairs and somebody finally clued in to call the fire department. I went back for Burke and yelled that his friend was out of it and the basement was on fire. Burke finally caught on or maybe finished getting his rocks off. He came flying out the door zipping up his jeans. The smoke was getting thick and he told the two girls to get the fuck outta the house. There were flames at the bottom of the basement stairs. Burke ran into the bathroom, doused himself with water and grabbed a wet towel. He jumped down the stairs and came back up carrying his pal, but it was too late. Stan was dead. Of drugs or smoke, I don't know. The fire department took over and Burke went outside and got sick. He had some burns but he was fine. There were a couple of drug charges laid, but nothing stuck to Burke. What else is new?" Malone pulled on his drink. "But his old man punched his lights out when he got home. He'd heard all about it, connected as he was to some cronies in the NYPD. You don't wanna cross old man Burke."

"A violent man, Brennan's father?"

"Depends on what you mean."

"Well, did that happen often, Mr. Burke beating his son?"

"Did it happen often that his kid laid there with a couple of floozies on top of him while his friend was frying himself to death downstairs? My old man would have done the same thing. So what? All fathers did in those days, to the boys anyway."

"So, would Brennan have fought back, with his father I mean?"

"I fucking doubt it. Hit his old man? Come on. He knew he deserved it."

I thanked Malone for his time and left some bills on the table to cover the beer. When I got to the door he called me back. "If you want to find out what Brennan was like with women, if that's what you're worried about, talk to Doreen Foster in Greenpoint. She's one of the hot tickets he was with the night of the party. Used to call herself Doree Dee. Stage name. If Brennan was some kind of sick fuck then, he's still a sick fuck now. And this Doreen'd know it. She's in the book."

I stayed in Brooklyn and got a pocketful of change for the pay phones, none of which had a phone directory on offer. When I reached someone at Doreen Foster's flat, the guy sounded as if I had woken him up, but he gave me Doreen's work number. She agreed to meet me at a bar near her office at five-thirty. I gulped down a sandwich and retreated to the sylvan glories of the Brooklyn Botanic Garden, strolling beneath the park's magnificent pink cherry blossoms till it was time to hail a cab to Greenpoint.

I waited for Doreen in the assigned bar, a dingy dump much like Jake Malone's. She arrived out of breath and plunked herself down with a sigh. She looked at the bartender and he brought over her regular drink, whatever that was, and took my order for a beer. Doreen was in her mid fifties, with harshly tinted dark hair. She must have been a looker in her younger days, but her face now bore the hardbitten look I had seen in too many clients after a life of being buffeted by unkind fates.

"Well, well, your name is Collins and you're here to talk about someone I knew thirty years ago. Brennan Burke, what a doll. Where is he these days?"

"He's running a choir school at the moment."

"Do I look like I just fell off the turnip truck? Gimme a break."

"I'm serious. You knew he became a priest."

"Yeah, I know that, but I figured he was boozin' it up and bangin' nuns. This is too much. Well, I'll let it go. What do you want to know?"

I explained that I was a lawyer from Canada. It occurred to me to use the house fire as my cover story so I opened with that. "These things have a way of coming back," I said. "Nothing ever really goes away, does it?"

"Tell me about it," she agreed. She lit up a cigarette and sucked on it greedily.

"I understand you were at the house the night of the fire."

"Oh, yeah, I was there." She took another drag and blew the smoke upwards.

"You'd known Brennan before the party, I take it?"

"Yep. I'd known him, as you put it, for years. He used to come see me when he needed a little female company."

"But he did have another girlfriend as well, I think?"

"Oh sure. He had girlfriends and I wasn't one of them. His main squeeze was Sandy. But she wasn't always —"

"Willing?" I interjected naively.

"She wasn't always available. I've been around long enough not to hold to that old fantasy, the one that says the guy's wife is frigid, or the girlfriend won't do this or that. I'm sure that's what keeps a lot of single girls hoping all night long. But I don't buy it. Sandy and Brennan did whatever they wanted to do. But if she was away or busy, and Brennan felt like having a good time, he came over to my place. If I wasn't otherwise engaged, we got together. Brennan always had a few bucks for a bottle and he was great in the sack. I missed him when he went all righteous after that fire."

"What happened that night?"

"Oh Jesus, it was terrible, that guy dying. You could smell flesh burning. What was his name? Stu? Stan. I don't know how the fire started. Me and Brennan and this other girl were in a bedroom with the door locked. We were all bombed. Some guy came to the door but we could hardly hear him over the music. He was calling Brennan to come out and help this friend of his. But Brennan was busy with me and this other broad. I remember what I was doing to him, but I don't know what she was doing further up the line. Maybe planting sweet little kisses on his eyelids. Yeah, right! Brennan did not want any interruptions and told this guy to get lost, fuck off, whatever." Doreen signalled for another drink and the bartender brought it over.

"Then we smelled the smoke. Somebody pounded on the door, so we all leapt up from the bed, drunk, stoned, half-dressed. Brennan went down to the basement and tried to bring his friend out. Everybody told him there was no point, that he'd just burn up himself, but he went anyway. He carried the guy up the stairs, but he was dead." Doreen stared past me, her glass halfway to her lips.

"What happened to Brennan?"

"He had some kind of burn or injury to his chest. Nothing serious. That boy's parents, Stan's, my God." Tears sprang into her eyes. "I have two sons. In the Navy. I heard the boy's father died not long after the fire, and he wasn't old. Their only son, a talented kid. That was the end of their child."

"So Brennan was in there with you and this other woman while his buddy was dying downstairs. Hard to come to terms with a thing like that."

"Yeah, but it would have been the same thing for Brennan if he'd been in the middle of a poker hand, or watching a football game. It wasn't what he was doing, it was that he didn't bother to get up. I don't imagine he blames it on sex, if that's what you're driving at. He didn't have any hangups on that score." She stubbed out her cigarette. "That was the last I ever saw of him."

I had to ask the kind of question I don't like to ask, especially about somebody I know, but these were unusual circumstances. And Doreen wasn't shy.

"His sexual inclinations . . . Was he into anything rough, or —"

"Whoa! This is getting more interesting by the minute. I don't know what this has to do with the fire, but no. Nothing rough with Brennan. Vigorous, maybe! Hot-blooded Irishman and all that."

"Did the matter of religion ever come up in a sexual context?"

"No way! What did he do, set fire to a church and then bring some babe along to watch the guys with the big hose?"

"Nothing like that. Did he have a temper? Did you ever see him angry?"

"Come on, 'fess up. What did he do?"

"He didn't do anything. He's a priest and choirmaster."

"If you say so. I never saw him lose his temper. Though, who knows, with the unnatural life he's leading now." She shuddered.

"Doreen, thanks. Can I get you anything before I go?"

She reached over and stroked the palm of my left hand with a finger. "A cute guy is always welcome to give me somethin' before he goes. Are you sure you don't want to hang around for a while, maybe go to my place? I can tell my roomie to buzz off."

"Thanks, Doreen, but I'm meeting my wife back at the hotel."

"That's funny. I don't see a ring."

"I'm not much for jewelry."

"Yeah, you and Brennan. Unadorned. My ex used to wear this big diamond pinky ring. Tacky as hell. But, takes all kinds. See y' around, Babyface."

III

I returned to my hotel so I could call Rowan in Halifax. He assured me there was no sign of the police moving in on our client. "Anything at your end?" he asked.

"Not really. Our man seems to have had more wine, women, and song than you or I might have had on any one occasion. Of course, I can't speak for you, Rowan."

"You weren't in wartime London, my dear fellow. But do go on."

"I heard a bit about that house fire. Our boy was having a party of his own upstairs at the time. Tried, but too late, to rescue his friend."

"Not much then. Ring me if you hear anything more. Hope you're having a spot of fun yourself while you're there, Monty."

"Baseball tonight, I hope. Mets home game."

"Splendid."

As soon as I hung up, I got a call from Burke in the lobby, so I headed down to meet him. It was a bit unsettling to see him in his black clerical suit and Roman collar. I had been hearing so much — too much — about his younger self that I would not have been surprised to see him as a twenty-year-old reprobate wearing nothing but a boozy grin. Not for the first time, I had to adjust to his presence.

"You're all dressed up, Brennan."

"I didn't wear this for you, Collins. It's for my mother. If you've a son who's a priest, he should look like a priest!" He declined my invitation to the Mets game because his parents were expecting him for dinner, but we made plans to go out the following night. Meanwhile he had time for a quick drink in the hotel bar. His mood had lightened since I had spoken to him last, the result, no doubt, of being home and out of a country where murder charges might be laid against him at any moment.

Chapter 9

I know for certain the one I love.
I'm thru with flirtin', it's just you I'm thinkin' of,
Ain't misbehavin', I'm savin' my love for you.
— Thomas "Fats" Waller, Harry Brooks, Andy Razaf, "Ain't Misbehavin'"

I

The last thing I expected the next morning was a call from Sandra Worthington. "There's something else I feel I should tell you. Can you come by around five-thirty or six?"

So, once again, I was on Sandra's doorstep in the East seventies. She came out to meet me and gave me a direct look. "It occurs to me now, Monty, that I've been a little too melodramatic getting you over here again. This seemed significant in the dark hours before dawn, but in the light of day maybe it isn't. I don't know what kind of trouble he's in so I don't know whether this is important or not. It's just that Brennan and I started seeing each other again after we broke up."

I braced myself for how much later, picturing them cuddled up in the Chester cottage in front of the fireplace, exchanging bodily fluids and fibres, then erupting into an operatic farewell scene two nights before the first murder. So it was a welcome anticlimax when I heard the relationship had resumed for a few months when he was in the seminary and she was studying at Barnard College. They carried on what sounded like a torrid love affair — my description, not hers — then parted again. Painfully. This would not look great on his character card, Burke as a seminarian having a woman on the side, but it could have been a lot worse.

"That's old news," Sandra announced. "I have more immediate concerns now. I'm starving. And you?"

"I could eat a thin gruel if someone put a spoon to my lips."

"There's a place over on the West Side that's unpretentious and has delectable food, in large quantities. Let's take a stroll across the park."

We walked to Fifth Avenue and down a few blocks to a path leading into Central Park. The park was filled with joggers and parents with their children. As we meandered along the pathways, I said lightly: "You may wind up as a character witness yet. Seems you couldn't bear to stay apart from my client."

"You could be forgiven for thinking so. We always ended up back together. The summer we were nineteen I was fed up with Brennan and started seeing a man a few years older. Wyndham was from an old New York family, the type of man I had been groomed to marry. One evening we attended a concert. I knew Brennan would be there because he was friendly with some of the musicians. I hoped to avoid him, but no such luck. Wyndham and I were in the lobby chatting with friends when in waltzed Brennan with an absolutely dazzling redhead on his arm. He was half-lit but looked quite dashing. As soon as he saw me, he sashayed over to show off the new Irish girlfriend. I tried to sound cool and sophisticated as I remarked: 'You look as if you've met the love of your life, Brennan.' He said: 'I have, yes.'

"He introduced her to me. Ignored Wyndham altogether. She and I made phony small talk. Then, as they were leaving to find their seats, he leaned over and whispered in my ear: 'And as soon as the love of my life decides to dump that Wall Street gombeen man, I'll be sending Mavourneen back to Erin. And the flame of love will burn anew.' But he didn't stop there. He never does. I had on a pair of diamond cluster earrings, clip-ons, that Wyndham had given me. Bren pulled one of them off with his teeth, popped it over to the side of his mouth and made a big show of barely being able to talk. Because the stones were so enormous, you see. 'If you want this back before anyone notices, meet me at intermission, by the box office.' He nodded pleasantly, returned to his date, and escorted her into the theatre."

"And?"

"Yes, I made my excuses and went out to meet him. To my ever-lasting embarrassment."

"What could be worse for a young daughter of privilege than the scourge of embarrassment?" I chided her.

"We met at the box office. He tucked my arm in his and we walked to the staircase like any two well-dressed, well-behaved people out for an evening of music. As soon as we got to the bottom of the stairs he started . . . well, it seemed important to him to know what my feelings were. 'Sandy, do you love me? Tell me if you love me.' Monty, I believe that what goes on, physically, between a man and a woman is private. So I normally wouldn't say this. But the flame of love burning anew in the bowels of an old theatre building? When anyone might have come along and seen us? Anyway we ended up standing against a wall at the end of a dark corridor, and he . . . Or we, it wasn't just him obviously —"

"I have to tell you, Sandra, there is something very fetching in the way you're blushing."

"Oh, don't make it worse! Anyway, when we had finished our romantic little interlude, he said something like: 'I can't promise you diamonds but I can promise you a horizontal surface in the future.' Of course my dress was wrinkled, my hair was all over the place, my makeup was smeared. I got my compact out and tried to fix myself up. He went to wipe the smudges of mascara off but he made it worse. So I tried that and he attempted to fix my hair into place. He had the comb and he said: 'Do you want me to try to tease it — *taze* it, as he pronounced it — a bit at the top?' He would have heard that from his sisters. It was so cute. 'No thank you, I'll do it, darling.' Then we started snickering and making dumb jokes about it all, and finally had to hold each other up we were laughing so hard. I got back to my seat just as the curtain went up. Wyndham kept turning to look at me. I told him I had met an old friend in the washroom. I wished he would disappear. I wanted Brennan beside me. That was the longest ninety-six minutes of my life, sitting through the rest of the performance."

"So? Did you get the earring back?"

"At the last possible minute, on our way back to the auditorium.

And that wasn't the last bit of theatre for the evening, either. When the concert was finally over, we found ourselves in the lobby. Brennan's date had gone to make a call. So he took that opportunity to insinuate himself between me and Wyndham, glaring daggers at him with those black eyes of his until Wyndham shrugged and backed off; he wouldn't cause a scene if his life depended on it. Brennan put his arm around my waist, bent me back so far that my foot was sticking up in the air, leaned over and kissed me for so long I nearly fainted. The spectacle brought wolf whistles from people all around the lobby. Then he set me upright and strode across the room, lit up a cigarette, and loitered casually against the wall until his date emerged. He nodded and said good night to Wyndham and me as they left. Is he still that much of an effing show-off?

"Wyndham didn't allude to the incident. And he never called me again. The next morning, my father looked at me over the *Wall Street Journal*. 'You're very chipper this morning, my dear. Has Wyndham livened up, or is that Burke fellow back in our lives again?' Then he went back to reading the paper. Though, if my memory is not playing tricks on me, he started whistling 'Some Enchanted Evening.'"

"So you were back together."

"Yes. Till the final parting, engineered by God Almighty." She snapped back to the present. "I'm famished."

We walked to the West Side, where we had a bite to eat, split a bottle of red wine, and gabbed about work and kids. She told me she was widowed; I told her Maura and I were separated. We turned to the subject of music and I ended up scribbling a twelve-bar blues on her napkin. I sang it to her on the walk back home, and made her laugh:

> Woke up this morning, got yo' earring in my mouth.
> Said, woke up this morning, woman, got yo' earring in my mouth.
> You don't give me nothin' else, babe, I take yo' diamonds and go south.

When we got to her front door she gave me a hug and a quick goodbye peck on the cheek. One of the strongest temptations I have ever faced, stronger even than the urge to stay and show Sandra I was no boy soprano, was the temptation to cajole her into a cab with me, and take her across the bridge to Brennan's. But I didn't say a word about my destination. I felt like a sneak.

II

I rode in the cab alone to Sunnyside in Queens. Brennan's family lived in a semi-detached, two-storey brick house with a steeply pitched roof; it had three windows up and two down on each side of a double doorway. The Burkes occupied the northern half of the house with a corner lot. Trees and hedges added a suburban touch to the neighbourhood.

I rang the bell and waited. I could see a small orange glow approaching the door window. The tip of a cigar preceded a full head of snowy white hair and two very cold blue eyes, which stared hard at me. Then the door opened and Burke Senior filled the entrance to the hall. A few inches shorter than Brennan, and stockier, the father struck me as an implacable force. The sense of power held in check was even stronger in the father than in the son. As was the clipped Irish accent. "Mr. Collins, is it?"

"Yes. Montague Collins. Good to meet you, Mr. Burke."

He put his hand out. "Declan. Come in. What's troubling my son?"

"I —"

"He tells me you're a friend down from Halifax. If that's the case, why aren't you staying with us? Whatever the real story is, you more than likely know what's eating him. His mother is worried. She finds him thin, and I find him a terrible card player. He's losing his shirt in poker and that never happens. But when his mother took him aside he told her there's nothing wrong. As usual, he's keeping his gob clamped shut and not talking about his troubles."

I could not imagine Declan Burke opening up about any troubles he might have — if he had troubles — and it was clear his son was made of the same stuff.

"Well, come in and have a drink. We're all downstairs."

I followed him past a pleasant, well-worn living room on the right to a set of stairs leading to a family room below. One corner of the room was set up as a bar. The dark green walls were covered with framed photographs and posters, all on an Irish theme. There were comfy couches along two walls, and a card table in the centre of the room.

"Gentlemen. And lady. I give you Mr. Collins."

There were five people around the table, and an empty chair where Declan had been. Brennan was in his clerical black but the collar had disappeared. He must have been on duty somewhere during the day. He and two of the other men had big stogies in their mouths. All had drinks, which appeared to be whiskey. The one lady at the table was sipping a glass of white wine, her cards in a tight pack in her left hand. Everybody rose. The woman was tall and elegant, her white hair pulled back in a chignon. She had an oval face and huge, dark eyes. She came over and took my hand warmly in hers. "Teresa Burke. I'm pleased to make your acquaintance, Mr. Collins."

"Please call me Monty. Everyone does."

"Fine then, Monty. You've met Declan." She gave her husband an admonitory look. "I hope he was gracious at the door. This is Tom Kelly, Vincent Graziano, and Domenico Antonelli."

"I'm going off with Monty here, if nobody minds," Brennan announced. He stubbed his cigar in the heavy ashtray beside him.

Domenico answered for everyone, in a thick Italian accent. "We don't mind. Most nights he wins. Tonight he loses. Either way he can go. Leave the cigars. We don't have the, uh, Havana connections you have, Brennan." Everyone laughed.

"These are legal in Canada," Burke replied. "I can smoke them any time I like. See you boys later. Win the farm back for me, Ma," he pleaded and we went upstairs. "I'll be ready in two minutes."

He left me at the door, then returned wearing jeans and a dark crewneck sweater. Declan and Teresa came to see us out. Brennan put an arm around his mother and squeezed her lightly. She looked up at him with concern. "You're a sight, Bren darling. Black circles under your eyes. You're exhausted. And look at this." She reached up and stroked the dark hair curling over his collar. "Don't they give you time off for a haircut? And you obviously haven't been eating —"

"The girls at the bar will think I'm a tortured artist. Might get lucky."

"Oh, Brennan! But really, my darling, I'm worried."

"Mother dearest, mother fairest, we've been all through this before," Brennan sang to her in the voice of an old-style crooner. He kissed her lightly on the forehead and opened the door.

"Till next time, Monty," said Declan. "A trip to Halifax may be in order, I'm thinking. Goodbye Brennan," he said and rested his hand briefly on his son's shoulder. Then he turned and went back to the game.

III

"So, where are we off to?" I asked.

"There's a blues bar on Queens Boulevard. Five minutes away." I noticed a bit more Irish in his voice. "You have a blues outfit of your own, have I got that right?"

"Yeah. I still play in a little band we formed in law school. Functus. We play for ourselves mostly. But then again, it's blues, so we're happy in our loneliness."

The bar was smoky and crowded when we arrived and the band was on a break. We found a table and ordered drinks, a Jameson's for him and a Czech beer for me. I could see that Burke was tense. Any relief the visit had offered seemed to be wearing off. But he made an effort to chat about his family. He was the second child, oldest boy, in a family of six: Maire, Brennan, Patrick, Francis, Terrence, and Brigid. When the band came back on, we ordered another round and turned our attention to the blues.

I became aware of two women eyeing us from the bar. One was very attractive with red hair, the other a rather blowzy-looking blonde who may have had one too many for the road. They were in their mid- to late thirties. When the band stopped between numbers, the blonde approached our table, half-dancing in time to a tune playing only in her head.

"Hi there. Mind if we sit down? I find a chair much more comfortable than a bar stool, don't you?" She addressed herself to Burke. He didn't say anything.

I looked at him, then said: "Sure. Have a seat." I got up to let the redhead go behind me. Burke stood as well, out of an old-fashioned sense of chivalry perhaps.

"What are you drinking?"

The blonde answered: "Tequila for me, and she's having club soda. She's my designated driver. If I end up needing one, that is." She looked across at Burke. He didn't crack a smile, but reached for a pack of cigarettes and lit one up. I signalled the waiter and ordered drinks for everyone.

"I'm Monty, this is Brennan. And you are?"

"My name's Louanne and this is Rosemary. We're here from New Jersey on a course, and we've had enough of the classroom, wouldn't you say, Rose? You don't sound like you're from here," Louanne said in my direction.

"I'm from Nova Scotia." She looked at me blankly. "Canada. You know, the country that runs for four thousand miles along your northern border?"

"Right. And what do you do, Monty?"

"I defend undesignated drivers."

"Oh, a lawyer?" She turned to Burke. "And you, sir?"

"I'm a fellow who's waited all his life to hear this band, the —" he squinted at a poster on the wall "— South of Blue. Sure and aren't they starting up right now?" Burke twisted in his chair so he could give them his full attention. Louanne was unperturbed and sat there with her tequila, moving unrhythmically to the music. Rosemary listened with a polite expression on her face and tried to be discreet as she checked her watch. I wanted to speak into her ear without getting too close and coming off as a lout. After a few preliminaries, to which she responded courteously, I was able to have a mouth-to-ear conversation with her and she began to open up. Rosemary was recently divorced and had a ten-year-old son, William, so we talked about our children. She recounted some entertaining stories about her work and the bizarre characters who people offices the whole world over. Never willing to take second seat when bizarre work tales were the order of the day, I told her some war stories of my own.

The instant the band announced a break, Louanne filled the silence. "So Brennan. What's your line? Are you a lawyer too? Or a client?" She laughed, and turned to Rosemary. "Kind of looks like a hit man, doesn't he?"

"You've never been safer in your life," he answered.

"Oh yeah? What do you do?" Louanne persisted.

"I'm a priest, an expert on the Holy Trinity. Is there anything you'd like to know about it?"

"You're shittin' me. I don't see any collar here —" She reached over and pulled at the neck of his sweater. He took her hand gently and put it back on the table.

"Is he?" Louanne turned to me.

"Afraid so," I confirmed.

Rosemary nudged me with her knee and whispered: "What do you know? For once I'm on the right side of the table. Any other time I've gone out for a drink with Lou, I ended up driving her and some guy somewhere and going home by myself."

"If you're alone at the end of an evening, it could only be by choice," I whispered back.

"Very gallant of you, Monty. But you're right for the most part. The type of man you meet in a bar — present company excepted, I hope — is not usually the type you want to go home with. And the more persistent they are, the more likely they are to be bad news."

"Well, I promise not to persist. But you don't have to go home by yourself if you don't want to. Is William taken care of for the night?"

"He's with a sitter." Music in my ears. Time to stop hitting the booze. I ordered club sodas for both of us.

At that point, our senses were caressed by a smouldering female voice. She started with a quiet, slow-burning little number I didn't know. Then she launched into a scorching, estrogen-fired version of "It's a Man's World." I took a break from chatting up Rosemary to give my attention to the tall, dark-haired siren at the microphone. I looked at Burke and saw that he was transfixed, oblivious of everything else in the room. Louanne sulked and downed her drink. When the woman brought the song to its blistering conclusion, the crowd went wild with applause. Everyone applauded, that is, except Brennan; the song hadn't ended for him. He continued to gaze at her, then nodded his head in acknowledgement.

Rosemary and I were doing a bit of a shuffle about whether to order another club soda. Brennan, after snapping out of his reverie, read the signs and leaned towards me. "Take both of them."

"Both of them!" I exclaimed, seeing not the upright priest of tonight but his younger self in the sack with two women while deadly smoke curled up through the floor boards.

"I mean," he said with exaggerated patience, "when you leave with Rosemary, take Louanne with you and make sure she's safely on her way home. She's had a skinful."

"What are you going to do?"

"Stay for the last set and head home to bed."

Rosemary announced to Louanne that the special bus was leaving. Resigned, she gave a theatrical sigh and made ready to leave. "Good night, *Father.*"

"Good night, dear. Safe home." He smiled at Louanne for the first time, and her eyes lingered on him before she turned and walked out.

The night ended for me shortly after that. When we got to Jersey, Louanne wailed that she had forgotten her bag, and her house keys, in the bar. Could she stay the night with Rosemary? She could, and I didn't.

But that bit of frustration was soon forgotten, as events careened out of control in Halifax.

Chapter 10

You got my attention, now go ahead speak.
What was it you wanted, when you were kissing my cheek?
Was there somebody looking when you gave me that kiss?
Someone there in the shadows, someone that I might have missed?
— Bob Dylan, "What Was It You Wanted?"

I

The call came on Victoria Day, five days after my return from New York. I was spending the late May holiday with Tom and Normie, playing catch and goofing around in the backyard. Now Rowan Stratton's announcement: he had reliable information that Brennan Burke could be arrested as early as the following morning on two counts of first-degree murder. The police had physical evidence tying Burke to both victims. And there was apparently a connection between a mark left on the bodies and the cross-shaped scar Rowan had described when this all began. A crucifix had imprinted itself on Brennan's flesh in the heat of the infamous fire back in 1960.

Brennan was not home when Rowan tried to reach him. I said I would take it from there, and I tried the rectory half an hour later. Father Burke was out for dinner. I did not hear from him until nearly ten that night.

"Monty. Brennan here. You called."

"Yes. I have something to discuss with you."

"Go ahead."

"I'd rather see you in person. At your place."

"Now?"

"Yeah."

"See you when you get here." Click.

I drove downtown at top speed and went up to Brennan's room. He came to the door in cut-off shorts and a worn black T-shirt.

"We have to talk, Brennan."

"Surely we do, if you've come all this way at night. But listen to this first. Have a seat." He moved some theological texts from a chair. "I've been asked to be guest conductor of the Halifax Symphony and the Recordare Chorus, for a segment of their concert next winter. Mozart's *Coronation Mass*, and the *Kyrie in D Minor*. Now if that *Kyrie* doesn't terrorize you back into the church, I don't know what will. The opening chord —"

"Brennan! Listen to me."

"You've got me troubled, Monty."

I took a deep breath. "First things first. Take off your shirt."

"*What?*"

"Let me see the scar. The imprint from that fire."

"You're losing me here."

"It's part of the evidence against you. Now show it to me."

He gripped the arms of the chair and slowly stood up, never taking his eyes off my face.

"Evidence? It's not evidence of anything. What the fuck are you talking about?" His quiet tone was more menacing than a shout as he moved towards me.

I stepped back. There was a real possibility that this man, a priest and a friend, was in fact a killer. I told myself not to be so melodramatic.

"Rowan's been in touch with the police, Brennan. You're facing arrest as early as tomorrow. Two charges of murder. Leeza Rae, Tanya Cudmore."

His eyes moved to the closed door and back to my face. He took another step towards me. "I can't be hearing you right."

"There's a mark on each of the bodies that matches what you're supposed to have. I've never seen it." I tried to put aside my apprehension as the news sunk in.

The next thing I knew he was stripping off his T-shirt, revealing a muscular chest and abdomen. Branded there just above his heart was the small, nearly complete image of a cross. The vertical bar was deeper and darker near the top, as was part of the crosspiece on Brennan's left. The rest of the image was more faint. It looked as if the original metal crucifix had been slightly off centre and embedded unevenly in his skin. I examined the image for a long while, then looked up at his face, which was drawn and grey.

"Get me out of this," he whispered.

"I need some information. Put your shirt back on. I have to know how many people have seen that scar."

"What can I tell you? Everybody knows about it. All the old souls in the parish back home loved the story, little Brennan Burke being given a clout by God on the way to Damascus. The prodigal choirboy. On and on and fucking on."

"I didn't ask how many people know about it; I asked how many have seen it."

"How the hell can I answer that?"

"Try. If it wasn't you who killed those two women —"

"Monty, for the love of Christ. You know I didn't kill anyone!"

"So it was somebody else. Somebody who wants to frame you or connect you to the killings. Now who would want to do that? I have to know."

"I have no idea. I can't imagine."

"All right. Let's go back to who could have seen the scar. I think we can leave aside, for the moment anyway, casual observers at the pool, or anything like that. We're looking for someone very familiar with that imprint. Now, tell me. Who?"

"Well, Monty, I don't get around much. Being a celibate priest and all."

I made an effort not to lose patience. "Very well. Let's start with people in this building. Do you go around with your shirt off here in the rectory? Would the other priests, the housekeeper, whoever is here, would they have seen it?"

"There's only one other priest in this rectory. Mike O'Flaherty. We don't sit around with our shirts off, but he may have been in here when I've come out of the shower. I don't remember that happening, but I can't say it never did. And the housekeeper? Never. She'd be shocked that there's anything made of flesh under the priestly garb."

"People you exercise with, lift weights, go to the gym with?"

"I use a set of weights in the basement once in a while. Alone. When I go out for a walk, guess what, I'm fully dressed."

On to the next set of questions. I did not see this — premeditated murder followed by mutilation — as a woman's crime. But if we could eliminate all female suspects, we could move on to the men. And of course the police had a man in the frame for these murders: Burke himself.

"Fine. Who have you slept with?"

"What the fuck? Nobody."

I lost it. "If you fucking lie to me, Burke, life as you know it ends tonight. I won't be able to defend you. I happen to know you're not exactly a virgin. So let's not hear —"

"Not a requirement of the job," he snapped. "You have to keep it in your pants afterwards, not before."

"We're not talking about before, are we? We're talking about the time after you got burned with that crucifix. When you decided to become a priest. From that time on —"

"Who have I shagged?" He looked as if he wanted to clock me. Then he sighed. "My girlfriend. Old flame. Way back. Would she fly to Halifax, find two strangers, murder them and carve them up in the hopes that someone would connect them with me? Is that what you're wondering? If she was going to carve anyone up, it would be me. Or would have been, thirty years ago. But she wouldn't. She's not the type. She didn't even shed a tear when we split up. She just said: 'If you're going, go. Don't waste any more of my time.' And gave me a withering look till I finally backed myself out the door. She wasn't one to put her feelings on show, especially in front of some cad who had just told her he didn't love her anymore."

"You didn't love her?"

"I told her I didn't. But it was bullshit." The expression on his face softened. "Of course I loved her. But I reasoned that she'd find it easier to write me off if she thought I was a complete arsehole who didn't care about her. Or some religious nut who didn't have normal feelings for a woman. She hadn't lost anything then. It was better than having her think of us as two star-crossed lovers separated only by the seminary walls."

"Which was in fact the truth."

"Which was the truth, yes."

"What women have there been since then?"

"None."

I didn't buy it but I'd have to let it go. For now. "All right. Men. Shagged any of those?"

"Oh, fuck off, Collins."

"Don't get prim with me, Brennan. I don't care how you get your tail —"

"What is it about 'fuck off' you don't understand?"

"Well, you must have crossed paths with some gay men —"

"I've crossed paths with Scotsmen. That hasn't given me any desire to blow the bagpipes."

I went on as if he hadn't spoken. "If there's anything like that, I have to know. The police aren't going to be looking for a woman. After all, they're looking at you. So help me here."

"There have been no men in my life, Montague," he said in a voice laden with sarcasm, then continued more calmly: "Like you, I don't care how people get their tail. I suspect God doesn't either. If I were banging all the Daughters of Mary Immaculate, God probably wouldn't give a shit as long as I was performing the sacraments and otherwise being a good priest. But I've signed up for the life, made my promises and tried to stick to them. I've done just about everything else in my time, but boys? No."

I made a note of that "tried to" for future reference, but I had heard enough on the subject for one night. I wondered whether Burke appreciated the fact that his inability or unwillingness to name anyone who had a grudge against him, and intimate knowledge of his body, only served to tighten the noose around his neck.

II

The first thing I had to do was head off an egregious show of police power at St. Bernadette's in the morning. Brennan sat straddling a chair

128

and gazing out the window, and I looked past him, imagining police cars roaring up to the door of the rectory at the break of dawn. I had no intention of seeing my client and his church humiliated by the drama of Father Burke being led out of the rectory in handcuffs and shoved into a police cruiser. I got on the phone to Rowan, who was already working the system so Brennan could turn himself in at the station. I could not imagine the police objecting; a surrender puts the accused on the cops' turf right from the beginning, which is to their advantage. It was just a matter of working out the details. My client retreated into his thoughts as the hours ground on. Rowan finally called to say the surrender had been worked out, at which point Brennan turned and asked through clenched teeth how long I thought he'd be away from home.

I was destined to be the bearer of bad tidings for as long as I could see into the future. I took a deep breath and began to outline just how little control he now had over his place in the world. "I'll probably be able to get you out, more likely than not, but . . ." His eyes were locked on my face; he wasn't moving a muscle. "But it's not a sure thing, and it won't happen right away. It could be a few days. Or longer. Because the charge is murder, the onus is on us to convince the judge there will be no harm in releasing you until your trials." I could almost see the animation leaching out of him as he listened to my words. "And that's another obstacle, it goes without saying. Two murder charges. If they consider you a serial killer —"

"*What!*" he yelped.

"Two murders, unrelated victims, three months apart. From their point of view —"

"I'm not a killer at all, for Jesus' sake, let alone a serial killer. I can't believe I heard that phrase coming out of your mouth."

"It's not me, Brennan. This is the situation you're facing. A serial — a person like that is obviously considered much more dangerous to the public than the guy who kills his drinking buddy. Now, as I said, there is a possibility you will be released."

"You said 'probably'!"

"Only if we can convince the judge you're not a flight risk or a danger to the public. You're facing the most severe penalty in the Criminal Code, life in prison with no chance of parole for twenty-five years." He looked ready to expire in front of my eyes. "This of course makes it more likely a person will flee rather than face a trial. And the likelihood of conviction has a bearing on whether you, or whoever, will make a run for it. So I assume the Crown — the prosecutor, that is — will lay out the case against you. We'll counter with your stellar character, the fact that you don't have a criminal record or a psychiatric history, if in fact those two statements are correct."

"Fuck you, Collins. I can't believe this. What do you mean 'if'? You think I've got a record, and a history as a psycho? How are you going to be able to represent me if you —"

"The only way I can represent you effectively is if I know you, and your life history, warts and all, so I don't walk in there like a little woolly lamb to the slaughterhouse. I intend to establish from day one our line of attack, that this is a miscarriage of justice, that an innocent man must not be made to sit in jail for months on end while the process drags on, the implication being there will be hell to pay for this later on."

"And my chances?"

"It's not a sure thing but I'd say you have a good chance if —"

"How long before I go to trial?"

"That will be months down the road. First there will be a preliminary inquiry, unless we waive —"

"Months! What's this preliminary? We can waive it? Skip whatever you can skip, if they bang me up in there for the duration. The sooner this is over . . ." He wound down, and sat there massaging his greying temples.

I did not have the heart to point out the obvious: that it might never be over.

"We'll request a ban on publication of all evidence adduced at the bail hearing, and the ban will be granted. If you're released, you'll need a surety, someone to put up some money to guarantee that you will not flee the country."

"God Almighty. This is where the old lady always signs over her house, isn't it?"

"There will be conditions, such as reporting once a week and surrendering your passport."

"Give up my passport? You mean I'll be spared one of Mike O'Flaherty's Blarney and Blather tours of the Emerald Isle? And here

I was thinking this was the worst day of my life."

You'd better hope and pray this is the worst day of your life, I thought, knowing all too well how much worse it could get. All I said was: "Wear a suit and tie, and for God's sake, if the media get wind of this, do not try to hide your face on the way into the station. Or on your way out of court if . . . *after* I get you sprung. Look dignified. Don't utter a word."

He did not utter another word to me but rooted around for his clothes, then headed into the bathroom for a shower. He was in there for twenty minutes, obviously prolonging the bliss of soap and hot water as if he thought he was going up the river for good. When he finally emerged in a cloud of steam, I was engrossed in writing notes on the many, many things I would have to keep in mind as the day went on. By the time I looked up, he was dressed in a white shirt and grey dress pants and was reaching for a belt. The pants looked too big. He had lost weight during the past few stressful weeks.

"Have you got anything smaller?"

"Smaller? What are you talking about?"

"Pants that fit more snugly around the waist?"

He regarded me with a touch of amusement. "You only represent nattily dressed clients?"

"When the sheriff escorts you from the courtroom down to your cell, he's going to take your belt and shoelaces. If your clothes don't fit, you'll be one of those guys who has to walk around all day holding his pants up."

He sank down in his chair, all questions of apparel forgotten. I prodded him, and he returned to his closet. He found a navy suit that promised to stay on when the indignities began.

"Now, you're going to eat."

"Eat?" He looked at me as if I had offered him hemlock.

"Breakfast. You'll need something in your stomach."

I drove him to the north end of the city, to Kempt Road where Jimmy's Homestead Restaurant sat amid a growing number of automobile showrooms. The place had a regular clientele ranging from judges to truckers. Jimmy had come to Canada from Sparta; the head waitress, Pat, was from Athens. But there were no lingering animosities. I ordered two large breakfasts of eggs, sausages, toast and home fries, coffee and orange juice. Brennan sat, squeamish and pale. I wolfed down my meal as if I were the one going on a jailhouse diet.

"Eat, Brennan."

"You sound like my mother, God bless her and keep her. Wait till she hears what's befallen her darling boy now. And Declan, well, it doesn't bear thinking about."

"Don't worry about that now. Rowan and I will handle your family. Your mother will know you're innocent. She'll know you've got clean underwear and socks on, and that you had a good, healthy breakfast. And Brennan? Listen to me as if your life depends on it. You are *not* giving a statement to the police. By a statement I mean anything at all. Keep your mouth shut. Even if you're innocent, it's never —"

"Even *though* I'm innocent."

"And I want to make something else clear: do not put yourself in the way of any needless aggravation from the police. Don't provoke them, don't needle them, don't argue with them, don't be a smartass. Be polite and cooperative, except where it comes to talking. Then be firm: you have nothing to say. Period."

He finally ate something. We pulled up to the police station just before eight o'clock. I got him in the door without seeing any reporters. Sergeant Ron Davidson met us inside and placed Brennan under arrest, then read him his rights. As soon as Davidson stopped speaking, Burke started: "You've got the wrong man —" I overrode him: "My client will not be giving a statement, Sergeant. He has nothing to say. Nothing," I repeated, with a warning glance at Burke. I had to leave him in their hands because I needed to prepare for court. I departed with misgivings.

It was a good thing Rowan accompanied me to the gargoyle-bedecked provincial courthouse for Burke's arraignment. The media were out in force, and I left them to my smooth-talking, silver-haired partner while I went downstairs to see Brennan. Despite twenty years of seeing my clients in jail cells, I found the sight incongruous and unnerving: a man from whom I had received Holy Communion was behind bars with the ragtag and bobtail of Halifax's underclass. I could hear a man babbling psychotically until he gagged and vomited; someone else reacted with a string of slurred obscenities. How had the priest's housekeeper described his work with prisoners? "The least of these my brethren." Well, he was amongst them now. He sat in the cell, arms folded across his chest, making a passable show of looking nonchalant. But I had come to know him well enough to see the intense hostility crackling beneath the surface. The sheriff gave us a meeting room, but there wasn't much to discuss. I assured Brennan that the arraignment would be brief. That was small comfort because, from the time he left the courtroom, he would be locked up, first at the courthouse and then at the Halifax County Correctional Centre. I left him and went upstairs to court.

The gallery was packed with reporters and gawkers when the priest was brought in to be arraigned on two counts of first-degree murder. To give him credit, Brennan managed to convey an impression of serenity. I jumped up to waive reading of the charges. There was no plea at this stage, and the proceeding was over in minutes. My client was returned to his cell in the basement.

Before he was taken to the Correctional Centre, I went down and gave him a warning: "Brennan, the place you're going will not give you any joy. Everyone is shoved in together. Remand is considered hard time. Please keep your cool, don't let anyone provoke you. We just have to get you through these next few days."

"It had better be just a few days, or —" But he was a quick study; he realized before he finished his thought that there was no "or else." From now on he had absolutely no say in the direction his life would take.

III

Brennan was in the Correctional Centre for a week and a half before we could be heard in the Supreme Court on the question of his release. I visited as often as I could. Maura made a couple of trips and came back exceedingly concerned. One minute he would talk about working with the other inmates as a priest; the next minute he would not plan beyond the end of the visit. When our court date finally came up, the hearing took two days. There was a great deal of case law against us and the Crown prosecutors hammered home the evidence the police had amassed against Burke: hairs matching his on both victims' bodies, the cruciform scar on both victims, his connection with Leeza Rae, her suggestions to friends that a priest was interested in her sexually, his connection with Janeece Tuck and his grief over her death. The Crown said it was likely Burke would be convicted. Because he faced life in prison, there was a high risk that he would flee the country rather than chance a trial. With two women dead — "so far" was the implication — the public was in danger if he was let out. I countered that he had lived for nearly half a century without hurting anyone or getting in trouble with the law; his life had been stable and exemplary all along; his actions after the murders, including talking to the police and giving hair samples, were those of an innocent man. My argument was peppered with the phrases "innocent man," "wrongful arrest," and "miscarriage of justice." Unspoken but audible nonetheless was "damages suit." Justice Angus Ross, a veteran nearing retirement, showed no reaction to the Crown's efforts or to mine, and reserved his decision. That was a Thursday; we would reconvene on Monday, June 4, to learn our fate. Brennan was led, dejected, to his cell.

The gallery was full again on the day of the decision. Brennan looked pale and wasted, nearly immobilized by stress, as he waited for the judge to appear. But the tide had turned in our favour. Justice Ross agreed to release him on a $20,000 recognizance with one surety, Rowan Stratton, and with a number of conditions, including that he stay within the boundaries of Halifax County, surrender his passport, and have no contact with any of the Crown witnesses. We amended the order to allow contact with the people at St. Bernadette's.

Brennan had the good sense to look humble and cooperative when the judge delivered his parting shot: "Don't make me regret this."

He refrained from giving malevolent looks or hostile remarks to the mob of reporters who dogged us till we got to my car and sped off.

"We'd better not go back to the rectory right away," I advised him as I shifted gears and pulled into Upper Water Street. "The press will be waiting for you. How about a walk in the park? Bit of fresh air and sun before the real work begins."

We made our way through the south end of the city until we were on Young Avenue, one of the city's most exclusive streets, lined with massive trees and stately old houses. At the end of Young was Point Pleasant Park, an oasis of nearly two hundred acres of trees, walking paths, picnic areas, and beaches lapped by the salt waters of Halifax Harbour and the Northwest Arm. The city still pays Her Majesty's Government a rent of one shilling a year for the property. Brennan and I pocketed our ties and slung our jackets over our shoulders as we walked the paths.

"So, did a taste of life on the inside focus your mind, Brennan? Any ideas about who's doing this to you?" He shook his head. "If not, all I can do is chip away wherever I can at the Crown's case. Raise a reasonable doubt. It would be infinitely better if you could come up with someone with a killer instinct, who is out to get you."

"This all sounds fantastical to me," he replied. "You have to realize that."

"And you have to realize that it sounds fantastical to me that you cannot identify a single person even remotely possible as a suspect." He looked blank. "For Christ's sake, Brennan, when are you going to start taking this seriously? After you're convicted and sent back to prison for good? It could very well happen. Wise up, and tell me who could have done this."

"You think I'm protecting someone, don't you? Which means you must hold me in very high regard." With a wry expression, he went on before I could reply. "'Greater love hath no man than this, that a man lay down his life for his friend.' But think about it, Montague. If I were protecting someone, to the point where I would risk spending the rest of my life in prison, that person would much more likely be a woman than a man, wouldn't you think? And although it's possible that a woman committed these murders — we can't rule it out, I suppose — it's much more likely to have been a man. Psychopaths tend to be white males, right? Do you think I'd protect someone like that?"

I had, of course, thought about it, in much the same way as he set it out.

We wound our way through the paths and came out at the southern tip of the park, looking out towards the Atlantic Ocean. A couple of sailboats glided by. After a while we hiked back to the entrance, got ice cream cones at the corner store, then made the journey back downtown in silence. We had nothing to say. But the police had plenty.

Chapter 11

What do I hear? Am I then sunk so low,
To have this upstart boy preferred before me?
— Handel/Jennens, *Saul*

I

Now that charges had been laid, I had access to the evidence — and I hoped it was all the evidence — the police had against my client. I looked at the first Information, much more accurately named in French as the *Dénonciation*. Sergeant Ron Davidson, a member of the Halifax Police Department, stated on the form that he had reasonable grounds to believe, and did believe, that Brennan Xavier Burke, on or about the 15th day of February, 1990, at or near Halifax, in the Province of Nova Scotia, did commit first-degree murder on the person of Leeza Dawn Rae, contrary to Section 235(1) of the Criminal Code. The second Information made the same accusation against Brennan Xavier Burke with respect to the murder of Tanya Jane Cudmore on May 10, 1990.

The crime lab report for the Leeza Rae killing indicated that hairs found on the body matched those taken the day after the murder from Brennan Burke. I spent a lot of time with the gruesome photographs of the victims' bodies. I had seen Tanya at Janeece's funeral but I had never seen Leeza. I had heard she was a good-looking girl; the photos showed only someone who had been brutalized. Both women had the initials IBR carved above the right breast, and a small crucifix carved above the left. This was an accurate facsimile of the cruciform scar on my client's chest. According to the medical examiner's evidence, the presence of blood in the markings indicated that the women were still alive when the mutilation was done. The cause of death was pretty well identical for both women, a depressed skull fracture in the occipital region (back) of the head. Pieces of the skull had broken off and become embedded in the brain tissue, resulting in contusion (bruising) of the brain, and intracerebral hemorrhage (bleeding) causing death. Leeza Rae suffered more blows to the head than Tanya Cudmore had.

There was much more witness information in Leeza's file than in Tanya's, which was not surprising given that Leeza had been killed after a dance where she had been seen by a hundred or more people. Personnel at the youth centre had been interviewed again while Brennan and I were in New York. The police were cagey when they asked about the dance. Physical contact was mentioned only in the wider context of how well, if at all, Brennan and Leeza knew each other. As to whether they had danced together, one of many questions about their relationship, the majority said yes. Eileen Darragh stuck loyally to no. She was quoted as saying: "I'm in that building every day, all day. As far as I could tell, Father Burke barely knew who Leeza was." The investigators, acting on "information received," also asked whether there had ever been any kind of argument or disagreement between Burke and Leeza Rae. Tyler MacDonald told the story of the confrontation in which Leeza's shirt was partly unbuttoned. My question was: *what information received?* Was there an anonymous tip? Leeza's file contained statements from two acquaintances, one male and one female, who said Leeza had boasted of a priest who "had the hots" for her and wanted to take her on trips out of town on the weekends. Junkets to Dorchester Penitentiary, I supposed.

The witness statements in Tanya Cudmore's file indicated that Tanya had been ejected from the home of Janeece's father immediately after the child's death but had returned, or been allowed back, two days before Tanya's body was found. Janeece's father had not been home at all the day before the body was discovered, so he was of no assistance as to where she was last seen. Neighbours in Tanya's apartment block remembered seeing her in the afternoon but nobody was sure whether she was around in the evening. She often went to bingo, they said, so it was not unusual for her to be out. Family witnesses recalled that Father Burke had driven Janeece home on at least one occasion in his car, and they believed Tanya had met Burke when she had arrived late to collect Janeece after practice. They knew nothing about any conversation Tanya and Burke may have had, and certainly knew of no physical contact between them. Witnesses from St. Bernadette's testified — reading between the lines I sensed their evidence was given reluctantly — about Burke's apparent fondness for Janeece in the choir, his grief at the funeral, and his failure to stick it out till the end.

The onus was on the Crown to prove its case beyond a reasonable doubt; it would be up to us to raise as many doubts as we could about the forensic and other evidence the police had gathered. It would be far better to come up with someone who might have borne a deadly grudge against the priest. Yet he could not, or would not, even provide me with the name of anyone on the North American continent who was familiar enough with his body (from the waist up was all I was asking) to be able to produce a facsimile of the cruciform scar above his heart. We desperately needed to find such a person. The next best thing would be to throw up another possible suspect as a smokescreen. So I directed my mind to the matter of alternative suspects.

II

I was standing by my secretary's desk when I noticed a small, stainless steel teapot beside her computer. I opened my mouth to tease her about possessing stolen property from a diner, when I thought of Mrs. Kelly at the rectory. Had someone stolen her teapot? No, that was a remark I made after she told me there had been a burglary. Not at the rectory, but at the archdiocesan office. I hadn't given the break-in another thought. But now, coupled with the vandalism directed at

Catholic churches in Halifax, it took on a whole new meaning as I struggled to fashion a defence for my client.

Jason, a young man who had been vandalizing Catholic churches, acting out of a rage against the Church and its clerics, could be the smokescreen I needed to conjure up a reasonable doubt for the jury. Something had happened to Jason, in reality or in his own mind; how else to explain why he had flinched away, not only from Burke, which was understandable, but even from Michael O'Flaherty? The Catholic Church had been around for two thousand years and had engendered more grievances than could possibly be tabulated. Jason could be, well, a godsend for our defence. It was a nice coincidence that, when confronted by Burke, he had jumped him and tried to strike him in the head with a heavy object, namely a full can of spray paint.

Jason would be good for us only if he had been in town when the murders occurred, in February and May. The fact that we did not have a full name for him would certainly hinder my efforts to present him as a suspect. But we had eyewitnesses who had seen and spoken to our vandal. I decided to call upon a forensic artist I had used in previous cases, to prepare a composite drawing from the description given by those witnesses. Time to reconvene the poker club.

It was a subdued pack of card players who turned up in the board-room of Stratton Sommers to share their memories with my forensic artist, Stacey Mallory. To a man, they rallied around Burke and claimed they were happy to do this and anything else he might ask of them. I held the door for our receptionist, Darlene, when she brought in a tray of coffee. Father O'Flaherty thanked her profusely and blessed her for her kindness; the others smiled their thanks; Burke looked right through her. On her way out Darlene whispered to me in theatrical tones: "He doesn't even know I'm alive!"

"You're an occasion of sin for him, Darlene," I whispered back, "and for all of us."

"Mean that?"

"Sure."

We got down to work. Michael O'Flaherty rose to the occasion, and had much to offer Stacey on the vandal's appearance and demeanour. Dr. Shaw, familiar as he was with human anatomy, was the most precise and helpful in describing the young man's facial structure. After an hour or so, Stacey had produced a sketch that looked remarkably like the man we had met in the church that night: a thin face with thin lips and small eyes, patches of light facial hair, and the inevitable ball cap.

In truth, though, I wanted to go only so far with the Jason factor, and no further. Jason was more useful to us as a shadowy, unidentified figure who may, or may not, have committed violent acts and tailored his crimes to look like the work of a priest. The real flesh-and-blood young man had probably done no such thing. And could likely come up with an alibi that would reveal our speculation for what it was. We would not want that confirmed in front of the jury. There was another very compelling reason I wanted to keep Jason in the shadows. He was obviously a troubled individual; I did not want to add to his problems. I would use the sketch, but I would keep it to a very limited distribution. It would not be provided to the police or to the media. All I wanted was someone to say this face had been seen in Halifax on or before February 14, 1990.

The first place I took the sketch was St. Bernadette's Youth Centre. I poked my head into the command centre of Sister Marguerite Dunne and Eileen Darragh. Eileen was not there but the boss was. Sister Dunne quickly confirmed that she had seen the young man. "I only remember one day when he was here at the centre, but he may have been around at other times."

"What day was this, that you saw him? And why does it stand out in your mind?"

"It was career day. Early December. Every year we take the young people out to the workplace, to observe people in various jobs. If somebody is interested in nursing, we set that person up for a day at one of the hospitals. Everybody wants to get in with an airline pilot, but we haven't had any luck there yet."

"So, what careers were on offer this time?"

"Let's see. I have the agenda here somewhere." I had no doubt that Sister Dunne knew exactly where every piece of paper was in her office. She found it in seconds. "Yes. Tyler took two of the boys to the Metro Centre to see how they run a complex operation like that. Father O'Flaherty — he does this every year — took a small group on a tour of the police station. I think the good father would like to come back as Sergeant O'Flaherty in his next life. Eileen took two girls to the law library. My niece is one of the librarians at the law school, so I set that one up myself."

"Were all the young people that day regulars?"

"Yes, except for this Jason. He was considerably older than the others, but he could obviously benefit from some workplace exposure. So he went out, too."

"What group did he go with?"

"He wanted to go on the police tour, but he missed it. Michael O'Flaherty had already left by the time Jason arrived. They never saw each other. I think Mike wanted to start the day at Tim Hortons, with an early dose of coffee and doughnuts. Getting into character. Jason went to the law library with Eileen and the two girls."

I was about to say goodbye when Marguerite spoke again. "Montague, how do you think our friend Father Burke is holding up?"

All I could do was shake my head.

"I see."

"Thank you, Sister. I may be in touch again."

"Any time."

I now had another potential witness in the law librarian if she remembered Jason being there, so I took a detour before returning to my office. The Sir James Dunn Law Library is contained in the Dalhousie Law School building. The library had caught fire several years before. Like other lawyers, judges, and students, I had been out on University Avenue, helping to salvage books from the wreckage. The library had then moved into a new, airier addition to the building. I recognized Rebecca Dunne behind the circulation desk.

"Ms. Dunne. I'm Monty Collins. I'm sure you've seen me in here, researching obscure points of law that never seem to do my clients any good. I was wondering if I could have a word."

"Hello, Monty. I knew your face was familiar. Come on back here." We went behind the desk and sat down.

"I'm working on a case and I think you may be able to help me." I pulled out a copy of the composite drawing. "Have you ever seen this guy?"

She looked intently at the sketch. "It seems to me I have, but I may just be remembering a similar sketch in the news somewhere.

I wish I could be more helpful."

"Would it refresh your memory if I asked you to think back to December? The St. Bernadette's Youth Centre had a career day, and —"

"Right. Marguerite sent a group over here. Yes. This could very well have been the lone male in that group. I can see the resemblance." Rebecca looked relieved, perhaps the natural reaction of a librarian who spends her days trying to help people find what they are looking for. I had all I needed, another witness who could say the church vandal was in town before the first murder. I already had him in place shortly before the second. But I might as well get more if I could.

"What was this fellow like, when he was here?"

"Quiet. Kind of moped around at the edge of the group. It was Ms. Darragh from the youth centre, and two girls ostensibly interested in library work. I gave them a rudimentary exercise in legal research. We looked at the cases in the most recent volume of the *Nova Scotia Reports*. Ms. Darragh was the only one who showed any interest in reading; well, I've always had the impression she's a bookish sort of person. And I mean that as a compliment. The young people were more interested in the Criminal Code: what would you get for this crime or that one? They had a giggle about 'assisting an alien to leave Canada.' But Eileen ignored them and stuck to the more dignified case law till it was time to go. It may have been my imagination, and I don't want to make false accusations. But I thought the young fellow tried to stuff the Criminal Code under his jacket! He saw me looking at him and he casually replaced it on the shelf. I may be wrong. I forgot all about it until now."

III

The next day I went to the offices of the Archdiocese of Halifax, where I was directed to see Father Eugene Cormier. I introduced myself and told him why I was there. The priest was in clerical black except for comfortable-looking brown suede shoes. He was a short, stocky, youngish man with prematurely white hair. He looked wary but greeted me politely.

"Father, I'll only take up a few minutes of your time. I'm looking for some information about the vandalism that has been going on in the archdiocese. And the break-in here at the office."

"Ask away."

"The break-in, when did it occur?"

"New Year's Day."

"The office was closed that day, I assume."

"Oh yes. We were all over at the bishop's New Year's levee."

"When did you discover the break-in?"

"Later that day, actually. I came in to pick something up from the office. I went to the room where we keep our personnel records, and I saw that some priests' files had been disturbed." Father Cormier looked as if the incident still troubled him.

"Are you able to tell me whose files had been opened?"

"Well, they are all men whose names are known around the archdiocese, though a couple of them are retired. Fathers O'Malley, White, Burke, MacDougall . . ." He rattled off a few more names.

"And Father O'Flaherty?" I asked.

"Father O'Flaherty's file isn't here."

"What do you mean? It's kept somewhere else?"

"It would normally be here. But it isn't. I mentioned it to him after the break-in, but he didn't seem interested in pursuing the matter. Doesn't surprise me. If you know Mike —" He shrugged. "I just let it go."

"Was anything taken?"

"Nothing that I could see. If there was anything missing from the files I might not have realized it, not knowing what they contained beforehand. But my impression at the time was that they had been hastily read, then thrown down when the person fled. It looked as if he left in a hurry."

"Was there anything taken or disturbed anywhere else in the building?"

"No. I checked around. Our secretary had left her wallet on her desk, and it wasn't touched. We confirmed this with her the next day. And warned her to be a bit more careful."

"Were you able to determine how the burglar got in?"

"No. We had the police here but they could find no sign of forced entry." I must have registered surprise because Father Cormier went on: "It would not have been an inside job, Mr. Collins. Everyone who works here has access to those files. They could have read them any time during the workday and nobody would have been the wiser."

"Do you have a lot of people in and out of the office, parishioners or people who need help?"

"Oh, yes. All the time. There is no way we could keep track of everyone who passes through here in the run of a week, not in retrospect anyway."

I asked about the vandalism and he named half a dozen parishes where anti-church, and anti-clerical, slogans had been painted. Nothing about the graffiti was especially notable; some of it had a Satanic theme but there was nothing to suggest the involvement of a cult. A few things had been broken, but there was no destruction on the altars. It sounded as if the perpetrator could not bring himself to desecrate the Church that was the source of his anguish. I showed Father Cormier the composite sketch of the vandal. He had never seen the man before. He invited me to take the picture around, and we went to the various offices and desks. One woman thought the face looked familiar but she could not say where or when she had seen it. When I turned away I heard someone say "One of our protests," but, when I turned back, the speaker busied herself with her papers. I thought about taking her up on it but decided it would get me nowhere.

I thanked Father Cormier and his staff and went on to the other parishes where vandalism had occurred. It was a splendid day to be out. Halifax is a city of trees and the streets were arched with green. In the end I found one caretaker and one housekeeper who thought they had seen the man around Church property in the winter months. I thanked them and took note of their names. I had what I needed, for what it was worth: a number of people who would testify that a man with a grudge against the Church had been in the area around the times of the murders. If he was the burglar at the archdiocesan office, what might he have found in the priests' personnel folders? What would be in Burke's file? Not much, I guessed, given that the bulk of his priestly life had been spent elsewhere. Could there possibly have been anything in the file about the cross that had been burned into his skin? This might warrant further investigation. But for now I had achieved my goal. I cruised to the office in the late afternoon sun, my arm out the open window, singing along with Louis Armstrong and "A Wonderful World." Once in a while in my work, things clicked into place and I could bask in the satisfaction of a job well done.

But I hadn't reckoned on my next encounter with Sergeant Moody Walker, and yet another damaging revelation about Brennan Burke.

IV

I worked cheerfully and late the day after making my rounds of the churches. I had made arrangements to meet my old friend Barbara, a Crown prosecutor, who was working at the other end of the province and who was in town for a conference. We met for dinner and a couple of drinks at a downtown bar that was a particular favourite of Crowns and police officers. I can barely remember what we talked about because, just as I put my fork down, uttered a little cuisine-related *bon mot*, and made to order another beer, Moody Walker lumbered in. He spotted me right away and smirked in triumph; his cherished suspect had finally been charged with murder. If his former colleagues had listened to Moody, they would have had Burke off the street before a second woman died. But they had him now.

When Barbara got up to leave, I distractedly said goodbye to her and waited for the inevitable. Moody Walker slid into her seat before she had cleared the building. "Looks like your man's not gonna make Pope after all, Collins. Nope. He'll be with his own kind soon. He knows some of the inmates already. Goes out and helps them with their problems. He better hope there's somebody gonna help him with his own problems. Hard to survive otherwise." Walker brought out his wallet and signalled the waiter for a drink.

"Moody, it wasn't Burke. He's being framed."

Walker let out a roar of good-natured laughter. "What else are you gonna tell me, Collins? I'll say this for you lawyers, you're loyal to a fault. Well, you have a job to do. But whoever is framing your client better 'fess up soon. A jilted lover, maybe? AC or DC? Nah, with him it's women. Or girls anyway." I had the impression this was not the first licensed establishment Walker had patronized recently — he was unusually voluble.

"What do you mean, Moody, girls? Surely, surely you're not talking about the little choirgirl, Janeece."

"Don't put words in my mouth, Collins. Nobody that young. Girls with a bit more shape to them, is what I have in mind. Like that Leeza Rae. These guys are all the same, whether they're RC or Baptist. They get these young girls —"

"There was nothing going on with Leeza Rae," I insisted.

"Right. She ran bawling from the building with her blouse flapping open, and then gave the finger to Burke for no reason, as he stood glaring at her from the window for no reason. Picture yourself wearing a trench coat, Collins, with a detective's badge in your pocket. You been listening to lies for thirty years. You just heard that story. Now tell me with a straight face you believe there was nothing sexual going on between them."

I tried to hold my ground. "There is a perfectly good explanation for any encounter Father Burke may have had with Leeza Rae when she worked at St. Bernadette's."

Walker leaned over the table and spoke urgently. "Rae wasn't the only one. Maybe you already know this, maybe you don't." I could feel my undigested meal turning sour in my stomach. I braced myself for whatever was to come. "This was back in the early eighties, 1982 or so. There was a girl at the college up there in New Brunswick, Mount Allison University. Burke was stalking this girl, a music student. Real talented little girl. That's how I figure he got onto her in the first place. Her band or chamber group — whatever it was, I don't know a violin bow from a drumstick — performed here in Halifax. He probably got a hard-on for her here."

The waiter brought Walker's drink. I didn't touch my beer.

"But there's more, Collins, a real jealous boyfriend scene. He'd been watching this young lady. A pretty little thing, who wouldn't want to follow her around? But most of us, grown-ups at least, go home to our wives. Only your guy doesn't have one. Anyway, on this occasion, she was out with her boyfriend, a real loser. But a good-looking loser, you know? The kind a girl would fall for and it would be the biggest mistake of her life. We know the boyfriend had beaten the girl on one occasion already. Your client's rental car was spotted outside the girl's dorm. Yeah, the local police checked the rental. You don't look so hot, Collins. Somehow I get the feeling this is news to you. It gets better. The boyfriend drops her off and gropes her for a while outside the dorm; she doesn't invite him in, so he starts to walk away. He's just picking up his pace when Burke squeals to a stop, explodes out of the car, grabs the little shithead by the throat, and slams him up against a tree. Nearly chokes him. The boy didn't want to spill this to the police, by the way. Fucking terrified. But they'd been looking at this kid for some other stuff, so he finally rolled over on Burke. Didn't have any idea who he was, of course, just this 'real scary Irish guy' who threatened to cripple him if, one, he went near the girl again or, two, he breathed a word of this encounter to anyone. Burke knew the kid's name and where he lived. What His Holiness said was: 'I'll fuckin' cripple ya.'

"The punk got lippy and tried to fight him off, and Burke pounded him so hard he broke a tooth and fractured three ribs. Burke gave him another warning, and took off. The kid didn't report it. And here's how dumb this little turd was: he told the police he took a souvenir from Burke, yanked a chain or something off his neck. The cop told him: 'You take a souvenir from a victory, asshole, not from someone who just beat the crap out of you!'"

I felt as if someone — it may as well have been Burke — had knocked the last breath out of me.

Walker paused for a quick gulp of his rum, then went on relentlessly: "Once the rental car was checked out, and found to be in the name of the Reverend Brennan X. Burke, the authorities in Sackville had a photo sent up from New York. Didn't tell New York why they wanted it, preferred to handle it without international complications. Anyway, this dirtball kid positively ID'd Burke from the photo. But the kid refused to press charges, and Burke had left the country by the time the police got the whole story. So nothing came of it. Unfortunately. A lot of bad luck and missed opportunities with this guy. As for the young lady who inspired this crime of passion, the police never brought it up with her. Saw no point in upsetting her once Burke was safely out of the country. But the local force had a couple of discreet interviews with her and her friends; they cooked up some story about a robbery on the campus. Showed the kids the photo of Burke. Cropped photo, no collar in view. The girl stared at the photo a good long time, but denied knowing him. So maybe he never got his hands on her. Just got his kicks by looking at her. Or maybe she was covering for him. If so, she did a good job of it."

I don't even remember how I extricated myself from Walker. I didn't know how to explain the fact that he laid it all out for me in detail. Was he drunk, or was he just determined to make me see Burke as he saw him, a twisto? Whatever the case, I had just heard something that rocked me to the core.

I had a sleepless night. As soon as I dragged myself into the office the next morning I knocked on Rowan's door. I did not divulge what I had learned from Walker; I merely asked for a bit of history. And it was simple: Rowan said Burke had been in Halifax from 1968 through 1970, and had arrived again last fall. If he had come to the province any time in between, Rowan didn't know about it.

What in the hell was going on? Father Burke wasn't stationed here in 1982. Could he have been in town for a musical event or a meeting? Had he seen the young Mount A student at a concert here, as Walker suggested?

It was time for another confrontation with my client.

V

I found him in the auditorium at the youth centre, alone on the stage, sitting on the piano bench. He was wearing his old grey Fordham T-shirt with jeans, and he had his half glasses perched on his nose. He was making notations on a musical score, stopping periodically to play a few notes on the keyboard. Even though the door had clicked shut behind me, he was unaware of my presence. I stood for a few minutes and listened. It was obviously the four-part Mass he had told me he was writing. If he had found a few moments of peace in which to compose music, I was loath to break in on him with such unwelcome news. But our choices, and our moments of peace, were running out.

Finally, he looked up and saw me. He knew that a visit from me at this point was not likely a social call, but he made an attempt at light conversation: "Monty. You're not here to correct my score, are you? Marguerite tried that a few minutes ago, and I put the run to her."

"Were her suggestions helpful?"

"Well-informed, I'll give her that. But misplaced in the context of the whole piece. You'll be wanting to add a blues riff to the *Benedictus*, am I right?" I looked at him without responding. "Time to get down to brass tacks, then, is it? What can I do for you, Monty?"

I pulled myself up onto the stage and straddled a chair. Burke turned on the bench to face me.

"Brennan, what were you doing at Mount Allison University in 1982?"

The colour drained from his face. He gripped the sides of the piano bench and stared at me with apprehension that bordered on fear. It was the last thing I expected to see in his face.

"Where did you hear about that?" His tone was belligerent but it didn't mask his trepidation.

"The police."

"Is this going to come out in court? It can't. That cannot happen." He put his hands up as if he could physically prevent the words from being uttered again.

"Explain it to me, Brennan. I have to know. Everything. I thought I'd made that clear. I can't defend you if I keep getting sandbagged like this. Now, what was going on?"

"It had nothing to do with this." He held up his hands again to ward off my objections. "It was not like these cases in any way. An isolated incident."

"There are no isolated incidents when the police are putting together a case for the murder of two women. You can be sure they know, or will know, everything you have ever done. That goes double for anything violent. So I'm asking you. Who was this girl you were stalking?"

"Stalking! What do you take me for?" I raised an eyebrow at him, folded my arms across my chest, and waited. He finally went on: "It was him, not the young girl. It was that shitheels I was after."

"If you were after some guy because of what he was doing to a young woman, if he was mistreating her, then you've played right into the Crown's motive for Tanya Cudmore's murder, avenging the death of a young girl who died because of the recklessness of a person close to her."

Brennan glowered at me. "I issued a warning to that worthless article of a human being. Then he made a remark that was unacceptable. I put a pounding on him. And if I ever see him again, I'll pound him twice as hard."

Jesus Christ. What had I got myself into with this man? I tried not to lose the last of my patience, or I would never get it back. I asked him calmly: "How did you meet the girl from Mount A?"

"Never mind how I met her."

Walker had told me the young woman denied knowing Burke. What was the story here? And how many more of these wretched stories would surface before this case ground to its conclusion?

"Brennan. You are not helping me and you are not helping yourself. You are facing life in prison. What else could possibly matter? If you had a girlfriend, or a crush on a young woman, even though you're a priest, doesn't that pale beside the murder charges? Let's get a sense of perspective here."

"I asked you," he demanded, as if he were the one trying to maintain his patience in the face of aggravation, "whether this is going to come out in court."

"It's highly unlikely that the Crown will apply to get this in as part of its case. It is so prejudicial to you that it would probably not be put before the jury."

His relief was palpable, but short-lived.

"However," I went on, "if we put your character in issue — if, say, you insist on testifying in your own defence — God forbid — and we claim there's no violence in your past, the Crown might raise this in rebuttal to our case. We just don't know. But they're not likely to raise it by themselves."

"Then don't mention it to me again. Ever."

I made no attempt to conceal my hostility. "It's going to be hell on earth trying to defend you, Burke. And if I can't, remember this: it will be on your head. You're a real piece of work, Brennan."

He got up from the piano bench and came towards me. I tensed.

He put his hands on my shoulders, looked straight into my eyes and said: "I'm not a killer. I have never raised my hand to a woman. There are no other violent incidents in my life —"

"What about that vandal you slammed down on the church floor? You were a quick draw that night."

"He jumped me and was trying to choke me. I didn't know what I was facing. There has been no violence apart from a few scraps I got into in my teens. And none of those were remotely like that business at Mount Allison, or the murders. Just barroom dust-ups and the kind of stupid things that happen when young arseholes have too much to drink. I told you before, Monty." He released me and gave me a little pat on the arm. "I'm just a choirboy."

"If I can come to believe that, and I hope I can, then I'll have no trouble accepting the truth of the Resurrection."

"Hell, I hope not. There's a whole book full of witnesses to that event, more than there will ever be testifying to my good character. A couple of books written by lawyers and judges too, you may be interested to hear, weighing the evidence of the Resurrection. I'll lend them to you. After my case is over. I don't want you distracted right now."

"Fine. Make sure I don't get distracted by any more sordid tales from your past."

As I turned to go I saw someone ease the door shut, but I could not tell who it was. It was impossible to say how long he or she had been standing there.

Part Two

Chapter 12

Oh, baby, don't you know I'm human,
have thoughts like any other one.
Sometimes I find myself alone regretting some foolish thing,
some little simple thing I've done.
I'm just a soul whose intentions are good.
Oh Lord, please don't let me be misunderstood
— Benjamin/Marcus/Caldwell, "Don't Let Me Be Misunderstood"

I

Brennan Burke was facing two counts of first-degree murder. The summer went by in a blur of preparation for trial. The Crown chose to proceed with the Tanya Cudmore murder first, most likely because it was so much easier in that case to come up with a motive: Burke's grief over Janeece's death and the inference of rage against the stepmother who had taken her from the safety of her bed to a vehicle driven by a man with a blood alcohol reading of .195. Normally, with more than one murder charge, especially if the defendant looked like a serial killer — I recalled how Burke had reacted to those words as if to a high-voltage shock — the motive for each killing would be similar. But the Crown believed the first murder, of Leeza Rae, was a sex killing. No rape, but the absence of rape is not that unusual in a killing related in some way to sex. In both cases the Crown was operating on the notion that Burke had a violent streak that got out of hand when he was severely provoked. I thought the two-motive theory a weakness in the prosecution's case but, with separate trials, the prosecutor would not have to address that problem. And the Crown had damning forensic evidence that seemed to link Burke to the murders. There had never been any direct physical contact between Burke and Tanya Cudmore, so the hair evidence was something we could not explain away, another reason the Crown had chosen to proceed with this charge first.

Our theory — and I wanted to believe in it — was that someone with a grudge against the Church, or against Burke, had committed the murders and planted evidence to put him in the frame. We had employed a private investigator in New York to find out whether anyone had been asking questions or burrowing into files that might contain a photograph or description of the crucifix scar, which had altered the course of his life when he was twenty, and might now alter it forever. The investigator had found nothing.

My client and I had a difference of opinion, to put it mildly, on a number of issues that fell within my area of expertise, not his. But he was the client, and he was paying the bills. So when he insisted on waiving his right to a preliminary hearing and going straight to trial, all I could do was put a memo in the file indicating that he had taken this decision against my advice. The purpose of a prelim is to put the evidence before a judge to see whether the Crown has a strong enough case to take to trial. Burke wanted nothing to do with the process. "Drag my name through the muck twice instead of once? You must be daft."

"You'd be daft to pass up the opportunity to check out their case and see where we can best attack it. None of the evidence will be reported. If we ask for a publication ban, the judge has to grant it."

"No. Let's go to trial, and have done with it."

"We don't just want it over with, we want the right result. Don't we?"

"No prelim. Waive it. Now, what's your next point?"

So he had his way. Not for the last time either, as we shall see.

The trial got under way on September 4, 1990, a golden late-summer day. We made our way with foreboding to the Supreme Court of Nova Scotia, located in a modern concrete building on the Halifax waterfront. Hearing the case was Justice Helen Fineberg, a courteous, fair judge with a razor-sharp mind. Judge Fineberg was a striking woman of forty-five who had chin-length dark hair with a dramatic streak of white along the front. The Crown attorney and I had been called to her chambers to deal with the question of my client's honorific. Father Burke would not, of course, be dressed in clerical garb. Even if there had been some reason to do this, he refused to "defile" his Roman collar by wearing it to such a "charade." I knew the prosecutor would not accord him the respect of the title "Father." Anything to demean and depersonalize him in front of the jury was a legitimate tactic. I of course would be calling him Father every chance I had. Helen listened to the arguments and decided she also would call him Father Burke. No matter which approach she took, she would be helping one side and hurting the other, but if there was the benefit of a doubt, it was going to the accused. The Crown understood this.

Karl Schenk was in his late fifties and, like a terrier, he never let go. He had short, bristly, greying hair and a moustache. The lenses of his wire-rimmed glasses were flat. I had always suspected he had perfect vision and the glasses were a prop used to glint at defence witnesses on the stand.

Brennan knew enough about Canada to know we don't execute prisoners. Or, as Maura had put it when the subject came up, "This isn't Iran. Or Florida." The stiffest penalty in the Code was an automatic life sentence for first-degree murder, with no chance of parole for twenty-five years. I had given my client a few lessons in courtroom etiquette. The judges in the province's Supreme Court were called "My Lord" or "My Lady," unlike the judges in Provincial Court, who were addressed as "Your Honour." Counsel would be wearing black gowns with white tabs at the throat. If the Crown prosecutor and I referred to each other as "my friend" we were not cozying up; it was a standard courtesy. The accused was to refrain from reacting to the testimony and remarks made by the prosecutor, no matter how aggravating. Don't show anger. Don't be aggressive.

The accused man walked into the courtroom with his head held high and showed no sign of the tremendous strain he was under. He was impeccably dressed in a charcoal grey suit, snowy white shirt, and dark tie. I was afraid the suit was too expensive and might, when combined with his usual unyielding facial expression, give the jury the impression that he was arrogant and overconfident. He confidently

157

shrugged off my concerns: "I buy half-decent clothes so they'll last me for years. When they see how often I wear the same things, they'll catch on. I'm not going out to buy a new outfit for these shenanigans."

The wood-panelled rooms in the Law Courts are not overly large, and ours was packed. Reporters, friends and relatives of the victim, spectators, and courthouse regulars sat crammed together in the oak pews. The judge's bench was raised and situated between the flags of Canada and Nova Scotia. The clerk sat at a table directly below the judge, the two Crown prosecutors at the next table facing the clerk. Working with me was Susan Drummond, small and delicate, one of the sharpest defence lawyers in the city. Sue and I were at the defence table directly behind the Crowns, with our client in the chair between us. Two sheriffs planted themselves behind us, at a discreet distance from the accused, poised to subdue him if necessary. After two days of jury selection, we ended up with seven men and five women of various religious and non-religious backgrounds. They took their places in the jury box to our left. Karl Schenk stood up, and the trial began.

The Crown took six days to present its case, and it was devastating. The prosecutors had disclosed their evidence to us, as they are required to do. As far as I knew, we had it all. But nothing prepares you for the effect on the jury of the deadpan police witnesses, the forensic experts, the medical examiner. They had the hairs linking Burke to Tanya. They had the cross carved over the victim's heart. Burke did a creditable job of looking unconcerned but I could read the signs of anger, impatience, and extreme stress as he sat listening to hour upon hour of evidence linking him to the murder of Tanya Cudmore. Much of the Crown's evidence seemed unassailable, and a failed effort on my part to discredit it would have done us more harm than avoiding it. I did what I could. The investigators had never been able to locate the scene of the murder; they had found the body where it had been dumped. They had not found the murder weapon. They could not trace the raincoat in which the body had been found. Having done my homework on this first, I got the Crown witnesses to testify that a small spot of blood had been found in the back seat of Brennan's car, and that it did not match Burke or Tanya Cudmore. I already knew it did not match Leeza Rae. I would deal with the blood when our case opened. In the meantime I did my best on cross-examination to point out weaknesses in the Crown's case. I suggested other ways the hairs could have found their way to Tanya Cudmore. Janeece had been with Father Burke on a number of occasions and Tanya had been at St. Bernadette's. I made much of the fact that no evidence of foul play, and no traces of the victim, had been found during the meticulous searches the police conducted of Burke's room and his possessions. It was impossible to tell how I was doing with the jury.

Brennan was anxious for our case to open. I did not know quite what he expected. I had character witnesses lined up, of course, and alibi witnesses to state that Father Burke was giving a lecture at St. Mary's University the evening of the murder, then got into his car and drove to the rectory, where he arrived at nine-forty-five and did not, as far as anyone knew, go out again. Father O'Flaherty would give evidence that he, O'Flaherty, had been out late that night. He was a little vague about where, and I would have to resist the temptation to sneak in a question or a remark about that. When he got home to the rectory, at twelve-thirty or so, Brennan's car was there. A member of Janeece's family would testify that Father Burke had been thoughtful enough to drive Janeece home once in a while after choir practice. The witness believed Tanya was home on a couple of these occasions, but could not be sure. We could offer nothing stronger than that, and we had come up with no way to explain away the cross etched into the victim's skin.

I said I did not know what Burke was expecting as the time approached for us to open our case. That is not quite accurate. True, I did not know what fond hopes he had built up about the testimony we would offer. But I knew one thing he expected and anticipated: his own appearance on the stand. If Burke was truly innocent — and, despite the evidence, every cell in my body wanted to believe that — then in an ideal world the best thing to do would be to put him up there and let him tell the jury: "I didn't do it and here's why it could not have been me." But in the usual course of events, in the real world, a client who insists on taking the stand is often a defence lawyer's worst nightmare. The accused as witness is an unmoving target who has given up his right to avoid cross-examination. The client, having chosen to take this risk, can, and often does, end up blowing his entire case away with a few unguarded words. We have all seen experienced counsel construct a brilliant defence over a period of days or weeks, only to sit helplessly as the client takes it all with him as he goes down the toilet.

Naturally, I was not surprised when the Reverend Brennan X. Burke, who had been speaking publicly all his life, told me that he must, simply must, take the stand. I put a cover-my-ass memo in his file: "Strongly advised client not to testify. He insisted and I warned him that this was against my advice." I told him things would go beautifully on my direct examination, as I took him through his exemplary life for a rapt jury of twelve. But whatever happened on cross-examination was out of my control.

"We have put your character and your credibility in issue. That makes every dark corner of your life an exhibit for the opposition. If the Crown turns up something I don't know, and if you are immolated up there on the stand, then I cannot help you. Don't keep anything from me. No surprises." Of course he insisted there was nothing he couldn't handle, and remained tight-lipped about his past, including the fire in New York when he had been marked with the sign of the cross.

"Answer only what is asked. Say nothing more. Keep your cool and be courteous at all times."

Was the man listening?

II

The day finally came to open our case. Sue, Brennan, and I sat in the office we had been allotted adjacent to the courtroom. We went over the lineup of witnesses we would call. I would forgo my right to make an opening statement, and would save all arguments for my summation at the close of the trial.

"Any other ideas, Brennan? Anyone come to mind whose carcass I should be throwing up there on the sacrificial fire?" I was on edge. "Feel free to open up to us about anyone who hates you so much he would commit murder in your name."

"Don't you think I'd have mentioned it before now?" he snapped. "I piss people off, there's no denying it, but I can't imagine what I've done to deserve this. Though maybe you two will be running amok by the time this is over, carving my initials into whatever gets in your way."

"Your initials?" Even I was surprised at the sharpness of my tone. But Burke just shook his head and waved me off with a dismissive hand. It was time to go back to the courtroom.

I stood and called my first witness. "Please state your full name for the court."

"John Jamal Habib."

"What is your profession, Mr. Habib?"

"I'm a barber here in Halifax."

"Mr. Habib, do you recognize the man on trial today?"

"Yes, I do. It's Father Burke."

"And how do you know Father Burke?"

"He comes to me to get his hair cut."

"Now Mr. Habib, I am going to show you a couple of items and then I'll ask the court to enter them as exhibits. Do you recognize these things?"

"Yes, my appointment books for this year and last. They have my name on the cover."

I had the books entered as exhibits, which would be examined by the Crown and the jurors. Then I handed them to the witness. "Please take the books and tell us whether there are any entries relating to Father Burke."

"There are some dates written in here when he came for a haircut."

"Why don't you start a year ago and read out the dates Father Burke came to you for a cut."

"Okay. For 1989 I have October 12, 5:00 p.m., Fr. Burke, and December 7, noon hour. Now this year's book. Here's the first one, February 6, 12:30. And . . ." he flipped through the pages, "nothing again until — right — twelve noon on May 19."

"What kind of shape was his hair in when you saw him May 19, can you recall?"

"Shaggy. Wavy. I asked him: 'Father, are you here for a trim or you want me to fix it in a ponytail?' He laughed and said he was in the mood for a perm, and did I know where he could get a cheap red car and a cheap —" his eyes darted nervously to Burke "— uh, leisure suit."

This brought laughter from Burke and everyone else in the room.

"And what did you do with his hair that day?"

"Gave him a nice cut."

"Thank you, Mr. Habib. My friend may have some questions for you." But Schenk decided to leave it alone, and affected a complete lack of interest in the witness.

Burke leaned over to me and spoke out of the side of his mouth: "I hope all our witnesses are as loyal as our man John here. What I really said to him was 'a cheap red car and a cheap dame.'"

"I figured as much," I whispered back.

I next called a forensic scientist who specialized in hairs and fibres. She gave verbal and photographic evidence of the difference, visible under a microscope, between the appearance of recently cut hair, which has a sharp edge, and hair that has not seen the scissors for several months. The ends become more rounded over time. Again, Schenk did not get up to question her. Our case had pretty well peaked at that point. The barber and our hair expert were the only witnesses who could offer substantive evidence to help us on the forensics.

These witnesses had not been in our original lineup. We had been waiting for the judge and jury one morning, when Brennan remarked that he had had to dissuade his father from flying up from New York to sit in on the proceedings: "Probably wanted to intimidate the jury." The image came back to me of Declan and Teresa Burke at the door of their house, Teresa reaching up to caress the face of her middle-aged son. And that is when it struck me. She had touched the hair curling over his collar and said: "Don't they give you time off to get a haircut?" That was only days after Tanya Cudmore was murdered. His hair was long and needed cutting. The hairs found on Tanya's body had been recently cut. They may have come from Burke, but not in May, 1990. I would make as much of that as I possibly could.

We did have a minor success with the tiny smear of dried blood that had been found in the rear seat of Burke's car. Our investigative efforts brought us to a grade six student at the choir school, who had been given a ride in the car with a couple of fellow students.

"So Mario, tell us what happened in the car that evening."

"Father Burke was driving us home, and he took us for an ice cream first. Jerry Doherty was sitting beside me and he knew I had stepped on a big rusty nail a couple of days before when I was just wearing sneakers, and it had gone way up into my foot and made a big hole. Jerry wanted to see it, so I put my foot up on the seat and took my shoe and sock off. I pulled the bandage partly away to show him the hole and a bit of blood came oozing out. Jerry was like 'whoa' and I told him to be quiet so Burke wouldn't know. I tried to wipe it off the seat."

"And why didn't you want Father Burke to know?"

"Because he probably would have stopped the car and tried to clean it off. And we might not have got to the ice cream place."

"What made you think he'd be keen to stop the car and get it cleaned up?"

"Priests don't like anything gross." This brought chuckles from the assembly. "Like one time, he got a gob of something on his suit in class. We were writing a test in music composition. He walked by this girl's desk and something white and gooey came off the desk and onto his priest suit. He just looked at it and made a face and walked right out of the classroom. During a test! And he came back a couple of minutes later with his suit wet where he'd washed off the goop. Like, everybody could have cheated on the test!"

"And did they cheat?" Not relevant, My Lady, but let's hear it anyway.

"No, I don't think so. I mean, it was composition. So, if you tried to copy off of somebody like Becky Fong, and you wrote down a complicated chord like B flat minor when the normal thing on your own paper would be the easiest chord, C major, Burke would — Father Burke would know, and he'd mark you down. Or he'd say something like: 'Ah. Very sophisticated harmony. Why don't you play it for us.' And you'd go —" The boy mimicked the playing of something discordant on the piano, and everyone in the courtroom laughed.

"So, this told you what about Father Burke?"

"He'd be grossed out by blood in his car and he'd want it cleaned on the double."

"Thank you, Mario. When was this car ride, do you remember?"

"Yeah, it was the first week of May because it was only two or three days after I hurt my foot, and that happened May the third."

So we had evidence that, as finicky as he was, Father Burke had not had the interior of his car cleaned between the blood-letting in the first week of May and the search of his car by police after May 10 when Tanya Cudmore was killed. This, plus traces of other people's hair, including two long, black curly hairs matching those of little Janeece, would put the kibosh on any suggestion that Burke had transported Tanya dead or alive in his car, and then cleaned the car afterwards.

We went through the motions over the next four court days with the rest of our witnesses, who testified in support of his alibi and his character. We also called evidence about the break-in at the archdiocese office and the rifling of the personnel files. Other witnesses testified about the vandal who had been seen in the area around the time of the murder. Schenk rarely bothered to cross-examine them.

III

Then it was showtime. On Tuesday September 18, my client rose and took the stand. There was a charming moment when the court clerk asked whether he wanted to swear an oath on the Bible, or make an affirmation. The jurors and spectators laughed along with Father Burke as he gave the clerk a wry look and took the Bible reverently in his hands. "Do you swear to tell the truth, the whole truth, and nothing but the truth? So help you God?" "I do." He sat down and crossed one leg over the other, unconcerned. I took him through his life story as I wanted the jury to hear it. An immigrant to the U.S. from Ireland, son of loving parents, brother of five siblings; the young choirboy whose voice broke their hearts back in the old parish; his wayward years when he turned away from the church (but never from God) and pursued the kind of fun all young men pursue, "dating" and going to parties, with a bit of high-spirited drinking and experimenting with other substances; his occasional performances at the church even then, when everyone gushed about how he sang as if he believed every word; his decision to give his life to God; his years at Fordham, the Jesuit University, where he excelled academically and played football (he allowed that he was no Vince Lombardi); his years in the seminary; his studies in Rome; his teaching in various universities and seminaries; his founding and re-founding of the St. Bernadette's Choir School in Halifax. Father Burke this, Father Burke that. His strict vows, his stellar character, his credibility. I asked him straight out if he had killed Tanya Cudmore. He assured us with quiet dignity that he had not killed her, that he would not kill or hurt anyone. The jury loved him by the time I sat down, and may even have been ready to explain away the forensic evidence that seemed to tie him to the killing. Surely such a man would not hurt a soul. Would the jury please, please remember this when the Crown gets up and proceeds to eviscerate him in front of us all.

Karl Schenk stood and made a little bow to the jurors. I kept my eye on the jury box.

"Mr. Burke," Schenk began.

"Father Burke," rejoined Brennan, as he straightened his suit jacket, and I knew then and there it was going sideways.

"Mr. Burke," Schenk repeated, "how long have you been a priest of the Roman Catholic Church?"

"Twenty-four years."

"And what vows did you take when you were ordained a priest?" The Crown was not wasting any time.

"Promises of obedience and chastity."

"And poverty?"

"I'm not a member of a religious order, so no. But we are expected to live a life of, let's say, 'simplicity.'"

Schenk gave him a once-over. I got the impression he was about to say something, then changed direction. "Where have you served as a priest since your ordination?"

"New York, and here . . ."

"Anywhere else?"

"Yes."

165

"Where?"

"Southeast Asia."

"And?"

"Sao Paulo, Brazil."

"When was that?"

"In 1986."

"What were you doing in Brazil?"

"Running a small parish, with an associated aid program. Shelter, food, clothing, education, and training."

"Kind of a missionary position? Bringing the Word of God to the heathen?"

"The people were not heathens, Mr. Schenk. And we didn't force religion on them. We had to turn people away from our programs because we could not meet the demand."

"Did you know a woman called Eliana DeSouza?"

A hesitation. "Yes."

What was this? I had never heard of the woman. Not for the first time, or the last, I wanted to throttle my client for leaving me out of the loop.

"And what did Eliana DeSouza do for you?"

"Do for me?" A trace of belligerence in Burke's voice.

"What was her role there?"

"She was my assistant."

"Did you sleep with her?"

I was on my feet. "My Lady, I see no relevance in this line of questioning. Whether my client was intimate with a woman at some point in his life —"

"As a priest," Schenk interrupted.

"— has no relevance here."

"My Lady," Schenk argued, "the defence has put the accused's character and credibility squarely in issue. The Crown has every right to examine him. Sex is not the point except as it relates to his character as a priest, his faithfulness to his vows, his honesty and credibility."

The judge ruled in the Crown's favour. Schenk then had the pleasure of repeating his question. "Did you sleep with Eliana DeSouza?"

Burke looked at Schenk with something close to hatred. I hoped the jury could not read it in his eyes. "Is everyone to be trashed in this proceeding along with me?"

"Just answer the question, Mr. Burke. Did you sleep with Eliana DeSouza?"

Father Burke glanced at the judge, who was without expression. "Yes," he said reluctantly. I didn't want to be caught sneaking a look at the jury.

"Would you describe Ms. DeSouza as your mistress when you were in Sao Paulo?"

"No, I would not," Burke snapped.

"Well, how long did your affair with her go on?"

"A few months. Or so."

"I see."

Burke tried for an exculpatory explanation: "If you know anything about Latin America, then you'll know that —"

"Just a yes or no answer to my questions, Mr. Burke."

"If you don't want *my* testimony, why don't you just read your own into the record? After all, if I'm just to parrot the lines you have written out for me . . ."

The last thing any defence lawyer wants is an angry defendant on the stand. He's likely to lose control and, of course, he makes it all too easy for the jury to picture him losing control with the victim. Keep it together, Brennan, I pleaded silently. This is only the beginning of a very long and damaging ordeal.

The judge leaned over and said: "Just answer the questions please, Father Burke."

"Mr. Burke. You lived in Rome as a priest of the Catholic Church, correct?"

Silence. Then, warily: "Yes."

"When in Rome —"

I was on my feet again. "Objection, My Lady. Irrelevant."

"My Lady, I'll move on," Schenk graciously offered. And that's when I knew I'd been had. Schenk may have known something about Burke in Rome or he may not have. It didn't matter. Either way, he knew I'd pop up and object. All he needed to do was plant that "when in Rome" before the jury.

Susan leaned over and whispered: "He got a free one off us there." I nodded. I would have to shape up.

"How would you explain the breaking of your vows, Mr. Burke? Or your 'promises' as you put it? Is it that you have a very strong need for sex? Would you say that about yourself?"

Burke leaned back in his seat and turned his face to the jury. "Hardly. Given my choice of profession." The jurors and others in the courtroom laughed.

"Yet, every once in a while, you just decide the hell with your vows and reach out and pluck —" Oh, Christ "— some woman or other from your surroundings, and —"

It was my turn to be outraged. "My Lady! I really must object. To my learned friend's tone, and to his question. There has been nothing established in the evidence to suggest that my client reaches out whenever he likes, and, well —"

"Mr. Schenk?" The judge raised an eyebrow, and he nodded in submission.

"All right. We'll leave your sex life for the time being, Mr. Burke. I'm sure it will come up again. Now —"

"Objection, My Lady. My friend is showing deliberate disrespect for the witness."

"Thank you, Mr. Collins. Mr. Schenk?"

"I apologize to the court. Now. Mr. Burke. You ran the music program at the St. Bernadette's Choir School."

"I run it, yes."

Schenk glanced at the jury as if to say: "I know you'll have the good sense to see that he never runs it again."

"You knew a little girl named Janeece Tuck, did you not?"

"Yes."

"How did you know Janeece?"

"She was a member of the children's choir."

"You had a nickname for Janeece, did you not?"

"I did."

"What was that nickname?"

"I called her Alvin."

"And why was that?"

"There used to be these cartoon characters that my brothers and sisters liked, the Chipmunks. One of them, who was always into mischief and never where he was supposed to be, was Alvin."

"That described Janeece, did it?"

Burke smiled. "Yes, it did."

"Now you heard Janeece's mother, Ms. Tuck, testify here in the courtroom earlier in the trial?"

"Yes."

"She told us Janeece lived with her father and Ms. Cudmore, but spent some days with her mother, Ms. Tuck. And she told us about Janeece coming home from choir from time to time, and talking about you. 'I was in trouble again today, Ma.' Or: 'Father Burke growled at me again today.'" This was raising the antennae of some of the jurors, but Burke was nodding. The Crown attorney continued: "'Father Burke was talking to me in Latin today. I think he was cussin' me out.'" There were chuckles throughout the courtroom at that. "Were you cussing her out?"

"Ah, no, I wasn't." Burke shook his head and I could see from the unguarded tenderness in his face that he was remembering whatever it was he had said to Alvin.

"Can you recall what you said?"

"I think I said: *Venisti huc ante tempus torquere nos?*"

"And what does that mean, for those of us whose Latin is limited to *habeas corpus?*"

"It means: Have you come here to torment us before our time?" Everyone, including the judge, broke up at that. But the moments of goodwill were fleeting.

"Would you say you had a special relationship with Janeece?"

Burke was on guard. "What exactly do you mean by a special relationship?"

"I can see why you would be concerned, Mr. Burke, but I just mean that perhaps this little girl stood out for you as a special member of the choir."

"Ah, yes. I did have a soft spot in my heart for her."

"And she knew that, do you think? Her mother's evidence about your 'growling at her' was that the little girl was 'more bragging than complaining, the attention, you know.' So Janeece knew how you really felt about her?"

"I think she knew. I hope to God she did."

"What was it you liked about Janeece?"

"She was a lively, funny, smart, outspoken, beautiful little girl. A real character. And she was going to have a wonderfully rich contralto voice when she got older. Which she never had the chance to do."

"You must have been upset when you heard about her sudden death."

"Of course I was upset." Heartscalded, I recalled Burke saying of himself after she died. "A nine-year-old girl with her whole life ahead of her, to die like that."

"You are aware, then, of how Janeece died."

"Yes," Burke answered shortly.

"Janeece was taken from her bed by her stepmother, put in a car without a seatbelt, with a drunk driver, and taken along on an errand Ms. Cudmore wanted to run for her partner, the child's father. The driver lost control and Janeece was thrown to her death. Is that your understanding of what happened?" Schenk was giving evidence, and repeating it at that, but an objection would just annoy the jury, so I stayed in my seat.

"That's what I understood, yes." Burke did not try to hide his disgust.

"This must have struck a chord with you, so to speak, Mr. Burke." I could see my client tense in his seat, as if waiting for a blow, but I couldn't prevent it. "A young person dying while those who were supposed to look after her were too preoccupied with themselves to bother?" Brennan was grey, and his hands gripped each other in his lap. "Would you agree with me?"

"Who wouldn't agree it's a terrible thing?"

"I'm interested only in you, Mr. Burke. You have my undivided attention. Did the manner of her death, through the thoughtless neglect of her caregivers, strike any kind of personal chord in you over and above the normal grief you would have felt?"

"You know it did," my client whispered.

"And would that be because of a fire that took place in or around New York City in 1960 when you were a young man?"

Burke licked his lips and nodded.

"The court reporter cannot pick up a nod, Mr. Burke. Please give an, um —" Schenk looked up at the accused "— an oral answer."

Brennan looked at the wall and answered: "Yes."

"Did you have a friend with you at that house in New York, a fellow a few years younger than you, named Stanislaus Dombrowski?"

"Yes."

"How did you know Stanislaus?"

"I knew Stan through music. He was studying at Juilliard. A very gifted young lad. He started going around with me, and some people I knew."

"The wrong people for Stan, as it turned out. Correct?"

Burke looked down at his hands. "Ah, yes."

"I won't get into all the sordid details of Stan's short life or the drug habit he developed while hanging out with your crowd," Schenk turned his glinting spectacles in the direction of the jury box "but I'll move ahead to the fire. What started it?"

"Stan may have been trying to cook the, em, the smack. The heroin. I'm not sure."

"Was young Stan on drugs that night?"

"Yes, I learned that he had shot up earlier and then —"

"You seem to know all the lingo, but then you would, wouldn't you?"

I was up. "My Lady! I ask that that remark be struck from the record. I have been sitting here, making allowances for Mr. Schenk's cross-examination, but this is going too far."

"Thank you, Mr. Collins. The last remark will be struck and the jury will disregard it."

The chances that the jury would disregard an implied connection between the accused and drugs were slim enough. But Father Burke chose that moment to give himself absolution and, in the process, kept the issue alive in the jurors' minds. "God forgives all kinds of sins, Mr. Schenk."

"God may render forgiveness but Caesar renders it not," the government lawyer retorted. "We're faced with earthly laws here, Mr. Burke. Your friend died in the fire, didn't he?"

"Yes, he did."

"Did Stan call for your help before he died?"

Burke lowered his eyes. "I believe he did. I didn't hear him at first, over the music."

"But you heard him later."

"Not him, but someone else at the party called out that Stan was in trouble."

"And where were you when all this was going on?"

Burke couldn't stop himself from glancing at me. His eyes went nowhere near the jury box. "I was in one of the bedrooms."

"With whom?"

"A girl."

"*A* girl? Would you care to elaborate?" No response from Burke. "Let me help you. Was it more than one girl?" The jurors leaned forward as did the press, pens poised over notebooks. "Well, Mr. Burke? How many girls was it?"

"Three?" he answered with trepidation. Jesus Christ, he doesn't know! I sat there remembering his terse refusal to discuss the incident. Two, Brennan, it was two, I berated him silently. Then, taking his cue from Schenk's obvious surprise, Burke got it right: "Two." I heard the sound of scribbling from the press gallery. Not a rustle from the jury box.

"A priest in bed with two girls —"

Burke exploded. "I wasn't a priest then, for heaven's sake! I was a kid."

"Lucky kid. Did pretty well for yourself."

I started to rise but Her Ladyship was already there. Once again, Karl Schenk made an insincere apology. And then: "I won't take up the court's time trying to elicit just what Mr. Burke and the two girls were doing, My Lady. We can all use our imaginations." He turned to the accused. "So, the upshot is: you ignored the call for help because you were having a better time elsewhere, and your friend died at age eighteen in the basement of the house."

Burke gave a slight nod and again Schenk jumped in. "As I explained, Mr. Burke, we need an —"

"Yes." Burke cut him off quickly.

"Something else happened that night, didn't it? Something happened to you in the fire."

"Yes."

"What happened to you, what mark was left on you?"

Burke looked at the far wall. "The imprint of a cross here." He pointed to the place above his heart where he had been branded by the crucifix.

"And this told you what? That you were chosen by God?"

"You know, Mr. Schenk, you have made some terrible accusations against me, and terrible implications about the effects you believe I've had on other people. I'll grant you one thing: I seem to bring out the worst in some people." He looked pointedly at Schenk, who was about to react when Burke went on: *"Durum est mihi contra stimulum calcitrare.* And of those, you are the most offensive." Gasps from the crowd and the jury. Somehow I managed to keep my head from banging on the table. Burke may have been right, and may even have earned some sympathy, but this attack would only serve, yes, to bring out the worst in the prosecutor. And what had Burke said to him in Latin?

In the meantime, Karl retaliated: "Well then, I am heartily sorry for having offended thee."

"Ah, a slur on my religion now, is it?" I doubted that Justice Fineberg recognized the words from the Act of Contrition, and I left it alone, hoping some of the jurors would be offended on Burke's behalf.

Schenk moved on. "All right, Mr. Burke. Tell us what this wound meant for you."

"In my mind, Mr. Schenk, it meant that in some mystical way I was being asked — ordered — to serve God. I did not enter the priesthood solely because of that, naturally. But it gave me the jolt I needed to get started in pursuing my vocation."

"But wouldn't that have happened to anyone?" The prosecutor assumed a puzzled expression. "Anyone who was wearing a cross around his or her neck, or some other piece of jewelry? If the person went too close to the flames, the gold would get hot enough to burn flesh, leaving an imprint of itself in the skin. Wouldn't that have happened, not just to you, but to anyone?"

"Yes, I suppose it would."

"Well then, how could you see it, in your own case, as a mystical experience, a sign from God?"

"I wasn't wearing a crucifix."

I bolted forward in my seat. I sensed the rapt attention of the jurors. I knew Schenk did not want to do this, but he went ahead and asked the question anyway. "What do you mean, you weren't wearing a crucifix?"

"You've painted me as a degenerate here in front of the jury, the judge, the press and the public. A dissolute youth, lying there in drunken, stoned bliss with two women giving me, ah, pleasure, while my friend was dying downstairs. What the hell would I be doing with a crucifix around my neck at that stage of my life?"

Chapter 13

Kyrie eleison, Christe eleison, Kyrie eleison.
(Lord have mercy, Christ have mercy, Lord have mercy.)
— *The Mass*

I

Father Burke was still under oath and I could not speak with him. He was escorted from the courtroom. Susan Drummond and I bolted for our conference room. I was about to shut the door behind us when I saw my wife coming towards me. "May I?" she asked, obviously in deference to Susan; otherwise, Maura would have made herself at home with nary an if you please. The two women knew each other and said their hellos.

"Let's start at the end," I said. "What was the reaction?"

Susan had been on the ball, I was relieved to learn. "The jurors were stupefied. We can't assume they're all believers and mystics. We know from jury selection that some of them are far from it. But every last one of them gaped at what Burke said. I can't believe Schenk left it like that. It's not often you see Schenk flummoxed."

"True enough," put in Maura. "And it wasn't just the jurors who looked poleaxed. The woman sitting beside me had just squeezed in a few minutes before. When she heard Burke say he wasn't wearing a crucifix, she looked as if someone had entered her from the rear!"

"Who was the woman?" I said.

"Don't know. She had short, straight dun-coloured hair, and she was kind of chunky. About thirty-five. She looked as if she was seeing God Almighty Himself. Her hands flew up to her face, which was the colour of oatmeal, and she didn't quite manage to stifle a little cry. She'll be saying her prayers with fervour tonight, whoever she is."

"That must have been Eileen," I answered. She had sat in occasionally during the trial. "Eileen Darragh. Assistant at the youth centre. She's always thought Burke was God. Now she knows for sure.

"What's the jury's attitude to our guy, do you think? I don't mean the mystical stuff. What about the sniping between him and Schenk? The woman in Brazil. Breaking the vows. That was only four years ago." Anger made its way into my delivery. "I asked him straight out. Who could have seen that scar? Had he slept with anyone? He said no. Lying to the lawyer. *De rigueur* for any client. I guess they like to keep us in suspense —"

"Lighten up, Monty," Susan said. "This is all the Crown can find on him in terms of character. Promises of chastity and obedience, he said. He didn't use the word 'vows.' They're not going to get a bishop to testify that he's disobedient. The poverty angle is too nebulous, and we can be sure they've looked into his assets. So all they have is celibacy, and his evasiveness and dissembling about it. And —" Sue mouthed the words "— Mount A."

Maura caught my warning look. I had not told her about the young woman at Mount Allison. My fear of the incident flared up again. It was exactly the sort of evidence Schenk might produce on rebuttal, to counter our evidence of Burke's good, non-violent character.

"What is it?" Maura asked. "Is there something else?" I waved her question off and shook my head. She knew enough not to pursue the subject, though it would not be likely to slip her mind.

"Priests are allowed to do everything else," Susan said, "so who cares if he gambles and takes a drink? He's not a lush. As for the sex, the jurors probably don't care. They understand. These guys are saddled with a vow of celibacy. If they break it once in a blue moon, it's just human nature."

"I hope so. It's character and credibility though. He's a liar, he breaks his vows, *ergo*, you can't believe his evidence, and what else might he do? I made him sound like a saint on direct. Now all this comes out. Jesus, if we have to go through a trial for Leeza Rae, they'll crucify him."

Susan held up a calming hand. "One step at a time, Monty. You men are so hysterical. This is the Cudmore trial, and sex is a minor sideshow. The jury loved him on the Janeece questions. They could see how deeply he cared for the little girl. Of course, that's the motive. But if he's that tender-hearted underneath the icy exterior, how can he be a killer?"

We returned to the courtroom and the cross-examination resumed. The witness was reminded that he was still under oath. The Crown prosecutor started his damage control immediately.

"In what year did this crucifix incident occur, Mr. Burke?"

"In 1960."

"And this branding, if we may call it that, changed your life, correct?"

"That's right."

"In what way?"

"I began to explore the idea that I had a vocation to the priesthood, I redirected my university studies to that end, I gave up some of my former activities, and I entered the seminary."

"What year did you go into the seminary?"

"In 1962."

Schenk took a sip of water. He cast a quick glance at the jurors to see if they were paying attention. They were. We all were. I tensed as he turned to the accused.

"Do you have any children, Mr. Burke?"

What? They say there are no atheists in a foxhole; I wonder if there are any at the defence table when the accused is on the stand. What was God doing to me now? My client was staring in horror at the prosecutor. He looked as if he might need medical attention. I heard pens scratching on paper, and voices murmuring.

I finally got it together and leapt to my feet. "My Lady! Objection! This scar is relevant only as it relates to what was found on the body of Ms. Cudmore. The mystical aspect, or the effect it may have had on Father Burke's life, is not relevant to this proceeding. My

Lady, Mr. Schenk is harassing the witness."

"My Lady," Schenk replied, "the accused has testified that this crucifix incident changed his life, made him mend his ways. The Crown has the right to cross-examine him on that issue."

I had to sit and watch while the most personal and confidential aspects of my client's life — so confidential that, once again, Burke had not confided them to me — were exposed to the merciless light of the courtroom.

"Mr. Burke. I'll repeat the question. Do you have any children?"

"I do not have any children, Mr. Schenk." His voice was caustic.

"I'm not asking whether you are raising a child as a single dad in the rectory, Mr. Burke. Let me be more precise. Have you ever fathered a child?"

Burke began massaging his temples with his left hand. He looked at Schenk with cold fury in his eyes. "Yes. Long ago." Again, the scribbling and murmuring behind me.

"What year was your child born, Mr. Burke?" Schenk looked blandly at the witness.

Burke waited a long moment. "It was 1963."

"So, you entered the seminary in 1962 and you had a child born in 1963?"

"Question asked and answered, My Lady," I snapped, barely rising from my seat. Surely this torment would end.

"Where was the child born?"

"New York."

"What happened to the child?"

"The baby was put up for adoption."

I heard a clamour behind me, followed by rapid footsteps and the soft thud of the courtroom door closing.

"The pregnancy, the birth, the adoption process. Very stressful, traumatic events. For the mother. Were you a pillar of strength for her during this difficult time in her life?"

No response.

"Let the record show there was no response from the witness. I'll try again, Mr. Burke. Did you send her flowers? A card?"

Burke did not reply. Just stared venomously at his tormentor as the flaying went on. I thought seriously of checking my client into a hospital for observation. We both might require medication if this didn't end soon.

"Do you ever wonder about your child, Mr. Burke?"

I saw a look of intense pain flash across the face of my client, then it was quickly masked. "Wherever my child is now, Mr. Schenk, he or she is in my prayers every day of my life." Schenk had made his point and knew it was time to move on lest Burke gain in sympathy what he had lost in credibility. We could infer, from the feelings he could not hide, that Burke was the kind of man who cared about children. And mourned their loss. Would he strike out in revenge at the loss of a child he treasured? Would his feelings be all the stronger because he had already lost a child of his own?

It ended with a whimper, not a bang. The big guns had been fired; all that was left was to carry the wounded from the field.

"I told you so" should be engraved on the last page of every trial transcript. I told you, I implored you, I pleaded with you to stay off the witness stand. But you knew better.

I left the court with Burke as I always did, but the media onslaught was especially hard to bear that day. The questions were pointed and painful, and the hunted man was pale and shaky after his ordeal. I refused all comment. Burke, following the script at last, exercised his right to remain silent. When I had him alone, anger blotted out all pity, and I launched into a lacerating attack on him as a client. He did not speak to me, but waved me off, got into his car, and peeled away.

That night I tried to reach Burke on the phone but he wasn't in. So I called Sandra Worthington in New York.

"Monty! I don't like the sound of your voice. And I don't like what I'm hearing about Brennan. How can there be so much evidence against him, if he didn't do it? I can't see him as a killer, I really can't. Anything else maybe, but not that."

"It's been sheer unmitigated hell from day one, Sandra, what can I tell you? And between you and me, he hasn't made it any easier on himself, or his defence team. One thing he seems to share with the least sophisticated of my clients: they all seem to think they're protecting themselves by keeping information from their own lawyer. How wrong they are."

"So, what's happened now to account for this phone call?"

"The Crown brought out on cross the fact that Brennan had fathered a child born in 1963. First I heard of it. I thought he was going to have a stroke right there on the stand."

There was a long silence, then: "I wouldn't have thought that would faze him in the least. He didn't care then, he wouldn't care now. But of course, it would make him look bad in front of the jury. So that would account for his alarm."

"I feel the same way you do about him right now, Sandra. But I have to tell you, I think it was more than that. It was obvious he found the whole subject very painful."

"If you say so."

"I'm sorry, Sandra. But I have to know what's going on. He didn't even speak to me after he limped from the stand."

"*He* didn't speak to *you?*"

"Nope."

She sighed. "Monty, this is what I was planning to tell you when I called you over here for that second visit. Then, by the time you arrived, I had second thoughts. I've always kept it private. I didn't tell the police either, in case you're wondering. They came to see me but I told them very, very little. I don't know where they got the information. The first time I saw you and we spoke about his ordination, I almost let it slip by saying how gratifying it would have been to bring his three-year-old child to the ordination. But of course the child was long gone by then. I gave the baby up for adoption, after all I went through to give birth. I was very ill. I didn't tell Brennan about the pregnancy until nearly the end of my term. And then he spent half the conversation asking why I hadn't told him as soon as I found out. I hung up on him. He didn't come near me after that phone call. I had the baby in Connecticut. When there's a scandal in the family — and in those days it *was* a scandal — it's handy to have relatives who live out of state. My grandparents, bless their hearts. Anyway I had an extended stay in hospital, with a condition called eclampsia. I was out of it. That really was the only good thing — that I hardly have any memory of it all. It took me weeks to get my health back." Her voice was laced with remembered pain and bitterness. "Not a word from Mr. Burke. He had gone on to a higher plane of existence."

II

I was torn between animosity and compassion when I saw my embattled client the next morning. He looked gaunt and desolate after being savaged by the prosecutor. None of it would have happened of course, if Burke had kept me informed. If he had, I would have taken a flame-thrower to the courtroom before I'd have let him take the stand. Now he was slumped in a seat in our regular room. He didn't meet my eyes.

I sat down without speaking and started going over my final argument. I would speak first, which is the procedure when the defence calls evidence; then the Crown would sum up. I had the right of rebuttal. The summations would likely take half the day, followed by the judge's charge to the jury. If the jury began deliberations that afternoon and failed to reach a verdict, they would be sequestered in a hotel overnight.

Silence from Burke should have been a blessing, but it had come too late. I couldn't bear it any longer. "Didn't it occur to you that I might want to speak to you last night, after the catastrophe you brought down on yourself in this building yesterday? I tried to reach you. Where the fuck did you go?"

I expected a belligerent reply but what I got was worse. He looked at me in silence and in his eyes I saw a depth of sadness and despair I could not have imagined in him. I asked him if he wanted an adjournment so I could take him to a doctor. He shook his head and looked at the wall. I checked my watch. "It's time to go, Brennan." He stood, adjusted his clothes and made for the door. We met Susan on our way to the courtroom. She and Brennan walked ahead of me. I had never realized how tiny Susan was until that moment. Her head only came up to his shoulder.

Susan noticed the state our man was in and looked up at him with concern. "Brennan! Dear. Don't give up on us now."

"As long as you two don't give up on me," he said, in a voice I hardly recognized.

It was my turn to be shaken. "Brennan. We're not going to give you up."

"Never," Sue assured him.

We had to get to court. I took a deep breath as we reached the entrance. "All right. Let's get our game faces on. Time to go." Burke managed to assume his usual self-assured persona and he strode into the courtroom as he always did.

There was a heightened sense of expectancy in the jurors' demeanour as they filed in. The courtroom was packed, and the press were in place with sharpened pencils. I leaned over to Burke and told him — again — not to react to anything Karl Schenk said.

I spoke for just over an hour. I emphasized the barber's testimony and portrayed the hair evidence as a fatal flaw in the Crown's case. I made the point that the Crown had failed to show any connection between Burke and the initials IBR carved above the victim's right breast. The crucifix scar, I argued, was a sign of Father Burke's innocence, not guilt. For him to carve his own cross into the body would have been tantamount to a confession. I referred to Father Eugene Cormier's testimony that during the break-in at the archdiocesan office, the only thing the culprit had done was look through personnel files. Somebody was obviously after intimate knowledge relating to priests. I mentioned the vandal who had been desecrating Catholic churches. I reminded the jury that Father Burke, like all of us, was a human being with weaknesses and flaws. But his history was one of devotion to the Church, to God and His people. He had no criminal record or history of violence. The jurors had seen Father Burke here day after day. They knew in their hearts he was not a killer. I did what I could in a bad situation. When I was done I reached over and gave Burke's shoulder a little squeeze. He nodded and gave me a slight smile.

Karl Schenk got to his feet and the defence team collectively braced itself.

"Ladies and gentlemen, there is nobody else in the frame for this killing. Brennan Burke's hair was found on the body, and there is no evidence that Mr. Burke had had any physical contact, at all, with Tanya Cudmore before the murder. The defence has made much of a discrepancy in the length of the hairs found on the body and the length they claim Mr. Burke's hair was at the time. Well, I'm sure all of us could pull hairs from different parts of our heads and find them different lengths and shapes, no matter when we had our last trim.

Who knows what he was wearing when he killed Ms. Cudmore? Old clothes perhaps, something he had last pulled over his head when his hair was a different length. The fact remains: Mr. Burke's hair was found on the body. Enough said on that subject.

"We do not know what the letters IBR stand for. Only the killer knows that. But we do know something about the crucifix scar. We have photographic evidence of it on Mr. Burke's chest. We have no evidence of anyone local who may have seen Mr. Burke undressed from the waist up in the years after the fire. The theory of the defence, apparently, is that somebody who knew about the scar may have held a grudge against Mr. Burke, and then killed, not him, but an innocent third party. And tried to frame Mr. Burke. We are left to wonder who this person might be. The mark is there on Tanya Cudmore's body; the only evidence we have tells us it must have come from the accused.

"In addition to the physical evidence, we have motive. It was well known that Mr. Burke was in mourning for little Janeece Tuck. And the next thing we know, the woman whose carelessness led to the child's death is murdered. We heard Mr. Burke testify on cross-examination about the fire that occurred during a party when he was a young man, and the death of Mr. Burke's friend in that fire. The accused admitted that Janeece's death struck a painfully familiar chord with him. Was the crucifix on Tanya Cudmore's body a mark of Mr. Burke's own feelings of guilt? We'll never know.

"The defence has conjured up a phantom suspect, a vandal with a beef against the Roman Catholic Church, a shadowy figure with no name who just may have gone out and murdered, not a Church official or a priest, but a complete stranger, the stepmother of a little girl who died in a tragic accident. Where did this no-name suspect get the hair and the perfect replica of the priest's cruciform scar? I won't waste any more of the court's time on this except to say that the unfortunate young man, whoever he is, had already chosen his method of acting out against the Church. His weapon was a spray can.

"The evidence has shown what kind of a man Mr. Burke is: a man with serious flaws in his character; a man with a past he tries to hide; a man who makes vows and breaks them whenever he feels like it; an impulsive and irresponsible man who lies about his behaviour."

Schenk went on for another two hours. Several times I had to put a cautionary hand on my client to keep him from showing anger in front of the jurors. Schenk ended by reminding the jury that all the elements of the crime pointed to Burke as the killer: motive, opportunity, means, forensics, signature, character. All of it fit Mr. Burke, and nobody else.

We broke for lunch. Burke sat, catatonic, in front of his untouched sandwich. "We all knew what he was going to say," I tried. "We just didn't know what *you* were going to say." But my words fell on deaf ears. I heard a soft knock at the door. I got up and opened it a crack. I mouthed the word "Maura" across to Burke and he made a "come in" motion with his hand.

"Professor MacNeil. What's the state of the law on fleeing to Paraguay without a passport the night before the verdict? Got a full tank of gas?" Burke asked. She sat down and took his hand in hers. For once, she was at a loss for words. He spoke again: "Do you think my reputation will be salvaged if I minister to prison inmates till I'm, say, seventy-five years old?" He closed his eyes and massaged the sides of his head. Nobody spoke. Then the break was over.

Justice Fineberg's charge to the jury took just over an hour and a half. And it was a good one, even-handed and correct in the law. The jury retired to begin deliberations at four o'clock. Not surprisingly, they had not reached a verdict by six o'clock, so they were bundled off to a nearby hotel where they would be sequestered. They would return to the courthouse for regular working hours, then go back to their hotel at night. Brennan's fate was in their hands, and all we could do was wait.

III

Brennan, Maura, and I piled into my car, and put behind us the garish lights of the cameras.

"Has either of you got your pilot's licence?" Brennan asked. "No? What's the good of you then?" He continued, with an obvious effort at normalcy: "I should stop by the choir school. Then let's eat. And drink."

"My place," Maura said.

I pulled up to the school, and we all went inside. "I'd better straighten out some choir stuff. Get things together." He strode ahead. Maura and I exchanged glances and followed. As we approached the director's office, we heard voices. Brennan didn't turn his head, but kept going towards the choir rooms. I halted and put a restraining hand on Maura's arm just before we got to the director's door. Someone was sobbing inconsolably within. I thought I heard words, something about a baby, but could not make out more than that. I peeked inside. Sister Marguerite Dunne was sitting on a chair beside a distraught Eileen Darragh. They turned their heads towards us. Eileen's face was puffy and streaked with tears.

Sister Dunne, all business, was the first to speak: "Eileen is worried about Father Burke. Did I see him strut by here?"

"Uh, yes. We just came from court. The jury has retired."

The weeping resumed. Eileen reached out blindly and Sister Dunne, dry-eyed and matter-of-fact, put a tissue in her hand.

"We're going to do our best for him, Eileen," I said. "I'm hoping the jury sees him the way you do. If they don't, we'll file an appeal immediately and we'll start all over again. We'll make sure nobody has any doubts next time."

She broke down, and Marguerite looked at us as if to say: "These young girls, what can you do?" She patted Eileen on the arm and stepped outside, closing the door behind her.

"What's going to happen?" she asked.

"I think the jurors like him. I just hope they have enough confidence in that feeling to hold the line against the forensics. There has to be an explanation, but we haven't been able to come up with it. Eileen's having a rough time with it, eh?"

Sister Dunne responded: "None of us understands the significance of the fact that he was not wearing a crucifix around his neck when that image was burned into him. Eileen was quite taken with that aspect of the story. There's even more to him than she had thought. Which, I suspect, was quite a bit in the first place. Then we heard about Brennan fathering a child when he was younger. I can't say I was all that surprised." She should be his lawyer, I said to myself. "I've never thought of Brennan as a tender virgin. Far from it. But that revelation seems to have set Eileen off. A child in his life, however briefly, and an old girlfriend with whom he was intimate. She's dying to find out more about it, but at the same time she can't bear to know. I'm not sure whether any of his other escapades sank in. We are all wildly unrealistic about the people we're infatuated with. I'm sure I'd be the same way."

I doubted that, but kept it to myself.

"I know I was," Maura volunteered, and gave me a look. "We haven't been introduced," she said to Sister Dunne. "And if we waited for Montague to do the introductions, we'd be here till the real killer came bounding in asking 'What time's confession?' I'm Maura MacNeil, formerly married to —" she jerked her head in my direction.

The nun's smile was back. "I'm pleased to make your acquaintance, Ms. MacNeil. I'm Sister Dunne, first name Marguerite. It's my job to run the school. And to keep Father Burke humble."

"I think that's been taken out of your hands now, Sister," Maura said.

"I suppose you're right. If there is anything I can do, at any point in this ordeal, please call."

We heard footsteps and we turned as one to watch Brennan striding down the hall towards us, a cigarette in his mouth. Marguerite pursed her lips and seemed about to protest. But instead she said: "Brennan. We keep missing each other these days, understandably of course, but here you are. I must say I think you are capable of many, many errors in life. Misinterpreting Holy Scripture; giving far too much weight to certain heresies in the first four centuries of the Church's life, instead of dismissing them and moving on with your analysis; not doing enough of the music of Purcell; and thinking too often with your penis and not your brain, like every other man. But all of that doesn't make you a murderer."

I saw Eileen standing just outside the office, her eyes still red, her mouth hanging open, appalled at the nun's remarks.

Brennan replied: "Why, Marguerite. I'm all choked up. Those are the kindest words anyone has said about me for as long as I can remember."

"You are in my prayers Brennan."

"And I know you have God's ear."

"You can bet on it. Good evening." Marguerite stalked towards the exit, nearly bowling Eileen over, and the younger woman emitted a little cry. Brennan turned around.

"Eileen is concerned about you, Brennan," I said.

"Do I look worried, Eileen? I'll be all right. You just keep this place humming and take care of my little angels. Don't let them sing anything by the St. Louis Jesuits if I'm gone for a bit." I thought I saw my wife give him a little shove. He went to the agitated woman and put his arms around her. She clung to him, still speechless, and looked even more wretched when he let her go. Without being conscious of doing so, I was sure, she wrapped her arms where his had been and hugged herself.

"Let's go," Brennan said.

"We'll go to the house," Maura said, "have something to eat and open a bottle of wine."

"Sounds good to me. I don't feel like meeting my public tonight."

I turned to Eileen, standing alone and bereft. I assumed that an evening with Brennan, dinner and wine, even under such terrible circumstances, was an outing she could only have imagined. Yet I could not bring myself to include her in the invitation. I did not, however, want to leave the woman in the state she was in. "You two go ahead," I called to the others. "I'll be right out."

Chapter 14

Listen to the engine, listen to the bell, as the last fire truck from hell
Goes rolling by, all good people are praying.
It's the last temptation, the last account, the last time you might hear
the sermon on the mount. The last radio is playing.
Seen a shooting star tonight slip away.
— Bob Dylan, "Shooting Star"

I

Seeing Eileen so distraught gave me cause to regret the moments I had smiled over the way she blushed in the presence of Father Burke. Her grief was obviously real and heartfelt. The prospect of losing him to a life sentence in a maximum security prison was too much to bear. Eileen had been helpful to us in our efforts to counter both murder charges, insisting as she did that Father Burke barely knew Leeza Rae, and did not know Tanya Cudmore at all.

"Eileen," I said. I took her hand and led her into her office, where we sat. "I know Brennan is grateful for your concern." She looked away. "He is dealing with a level of stress we can hardly imagine. And I know it's not easy for you, or me, or any of us." She turned her tear-streaked face in my direction. "But he appreciates what we're trying to do for him. You've known Father Burke a long time, longer than any of us."

She looked at me warily. Was my attempt to salve her ego just a little too blatant? No doubt. But she replied: "Yes, I have."

"You seemed upset in court, when you heard Brennan testify that he had fathered a child in his early years." Her face flamed red, and she kept her eyes on her hands, which were clasped tightly in her lap. I went on: "People don't tend to think of a priest —"

Eileen's response took me by surprise, as much for its intensity as for its content. "I was supposed to be adopted, you know." Her voice seemed unnaturally loud in the small room. "I was meant to be adopted."

"What happened, Eileen?"

Her story came out in a rush of words. "I was here at St. Bernadette's, when it was an orphanage. We lived for one thing, and one thing only, that some nice Mum and Dad would come and take us home. There were nine or ten of us living here at the time, and I was eight years old. We were all 'hard to place,' mainly because we weren't babies anymore. Other reasons maybe, too. Whenever adults showed up, husband and wife together, we all went into action. Straightened our clothes, patted our hair down. There was a mad scramble for the piano. Any child who could play a tune would try to perform. Sometimes there would be a shoving match on the piano bench. Whoever got shoved off would try to look wounded and hard done by. The kid who had the piano banged away ferociously, hoping talent would cancel out the sin of knocking the other child out of contention.

"The Kernaghans were coming around. You must know them. He's a BCL — Big Catholic Layman. She's involved in the CWL." Eileen seemed to assume that I was part of the world of St. Bernadette's. "They pretended they were just dropping in, visiting the nuns. But I knew. They were going to adopt one of us. You hear about this one and that one being traumatized when they find out they're adopted. Try *not* being adopted. Ha! Try *not* having a family."

"So the people here at St. Bernadette's are your only family." She nodded distractedly and I continued: "Well, we'll have to work extra hard to make sure the black sheep of the family doesn't get sent away." But she had returned to the past.

"I knew the Kernaghans were looking at me. I was a great one for sneaking around and listening to the grown-ups talking. One night I even found my file in the director's office. I never got to read it all because I heard Sister swishing along the hall towards the office, rosary beads clacking. I had to stuff the file back in the drawer and hide. But I read the notes about myself: 'Eileen is bright, significant potential, keep giving advanced work — approaching hard-to-place category — Kernaghans interested.' The Kernaghans visited, more than once, and I was on my best behaviour. He was tall and had a big laugh. He brought us licorice cigars and ruffled our hair. He called all the kids 'dear,' even the big boys. Mrs. Kernaghan was a kind person. 'Are you warm enough, Eileen? Do you have a sweater?'

"It was a done deal, in my mind. A child's mind. I was Eileen Kernaghan. I had perfected my new signature. I was so far beyond my old life at St. Bernadette's Home for Children that I was on my way back, puffed up with a sense of patronizing goodwill towards the inmates I had left behind. I was on a mission, to lift them out of their miserable little lives. Poor things."

Eileen got up slowly and walked out of her office as if in a trance. I sat, uncertain whether to follow. A few minutes later she was back, with a paper in her hand. I peered at it and could see a childish but very detailed picture drawn and coloured on lined paper. It was a winter scene with a large colonial-style house, its front windows glowing a warm golden yellow. A small girl stood stiffly in front, bundled in a dark blue snowsuit with a red hat, one red mitten and a red scarf billowing in the wind. A big yellow dog sat at her side, gazing at her with the other red mitten in his mouth. Eileen began to read.

> "Jennifer dressed with a lot of care for her trip back to St. Bernice's Orphanage. It had been so long since she had been there she could hardly remember what it looked like. Were there snowbanks in front? Were there railings to slide down on the front stairs? She honestly could not remember. Just then, Jennifer's mother came into Jennifer's big bedroom, which she had all to herself except when her parents came in to kiss her goodnight or gently wake her up in the mornings, and it had wallpaper with little tiny yellow, blue, and pink flowers, and a cozy bed with too many pillows on it. Jennifer's mother was in by this time and

said 'You look beautiful darling!! I'm glad you're wearing the new dress we bought you for Christmas. It will be perfect for your trip back to that orphanage. Oh, there's the phone. It could be an important call.' Jennifer's mother gave her a quick kiss on the cheek and went into another room to answer the phone, which had started ringing just after she (Mother) arrived in Jennifer's room.

"Jennifer looked at herself in the mirror. Her hair had grown in the long time since she had left the orphanage and it had a bit more curl in it now. It looked pretty in the red headband that matched her red velvet Christmas dress with the white lacey collar. All of a sudden Jennifer realized something. She could not wear that dress to visit the poor children at the orphanage!! It would not be fair! Jennifer quickly changed into an old skirt and sweater and put her hair in a ponytail. She stuck her list of Things To Do To Get Adopted in the waistband of her skirt. She would not leave St. Bernice's till she had told every kid — even Albert — how to make grown-ups like you and take you home. She would put Molly in charge of getting the kids to change into perfect girls and boys. Or at least tidier and more polite. Then she would tell her Mum and Dad to tell all their friends — some were lonely and old with no kids — to go visit St. Bernice's. Surprise! 'What cute youngsters you have here!' Mum, I'm ready!"

I didn't dare speak. Eileen looked up from her story, eyes blazing. "Of course, it never happened. I spent my life in that place. Well, this place. The orphanage. In a dormitory with other kids crying and snuffling and hacking and fighting all night long. I never went to university. I never became a teacher, even though I had the aptitude. Where was the money going to come from for that?"

"What happened, Eileen? Was there really going to be an adoption?"

"Oh, there was an adoption all right," she recounted in a hollow voice, "but not for me. They chose another child. So. I never became a Kernaghan. I never set foot in the Kernaghans' house. And they've never set foot in mine! I live in a noisy, rundown apartment in the basement of a frat house. A bunch of drunken fraternity boys for housemates. Well, I can't complain that I don't have a man around the house." She tried for a laugh. "Just not the man of my dreams. Ha!"

"The man of your dreams is not available, is he, Eileen?" I said softly.

She looked at me, and I saw a trace of bitter amusement in her reddened eyes. "And if he were, he would not be available to the likes of me," she replied, with self-lacerating insight. "But you know that already, don't you? You know I would be the last woman he would notch up on his belt, or whatever that notch business is with men. You think I'm ridiculous."

"No, I don't." Not anymore.

Eileen stood up, wiped her eyes, and scraped her damp hair from her face. "I have to get — home," she announced, "such as it is." She took a deep breath. "Monty, I promise I'll be all right in the morning. No more self-pitying outbursts from me."

"We're all entitled to let it out once in a while, Eileen." I got up to leave.

"Take care of the good father, Monty. Some of us here — I won't mention any names," she said, in an effort at lightness, "but some of us could not bear to lose him."

"I know. Thanks, Eileen. Goodnight."

II

Brennan and I yanked our ties off when we arrived at the house on Dresden Row, and Maura went to the kitchen. I followed her, opened the fridge and a couple of cupboards. "What did you do, hijack the Sobeys truck? I've never seen this place so well-stocked. Expecting company?"

"I have company. I did what you are never supposed to do. Shop while starving. And you're not going to lug any of this stuff to your place. Last time you were here, we looked the next day for a box of pasta and poof! It had disappeared."

"That was months ago, and the kids ate it. If you're going to keep track of all my —"

"Are we going to eat, or are you two going to have a row?" Brennan had come in behind us. "In our house, when the women hijacked the grocery truck, the men did the cooking. So give me a cleaver and some living things to chop."

"Get Brennan some lettuce and veggies to hack at, Collins. I'll make a sauce, and you can put the pasta on to boil. But keep your hands and the package of pasta where I can see them. Tom! Normie! Have you two had your dinner?" From somewhere upstairs came an affirmative reply. "We have company. Come down and say hello."

Normie flung herself down the stairs, missed the last few, skidded to the bottom and hit the ground running. Brennan and I had gone out to meet her, and he grabbed her around the waist as she careened by. Her legs kept going, like those of a cartoon character who had just run off the edge of a cliff. Brennan squatted in front of her.

"Evening, Stormie!"

"Good evening, Your Excellency!" she answered, giggling.

"Excellency, is it now? So, Stormie. What happened to you, did a tornado go through your hair?"

"What happened to you, your Grace? I thought you were only allowed to wear black and white."

"Maybe I just felt like bursting out in a riot of colour today."

"But it's really just a dark blue you have on, with white again. I could show you some other colours if you like."

"I'll bet you could." They smiled at each other and then my daughter's small face grew solemn. She stared at Brennan and one big tear rolled down her cheek. She suddenly clasped him in a fierce hug, then broke away and pounded up the stairs. I gaped after her. Brennan didn't move.

"Hey, Father!" My son had joined us. Brennan didn't seem to hear him; then he made an obvious effort to shake off whatever he had been experiencing.

"Hello there, Mr. Douglas."

"Are you doing okay, Father? We're all rooting for you."

"I'm fine, Tommy. I'm on the pig's back. Don't you worry."

"All right. Well, I'm on my way out. Mum, I'll be late. Yes, I'll be careful. No, I won't have anything to drink. Yes, my clothes are clean. No, I won't —" Tommy's voice was cut off as the front door closed behind him.

Then we three adults busied ourselves in the kitchen, preparing a dinner with a high quotient of garlic. We opened a bottle of red wine and spoke about inconsequential things. Anything but the trial. And the impending verdict.

"Oh, Mum!" Tommy Douglas popped his head in the door again. "I forgot. You had a phone call from some guy who can hardly speak English. But he said he'll call you back. His name was Jackabo."

"Must be Giacomo," she murmured, and I saw a rare blush creep up my wife's cheeks.

"Giacomo?" Simultaneously from me and Brennan. I realized I was staring at Maura, and looked quickly away only to find Brennan regarding me with shrewd eyes. No doubt mistaking curiosity for something stronger.

"Yes. Giacomo. He's from Italy."

"So, how did you meet this Giacomo?" I asked out of politeness.

"How did I meet you? How do I meet anyone? I get out of the house once in a while."

When the meal was ready, we carried things into the dining room. I scooped a large pile of the kids' junk from the old cherry wood table, checking to make sure there was nothing on the chairs that would stick to us unbecomingly when we got up.

We had just sat down when the telephone shrilled in the kitchen. Maura jumped. But Brennan was quicker. "Don't trouble yourself, my darlin'. I'll get it." He rose from his chair and picked up the receiver as if it were his own, then turned to face us in the archway.

"Prrronto!" he said into the phone.

Maura, both hands tensed on the table, looked on as Brennan began speaking to the caller in rapid Italian.

"Chi sta parlando? Mi spiace molto, ma la signora MacNeil non può venire al telefono proprio adesso. Stiamo molto occupati qui. Questo non è un momento conveniente per essere chiamati da un ragazzo. Cosa? Oh — L'ho chiamato ragazzo perché la sua voce mi dava l'impressione che Lei è molto giovane. La prego di scusarmi. Chi sono? Sono il padre Burke, il confessore della signora MacNeil. Si. Non mi piace quello che

ho sentito dire, e nemmeno deve piacerle. Credo che rimarremo qui per tutta la notte. Adesso devo lasciare il telefono. Ciao."

He hung up with a soft click, came to the table and picked up the bottle of wine. *"Vino,* anyone?"

"What did you say to him?" Maura hissed.

"Oh, I just told him that you're with me now and you have no need of other company. I thanked him for calling." He flashed her a look I could not interpret, then sat down and tucked into his pasta.

My wife looked at him for a long unguarded moment, wondering, I knew, what it would be like to be with him now, with no need for other company. I had the fleeting impression that there was something intimate, something knowing, in their prolonged eye contact. But these were freighted moments for all of us. I didn't dwell on it.

In the next instant, she retaliated.

"Bullshit. Did I hear the word 'confessor' in there? And what does *ragazzo* mean?" She gave him a look that would have reduced a less assured man to a quivering heap on the floor.

"Ah, that's right. My memory is not what it used to be. Stress, you know. I told him we were busy here and you couldn't come to the phone. I explained that I am your confessor and that I didn't like what I was hearing from you. He wouldn't either. And I believe I used the word *ragazzo,* which means 'boyfriend' or 'boy,' because he sounded very young. He got a little huffy over that, but I apologized. As I always do when I'm wrong."

"So apologize."

"When I'm wrong, I said." Brennan smiled and raised his glass to us.

"How very Old World you're being tonight, *Father."*

Brennan nodded and went on with his meal. *"Delizioso."*

"Where did you learn to do that?" my wife asked, without looking overly impressed.

"I lived in Rome when —"

"Not that. Where did you learn to be so presumptuous and overbearing?"

"Ah. Well, it's part of my calling isn't it? God's representative on Earth," the padre said, helping himself to a piece of bread.

"From my limited reading of scripture, done mostly to pick and choose the commie bits, I did not find Jesus Christ — who, unlike you, really *is* God — to be anything like you in high-handedness and self-assurance."

"No? Not even when he went storming into the temple and overturned all those tables? Jesus wasn't a little milquetoast, despite what you see in a certain class of religious kitsch. He was, after all, a carpenter in the days before power tools. But if you find me hard to take — and you, not being a shrinking violet yourself, seem to have no trouble putting me in my place — you should have met the parish priest I had as a kid in New York. Old Father Butler. He was forever finding me somewhere I wasn't supposed to be, and booting me home."

Brennan stopped to refill his wine glass. "I remember one day when I was around twelve. He was out for his daily walk, patrolling the neighbourhood really, at six in the morning. He spied me and a few pals outside an abandoned building where we had gathered overnight with an illicit case of beer. He picked me up by the scruff of the neck and dragged me over to the rectory. The poor old housekeeper, who of course was up because he was up, was instructed to 'phone over to the Burkes and tell them I have the little Christer here. If his poor mother hasn't already died from worrying.' He told me I was going to serve the seven o'clock Mass, and sing at the nine. And I was to sing 'like the angel I know you really are, you little gobshite.' He gave me a cuff on the head on his way out. You should have seen the smug look on his face when he got to see me prostrate myself before the Almighty on the day of my ordination." Maura and I were quiet for a few minutes, trying to reconcile that image of abject submission with the Brennan Burke we knew.

I found it difficult to make dinner conversation when all I could think of was the ordeal of a jury wait the next day, with a result I could not predict. If I were to bet, though, I would not be betting the farm on my client. Burke seemed determined to avoid the subject altogether. I couldn't refrain from one comment about the proceedings, however.

"What was it you said to Schenk, in Latin? I thought he'd be sticking the transcript under our noses the next day, but we never heard about it."

"Oh, who knows?" Brennan answered offhandedly.

"*You* know, so get on with it," said Maura.

"I think I called him a prick. Or I said it was difficult for me to kick against the pricks, I guess is how you'd translate it. Doesn't have quite the same connotation in Latin, but it felt right at the time."

"You're not exactly a 'turn the other cheek' kind of guy, are you Brennan?" Maura observed.

"I do struggle with that part of the Lord's message, I'll admit it. But, believe it or not, I'm infinitely more mellow in that respect than I was when I was a kid."

"Little scrapper, weren't you?" I said.

"My parents repeated the same thing till we nearly expired of hearing it —" and here, the Irish accent thickened — "'Brennan was the last one of our boys we ever expected to become a priest.' My brothers were much more likely prospects. But here I am. A kindly light, to lead you both." He favoured us with a deceptively beneficent smile.

"Sister Dunne certainly has your number," Maura remarked.

Burke rolled his eyes heavenward and shook his head. "She's a tough cookie, I'll say that for her. There was a news clip out of Central America some years ago; I saw it on tape when I came up here. A village being evacuated under armed guard, as the opposing forces reached the gates. You could hear the gunfire as they brought the children and their mothers out, and shoved them into anything with four wheels. If you looked closely, you could see Marguerite standing sentinel over the crying children, ready to throw her body over one of them if need be. Absolutely fearless."

We sat around the table for a while making desultory conversation, but I sensed Brennan becoming restless, until he announced: "It's time I was off." St. Bernadette's was only a few blocks away, but I said I'd walk over with him. Maura looked up at him as he stood in the doorway, and I could see the effort she made not to fall apart. Then he took her by the hand and pulled her towards him. He held her tightly for a few moments, gently released her and walked with me out into the night. I turned and looked at my wife, standing in the doorway, desolate.

When Brennan got to the sidewalk he stopped to light a cigarette. We went to the corner, turned left and walked east on Morris Street. The city was enveloped in fog, and the street lamps had a gaslight effect. A foghorn sounded in the harbour.

"A container ship leaving port? Wonder if I can catch it," he said. "What would you do on your last night as a free man, Monty?" He spoke as if he were asking me what brand of beer I would order in a pub.

"Don't talk that way, Brennan. Don't talk about last nights."

"Lots of things come to mind," he continued as if I hadn't spoken, "but some of them would just get me in more shit than I'm already in now. If such a thing were possible. Do you think a bit of female company would be in order for me tonight, Monty?" He looked theatrically at his watch. "Did I leave myself enough time to sweet-talk somebody into the crib? Maybe. But then, when I light up a smoke afterwards and ask her if it was good for her, she'll probably answer: 'No, Bill, if that's really your name, I didn't like it when you curled up in the fetal position and begged me to hold you. That got boring after a few hours.'"

"I know you'll keep it together, Brennan. Marguerite isn't the only tough cookie in the jar." I hoped I sounded more confident than I felt.

We arrived at the church. Brennan took a deep drag from his cigarette, dropped it, and ground it out with his toe. "I'm going in here. To pray for the strength to handle what's coming. 'Out of the depths I cry to thee.' If this works for me, then here is where I'll spend the night. If it doesn't, who knows what charges will be pending against me by morning? Go home Monty, to one of your houses. Wouldn't it be grand if you picked the right one. But wherever you are, get some sleep. One of us will have to have his wits about him in the morning." He gave my arm a little squeeze and unlocked the door of his church. I stood outside for a few moments, picturing my friend on his knees before his God. I could not begin to imagine the conversation. Then I headed back to Dresden Row to pick up my car.

III

The next day dragged by without a verdict. I was in the office all day and the tension was nearly unbearable. I had done my share of jury waits, but this was the worst. I didn't want to think about what it was like for Brennan. I gave him a call when the jury was sequestered for a second night, and asked if he wanted company. He declined in a voice that was barely audible. I assumed he would be spending much of the night in church again. If indeed that was where he had spent the night before.

The next day, Friday, the wind blew the cold autumn rain in sheets parallel to the pavement. We heard nothing all morning. I tried to concentrate on other cases but soon gave up the pretence. Rowan, too, paced uselessly around the office. I restrained myself from calling Brennan because I did not want to subject him to the unnecessary jangling of the phone. I did not think it a good omen that the jury was taking this long. It felt to me as if they were doing something they didn't want to do, and couldn't bring themselves to finish it off.

The call did not come until four-ten in the afternoon. I phoned Brennan and said I'd pick him up. On the way out of the office I asked Darlene to call Sue Drummond and Maura, and not to give up till she reached them.

Brennan's face was the colour of Wednesday ashes when I opened the car door for him. Tension radiated from him in waves. He didn't speak, and neither did I. After I parked, we pushed our way through the waiting reporters and entered the courtroom. Schenk was already there. Susan came in, followed by Maura, who put an arm around Brennan's shoulders. He looked at her and tried to smile.

The jurors filed in. Not one of them looked at the accused man. A couple of the women and one of the men looked as if they had been weeping. I caught my wife's eye. We both knew it was going to end badly.

As the press reports always say, the accused showed no emotion as the verdict was read: guilty of second-degree murder. I asked that the jury be polled and they stood one by one to confirm the verdict. Brennan looked at the jury box and smiled sadly, almost lovingly, at his jurors, as if granting them the clemency they had denied him. This would later be interpreted in one of three ways: acknowledgement by him that they had done the right thing in finding him guilty; appreciation for reducing the verdict to second degree; or absolution for their wrong — forgive them, for they know not what they do. I spoke to Brennan, assuring him I would see him as soon as I could. Two sheriffs, one on either side, took his arms and led him from the courtroom. As soon as the door closed, I knew, they would have him in cuffs.

The reporters and the onlookers filed out. Maura, Sue and I stood in the courtroom in utter silence. The enormity of the verdict began to sink in. I could not shake the feeling that, if Burke had not insisted on waiving the preliminary hearing, this trial would have taken place a year or so after the charges were laid instead of within a few short months. A greater delay would have given potential jurors more time to forget what I suspected was very much on their minds: the fact that there were two murder charges, not one. They were instructed of course to base their decision only on what they heard in the courtroom. But how could they ignore what they must have heard every single day: "You're on a jury? Oh, Burke, right, the priest who killed two women."

Conviction on the charge of second-degree murder meant a sentence of life imprisonment, but Brennan would not necessarily have to wait twenty-five years to apply for parole. He could serve anywhere from ten to twenty-five years. I took some comfort from this, but not much. He could be in prison till the age of seventy. If he survived that long. And I was worried about the hard-nosed judges of the Court of Appeal. I thought the jurors had been sympathetic to him; they probably saw a lot in him to like, and they didn't want him to go down forever. Yet, they couldn't find it in their hearts to acquit him. They were convinced he had killed Tanya Cudmore.

Chapter 15

Somewhere up the coast near the Bay of Fundy
There's a place called Dorchester town.
In a cell in a block behind the walls of the prison
There's a man on a real come-down.
— Matt Minglewood, "Dorchester"

I

I made my way through the courthouse with dread. I had to face my client. And I knew that, given the late hour, the van would be waiting to take him to the Correctional Centre, where he would be warehoused for two or three weeks till he could be processed as a federal inmate. Then he would be assessed and shipped to a federal institution to begin serving his sentence. It spoke volumes about his future that I hoped he would be sent to the forbidding Victorian fortress known as Dorchester Penitentiary. There were places that were even worse, and Dorchester was less than three hours away, just on the other side of the New Brunswick–Nova Scotia border.

He was sitting absolutely still in the interview room downstairs; his face lacked all animation. His eyes followed me when I entered on my side of the partition, and began speaking through the metal grate. "We'll start the appeal procedure right away. Sue and I will sit down this evening."

"Will I be out of jail while I wait for my appeal?"

I swallowed, and delivered the latest in a long litany of unwelcome opinions: "It's very unlikely, Brennan, I'm sorry. The Criminal Code allows for release pending appeal but in practice it's extremely rare for someone convicted of murder to get out. You see, you no longer have the presumption of innocence working in your —"

"How long before my appeal will be heard?"

"Several months at least." He started to speak. I waited, but whatever it was died before delivery. "But Brennan, we're going to try for release anyway. First, though, we have a hearing to determine your, uh, parole eligibility date. To see how many years you'll have to serve before you may apply for parole."

"Jesus Christ! I believe in an entire world of things that can't be known through the five senses, but I can't believe what I'm hearing today. We can't really be sitting here discussing how many years of a life sentence I'll have to serve for something I didn't do."

"I understand. But this is what we have to deal with. Immediately after the sentencing, we'll set a date for your release hearing. We'll do everything humanly possible to get you out."

"I know, Monty. And I know whose fault it is I'm in here. Not yours. Mine. You warned me, you beseeched me, not to take the stand. I guess a mick just can't resist getting into the dock and making a speech." He lapsed into silence as his left hand massaged his temples.

"The fault, Brennan, lies with whoever killed those two women and carved your crucifix into the bodies. We'll be fighting on several fronts: the release, the appeal, and the investigation. I am going to find the individual who is doing this to you. And he'll be put on trial."

"And your wife will carry out the sentence."

"Nothing would please her more. Nothing else would please her at all, at this point. You have to go now. You've been in the jail, so you know what remand time is all about. Stay calm and take care. You got through it before, you'll do it again."

"I'll live," he said tersely, in a tone that belied his words. "And Monty. Thank you for all you've tried to do. I know I haven't been the ideal client."

And the Ides of March hadn't been the ideal day for Gaius Julius

Caesar to meet with the Senate. "The ideal client doesn't exist, Brennan." I tapped on the grate between us. "You've given me one hell of a ride."

II

Sue Drummond and I met over dinner to plan our strategy. We had to show that our appeal was not frivolous, that our client would surrender himself when he was supposed to, and that his detention was not necessary in the public interest. This meant public relations as much as public safety; what would people think of a justice system that set a convicted murderer free amongst them? Sue would draft the documents; I would look for cases, if there were any, in which people convicted of murder had been released by the courts. I was in the office till three in the morning, only to go home, lie in my bed, and endure nightmares about endless appeals, which were blocked time and again by technical glitches only the Crown and the judge understood.

I rose at eight, exhausted, and had a quick shower before heading downtown. Fuelled only by coffee, I sat at my desk and stared wildly at Brennan's file, wondering how things had gone so far without giving us any inkling of who was behind the murders. I read the file again, with no new insight. My phone rang just before noon.

"Yes?"

"My God, Monty, you should see him." It was Maura, in tears. "He has a black eye. Just shrugged when I asked what had happened. There's no life in him, no personality. It was only a few nights ago that he had dinner with us. Even with all the stress of a jury wait, he managed to be so cocky that night. That business with Giacomo."

"Did you think that was cocky of him, Maura?"

"It was very male of him, let's put it that way."

I don't know what made me say what I said next. It may have been the look that passed between them over dinner; it may have just been stress. "You know I wasn't sure at the time if he was clearing the decks for me or for himself."

She practically leapt through the wires at me. "What in the hell is wrong with you Collins? How can you say that? He's your client and your friend. He's wasting away in jail. And you make an accusation like that. I'm not through with you yet, but here comes Normie. I don't want her to hear this shit and I don't want her to hear about Brennan. She's very worried about him, very subdued. I'm in here, Normie sweetheart,"she called out to our daughter. And then to me. "Go to hell." Click.

I sat there wondering why I had made such a nasty remark to my wife, when she had called me in tears looking for consolation. I blamed it on exhaustion and dialed her number to apologize, but she wasn't taking calls.

I stared at the papers on my desk and tried to decide what to do. Hire private investigators to dig into the lives of all Brennan's acquaintances? Who? Father O'Flaherty? Sister Dunne? Eileen Darragh? Tyler MacDonald? The other young staffer, Erin? Mrs. Kelly? Jason? The poker club? The choir? All the angels and saints? It sounded preposterous when I ran the parade of names through my mind. The phone rang again. It would be like this all day, I knew. This time it was Rowan. And if I thought my day couldn't get any worse, I had once again miscalculated.

"Monty, my dear fellow. You sound all in."

"I am, Rowan. How about you? Did you spend the whole night fielding press inquiries?"

"I'm sending someone over there, Monty. Wants to see you."

"The real killer perhaps?"

"No. But primed to be the next killer by the sound of things. I shouldn't be flippant. Brennan's father just called me. From the Lord Nelson."

"He's *here?*"

"He is here, yes. At the hotel. I've never met the man. I should like to, of course. But that will be your privilege today. I told him I'd ring him back once I determined whether you were in the office. Sit tight."

I sighed. "The door's open. Tell him to take the elevator up."

I clicked off and sank my head into my hands. All I needed was old man Burke on my case. It wasn't long before I heard the elevator. Next thing I knew, the stocky and imperious form of Declan Burke was at the threshold of my office. I got up and made a face that was meant to express delighted surprise at his arrival. I opened my mouth to say something insincere but he spoke first.

"Mr. Collins. What the hell is going on with my son?" Anyone who found Brennan a little brusque should meet the original. "I want to see him."

"I'll be happy to take you out there," I lied. "When did you get into town?"

"I have a son in jail for a murder he didn't commit. If I haven't seen him yet, that can only mean I've just arrived."

"Right." If there had been a trap door to hell under my desk, I would gladly have pulled the plug and consigned myself to the flames.

A few minutes later I was crossing the MacKay Bridge on my way to Lower Sackville, with a glowering Burke Senior as my passenger.

"What the hell went wrong, Monty?"

"Whoever did this came out of left field. Brennan has no idea who it is."

"But how could a jury possibly think he's a killer? A priest, for Christ's sake."

"They couldn't get out from under the forensic evidence that was planted to make it look as if Brennan had been with the victim."

"He called and told us it would all work out in the end, that he'd be acquitted."

"He likely assumed that, once people got to hear him, they'd know he was innocent."

"Then all hell broke loose. What the fuck happened to him on the stand?"

"He testified in his own defence, we put his character in issue, and this opened up his whole life for the Crown to attack."

"So why the hell did you let him testify?"

"It wasn't my idea."

"You're his lawyer, for the love of Christ. Why didn't you stop him?"

"Think about it." I looked at him. "Would I be able to stop *you* from climbing up into the dock if you were of a mind to do it?"

There was a hint of amusement in his eyes as we exchanged glances. "He insisted, against your advice, is what you're telling me. I can well believe it. He was always hard-headed."

"Declan, what kind of a person would do this to your son? Has he ever confided in you about anyone who had a grudge against him, or someone you can think of who might have been provoked to this extent?"

"If Brennan had a problem with anyone, he kept it to himself."

Of course.

Fifteen minutes later we were seated in front of a partition, waiting for Brennan to appear on the other side. When his son walked in, Declan gasped at the sight of him. Brennan tried to give his father a smile, but it barely registered on his face.

"Jesus Christ, Brennan! What have they done to you, drained your blood?"

"No, Da. It's these colours. Green doesn't do a thing for me."

"Is that a black eye you have there?" his father asked, his voice growing more agitated. "What the hell happened?"

"Nothing."

"Nothing? When did I ever believe you when you came home with a black eye and told me 'nothing'? Now what the hell happened to you?"

"A fellow gave voice to a misconception about the priests of the Holy Roman Church. I started to give him a snap course in theology, and he drew off and hit me. I shoved him away from me. That was it." He turned to me. "I know better than to get into any shit with a bail hearing coming up, as hopeless as it might be. Now, a lot of the other fellows are fine. I know quite a few of them from the times I used to come here dressed in black."

"Be careful, Brennan, for Christ's sake," I warned.

"How long are you here for, Da?"

"Just till tomorrow. I have to get back to head off a visit by your mother. I had a hell of a time persuading her to sit tight. It goes without saying that she sends her love, but I've said it anyway."

"Don't let her come up, whatever you do. I don't want her here."

"I know. Now. What are we going to do about all this? Who hates you enough to take your life away from you? I'd certainly know who was out to get me."

Brennan looked amused. "Think so?"

"And don't sit there and tell me you have no idea. Go over everyone you ever met and come up with a few possibilities by the time I come out here again tomorrow."

"What are you going to do then, Da?"

"I'll make a few inquiries in New York, if you think somebody was studying a picture of that crucifix of yours. That is, if you still insist nobody has seen it. I don't get it, Brennan. That mark isn't between your legs, or on your arse; it's on your chest. That kind of opens up the field a bit, doesn't it? Hell, maybe you've been swanning around in a see-through silk shirt."

"No swanning, no silk. The only one who's ever been able to see that mark when I was fully dressed was Monty's daughter." Declan turned to me and glared. "She's only seven, Da. She has the sight."

"Ah. Rocky road ahead of her then."

So that's what Maura had observed at Strattons' party; that's what Normie had been trying to imprint on her hand. It seemed like a lifetime ago.

Brennan asked for news about the family and Declan obliged, but it was clear he was just going through the motions. "It breaks my heart to see you like this, Bren. As soon as they spring you —" he turned to me and raised an inquiring eyebrow, then turned back to his son "— get to work finding out who did it. Turn over some tables, raise hell. Don't repeat the mistake of thinking the courts are going to solve this for you. If they can't find any errors on appeal, you're fucked. I'll be out to see you tomorrow. For Christ's sake, take care of yourself."

Declan didn't speak until we were halfway to Halifax. "Thank God he's not the same little hothead he was at fifteen. He'd be scrapping with them all. And who could tell what would happen? You know what these arseholes are like. Look at them the wrong way, or throw them a punch, and they'll hold a grudge till they're clomping around in walkers out at Whispering Geezers Villa. How many children do you have, Monty? Just the little girl?"

"No, I have a teenage son, Tom."

"Nothing like it, is there? Being a father. You see a client in that jail. And a friend, a man a few years older than yourself. To me, that's my little son in there."

We made arrangements to meet at my office the next day, and

head out for another visit before Declan returned to New York. I went back to my preparations for the bail hearing.

III

Sunday was bright and cold. Declan called just before noon to say he was on his way to the office. I made a quick call to Dresden Row and reached Tommy Douglas. "Tell Mum I'm heading out to the Correctional Centre if she'd like to come with me. I'll be here for half an hour or so."

As soon as I got Declan settled in a chair with a cup of coffee, I heard someone get off the elevator and assumed it was Maura. I went out to meet her. Her cheeks were as red as her scarlet coat sweater. I tried to head her off outside the office so I could apologize for the remark I'd made the day before. But she started in before I could part my lips.

"I simply cannot believe what you said to me yesterday, about that little scene with Giacomo and Brennan. You know perfectly well that Brennan's heart is in the right place." We were in the office by this time, her marching ahead, throwing her voice to make sure I got every word. "He thinks, for some unfathomable reason, that you and I should be back together. He may not look it, but, underneath it all, he must be a hopeless, a terminal romantic. But I can tell you, you'll be riding a Zamboni in hell before you'll ever get in my bed again."

An amused Irish voice rang out from a dark corner of the room. "My son told me you've a tongue on you that could slit the hull of a freighter. His observation has been confirmed." Maura stood stock still. She stared as Declan rose and came towards her, blue eyes sparkling with delight. "I can see he was right about your other qualities as well. I'm Declan Burke. And I cannot possibly say how it pleases me to meet you." He put out his hand, and she took it.

"Mr. Burke. It's not the way I'd have chosen to present myself to you. I'm sorry you had to hear all that. But clearly you're not." A smile made its way to her eyes.

"Bren spoke to Teresa and me about the two of you, when he was home in the spring. His good friend Montague and Monty's lovely wife,

Maura. He neglected to say you were on the outs with each other."

"That's all there is to know about us really," Maura was kind enough to say. "As for you, I can't quite take in the fact that I'm finally meeting the patriarch. Brennan looms so large in our lives these days I tend to think we've got the whole Burkean universe here. Now there's you."

"A parallel universe. I went to Brennan's church, by the way. There was no choir at the early Mass. Just as well. Wouldn't want to see them without Bren directing."

"Who said Mass?" I asked.

"An old fellow. Another Harp. Said a nice Mass." O'Flaherty, several years younger than Declan.

"That's Father O'Flaherty. Were you talking to him?"

"No, I wasn't."

"Too bad," I said. "He'd love the chance to talk the ear off you. He's very keen on his Irish heritage. Organizes trips to the old country. Have you been back there once in a while to visit?"

"No."

"I see. Well then, let's get moving."

When we arrived at the Correctional Centre, I suggested that Declan go in ahead for a private visit; Maura and I would join him in a few minutes. Hoping to avoid a return to our earlier argument, I asked her what she thought of our companion.

"Formidable. Merits further study."

"Doesn't give much away, does he?"

"The apple doesn't fall far from the tree," she agreed. "I remember you telling me about Brennan when you first met him. Said you could barely get a word out of him."

I shook my head, remembering our first few meetings. "What a prick."

"Halcyon days," Maura quipped, with a hint of a smile.

When we entered the visitors' area, I couldn't reconcile the commanding figure I had been remembering with the sallow, black-eyed wraith behind the partition. Brennan and his father were regarding each other morosely, not saying a word. They both looked relieved to see us come in.

"Are you two just going to sit there? Talk to each other, for Christ's sake," Maura chided them. "Now. Declan." She looked at the older man but addressed her remarks to the younger. "Did your lad here give you any ideas you can pass along to us about where to start looking for the real perp? Murderous bishops? Frustrated nuns? Envious choirmasters? Temperamental sopranos? Sore losers at the poker table? Jilted lovers? Jealous husbands?" Surely that wasn't a dig at me.

"Maura, how the hell can you laugh about this?" Brennan looked pained as he ran his fingers through his hair.

Declan turned to her. "You're not doing a bad job there, darlin'. I've been pegging the same questions at him, word for word in some cases. He just sits there."

"Look, he's exhausted and run down," I cut in. "Let's ease up, all right?"

"I hear you," said his father. "But it's so frustrating just sitting here, not being able to help him. I asked him how it's been for him in here. Do you know what he said to me? He doesn't like the soap! Typical. He's encircled by psychopaths and his nose is out of joint because he smells like disinfectant. He was always a fastidious little Christer."

"Da. We'll talk when I get out, all right? MacNeil, tell me something funny, without me as the butt of the joke."

"All right. Speaking of butts, did you know I am distantly related to the Proud Arse MacNeils? So named because they were the first family in their community to have an indoor toilet. Can you claim any comparable distinction? I doubt it. No offence, Declan." She brought out some more classic Nova Scotia nicknames and kept up a line of inconsequential patter till it was time to get Mr. Burke to the airport.

"Declan. Maura. Could I just have a word with Brennan?"

They said their goodbyes with promises of phone calls in the days ahead. When the prisoner and I were alone, I wasted no time. I had been struck by something his father had said the day before, about throwing a punch and being the object of a long-lasting grudge. "What's the name of that greaseball you punched out at Mount A?"

He rocked forward in his chair and rebuked me with some of his old fire: "I told you I never wanted to hear about that again."

"It's worth looking into."

"No, it isn't."

I persisted. "I'm sure you remember everything about him, so give me his name." Silence. What had Moody Walker told me? A souvenir. "The way I heard it, this guy took something from you. Yanked it off your neck."

"He did what?" I had his full attention.

"Was it a medal?" He stared at me but didn't answer.

His eyes slid away from me and he focused on something in the middle distance. Replaying the scene in his mind? Had I finally broken through? He parted his lips and was about to speak. But by the time he did, he had recovered himself.

"There's nothing there. Get it out of your head." Then he rose, walked over to a guard, and was escorted from the room without looking back.

"Jesus. What happened?" Declan asked when he saw my face. "Is everything all right?"

We began walking to the car. "Clients, Declan. They're all the same. Their own worst enemy." I unlocked the car, we got in, and I wrenched the key in the ignition, then spun out of the lot like a jailhouse regular.

"Well, what is it?" Maura wanted to know.

"It's just some information I wanted from him. He won't tell me. That's all."

"Do you think it's something he would tell me?" Maura asked.

"Definitely not," I answered, which provoked a stare and a spate of unasked questions.

We got Declan on the plane and promised to keep him posted. Then we drove to the city in silence.

The first thing I did the next morning was call a private investigator. I told him what I had heard from Sergeant Moody Walker about the fight at Mount Allison University in 1982. I wanted the guy's name. I intended to track him down.

Part Three

Chapter 16

Ah, well I rolled in late last night.
Would you believe I would like to die now?
There was my lady lying with a man. Not another one, oh no.
Would you believe that it happens more often than not?
Here's to all the ladies that fell for me tonight, whoever they were.
— David Wiffen, "More Often than Not"

I

The days went by, and Brennan's physical and psychological health deteriorated with every hour he lost behind bars. My efforts to keep his spirits up were seen as the empty gestures they were. He fretted about where he would be sent to do his time, but when I tried to discuss it he tuned me out. His state of mind was not enhanced by the results of the sentence hearing: the judge told him he would have to serve eighteen years of his life sentence before he could apply for parole.

Then it was time to move ahead with the application for release. Susan and I prepared our submissions to the Appeal Division of the Nova Scotia Supreme Court. A country-wide search had netted me very few cases in which a person convicted of murder had been released pending appeal. Karl Schenk had a trunkful of cases to support the Crown's position that Burke should stay in jail.

Decision day finally dawned. We would be facing Justice Dennis McTiernan. This could be bad or it could be good; there was no way to predict, because he was notoriously unpredictable. The only predictable thing about him was his nickname, Dennis the Dissenter, so named for his willingness to buck his fellow appellate judges and write dissenting opinions. He didn't always dissent in the same direction; sometimes he was for the Crown, sometimes for the defence; sometimes for the little guy, sometimes for the powerful. He had done very little criminal work before being appointed to the bench. Expecting the worst, Susan and I prepared not only for this hearing, but for an application to the Chief Justice of Nova Scotia for a review of McTiernan's decision if things went against us, as they likely would. I decided not to share this bit of the planning with Brennan, whose mood had been alternating between depressed and belligerent in the days leading up to the hearing.

But first things first, and here was Dennis announcing his decision. I had to look at Sue to make sure I was not hallucinating. McTiernan stunned us all by ordering Brennan's release. The conditions were similar to those imposed on him before his trial, except that the amount of the recognizance was $100,000. We were fortunate indeed that Rowan Stratton was able and willing to act as surety for his long-time friend. I immediately began to worry that Schenk would apply to the Chief Justice in an effort to have the decision overturned.

For now, though, Brennan was free. I drove him to my house. He sat in the car with his head back and his eyes closed as I spoke of the next few days: "I don't think you need to deal with the rectory right now, and you certainly don't need any attention from the press. Tell me what you want from your room. Clothing, books, music, wine, whiskey, your favourite *soap*, whatever you want, I'll bring it to you here. I'll get you some groceries. Then I'll go back to work. So, sit out on the lawn and gaze at the water, go for a long walk, get tanked, or sleep all day. It's up to you. The house and everything in it is yours. The key is on a hook under the eaves of the shed. It's always there for the kids, just in case. I'll stay out of your hair for a couple of days and let you unwind."

"Where are you going to be?"

"I'll be working long hours and going out afterwards. Getting out early and getting in late."

What I didn't tell him was that if I didn't blow off steam in some way, I'd be the next one convicted of a violent crime. That night, Monday, was blues night at the home of Ed Johnson, lead vocalist for our band, Functus. If ever there was a time for singing the blues, this was it, and what I couldn't say in words I would express through some fiery blues harp and slide guitar. I was interested to see, when I arrived, that Ed's friend Bev was on hand, as she sometimes was, to hear the band. Bev was around my age, small, quick, and dark; very attractive in a jaded kind of way. She had made no secret of her interest in me, but I had always put her off. Tonight I was ready to take her up on her offer. There would be no Maura, no Brennan, no Declan, in my life this night.

We all wailed and swilled our way through the evening, and somebody passed around a veggie tray that contained nothing but cannabis derivatives. I stole the show with an over-the-top rendition of Bo Diddley's ode to male prowess, "I'm a Man." Shameless. Living it down would not be easy, but I'd worry about that later. Between numbers I made a point of pulling Bev onto my lap, wrapping my arms around her and generally being much more physical than I would normally ever be if there were more than two of us in the room. I cut back on the booze fairly early so I wouldn't blow it. Bev and I began to get better acquainted in the back seat of a cab. I spent that night and the next at her place. I slumped over my desk during the days and had two long nights of mindless, loveless, heedless physical release. It was just what the doctor ordered.

I dragged myself to my house Wednesday evening, after another wasted day at the office. There was a light on so I knew Brennan was still my guest.

"Honey, I'm home!"

He came out to meet me. The improvement in him was astonishing. "It's about time. I've been slaving over a hot stove all day and what thanks —" He peered at me. "You look like shit. Are those the same clothes you were wearing two days ago? Can't you break down and leave a spare set of clothes over there?"

"Over where?" I said, bewildered.

"At your old place. With MacNeil."

"I wasn't at Maura's."

"You weren't? Oh. I called over there last night and Tommy said: 'They're out till late.' I assumed he meant she was out with you."

"No."

"Ah."

Who was she out with, I wondered, late on a school night? "Did she call you back?"

"No. Well, not last night. She called this morning. Gabbed a lot, but she sounded like hell. Worn out. I figured that you —"

"I wasn't anywhere near her. So. What did she say?"

"Nothing really."

"Nothing? You just said she gabbed a lot. She doesn't tend to prattle on about nothing. Especially if she's worn out. It's not her style."

"Right. Where's your gear?"

"Huh?"

"Your guitar, your harmonica. When you left here on Monday you were going to blues night, remember?"

"Oh, we had blues night, all right. Shit. I left my stuff at Ed's. I hope." I had picked up my car on Tuesday but I hadn't gone in. Hadn't even thought of it.

"That may have been the other call. Someone phoned last night, didn't leave his name."

I went to the phone. "Donna? This is Monty. Ed around? Very droll, Donna. Yeah, I was pretty wound up. Hey, Ed. Did you call here last night, about my guitar? Oh, him? No. Irish exchange student. Mature student. Listen, I'll stop by and get my stuff tomorrow. No, no. Really. There's no hurry. Well, if you're coming this way, but otherwise — okay." I hung up. "Shit. Now he's coming over."

"And?"

"Nothing."

"Go get cleaned up. And put those clothes in the laundry, for Christ's sake. I do have dinner for you."

"Smells good. What is it?"

"Irish stew."

"What's in it?"

"Lamb. What else would it be?"

"Where did you find the lamb?"

"Are you well, Montague? What do you think I did, go out and slaughter one from your herd?"

"Flock, I believe the word is. While shepherds watched their flocks by night."

"Right. I should know that. But no, you do have a supermarket out here."

"It's a good walk."

"I'm a good walker. That's all I did. Walk, eat, sleep. Just what the doctor ordered. I feel great."

"You look great. Big improvement over what I saw out at the Correctional Centre."

"You, on the other hand, look knackered. Now hurry up. Before my stew is *ruined.*"

I took a long, hot shower, brushed my teeth and stuffed my clothes in the hamper. Feeling considerably more chipper in fresh jeans and a comfy sweater, I sat down to a surprisingly delicious Irish stew. The doorbell rang. Ed. I nearly knocked my chair over, trying to head him off at the front door.

"Hey Bo Diddley," Ed sang, loudly.

"Can it, Edward. I'm beat."

"No wonder. Didn't know you had it in you, Collins. You're usually content to blow the harp and play guitar. But those vocals on 'I'm a Man.' Whoa! That's your signature tune now, my friend. The girls sure lapped it up. Just like the old days, eh? Walked out with more than your harp in your hand after those gigs."

"Just give me my gear and piss off."

"Jesus. Something smells good in here. Is Bev so in love with you now that you've got her cooking for you? I would have taken her for a wing-nite kinda girl."

"Bye, Ed. See you next time."

"Can't wait. For the blues and the social dynamics."

Then I had to face Brennan who, I knew, had not missed a word. He was beaming, the last harrowing weeks momentarily forgotten. "B. O'Diddley. A Celtic musician, would he be?" I ignored him. But he was on a roll. "I don't believe I've been introduced to this Bev. Why don't you give her a call? This will be much better for her than the greasy chicken wings she's used to gobbling between —"

"Father?"

"Mmm?"

"Fuck off."

We resumed our meal in silence.

"This is good," I had to concede. "I didn't know you could cook."

"I can do a lot of things you don't know about."

"All as wholesome as this, I'm sure."

"Right."

We moved into the living room after dinner. He took my easy chair and I sat on the chesterfield. The last thing I remember was Brennan lighting up a stogie and regarding me through the smoke, with the look of a man mightily amused. When I awoke, daylight was streaming in and I was lying on the chesterfield with a quilt over me, a glass of water on a little table beside me, and, tucked under my right arm, a black-and-white cat. Cat? I did a double take. It was one of Normie's stuffed animals. Burke was up, showered and dressed. I could smell coffee.

"Brennan? I think I'll keep you. I never got this kind of treatment from my last housemate."

"Who was that?"

"Professor MacNeil."

"Well, maybe if you weren't forever getting up on other women, MacNeil would —"

"That's not a very priestly remark. But then again, you're a little more worldly than most of the saintly fathers I grew up with. As for me, being with another woman is hardly an everyday occurrence. Getting anything more than a dirty look these days is a rare treat. Maura told me I'd be riding a Zamboni in hell before I'd get near her again, so —"

He put his hand up. "Don't be telling me that."

"Where do you suppose she was Tuesday night?"

"How the hell would I know? Is she seeing anyone that you know of?" he asked offhandedly.

"I don't know. And I don't care."

"Is that a fact? Maybe this Giacomo has ventured onto the scene again. I thought I had put the run to him."

"Oh, Jesus. Don't mention that."

"Why not?"

"Never mind."

"Monty. Get up off your arse, have some coffee, and drive me home."

"You're leaving?"

"What did you think? I'd moved in?"

"Never know with you."

"You said a mouthful there."

I dropped him off at the rectory, the portals of which he would now enter as a convicted murderer. I headed to the office. The party was over. And the investigation was on.

II

The day after Brennan returned to St. Bernadette's, Maura and I were having a family dinner at the old house with the kids. The evening got off to a rocky start.

"How was blues night?" Maura asked.

"It was fine."

"Did Burke go with you?"

"No. Why?"

"A night of music. Why not?"

"Because he was wasted after his spell in the clink. I dropped him off at my place for two days to sleep."

"You dropped him off? What do you mean? You weren't there?"

"I didn't say that."

"I see."

"Do you? Well then Maura, how was Tuesday night?"

"What do you mean?"

"Well, did you go out and have a big bang-up time with some-body on Tuesday night?"

"Since when do you bother to keep track of my activities?"

"I just wondered if you're seeing anyone these days."

I had brought wine to the festivities and I fumbled around in the kitchen looking for a corkscrew. It was never in the same place twice. I spied it and snatched it up.

"If I went out with someone Tuesday night, what difference does it make to you? Somehow I suspect I didn't cross your mind that night. And if I'd known you were going to dump Brennan off alone after his ordeal, I might have postponed my date with . . . postponed my date, and taken Brennan out to dinner somewhere private and relaxing. I owe him one anyway."

"I'm sure he wanted to be alone, especially after being cooped up with a bunch of jailbirds. He was probably relieved to be 'dumped off,' as you put it. What do you mean, you owe him one?"

"He treated me to a night out, so —"

"You and Burke spent a night together? Is that what I'm hearing?"

"Evening."

"When was this?"

"I don't know. Couple of months ago."

"Funny it never came up in conversation. With you, or with him."

"There's a reason for that."

"Yeah. I can imagine." I drove the corkscrew like a dagger into the wine cork.

"It's not what you think." She sighed. "I never told you because Normie got hurt that day."

"What? Hurt how? Did somebody hurt her? What the hell happened?" This revelation blotted out any concern I had about what Burke might have been up to with my wife.

What followed was a long story about Normie falling from a slide at a playground where Maura had let her go, after we had agreed she would not be allowed to go there; Normie going for a sleepover that night; Maura wanting her checked beforehand at the Children's Hospital just to be sure; Tommy needing a ride to a friend's camp half an hour away; Maura having to be two places at once; me incommunicado somewhere; nobody else around, Maura thinking of Brennan living a few blocks away; Brennan coming over to help her; Brennan taking her out for a late evening dinner at a restaurant on Spring Garden Road.

"So Brennan and I spent the evening eating, having a few drinks, and talking."

"Right. So, is he a fun date?"

"Oh, yes." She smiled. "Very gallant. And he can be very funny. We had lots of laughs."

"And then what?"

"And then we came home and he left."

"Well, did he come in with you?" Why couldn't I stop myself from sounding like such a jerk? A sizeable portion of my criminal clientele were guys who just would not let their wives or girlfriends go. They would harass them, or follow them, or assault them. And I always asked: "Why would you want to be with a girl who doesn't want you around? Leave her alone." I had no desire to see myself in the same light, but I wasn't ready to let the subject die. Maura was getting pissed off and, objectively speaking, I could hardly blame her. We weren't living together, I had the occasional girlfriend, she had the occasional boyfriend, or so it seemed. And why not? I had no right to interrogate her. But, Burke? My mouth opened again. "How long were you two together that night?"

"I don't know why I'm submitting to this barrage of questions. I guess I'm just too sweet and good-natured to tell you to get stuffed. We were at the restaurant for a long time, two or three hours. Then we came back here and he stayed for a while. I wasn't looking at my watch."

"You probably didn't even have it on by then."

"You should hear yourself! I'll try to ignore what you're insinuating about my character, that at the first opportunity I would be all over a man who's a friend of yours, and a client, never mind that he happens to be a priest. But what does this say about the way you regard Burke? It's not much of a stretch to picture him breaking his vows, but I cannot imagine him betraying you in that way. And yes, before you have a good laugh, it would be a betrayal from his point of view. The dear, sweet, deluded man is determined to believe, in the face of all the evidence to the contrary, that there is still something between you and me, and that our marriage can be salvaged. I could be the most gorgeous, most ravishing temptress on the planet, and I'm sure he would still have contented himself with a goodnight kiss —"

"Oh? And while this kiss was going on, just how much —"

"— because of his respect for you, and because of everything you've tried to do for him and his case, which has obviously taken its toll on you, Montague. This really is not like you. I thought you were burnt-out when you were with Legal Aid, but this is pathetic."

I was not through being pathetic. "And then what?"

"And then nothing. Well, he sent me flowers the next day."

"Flowers! And just why —"

"When I came downstairs for dinner, he was eyeing a bouquet of pink roses on the mantelpiece. 'Who sent you these?' he asked me. I told him it was none of his business. And he said: 'Well, they don't suit you.' I gave him a bit of a rough time. 'So I suppose you, a lifelong bachelor, know all about what kind of flowers to send a woman.' He said: 'Wait and see.' Off we went to the restaurant. The next afternoon, a delivery guy came to the door with a potted plant."

"Oh? A flower that suited you?"

"You tell me. It was a snapdragon!"

She laughed, and I wanted to join her, but I couldn't stop bickering: "Back to this —"

"Oh, stop being such a flaming arsehole!"

"I'm sorry. I know I'm being primitive. I'm stressed out and exhausted."

"Mummy, I heard you! You said the R-word to Daddy!" Normie came in, and stood staring at her mother, wide-eyed.

"The R-word? What's that, Normie?"

"Arsehole!"

The arsehole and his naughty wife looked at each other and tried to stifle their laughter. The tension was broken, for the time being. I reserved the right to brood later. We sat down to dinner when Tommy Douglas came in. He told us all about a girl he liked at school and Normie teased him. He teased her back. And so on. Although Maura was not by any stretch of the imagination a cordon bleu chef, we laid waste to her roast chicken, potatoes, ersatz-gravy, and bakery-made butterscotch pie. When there was nothing left, Tom excused himself, and Normie grabbed all the napkins from the table. She went into the living room and busied herself making doll clothes out of napkins and paper clips. MacNeil and I split the bottle of wine, and half of another, and sat in a post-dinner stupor, more mellow now, *Deo gratias.*

III

As I watched Normie playing happily in the next room, I thought of the Crystal Green case, when I had, for better or for worse, taken apart a mother's life on the witness stand, in front of her family, friends, and all the courthouse busybodies. I started to tell Maura about it, leaving out only the names.

As usual, she interrupted, but this time she was on my side: "She goddamned well deserved it! Picture for yourself what I would have done to someone, anyone, who hurt or abused Normie or Tom in any way. I would tear the guy limb from limb from limb —"

"I get the picture."

"Any woman would. Except that one. And she's the child's mother no less. The one person on this earth who should be protecting the child with her own life. But she not only lets the abuse go on, she stays with the child molester, and sends her own daughter away!"

"That's the way I felt. I couldn't stop myself when I had her on the stand."

"It's just like little Janeece," Maura said, "and the failure of the step-mother to protect her. I suppose the wretched woman didn't deserve to be murdered for it, though somebody obviously thought so." Flushed with anger, Maura reached for her wine glass and drained it. "Same with the other one when you think of it," she continued. "The only woman in the room except for the poor victim, who was what, fifteen? What kind of woman would pander to her boyfriend by encouraging him and his little band of losers to gang-rape another girl? Couldn't she feel the terror every woman feels at the idea of rape? How could she not have put herself in the victim's place and gone for help? Instead of cheering them on —"

"I'm sorry, but who is this you're talking about, Maura?"

"That other one who was murdered. The gang rape one."

I felt time slow down. I knew I was hearing something of enormous significance but I could not work it out in my mind. "You don't mean Leeza Rae?"

"Of course I mean Leeza Rae. What did I just say?"

"Well, what's this about her being part of the rape?" Every cell in my post-prandial brain was on alert. "Where did you get this?"

"Collins. If you had been listening to me over the past six months —"

"I'm listening now."

"I am working on a Charter of Rights case. We lost at trial. We are going before the Court of Appeal in January. We have two fairly new judges on the court, Vitelli and MacLeish. I'm not familiar with them, so I'm reading every one of their decisions as it comes out." She paused and I waited in tense silence.

"So. Justice MacLeish wrote the decision of the Court of Appeal in that goddamned rape case. Vic Stillman. Leeza Rae's boyfriend. It was a jury trial. The lead rapist, the alpha rapist I suppose he'd want to be called, this Stillman creature, got seven years. His sidekicks got less time, and one guy got off. Stillman appealed his conviction and sentence. Appeal dismissed. Unanimous decision, written for the court by MacLeish. The appeal judges made a lot of references to the transcript and that's where all the details are about the rapist's girl-friend Leeza — who has since been taken out by our unknown killer — Leeza encouraging these clowns to rape and humiliate this little girl. Leeza Rae not only encouraged them but laughed at the victim while it was happening, paraded around with the girl's clothing on. She wasn't charged with anything. It was horrible, just terrible." Maura's voice broke and there were tears in her eyes. She looked at Normie, who was singing to her dolls in the next room without a care in the world.

When Maura had recovered, she said: "And you didn't know any of this?" I didn't. I had read the newspaper reports of the rape trial; the reporters had concentrated on the chief villain and his sidekicks. If there had been a reference to the girlfriend, I had missed it. And Leeza Rae had not become important to me until long after the boyfriend's trial. Before her death, everyone had thought of Leeza as a victim of her brutal boyfriend. Now, I wondered whether a friend or family member of the rape victim might have acted on a grudge against Leeza. Suddenly the case opened up in a way I had not anticipated.

"When was the Court of Appeal decision reported? I'll look it up."

"Last November or December. MacLeish's first decision."

I decided to read it the next morning. And I would have, if I had not been distracted by another development in the case.

Chapter 17

Whatever you wanted, what could it be?
Did somebody tell you that you could get it from me?
Is it something that comes natural? Is it easy to say?
Why do you want it? Who are you anyway?
— Bob Dylan, "What Was It You Wanted?"

I

When I got to the office in the morning, a message was waiting for me from my private investigator. I called and he filled me in on one Trevor Myers, twenty-nine years old, originally from Amherst, Nova Scotia, up near the border with New Brunswick. He had a violent criminal record dating from the late 1970s, and had served time in Springhill, Dorchester, and the Correctional Centre in Lower Sackville. Myers's favourite hangout, when he was not incarcerated, was the Miller's Tale, a bar in Dartmouth. That afternoon I gave the place a call.

"Lemme talk to Trevor."

"Who?"

"Trevor. Put him on."

"Trevor who?"

"Like you never heard of him. Trevor Myers. Is he in there or not? Stop jerking me around."

"Back off, man. Myers isn't here. I haven't seen him all day. Try again." Click.

I did not look forward to asking Brennan whether he had had any contact with Myers during his ministry at the Correctional Centre.

My client and I could not get together that day so I invited him over for a meal on Saturday evening. We had wine, whiskey, and stout, and were well-oiled by the time we moved from the kitchen to the living room, and the conversation switched from pleasure to business.

I took a deep breath and plunged in. "Have you ever seen Trevor Myers out at the Correctional Centre, or anywhere else in the last eight years?"

I could see him shutting down on me. There was so little expression in his face that he could have been sitting alone in a bus terminal. Then he unfolded himself from the chair and left the room. I jumped up to head him off.

"Brennan, where the hell do you think you're going?"

He turned and shot me a look that added sixteen centuries to my time in purgatory.

"I'm just getting a smoke. I am not leaving. Because, one, I might *kill* someone if I drive in this condition and, two, the subject you just brought up will not be mentioned again. You are my lawyer. I am your client. I am instructing you not to pursue that line of inquiry. It is not connected with the murders. Now let's sit down again and be civil." He got his smokes, returned to his chair and made himself comfortable.

"Burke, I can't fucking help you if you won't let me track down other possible suspects. Including this clown who may bear a grudge out of all proportion to what happened between you." He shook his head, and I sighed.

"Move on, my dear Montague. Let's find more promising suspects."

"All right. This DeSouza woman in Brazil. What's her nationality?"

He looked dumbstruck. "You're having me on, aren't you?"

"No. A woman you've admitted having an affair with. Unlike the woman or women you won't admit to —"

"You, Monty, have women on the brain. I live in a world of men, not women, for better or for worse. You're putting me in mind of Karl Schenk, trying to portray me as some kind of womanizer. Which I am not. I resent that."

I started to laugh, in spite of myself. How many poor schmucks in this world would give their last dime to be branded as a womanizer, by anyone, anywhere? And this guy, who from what I gathered was memorable for his abilities in that regard, found it oh so tedious to be questioned about it.

"What have I said to amuse you now?"

"Don't ask."

"But I do know this much." He leaned forward in his chair and gestured to me with his glass. Some of the liquid spilled onto his pants but he ignored it. He locked his black eyes onto mine and said: "You're going to wind up a big fucking loser if you don't smarten up about your wife."

I shot forward in my seat. "Just what the hell are you trying to get at?"

"You're throwing it all away, Collins."

"What do you mean, *I'm* throwing it away? It takes two to wreck a marriage. And, for your information, she was the one who insisted on the separation."

"And why was that?"

"How is this any of your business?"

"You've been asking me about my affairs, so now I have a few words for you."

"I ask about your affairs because I'm trying to defend you on a murder charge."

"Well, I'm trying to defend you on a charge of shooting yourself in the metatarsals. Now, what's your problem with Maura?"

"What's my problem? You've met her."

"She's a bit fierce, to be sure. But you're up to the task. Wise up, or you're going to lose her to someone else."

"That sounds like a threat."

I saw a flash of anger in his eyes, then he looked away, shaking his head. "It's plain to see you're not indifferent to her. So, make a move. Don't waste any more time. Yours or hers. Stop being such a fucking bonehead."

"You act as if it's all me. She's the one who runs up one side of me and down the other as soon as we've been in the same room for five minutes. If you think that's love, Burke, you move in with her."

Burke sat back in his chair and smiled. "Have it your way then, you stubborn gobshite. Maybe in time, you and I can take turns paying her visits. You the forlorn ex-husband, me the kindly parish priest, invited to Sunday dinner with her and Giacomo and his two adorable stepchildren."

"Fuck you!" I had one hand wrapped around my glass; the other was clenched in a fist. I'm not a violent man. But I had the urge to beat the crap out of Brennan Burke. It was all I could do to remain seated and keep myself wrapped in the mantle of a civilized human being.

He got up from his chair and wove unsteadily from side to side, raising a warning hand in my direction. "We've had a skinful, Montague. And we'd better not say another drunken word. Let's find something to sober us up. Coffee? Tomato juice? Ambulance?"

I let a minute pass without speaking, willing myself to cool down. "There's tomato juice out in the cupboard, but you'll never make it. You can't even walk."

"Well, get up off your arse and find it for me. I'll get the Waterford crystal."

I poured two tumblers full of what I hoped would be the cure. We sat down heavily at the kitchen table and drained the juice. I put my head down on my arms.

I do not know how much time passed, perhaps an hour or so, but when I returned to awareness I saw that Brennan, too, had conked out at the table. It was a few more minutes before he stirred.

"This was supposed to be a working dinner," I said, the clarity of my speech having been restored somewhat by my little nap. Perhaps we had lost more time than I thought.

"So we worked each other over." He sounded a bit more sober too.

"Without solving anything. Like the case." By that time I felt able to give a little speech. "And to think that I had unkind thoughts, every working day, about my clients at Legal Aid. They wouldn't help themselves. They wouldn't help me. I lost patience with them. Failed to appreciate them. Till now. Because now, I have to put up with *you*."

"You're finding this client a bit too rich for your blood. Ever think of going back to Legal Aid?"

"No, Brennan. I think not. By the time I get finished with you, the way things are going, the billings from your case alone will fund my early retirement. I know this is going to sound insulting —"

"That seems to be a recurring theme here tonight."

"But where is the money coming from, to pay my fees? I didn't know you guys made enormous salaries. Spirit of poverty and all that. And Rowan gave me to understand that this is you, not the church."

"I don't have a mortgage. I don't have alimony payments. My sisters insist on buying me clothes. And I take Mike O'Flaherty's money every Wednesday night at poker. Shit! Mike asked me for something and I forgot all about it. We're having a Knights of Columbus gathering on the weekend, and I promised to help with the music. I'll give him a call."

Burke picked up the phone, punched in the number, and waited. "Mike. I didn't wake you, did I? Ah. It is rather late, yes. What? Yeah, I've been lifting a few. I'm with Collins. Anyway, you wanted some of those old song books. The Irish stuff? They're on a shelf in my room with a bunch of other music books. Take what you want. It's open. Yes, I suppose you're right. It could have waited until tomorrow. I'm legless here, not thinking straight. So, when is this crowd rolling into town? Friday, right. I'll help you this week. Good, then." Click.

"What the hell time is it?" he asked me. He peered at his watch in the dim light. "Jesus! It's well into morning here. Poor Michael. O'Flaherty and his Knights. He's going to lead them in song. Better him than me. And he's recycling that variety show for their edification. Did you see it? They have it on video." Brennan was at the sink, pouring us glasses of water. We went into the living room and he made himself at home in my comfy chair.

"Oh, right. I did see the video, or part of it. I remember being surprised you agreed to take part. You didn't strike me as a very humorous guy when we first met."

"I was a little tense. But now, having had a jury of my peers find me guilty of murder, I'm a million laughs. An old Hibernian quirk. *Sláinte,*" he said, raising his glass of tap water.

"It was a cute skit, though, with the kids singing. And you were fearsomely Teutonic with that accent and the Beethoven wig," I observed.

Brennan rubbed his head. "Yeah, I remember."

"It's your own hair, Brennan. You're not Ludwig now."

"No, but I must have lost half my hair when he yanked that wig off my head." He laughed. "All in a good cause, though. We managed to raise —" He looked at me. "What's got into you, Collins?"

I reached out blindly and found a spot to rest my glass, never taking my eyes off his face. "Tell me that again."

"Tell you what?" he asked.

"What did you say about the wig?"

"Just that ham-handed O'Flaherty grabbed a fistful of my own hair when he tore the Beethoven wig off — Jesus Christ!" He held his glass in mid-air as he returned my gaze.

I was no longer aware of anything other than our voices. "Tell me exactly what you remember about it. Don't leave anything out."

He recited the story as if in a trance. "The children finished their song. Well, I finished directing it. We took our bows, and walked off the stage. The next performer was somebody from the church, I don't remember who. The children and I went to the little room where the costumes and props were kept. I sat in the only chair. Eileen and Mike were right behind me, helping the children off with their choristers' robes. The space was cramped and they were all bumping into each other. I was hunched over reading the program, wondering how much longer it was going to go on. All of a sudden, my hair was being pulled, the wig being yanked off my head. And I heard Eileen laughing and saying 'Easy there, Father O.' He said something like 'Why don't you just call me Daddy-O, we're not formal around here.' Some little joke."

He stopped and took a deep breath.

"What happened to the wig after that?"

"I have no idea. I don't even know where it came from in the first place."

"Did you see Mike do anything with it after taking it off your head?"

"No. I wasn't even looking at him, just rubbing my head and reading the program." Brennan's knuckles were white where they gripped his glass. I nodded at the glass, afraid it would shatter. He followed my eyes and absently placed the glass on the floor. "Monty, I can't believe Mike would —"

"That's the hair taken care of. And you told me it was possible Mike had come into your room some time when you were getting out of the shower, so he could have seen the scar. Brennan, I'll have to get moving on this right away. But please, please listen to me." The words "this time" hung in the air unspoken. I felt instantly sober. "Don't say a word to Mike or to anyone. Try not to behave any differently. We have to be one hundred percent correct in the way we handle this. There's no room for error. And don't let that videotape go astray. It's evidence."

II

Brennan slept it off at my place and left early Sunday morning, before I regained consciousness. The instant I awoke, the revelations about O'Flaherty began spinning around in my head. The urge to question him was almost overpowering. But it would be rash to confront O'Flaherty before I had more information. Fortunately there was another adult witness to the scene, Eileen Darragh. I could talk to her first. But not today. It was my week with the children, and I was anxious for them to appear so I could direct my attention to them and away from the case. When Maura dropped them off, she didn't miss the fact that I was all keyed up.

"You're not usually this agitated, Collins. What happened? Still got the shakes from a rough night?"

"In a way."

"What did you do?"

"Got tanked with Burke."

"Oh? And what kind of experience was that?"

"I spent the night insulting him."

"How did he take that?"

"Some of it he wisely refused to acknowledge."

"Did he insult you back?"

"He went after me a bit. But he meant well."

"Booze must have a mellowing effect on him. I find that comforting somehow. So what's got you all worked up today?"

"I'll tell you later in the week."

"Something to do with His Excellency?"

"Yeah."

"Good or bad?"

"Good for us. Bad for somebody else."

She wanted to ask more, but she let it be. "All right. I'm off."

"Where are you going?"

"Where do I always go? See you tomorrow. Can you barbecue turkey?"

"I beg of you, don't do that. If it's too hot for the oven we'll go out." Tomorrow was Thanksgiving, but it felt more like August than early October.

The kids and I read stories, played games, ate treats, got out the guitars and harmonicas and had our own wholesome little blues day. On Monday we ate turkey, properly roasted. It was a fun weekend and it took my mind off the murder investigation. Once I got Tom and Normie to school on Tuesday, though, I had only one thing on my mind. I headed immediately to St. Bernadette's, only to hear that my witness, Eileen Darragh, was out of town for the day on a course. She might, however, be in the office that evening. I would have to wait.

I thought over everything I could recall about Father Michael O'Flaherty: his keen interest in violent crime; his heated discussion with Moody Walker in Tim Hortons about a priestly connection to the Leeza Rae murder; O'Flaherty's mysterious walks at night; his love of dancing with the young women. What had I been told about O'Flaherty's whereabouts the night Leeza was killed? All I could remember was Brennan saying he and Mike had a nightcap after the dance, and he assumed Mike had gone to bed. None of it had added up to murder — until now.

III

It was nearly nine o'clock before I got Normie settled in bed, and put Tommy in charge of the house. I drove to the centre. Would Eileen be there? I saw only one light, but the door was unlocked. Lax security. That suggested Eileen was not on the job. I went in. The light was coming from the director's office, so I peeked inside. I heard the voice of authority.

"Who is it?"

"Good evening, Sister Dunne. It's Monty Collins. I was just wondering whether Eileen was around. I forgot to check something with her last time we talked."

The nun, as crisp and alert as if she had just commenced her work day, came out to meet me. "The last time you talked to Eileen Darragh that I know of, she was in no condition to answer questions from you or anyone else."

Obviously, I was not going to be able to slip anything past Marguerite. "Right. She was a little overwrought."

Suddenly I remembered there was something the nun had said that night. It had struck me at the time, then vanished in the stress and turmoil of the following days. What was it?

"How is he getting along?" Marguerite asked. "I catch a glimpse of him once in a while, but he doesn't stop by to chat."

"I cannot imagine how he's holding up as well as he is," I answered.

"He's made of sterner stuff than a lot of us."

"He said something similar about you," I told her. She emitted a short bark of laughter.

"What is your take on these murders, Sister? Have you any idea who would kill two women and make it look as though Brennan had done it?"

She was shaking her head before I had finished speaking. She answered softly. "I don't know. I have thought about this over and over and over. I can't see it being anyone here. There could have been people in these women's lives who had a motive, but where is the tie to Brennan? I do not deal well with this kind of frustration, with being unable to solve a problem. I've felt utterly useless all through this."

I decided to take a chance. "What do you make of this interest Father O'Flaherty has in crime and police work?"

If I had expected her to be offended on his behalf, I was wrong. She answered as if I had inquired about his enthusiasm for standing with a microphone at the head of a tour bus, answering the same dumb questions about Ireland, year after year.

"I've always thought it a harmless diversion, like reading murder mysteries. Who isn't interested in what the police are up to? He has some cronies on the force. It never occurred to me that there was anything untoward about it. Any more than there is in his devotion to the Blessed Virgin. Or the pleasure he seems to take in making his hospital rounds. You won't get me in a hospital unless you knock me senseless and strap me to a board." This from a woman who had stood unflinching in the crossfire, while women and children were being evacuated in war-torn Central America.

"This devotion of his to the Virgin Mary —"

She interrupted. "Does it mean he holds the Virgin Mother up as the ideal, against which all other women are measured? And lashes out with violence when they turn out to be neither virginal nor motherly? I never thought of it."

"Right. Does he think that way, do you suppose?" I persisted.

"Father O'Flaherty is an old-fashioned kind of man in many ways. A product of his generation, certainly. But I have always had the impression that he loves — truly loves, I mean — women. I have to get going. Shall we go out together?"

It was only when we reached her car that I remembered what the nun had said the night the jury went out. "Sister?"

"Mmm?"

"You said something that last night we were here, and I meant to ask you about it. You were talking about the fact that Brennan had fathered a child and you said: 'A child who was in his life, however briefly.' That struck me as an odd phrase. It was my understanding that he and his girlfriend had broken up during her pregnancy, long before the baby was born." I was not about to recount my telephone conversation with Sandra Worthington. "Wouldn't it be stretching things, under those circumstances, to say that the child was briefly in his life?"

Sister Dunne looked distinctly uncomfortable. "A careless choice of words on my part."

I was not about to drop it. "Careless in that you were inaccurate, or careless in that you revealed something you had not meant to reveal?"

She got into the driver's seat and spoke to me through the open window. "Come around and have a seat, Monty." She leaned over

236

and unlocked the passenger door. I obeyed. "I don't see how this can hurt him, at this point. At least not beyond the hurt suffered by a very private individual when anything personal is hashed about by others. I got a phone call, near the end of the trial. After that torturous cross-examination. The call originally went to the rectory and Mrs. Kelly, thick as she is in many ways, caught the scent of something complicated and directed the caller over to me." I sat immobile beside the nun, bracing myself for whatever was coming. "The woman was a home care nurse in Connecticut. She wouldn't tell me much, but she wanted someone up here to know that Brennan was not the kind of man — she said 'young man,' actually, so it was clear she was talking about the past — not the kind of young man the prosecution was making him out to be."

"Is this yet another old flame of Brennan's?" I asked.

"No. She is a former maternity nurse. She was on duty the night Brennan's child was born." I stared at Marguerite. Sandra had made it painfully clear that Brennan had left her to face the birth all by herself. Marguerite spoke again. "Brennan 'cared.' That's all she would say. 'The young priest cared.'" Sister Dunne sighed. "I don't see what good this can do him now. It may even complicate things for him in ways we cannot foresee. But if you want to talk to her, she left me her name and number. Call me at the office tomorrow." I got out of the car and closed the door and watched Marguerite drive off.

When I turned to go to my car I looked at the centre and realized that the place was not in darkness. A light was on. I hesitated, then started for the door. Had Marguerite locked it after us, or not? I reached for the door and it opened.

IV

The corridor was dim, the only light coming from a room down the hall and around the corner. I headed in that direction. Suddenly the building was plunged into darkness. I turned to leave, then heard footsteps rapidly approaching. I whirled and came face to face with Father O'Flaherty. As dark as it was, I could read his body language; his usual good cheer was gone. He barked out something I could not catch, and raised his right arm. He had something in his hand. I backed up and put an arm out to fend off a blow.

"How in the hell —" he was nearly shouting "— could something like this blow a fuse, just by being plugged into the wall? It's an adapter, isn't it? What else are you supposed to do with it? Monty, do you know? Here, have a look. If you can see without light."

I willed myself to resume normal breathing.

"I've been trying to set up the equipment for our big weekend: a slide projector, VCR, some other damnable stuff. Maybe I plugged too many things in one outlet. I'd better leave it till the young fellows come in tomorrow." For the first time, he questioned why I was there. "What brings you out tonight, Monty?"

I made a split-second decision. "I was looking for Brennan, but why don't you and I have a seat for a few minutes? Leave a note on Eileen's desk, telling her there's a fuse that needs replacing. Then let's have a word."

He nodded and went into the office. When he returned, I took him by the elbow and sat him in a chair in one of the meeting rooms. I managed to arrange things so his face was illuminated by a street light just outside the window.

"Knights of Columbus are coming to town, I hear. Are you expecting a big turnout?"

He started to describe the weekend plans, and I listened with half an ear. When he paused, I asked what kind of entertainment he would be putting on. He made a crack about buying out the Clyde Street Liquor Store, then talked about Masses and a movie. Finally, the variety show.

"The variety show I saw, you mean?"

"Oh, were you there Monty?"

"I missed the stage production, but I saw the video."

"Sure, I remember now. At the church fair. Yes, yes." His mood was lifting.

"The children's choir was the highlight for me, I'd have to say." I didn't take my eyes from his face. "Brennan does a wonderful job with those children. This is a dreadful business. I hope I'll be able to get it straightened out when it goes to the Court of Appeal."

Father O'Flaherty focused innocent-looking light blue eyes on me. "Surely, they'll see reason in the Appeal Court. I've often wondered about the jury system, to be honest with you, Monty. Wouldn't you think, if they couldn't find first degree, they would have acquitted him? A priest, for goodness sake."

"You don't think a priest would be capable of murder, Father?"

"Of course not! Not unless there was something wrong with the man."

"What if the priest thought someone had committed an unforgivable sin, or an evil deed, and should be punished?"

"It is God who forgives and God who punishes," O'Flaherty said urgently. "It's not up to us."

"Back to this variety show, Father. Do you think you'll put on another one any time soon?" I asked with feigned enthusiasm.

"It would be fun to do again, but a lot of work for sure." He seemed to mull the idea over.

"Where do you get all the props and the costumes? The wigs and things?"

"Oh, people bring them in, donate things. That's the least of it."

I tried to move so my face was in shadow, while the priest's was still in the light. "That Beethoven wig was very effective on Brennan."

"Yes, wasn't it! He was a dandy Beethoven." Father O'Flaherty smiled.

"Somebody told me the children had a good laugh afterwards, when the wig was pulled off. It had got itself pretty well affixed to Brennan's head. You just about yanked him to his feet by the hair, as I heard it." I watched him intently.

"Did I now? The poor lad. I don't remember it at all." If he was lying, it was impossible to tell.

"What became of the wig? I'm sure it would be useful again."

"Oh, I don't know. You'd have to ask the young girl. Erin Christie. I think Erin brought it in. She played the part of Father Burke in the show. Excited about the role, she was. Brennan was very good to her when she had some sort of trouble. Man trouble maybe. She didn't confide in me. Probably thought I was too old to remember things like that! You know young people, how they are. You're not much more than a lad yourself. Well, I've had it for one day. Off to dreamland. I'll tell Brennan you were looking for him, shall I Monty?"

"No, that's all right, Father. He'll only worry that it's something urgent. I'd better wait till tomorrow."

We said our goodbyes and left. What was I to make of the conversation? I wasn't able to detect even a glimmer of a guilty conscience in the man. But then some murderers have no conscience and can face the world with a brazen countenance knowing there is no guilt to be seen flickering behind their eyes. All night, when I should have been catching up on my sleep, I went over and over the conversation with O'Flaherty, trying to figure out whether I had missed something.

V

The next morning I dropped in on Eileen Darragh. "Oh good, Eileen, you're here."

"I've always been here, Monty," she quipped, as she stuck papers into a two-pronged file clip. If she was embarrassed about our last encounter she gave no sign of it.

"True enough in your case. I'd just like to ask you something in confidence. There's probably nothing to it." She looked wary. "You remember the variety show the centre put on last Christmas?"

"I sure do."

"I enjoyed the Beethoven skit, by the way. I was told that was your idea."

"Thank you. Yes, it was. Erin and I put it together. We saw it as a way to get the choir into the show and have a bit of a lark at the same time."

"And poke a bit of fun at the choirmaster in the process."

She turned slightly pink. "Yes, that too." She avoided my eyes but she laughed. "Didn't hurt him in the least!"

"After the skit was over, Eileen, I understand you and the other cast members were in a little room, getting the costumes off, and . . ." I heard the sound of paper sliding to the floor. The file on Eileen's lap had fallen, and she looked at it as if she had no idea what to do with it. "Father Burke says Mike O'Flaherty was a little rough removing the Beethoven wig."

"Father Burke told you that?"

"Yes, he did."

"Oh, thank God!"

"Is that what happened?" I asked.

"Yes, that's what happened."

"Did you say anything at the time?"

Eileen tilted her head and directed her gaze somewhere above the door behind me. "I just can't remember what I said." She returned her focus to me. "I've thought of that since, Monty. Well, you can imagine. I've relived the scene in my mind, over and over. Just the thought that Mike . . . Father O'Flaherty . . . it's impossible! I didn't even remember the wig until Father Burke's trial started, then it came back to me. I should have said something. But I didn't know what to do." Her voice faltered. "It may have been completely innocent on Father O'Flaherty's part. Must have been. I mean, Mike, of all people. You can't really think . . ."

"You're right, Eileen. There may be a completely innocent explanation. So it's vital that we keep this conversation between the two of us."

"Of course," she agreed, her relief plainly visible. The secret was no longer quite as much of a burden now that it had been shared.

"Monty?"

"Yes?"

"Thank God Father Burke remembered! If he had forgotten and I had just sat here, I would never be able to forgive myself." She must have been under a great strain, not knowing whether to come forward, not wanting to pit one beloved priest against the other.

"No, you're covered there." I smiled as I got up to leave, my mind already on my next move. "Oh, one more thing." She looked alert. What was I going to unload on her now? "What became of the wig after the show?"

"I don't know. I took all the costumes and props and put them in the basement with our other junk. Someone was helping me. One of the girls. But I don't think the wig was there, because Erin mentioned keeping it for some other project she was planning. If it was there, she probably would have . . . oh, I just don't know, Monty. I can't remember."

"All right. Just leave everything where it is and make sure nobody touches the stuff until, or unless, I speak to you about it again. Who goes down to the basement?"

"People don't go down there very often. I do once in a while. The priests might. Sister Marguerite? I'd say not. Maybe the youth workers."

"Where did it come from, the wig?"

"Tyler bought it. With a lot of the other costumes for the show. I sent him off to Frenchy's with fifteen bucks in his pocket." Frenchy's, the chain of Maritime second-hand clothing stores, where unemployed fish plant workers and doctors' wives shopped for everything from cleaning rags to designer garments for prices as low as a couple of dollars.

"All right, Eileen. I'm off. I know I can rely on you."

As soon as I was in my office, I called Brennan to fill him in. "Eileen confirms what you told me about O'Flaherty pulling the wig off, and it's eating away at her that she didn't speak up about it. Though I'm sure we can both understand why she wouldn't want to rush to judgment about Father O'Flaherty."

"Exactly. Here we are in the sober light of day, and it seems absurd to have suspected Michael. Of all people."

"But we've got him pulling the wig off, with the inevitable hair samples the killer wanted. What kind of a liar do you think O'Flaherty would make?"

"What do you mean?"

"I questioned him about it." Silence at the other end. "I put it in the context of the entertainment planned for the Knights of Columbus. I caught up with him last night at the centre, sat him down with a light shining in his face. So to speak. And brought up the subject of the skit and the wig. He didn't deny it." I waited for a reaction. "Brennan?"

"I'm listening."

"He didn't deny that it happened that way. But the thing is, he didn't look the least flustered. 'Oh, did I now? I don't remember.' Is he capable of being that cool under fire?"

"I wouldn't have thought so. You've played poker with him. You know every card in his hand just by the face on him."

"Right. Well, we're going to have to go deeper into this. But in the meantime, carry on the way you always **do.** And, though it sounds preposterous, be on guard."

"You're right. It does sound preposterous. But I hear you."

Chapter 18

How long a distance covered since we lost that line.
An answer hovers in the air.
Fingers recall numbers that have slipped the mind,
almost hoping no one's there . . .
If we could trace our steps — recreate the crime —
Find our way back through the woods,
If we could focus on the finest point in time
where we were both misunderstood.
— Lennie Gallant, Chris LeDrew, "Something Unspoken"

I

I wanted to give myself a break from thinking about the case. The night after I spoke to Eileen about the wig I was sitting home, picking out a tune on an old acoustic guitar, determined to relax. But the case continued to occupy my thoughts. We had confirmation of Brennan's revelation about O'Flaherty yanking the wig off his head, and pulling Brennan's hair out in the process. We had O'Flaherty claiming he could not remember, but not denying it. Not bothering to deny it, was a more accurate description. Was he an accomplished and ruthless liar? Was it possible that something so significant, the wig incident and the potential for obtaining the needed hair samples, was not even a factor in the case? No. It had to be a factor, a key element of the planning, at least for the first killing. But how did it fit in with the other pieces of the puzzle, the scar and the initials?

I did not know what experts the police had consulted about the meaning of IBR. The Crown had not led any evidence on the point. How could they? The only person who really knew what the letters stood for was the killer. And the police didn't need an explanation; they had the sign of the cross, carved into the bodies of the two victims, a symbol identical to the one branded on the chest of the accused. Burke could think of no one who knew the scar intimately. The facts were stark: if there wasn't anyone else, then he had killed the women. I desperately wanted to find another explanation.

I decided to look at those confounding letters. Every time I had put my mind to them, I had considered and rejected the idea of asking Burke to participate. If he was guilty he would lead me on a chase from here to eternity to keep me from solving the riddle. Finally, after trying every alphabetical and numerical combination my tired brain could produce, I made up my mind to hash it out with him anyway. It might not bring me any closer to establishing a defence — in fact, I could end up facing the possibility that there was no defence — but I might be an older and wiser man by the end of the night.

It was nine in the evening when I called the rectory, and Mrs. Kelly told me Father Burke was in his room with some other priests, but she graciously offered to take a message from me, a mere layman, asking him to call me. I sat by the phone with a pen and paper making up crosswords and other puzzles with the letters IBR. The phone rang at 9:15.

"Monty. Brennan here."

"I know your voice now, Brennan. I have for some time."

"Ah. I suppose you do. Mrs. K. just came up with your message." I could hear conversation and laughter in the background. If there had been any strain involved in a meeting with fellow priests after his conviction, it must have eased. I had little doubt that, as painful as it would be, he would have proclaimed his innocence to everyone he had to see. Otherwise, social intercourse would have been impossible.

"Can you spare me a few minutes, Brennan? If so, I'd like to scoot in to see you."

"Sure thing. I'm trying to keep order here with a bunch of football hooligans. Come on over."

He was still in his black shirt and Roman collar when I arrived, as were his guests. Burke and three priests I didn't know were sitting around a table with books and papers spread in front of them. They appeared to be working, but they had a football game on television.

Notre Dame and Purdue. I did a double take. I had seen the game Saturday afternoon. Then I noticed the VCR and concluded somebody was a gridiron fanatic. One priest knew every play and was cuing the others about what to expect. It took me a moment to realize that I had never seen a television in Burke's room before. The Notre Dame enthusiast saw me looking at it and explained: "O'Flaherty's. He's out, so we heisted it. It's going back after the game. Brennan doesn't deign to watch television." The priests each had a beer in front of them, and were quick to offer me one. Brennan and an older man were smoking.

"Good evening, Montague," Brennan greeted me. "Something on your mind? Come on." He put an arm around my shoulder, held the cigarette away from me with the other hand, and leaned his ear in towards me. "You remember how it goes: Bless me Father, for I have sinned. It has been thirty years since my last confession."

"You're a card, Brennan. I want us to put our heads together and try to decode this IBR business."

His face clouded over. "All right, all right. These guys won't be here much longer. Have a seat." I nursed a beer and listened to the priests planning a theology seminar. We were a long, long way from the Baltimore Catechism; it was Johannine this and Christological that, and something called the "hypostatic union," which seemed to relate to the dual nature of Christ as human and divine. Not for the first time, I was struck by how much there was to know in this world, and the next. And how, after twenty years of formal education, I was well versed in some subjects and not even literate in others. I tuned in to the game, just as Purdue's quarterback got sacked. Click, whirr, the tape rewound and Purdue got sacked again.

When the game was over, the guests unplugged the television and made ready to transport it to its rightful home. I leapt up to offer my services because I could not resist the chance to see O'Flaherty's room. It was at the end of a corridor that ran at right angles to Brennan's. A little bit of Ireland on North American soil. Mike had Irish posters, a calendar, books, a wall map, and a 1950s record player, with an LP by Paddy someone on the turntable. One bureau held a collection of Celtic crosses, carved of stone, ranging in height from ten inches or so to nearly two feet. One of the priests bumped into the table on his way by and knocked one of the crosses onto the floor.

Luckily, it didn't break, and he moved his foot out of the way just in time. "Would I get Workers' Compensation if I lost a toe returning a stolen TV?" The only non-Irish items on display were some pre-Vatican II missals, a wall devoted to group photos of children making their First Communion, and a little shrine to the Blessed Virgin with fresh flowers (costly at this time of year, I would have thought) placed where their fragrance could be enjoyed by the Holy Mother.

When I returned to Brennan's room, he and I sat down and faced each other across his table. "You're back in uniform."

"I am. If I take the attitude that I don't want to disgrace the collar, that's tantamount to saying I'm guilty. Which I'm not. And He knows it." His eyes looked heavenward. "So I dress like the other fellows around here."

I got to the point. "I assume you've tried your hand at decoding IBR already, applying arcane principles of biblical interpretation?"

"No, I have not. It's some psycho's initials. Or the initials of his other personality." He leaned back and crossed his arms. "We could be here all night and be none the wiser at the end of it."

"Let's give it a shot. So to speak." I raised my eyebrows in the direction of the drinks cupboard.

"Divest ourselves of a few brain cells and we may start to think like the killer, you're suggesting." He poured us each an Irish whiskey and freed himself of his clerical collar. "Let's get to it."

"All right," I began. "IBR. It could be someone's initials. It could be 'I, so-and-so.'"

"Yeah. 'I, Brennan.' Oops, I forgot. There are five more letters in my name and I don't have room for them on this small body. Because I have to carve a crucifix on the other side. Next time I'll pick on someone my own size."

I ignored him and continued. "That I. Doesn't I appear on the real crucifix?"

Brennan went to a drawer and pulled out an old wooden cross with the crucified Jesus on it in ivory. "Comes from home. Ireland, I mean. Very old. See here? INRI. J in Latin is of course I. *Iesus Nazarenus Rex Iudaeorum.* Jesus of Nazareth, King of the Jews. A mocking tribute."

"So, this could be a J. If the person was thinking that way, he'd probably be talking about Jesus, right?"

"I suppose so."

"It could be Jesus, B something, then R, maybe Rex."

"It could be anything. And we're not on the same wavelength as whoever wrote it," my client snapped.

"Come on Brennan, it's either this or the crucifix scar, and I got nowhere with you on that." I sipped my drink. "Now, it may be letters or it may be numbers. What letter of the alphabet is I? Nine, correct? B is two. R is, let me count here, eighteen. Nine, two, eighteen. Nine times two is eighteen. Eighteen divided by nine is two. Do any of these numbers strike you as significant?"

"Not me, but I'll bet they set off murderous impulses in somebody." The priest sighed with exasperation and stared out the window into the darkness.

"Could it be an address? Someone's birthday? Somebody born in 1918, now aged seventy-two? Ring any chimes for you?" No reply. "Can you think of anything significant that happened February ninth or September second of 1918? First World War." Again no reply. "What was going on in Ireland in 1918?"

"Everybody was drinking and shagging and having babies. Or was that some other year?"

"Politically. Historically. What was happening?"

"The Easter Rising was over. The Troubles had yet to begin."

"Which troubles were these?"

"Anglo-Irish War, 1919 to 1921. The IRA versus the Black and Tans. Before your grandfather Collins signed the Treaty."

"Mike O'Flaherty seems to think there's a bit of Collins blood in you, Brennan. A resemblance when you were younger."

"Could be, but it must be fairly indirect. The man died in 1922."

"All right. Let's move on. Add all these figures up and you get twenty-nine."

I looked at Brennan's watch. It was eleven-forty-five. In Roman numerals. "What if they are Roman numerals?" I tried. He looked at me as if I were the class dunce. "I is one, but there's no B or R, is there?"

"You shouldn't spend so many nights without sleep. Your mind is not working in top condition here, Monty."

"What if one of them, the I, is a Roman numeral, and the others are —"

"With so little time and so little space to work in, do you think this kook is going to get complicated?" Brennan asked.

"The first thing one would think of is a Bible verse, but not with this combination. I mean Bible verses would be cited like John 3:16, right?"

"Very good. You've opened the Bible at some point in your life. You give me hope, Collins."

"Nah. There's always a guy holding it up for the cameras at the Super Bowl."

"Ah. Well, I have to get up very early in the morning."

"Go ahead. Pour me another on your way by." He poured me a whiskey, then went into the bathroom. I could hear water running, teeth being brushed, something falling and skipping across the floor, Brennan cursing. He came out, stripped down to a pair of blindingly white gym shorts, and climbed into his bed.

"Do you always sleep like that?"

"Like what?"

"With just a pair of shorts on?"

"What were you expecting, jammies with pictures of the BVM all over them?"

"BVM?"

"Blessed Virgin Mary! I thought you were brought up Catholic!"

"Are you a light sleeper? Or are you out once you're out?"

"Goodnight, Montague. Don't let the door bang you in the arse on your way out," he advised, and turned away.

I got up and paced around the room. I looked over the music collection and the shelves full of books I had never heard of, in English, Italian, Latin and German, along with several versions of the Bible.

"Brennan!"

"What?" he moaned from the edge of sleep.

"Who wrote the first book of the Bible?"

"New Testament or Old?"

"New Testament, for starters. Who wrote the first gospel?"

"Mark."

"What does Mark 2:18 say?"

"How the hell would I know?" This from a priest.

"I thought you guys knew the Bible front to back."

"I'm not a Jehovah's Witness. Though I think it may be something about the Pharisees." He sat up and reached for something in the drawer of his bedside table, then turned on a small lamp and waved a Bible at me. "This is the one I'd recommend you read when you finally grow up and realize you've been missing out on the Word of God. Don't quote me on this, but do not get one of the new dumbed-down versions. Mark 2:18 is all about John the Baptist and fasting. I can't see anything for us in that, can you?"

"Not really. Is there a book of the Bible that starts with an I?"

"Is Isaiah, like the BVM, unknown to you, Montague?"

I took the Bible that was dangling from his hand, and thumbed through the Old Testament. I stared at the verse. "Brennan. This could be it. Isaiah 2:18: 'And the idols he shall utterly abolish.'"

"Ah."

"An idol is something worshipped," I began. "An image . . ."

"Speaking biblically, an idol is a false god."

"So somebody thinks . . ."

"Somebody thinks Leeza Rae and Tanya Cudmore were setting themselves up as false gods? I doubt it."

"Maybe you're the false god."

"If I'm the false god, why didn't the killer abolish me, utterly? Goodnight, Monty."

I wasn't ready to give up on the false god angle. It struck me as exactly the kind of verse a religious zealot would fasten on. Burke had fallen asleep. I was lost in thought, flipping the pages of the Bible. Then I noticed something.

"Brennan!" I exclaimed, and the form between the sheets jolted awake again. "Matthew is the first book in the New Testament. Look!"

"I don't have to *look*, Collins. I know where it is," he said, in his talking-to-an-imbecile voice.

"But you said it was Mark. It's really Matthew. I remember now: Matthew, Mark, Luke, and John."

"Matthew is traditionally placed first in the New Testament. You asked me who wrote the first gospel. It was Mark. Chronologically. Biblical scholars have long known —"

I interrupted. "But the layman, or someone wanting to send a message to the laymen of the world, would likely use Matthew.

Numero uno, in Roman numerals, at least to the non-scholar. Let me see. Matthew 2:18 . . ."

But Burke was ahead of me, sitting up and wide awake: "This one I know. 'In Rama was there a voice heard, lamentation, and weeping, and great mourning, Rachel weeping for her children, and would not be comforted, because they are not.'"

II

"It's either a woman or it's a man who can easily identify with a woman."

It was the morning after we solved the IBR riddle; Brennan and I were closeted in my office with a "hold all calls" order in effect. I pursued my line of reasoning: "How often do guys do that, do you suppose? Identify strongly with female characters in a story. I suspect women are better at understanding male figures, if only because they are so used to seeing males in the leading roles in a culture dominated by men. But I may be talking through my hat. What do you think?" Brennan shrugged. "Something tells me a religious man might have less trouble here, being steeped in the Bible and its figures, the saints, whatever. That's just a hunch. Probably a preconception, given all the religious trappings to this case. And it's obviously someone with strong feelings about children." Burke had nothing to say.

"Let's look at women then." Silence again. "What's the matter, Brennan? Has this given you some ideas about a suspect you're not sharing with me?"

He shook his head.

Although there could have been any number of women saddened by the death of little Janeece Tuck, or outraged by the violation of the young girl who was the victim of the rape aided and abetted by Leeza Rae, we both knew there could only be a very small number of women weeping for both. The pool of suspects was especially limited when one factored in the connection with Brennan Burke. It had to be someone at St. Bernadette's.

"So we both know who we're talking about: Eileen Darragh, Marguerite Dunne, and possibly Erin Christie. There must be other young women at the centre from time to time. Perhaps we'll have to take a look at the teachers. You can fill me in on them. What you know about them and what you think they know about you. But let's start with the known quantities, Marguerite and Eileen. Maybe Erin. I take it there's no need to throw poor old Mrs. Kelly into a dank room and shine a bright light in her face."

Brennan looked as if he had spent a long night with a cruel and merciless light shining in his face. He finally spoke: "Eileen Darragh? How can we be sitting here speaking calmly of the notion that she's a killer? And Marguerite? She'd kill you with sharp words, not with a blunt object."

"But think about it, Brennan. Take Eileen —"

"She's spent her life helping young people at St. Bernadette's. She's not going to start killing them. Let alone go off the deep end and try to pin it on a priest. The whole idea is daft."

"Well, she can probably identify with children. She told me some time ago that she was supposed to be adopted as a child, but it fell through. Did you know that?"

"No, I didn't. What a shame."

"Yeah, so she'd be sympathetic to children."

"She'd be sympathetic to people who had a hard life. Like the two victims, both of them disadvantaged women with very unfortunate backgrounds."

I could not argue with that. But maybe there was another angle to be played here. "Brennan, you must know Eileen has strong feelings for you."

"What are you on about now, Collins?" He seemed genuinely confounded.

"Do you mean to tell me you have never noticed that she is in love with you, or infatuated, or has a crush?"

"Don't be telling me that!" He put a hand up to ward me off.

"Very strong feelings on her part. Frustrated longing —" He had his hand up again but I persisted. "You don't need me to tell you that kind of thing can be transmuted into a white-hot flame of hatred."

"Where did all this come from? How do you know this?"

"It's obvious to everyone but you, Brennan. Even the young people at the centre have noticed that she's tongue-tied around you. I've seen her blush painfully in your presence. And how could you forget the night the jury went out? She was sobbing uncontrollably. You had turned your back, so you didn't see how she wrapped her arms around herself after you had held her for a few minutes."

"Listen to yourself, Monty. You started out by saying she's a murderer who wanted to pin the killings on me, and you ended up saying she was crying because she was afraid I'd be convicted. You've ceased to make sense."

"I don't pretend to understand the woman. But unrequited love —"

"Will you get off that? Even if there is something in it, what are you suggesting? She killed Leeza Rae in a jealous rage? Because I danced with her? I didn't even like the Rae girl, to be brutally honest. I tended to avoid her. Eileen could probably see that, being at the centre every day. And what about Tanya Cudmore? What would be Eileen's motive there? And do not, do not try to tell me Eileen was doing me a favour by killing off the stepmother of little Janeece. One killing out of hate and the other out of love. And if it's love — as you put it, not I — what would be the point of having me locked away somewhere for the rest of my life? She'd never see me again."

"She could start paying you regular visits. Have your undivided attention," I needled him.

"You're not a well man, Montague. Eileen can have my undivided attention any time she wants it. All she has to do is ask me to be a spiritual adviser. I do that for a few parishioners. One of the young girls at the centre, and other people. Have private talks with them about their faith, theology, all the rest of it. She knows that. But this is sick. So spare me."

Brennan had both arms across my desk by this time and was leaning over as if to persuade me through sheer physical presence. "And besides, I can promise you that Eileen Darragh never got within sighting range of this thing on my chest. You asked me way back what women might have seen me undressed. Sex with Eileen? I'd have to go upstairs and get it stiff first. I only wish you hadn't put me in a corner, where I have to speak of her that way.

"And what are you trying to say, that she rubbed up against me in the corridor in the hope that some of my hair just might fall out at that moment and stick to her, and that she could then transfer it to two separate victims, three months apart? The second victim being Tanya Cudmore, who hadn't entered anyone's mind until after Janeece died? Oh Christ, Monty. Let's get a grip."

"All right, all right." I gave him a few minutes to wind down. "We have to come up with a woman who is intimately familiar with the scar. But I don't have any trouble finding a female motive. Maura linked the two cases without hesitation when we were talking about something else entirely. I'm trying to remember the conversation now. We were having dinner the other night, after a lot of bickering, and I brought up that case you sat in on, the mother who gave her child away and stayed with the child abuser."

"Don't be reminding me of that again."

"Maura got all worked up and started talking about the two murder cases. 'It's just like Leeza Rae. It's just like Tanya Cudmore.' Same thing to her. Once again the female mind displays an advantage we don't seem to have."

Brennan allowed himself a smile. "So we're looking for a woman who thinks like Maura."

"I wouldn't put it past her to murder with her bare hands someone who had hurt a child. Or who had stood by and let a child be hurt. If you can find a way to link her to the crimes, Brennan, I'll turn her in myself."

"I appreciate your dedication to your clients, Collins."

"But for the forensics to work, particularly the scar, you would have to have slept with her."

He raised an eyebrow at me, looked at his watch, and said: "Can you put off her arrest till morning? But, seriously, let's get our brain cells in gear."

"Marguerite. She withstood gunfire to bring women and children out of a battle zone in Central America. She was willing and ready to give up her life for them. How do you suppose she would view the way Janeece and the young rape victim were treated right under her nose?"

"She would take a dim view of it. But she didn't go out and kill anyone. She likely didn't even know the stories behind the rape or the death of Janeece. She probably wouldn't have known Tanya Cudmore from . . . Oh, wait, I guess she did know Tanya after all. I remember now. Tanya fell afoul of the good sister one day after choir practice, when she showed up two hours late to get Janeece. Marguerite gave her a tuning, the way I heard it. Flayed the hide off her. Mike O'Flaherty filled me in, in great detail. This was a verbal attack, I mean, as I'm sure you know. The woman has a tongue that would leave you skinned alive like St. Bartholomew."

"So, we have Marguerite already clued in to the fact that Cudmore was a negligent stepparent. And she did know Leeza Rae."

"But she didn't know me, Montague, not without my clothes on."

"Do you think it's possible she came into your room some time to pick up a book when you were asleep?"

"For Christ's sake, Monty."

If anyone had the wherewithal to work her way around the church bureaucracies in New York, and unearth a photo or a description of that mysterious mark, it was Marguerite Dunne. But we had employed an investigator in New York to question anyone who might have access to old files or photographs of Brennan, and he was satisfied that nobody had been fishing for that kind of information.

"I have a new-found respect for the police, Brennan. How do they ever figure this stuff out? I'll be quite happy to stay on the other side, picking apart whatever case they have made, rather than trying to make a case myself."

Brennan was sitting back with his eyes closed. "Do you suppose we gave up too soon on that poor devil we caught in the church? That vandal. You said somebody had been rifling through the personnel files at the archdiocese office. And didn't you once tell me he was at the law library, reading cases?"

"He wouldn't have known the victims."

"If he had been hanging around here, he might have met Leeza."

"But not Tanya Cudmore. Everywhere we go we come to a dead end."

"He wouldn't have to know Cudmore, Monty, just my connection with Janeece. He could have seen that news story about the funeral."

There was some truth in that. And, if he had been hurt in some way himself, he may have sympathized with young people being mistreated. Certainly something had happened to set him off. And someone at the archdiocese office said Jason had participated in a protest. An older woman who had looked away when I turned towards her. I wondered if she was talking about a demonstration at the local abortion clinic. I would have to check it out. In the meantime, my client looked as if he needed a break. Brennan and I called it a day and went our separate ways.

Chapter 19

Will I go to the Highlands with you sir?
Such a thing it never could be
For I know not the name you have taken or
why you roam ragged and free.
— Cameron/MacGillivary, "Elizabeth Lindsay Meets Ronald MacDonald"

I

My client wasn't the only one who needed a break. That Saturday I read for a while and watched a football game. I called Maura just before suppertime, with the idea that we might have a family meal and watch a movie. Then she and I could take in Matt Minglewood's "Rocking the Blues" gig at the Dirty O. But the kids were out, Normie at a friend's for a sleepover, and Tommy at a party. My wife obviously had plans, and she did not share them with me. I was disappointed, but I would see the kids tomorrow. I didn't so much decide my next move as sidle into it. I knew a lot of my fellow bluesmen would be at the Dirty O, so that's where I went. Ed, fellow Functus member, and his wife Donna were there, and so was Bev, with another woman named Cheryl. The music was great, as always, and everyone was in a party mood. I kept my alcohol consumption down. My judgment wasn't one hundred percent, however, because I ended up breaking a rule I had made for myself long before. I brought Bev home to my place.

We spent the same sort of night we had spent last time, though on this occasion we didn't get past the living room, and we did not wake up until the sun was high in the sky. At least, I woke up. And when I did, I thought I was hallucinating. So I clamped my eyes shut and prayed that the vision I had just experienced wasn't real. Sitting across from me, in the living room, smoking a cigarette, with what looked like my spare key dangling from his pinkie finger, was a smiling cleric in black with a little white showing at the collar. The Burke case had finally, perhaps inevitably, pushed me over the line into psychosis. I pulled the quilt over my head, groaned, and looked again. But he was still there, as he would always be. Bev was lying on her back farther up the couch, sound asleep, an arm dangling to the floor. The quilt was over her hips. She had something draped over her from the waist up: a leather jacket. Brennan's?

"Can you possibly be here?" I rasped. "Or did I finally shoot myself and wind up in hell?"

"You really shouldn't leave this key hanging out there on the shed," he replied. "The worst sort of people could get in here." He leaned over. "Are you awake?"

"I hope not. How long have you been here?"

"I found new graffiti in the church."

I eyed Bev with unease. She was beginning to stir. "Really. Was there a break-in?"

"Broken window."

"Not the stained glass!"

"No. A window in the sacristy."

"Did you call the police?"

"Are you *well?* I don't want the police anywhere near me."

"All right."

It was at that point that Bev came to. Her eyes opened and she squinted at me as if she couldn't quite place me. Then she caught sight of Father Burke in the chair across from us.

"What the fuck?"

"Morning, sunshine," he chirped.

She looked at me accusingly. "What did you do?"

"Nothing! He just showed up."

"Like hell."

"Really, he —"

"I want a shower. Where is it?" I pointed upstairs. She wrapped Burke's jacket around herself and left the room.

"Did I come at an awkward time?" Insufferable. "I'm afraid I woke your wife from a sound sleep this morning."

"You did? That means you're not very popular anywhere today, doesn't it?"

"She wasn't too bad. Said she wanted to get the kids going early anyway. I tried you first but you weren't up yet. I tend to forget that not everyone is up for early Mass on Sunday the way I am. Of course, my Saturday night companions were the Knights of Columbus, so I begged off for an early retirement." He smiled the smile of the righteous.

"Yeah." My eyes started to close, then jerked open. "Jesus! What time was that?" I looked at my wrist, but my watch was not in evidence. I groped around in the quilt, found my jeans, pulled them on, then staggered to my feet and batted at my hair.

"When was what?" Burke asked. "When did I call Maura? Around nine-thirty, I suppose. Then I stopped for a bite to eat and came out here. You know, I can't decide which is the real you, Montague, the woozy half-dressed degenerate or the lordly barrister in his gown and tabs."

"You may find this hard to believe, Burke, but I've had a similar problem trying to get a fix on you — did you say 'get the kids going early?'"

"That's what she said. Where would they be going?" There was no need for further speculation. We heard the crunching of gravel in the driveway.

"Shit!" I exclaimed. "I'll get into —"

"There's somebody in the shower, remember," Brennan said helpfully.

And in they barged. Normie launched herself at my neck and clung. I swung her up and kissed her. Tommy got down to business. "Hey, Dad. Hi, Father Burke. How ya doin? Dad, I have to use your Fender. Now. Before I lose this riff."

"Go right down, Tommy." Whew. One down, two to go.

Normie spotted Brennan at that point and wriggled to get down.

She went over and held her arms up for a hug. She snuggled against him. "You smell good," she said. I was left to conclude that I didn't. "You're going to stay out of that place now, aren't you, Your Grace?" she asked Brennan, staring at him with concern.

"I think so, Stormie. I hope so."

"I can play 'Michael Row the Boat Ashore.'"

"On what?"

At that point I jumped in. "On anything, right, Normie? Why don't you go down to the music room and practise it. On something. Then you can play it for us later on."

"Okay." And she was off. That just left — Maura. And here she was now, standing in my living room.

"Ministering to the drunk and disorderly now, are you Father? And two-handed swilling, by the look of things. Unless, unless, those two glasses mean . . ." Her voice drifted off and she affected a look of puzzlement. "You don't look as if you spent the night here, Brennan, so . . ."

"You're a great one to talk," I countered. "I called you last evening, remember? To suggest an evening of nice, clean family fun. Followed by Matt Minglewood. But no, you had shipped the kids off and were about to embark on an adventure of your own. Care to tell us about it?" Brennan's amused dark eyes left me and homed in on my wife with, I thought, some loss of amusement.

Maura said: "Look at me this morning, then look at yourself, if you dare approach a mirror. And ask yourself whether it is even remotely possible that I spent the kind of night you obviously did."

Then the morning lurched to its next, unavoidable scene. Bev came into the room, wrapped in an ancient frayed bath towel. She tossed Brennan's jacket to him and he caught it. I opened my mouth, but discovered I had nothing to say. I shut it again, plopped down on the chesterfield, and stared at the wall.

When no one else spoke, Bev turned to Maura. "Which of these guys are you here for?" Maura gave her a look that could have bored through a lead shield.

"Do you have any clothes?" Brennan asked.

Bev looked around the living room. "Yeah, well, I . . ." Maura gave a sigh of disgust and left the room. Bev quickly gathered her clothes, then looked from Brennan to me. "So, where should I . . . ?"

"The little bathroom," I said, jerking my thumb in the direction of the hall. She left.

"You're in the shithouse now, Collins," Brennan remarked.

"I don't see why, really, any more than she should be." I inclined my head in Maura's direction. But I knew there was only one hole in the shithouse and it was for me alone. Whatever Maura may have been up to in her own life, and I wasn't sure what or who it was, she would never have stooped to carrying on at home where the kids could catch a glimpse of it. She had poured herself a glass of juice and was drinking it with her back to us all.

Bev returned fully clothed. "Can I give you a ride somewhere?" Brennan asked.

She looked at him. "Is it true that in Ireland 'ride' means —"

"Here it means a drive, on the right-hand side of the road. Let's motor." He ushered her out my front door without a backward glance.

Maura turned to face me. I was once again without words, so I decided to make for the shower, without, I hoped, being subjected to a verbal or physical attack. By the time I was clean and dressed, the kids were with Maura, who looked for all the world as if nothing had happened. I didn't like it. Wasn't this an occasion for subjecting old Monty to the tongue-flogging of his life? Was this indifference I was seeing? Had she moved so far from me in her life now that she couldn't even be bothered?

"Where's Father Burke?" Normie asked, wide-eyed and on the verge of a major disappointment.

"He had to leave, sweetie," Maura explained in a saccharine voice. "He had to give a ride to a lady who can't walk very well this morning."

"That's very kind of him, but I wanted to play for him on the keyboard."

"Sweetheart," I said, "I have to talk to him later on. Maybe you can play it over the phone."

"Great!"

Surprisingly, Maura stayed for the afternoon. Guilty conscience on her part? I chided myself for being an asshole and started to relax, and we had some good wholesome family fun playing Scrabble and charades. I went into the kitchen and put together a pot of chili. While it was cooking Tommy asked me to go downstairs and listen to something he had written for the guitar. I listened and was delighted. He was way ahead of his dad when it came to composition.

The phone rang. I ran upstairs and grabbed it. "I see trouble ahead with this one, Monty," Brennan said.

"We're not planning a future together, for Christ's sake," I whispered into the phone. "We just met each other's needs for a night or two! Now, tell me what happened in the church."

"The vandal wrote: 'Home of the Fighting Irish=Hell!'"

I thought about the vandal, Jason. He'd called Burke, or maybe it was O'Flaherty, an "Irish bog-trotter." And we had reports that he'd been asking about priests and where they were from. He had called someone a "real scary Irish guy." No, Jason hadn't said that; it was Myers, the guy at Mount A. It was all becoming jumbled in my mind.

"All right," I said. "Let me have a look at it and then I'll call the police. You can make yourself scarce."

"It's gone."

"What do you mean, gone?"

"I painted over it. It looks like shit but at least you can't see —"

"You *what!*"

"I could hardly leave it there for Sunday Mass! Luckily I found it early in the morning before anyone saw it."

"You destroyed evidence that may very well have come from the killer? Can you really be that stupid? I don't believe I'm hearing this!"

"It's not evidence of anything!"

"The police could have photographed the handwriting, possibly traced the spray paint. We'll have to hire a paint removal guy to get your paint off, and read what's underneath it."

"Waste of time. Won't get us anywhere."

"We don't have anything else!"

"I was incensed when I saw it. All I wanted to do was blot it out. I scraped most of it off before I painted over it, so there's nothing to uncover. And you know as well as I do, it wouldn't have got us anywhere near the real killer, so spare me any further recriminations. I won't have my church desecrated."

"Burke, I can't believe you would —"

My daughter pulled at my sleeve. "What is it, sweetheart?"

"Is that Father Burke on the phone?"

"Yes, it is."

"Give me that." She swiped the receiver from my hand. "Father? This is Normie Collins. I'm fine, thank you. Remember what I said I could play? That's right. Well, here it is. Daddy, hold the phone up. I'm going down to the keyboard. I'll play loud." She barrelled downstairs and played a creditable version of 'Michael Row the Boat,' then came up, beaming. She nodded and signalled that I could terminate the call. I did so without another word.

We had dinner, and Maura announced that it was time for her to go. "Don't let Normie stay up too late. You know how she gets." She kissed the kids goodnight.

"Do I get a kiss too?"

"I don't know where that mouth has been."

I took a deep breath and began to address the first crisis of the day. "About this morning, I —"

"This morning, Montague, was such a pathetic balls-up on your part that I look at you more in sorrow than in anger."

II

Monday I was in the office making half-hearted efforts to catch up on other files and fill in my time sheets. Several times during the day I tried Burke's number and left messages with Mrs. Kelly, but didn't hear back from him. I knocked off work in the mid-afternoon so I could stop by the rectory before picking up the kids at Maura's.

Mrs. Kelly came to the door when I rang the bell. "Is he in, Mrs. K.?"

"I know he's up there but he hasn't been out of his room all day and he hasn't taken any of his calls. And meals? All gone a-wasting."

"I'll go roust him out."

"Well, I don't know," she fretted, eyes looking to the second floor. I smiled at her and went on up.

I rapped on the door. No response. I rapped again, more violently, finally provoking a bark from within. "Who is it?"

"Your long-suffering attorney."

"Open it."

He was lying on his back on the bed, uncombed and unshaven, wearing worn jeans and a sweatshirt. One hand was behind his head, the other held a long-ashed cigarette. There was an overflowing ashtray and a glass half full of amber liquid on the bedside table. Dismissing any thought of tact, I picked the glass up and sniffed it. Ginger ale. His face was devoid of expression.

"You'd better cut down on those coffin nails or you won't be singing Palestrina."

He didn't respond. I walked to a window and ostentatiously opened it wide, letting in a blast of glacial air. "I came by to apologize for giving you grief yesterday. Even though you really should have . . . Well, you don't need to hear it again."

"I photographed it before I cleaned it up." His voice was lifeless.

"Oh! Why didn't you tell me? It's not the original but it's better than nothing."

"O'Flaherty says the camera's not working. The flash went off so I thought it worked, but he says it may not turn out. He'll let me know." He sounded as if he'd been condemned all over again.

"O'Flaherty has it?"

"Yeah."

"Well, we'll wait and see. Why don't you get up?"

"I'm not getting up. There's nothing —"

He was interrupted by a tentative knock on the door.

"Christ," he growled, not moving.

"Come in," I called out.

The door opened and there stood a vision from a Botticelli masterpiece. In her late teens, she was petite and sweet-faced with long, curly golden hair cascading to her waist. Perched at the end of her nose was a pair of rimless spectacles, which did nothing to detract from the beauty of her light hazel eyes. She wore a long, cream-coloured dress and had a blue coat over her arm. She was looking uncertainly towards the bed, where Burke was still supine and I was sitting. I realized we were both staring at her, stupidly.

She began a nervous opening spiel. "Father Burke?" She looked from me to him and back to me. "I'm Lexie Robinson. I just moved here. I'm studying music. And, um, I've volunteered to start a children's choir at my church, St. Malachy's, but I didn't know how to go about it. Nobody had done it there before so, well, I thought it would be a good idea to call the choir school and get some pointers, and I talked to, uh, Sister Dunne, and she said to phone you." She was still directing her comments at me. I suppose a clean-shaven lawyer in a business suit looked more priestly than the wretch lolling in the bed beside me. Suddenly picturing the scene from her point of view, I leaned over and dug an elbow into Burke's leg to get him to sit up, which he did, but not without emitting a smoker's hack. The lovely girl was going on: "So, I dialed your number a few times but I didn't get any answer, and then since I was downtown anyway I thought I might as well come here." She wound down. Her cheeks had blushed to a shell pink. Her eyes were still fixed on me.

Then Burke stood up, stretched, and moved towards her, starting to speak in a raspy voice. She looked up at him, startled, and backed away. He stopped and put up his hands in a gesture that said "You have nothing to fear from me." I couldn't look at his face. He stood at a respectful distance, then cleared his throat. "We'll go over to the church. The music's in the choir loft."

Her eyes darted to me, and I nodded, pointing a discreet finger in Burke's direction. Yes, he's your man. I said: "Why don't we all go? I'll call the house and have the kids meet us at the church."

"You have kids?" she asked, bewildered.

"Angelface here is not a man of the cloth, Miss Robinson," Burke said, somewhat tartly.

"Oh. I'm sorry."

"Quite all right. Just give me a second." He rooted in his bureau, grabbed some clothing and went into the bathroom where we soon heard the sound of the shower.

And at that moment I became aware of a new dimension to my feelings about the case. Images from the past weeks flooded my mind: Brennan on the witness stand, watching helplessly as his life was ripped apart before all the world. The unmasked pain I had seen in his eyes on the day we were to leave the case to the jury, when, all defences down, he asked us not to give up on him. The gaunt shadow that sat across from me in the jailhouse. The choir director bringing forth from the children the music of the spheres. Father Burke facing the congregation in his white vestments and singing the *Agnus Dei* from the *Mass of the Angels,* the particular favourite of Janeece Tuck, when I knew it took every ounce of strength to keep his composure after his little friend's death. Images from his early life in New York came to me, some of them unedifying and some of them, in spite of Sandra's sardonic recitation, endearing. I contemplated what he had given up, the pleasures of the flesh that he enjoyed every bit as much as I did, and the chance to have the comfort of a wife and family.

And I saw him as he had just appeared, an unwashed layabout, convicted of murder. I had witnessed the effect he had on a young musician who had come to him for help, then backed away in fear. What kind of strength did he have to muster, to get up in the morning and face the world? Did he beseech God in prayer every time he had to face a new group of parishioners, students, parents? That cocky self-assurance that I had often found so irritating, was that what was keeping him going now?

I was filled with a sense of outrage that was nearly overwhelming. Throughout this long ordeal, I had experienced, in turn, doubt about his innocence; suspicion of other things he might be up to when I was unable to reach him at night; frustration with him and with myself, and with the inability of all of us to penetrate the secrets of the case; ambition to win the case and solve the mystery behind it; profound sympathy for what he was going through; an appreciation and enjoyment of the friendship developing between us; complicated feelings about that friendship and his place in our lives. Had I told him recently, perhaps more than once, to fuck off? But now, what I was most aware of was the outrage I felt at whoever had done this to him. He wasn't a saint, he wasn't an angel; he was a bright, talented, complex, at times exasperating man who was trying to do the right thing. And someone was determined to take it all away from him in the most barbarous way imaginable. Whoever did this was going to be hunted down, taken before a judge, and put away for life. We had all had enough.

I came out of myself and focused again on Lexie, who had nearly flattened herself against the door, looking as if she would rather be anywhere else on the planet. I gave her what I hoped was a reassuring smile and picked up the phone to call Maura.

"Hi. Can you ask the kids to walk over to St. Bernadette's? Not great. He'll perk up. He's going to do some music over at the church with a young lady who's just taken on a children's choir. Yeah, I'll tell you later."

When Burke emerged, scrubbed and shaved, the three of us set off. Nobody spoke till we were outside the church in the sunshine of a mid-October day. Then he began to sing: "Now lady, your mind is mistaken if it sees but a beggar in me. For my name, it is Ronald MacDonald, a chieftain of highest degree." Lexie looked at him and laughed, and he gave her a rueful smile in return.

"Good to know you've learned the local music," I remarked.

"Well worth learning, wouldn't you say, Lexie?"

"Oh, yes!" Her apprehension was starting to ease.

We entered the church and Brennan genuflected deeply, making the sign of the cross. Lexie followed suit. The choirmaster unlocked the door to the loft and we went up. "I keep most of our regular music up here, in file cabinets. Some of course we use at the school, but you can look over what we have here. More than enough for your purposes, I'm thinking." He pushed open the door to the music room. "You'll be starting in unison, I expect?"

"Yes."

"Is this a choir for everyone, or will you be holding auditions? Makes a big difference in what music you'll want to attempt."

The choir directors got into a groove. A few minutes later I heard a commotion below. My children, I presumed, and went to let them in. Normie was obviously pleased to be in the church again. "Can I run around?"

"You may walk around. Respectfully. And don't go on the altar. Then come up to the loft. Quietly." She nodded and started to walk up the centre aisle, one halting step at a time, like a nervous bride in an old-fashioned wedding ceremony.

I hid a smile and motioned for Tommy Douglas to follow me upstairs. Brennan and Lexie were out of sight. Tom had the massive pipe organ to himself. "Cool!" He sat down at the bench. "Can I try it? How do you turn it on?"

Burke came out of the music room and switched on the organ. "Go ahead. Pull out all the stops, as they say."

"That's where that expression comes from? Guess I should have known that. But I didn't know till the other day that 'getting down to the short strokes' means . . ." he stopped, reddened, and looked at me, ". . . golf." The three of us laughed. Tommy started to play a tune, as he would on any keyboard. He experimented with a few stops, and enlarged the sound. "You play that a helluva lot better than I do, Mr. Douglas," said Burke.

Tom looked like a man who had found his calling. In the next instant, he had found the love of his life. Lexie emerged in the light of the late afternoon sun as it streamed through the stained glass windows of the church. Her beauty was unearthly. She smiled at Tom and he gaped. Two men thirty years his senior had recently done no better.

I introduced them, and my son found his voice. "Tell me everything bad about yourself, so I can start getting over you." Burke shot him a glance of amused appreciation.

Lexie looked at Tom over the tops of her glasses and said: "Why don't I start with a few sour notes on the organ?"

"You can play this thing?" She nodded and he said "Show me" and slid over to make room for her on the bench. She went right into a Bach fugue and my son was transported.

"Ah. Let's go below and listen," the choirmaster suggested.

We met Normie coming up the stairs. "You're staying downstairs with us," I commanded.

We listened to Bach until it was time for me and the kids to head home. I sprinted up the stairs to get Tom and practically had to wrestle him off the organist's bench. He smiled mysteriously when his sister asked who was up there. As we made our way out we heard Burke and Lexie discussing repertoire, then they began to sing together. Tommy had a sudden urge to even up the laces of his sneakers and so he stopped, holding the door open with his bum and listening to every sweet note. All the way home in the car he talked about getting his driver's licence. To get to Mass no doubt. Out at St. Malachy's.

I was tied up with other cases until Friday noon. I called Burke to ask whether he'd had any luck with the photos. O'Flaherty had taken the film in, and reported it was blank. I restrained myself from reacting to the news. Instead I said: "You know, that scene in your room may have been one of the saddest sights I've ever witnessed."

There was no need to ask what I meant. "Oh? You think having dear little girls cringe in fear is depressing in some way, Montague?" He seemed to hesitate, then: "That's not all. Listen to this." I heard him rattling papers. "'Dear Father Burke, I don't think you killed that girl, but I want you to know it doesn't matter to me. What's past is past. What you need now is closure. I feel I have come to know you over the course of this trial and I want you to know I love you like nobody else could ever love you. I would like to come and visit you even if you are in jail and even if you are still a priest.' Here's another one: 'Dear Brennan. If you did it, it's because she fuckin asked for it, excuse my French. Otherwise you wouldn't of been prevoked beyond indurence!! I would never do anything to push you over the brink. I know how to please a man, especially you. Take my word for it, believe me!!!, you would be happy with me.' Blah, blah. I got a similar one from a male. What the hell's wrong with these people? What did I ever do to bring all this shite down on my head?"

"We'll get you out from under this, Brennan. I promise you."

If I wanted to reach him in the next few days, he informed me, I would have to stop by the church. No, he wasn't embarking on a prayer marathon; he was going to paint the interior. The patch of mismatched colour over the graffiti was a blessing in disguise, Mike O'Flaherty averred. He had been putting off a badly needed paint job because of the cost. Brennan, having tuned him out until now, tuned back in and volunteered to do it himself. Convict labour, he called it. They had commandeered one of the church ladies with a good eye for colour, and the paint had been selected and lugged to the site.

"It will give me something useful to do as I wait out this painful episode in my life," Burke said. "But if one person says 'it will be good therapy for you, Brennan,' I shall fall upon that person from a great height."

"When do you start?"

"I'm heading there now. But I'll have to take a break for a while from, say, four to six, because little Lexie Robinson is coming over for some more assistance with her choral music. And by the way, I could use an extra hand with a brush."

"I know just the lad for you."

"Thought you might."

III

Tommy Douglas cleared his Friday after-school schedule, showered, and donned his painting apparel, a sharply creased pair of khaki pants and a handsome Shetland wool sweater. "You can't wear that for painting, Tommy! It will be ruined in the first five minutes. Get back in there and put on an old pair of jeans and a T-shirt."

"But that's what I had on when we met. She'll think I'm always a slob."

"She'll think you're an idiot if you wear good clothes for a paint job."

"Really?" I nodded. "Okay." So he dressed down and we walked over to the job site.

Lexie was already there when we arrived. She and the choirmaster were hard at work in the loft.

"Do you want me to start where you left off, Father?" Tom called loudly.

"Oh, good, Mr. Douglas, you're here. Why don't you pop up and we'll figure out the best way to go about it." Tom bounded up the stairs, and was greeted — enthusiastically, I thought — by Lexie, who was clad in jeans and a T-shirt. Her glorious hair was tied in a ponytail.

I looked around. Burke had a huge job in front of him. If he had begun painting when we finished our call at noon hour, he was making slow progress. He had done one segment of the south wall in the new creamy paint, several shades lighter than what had been on it for decades, and it was clear it would brighten up the church immeasurably. But the pillars had not been touched yet. And there was all the remaining wall space, as well as the ceiling. Scaffolding was in place for that daunting task.

"Brennan, how many hours did you put in here?"

"Four hours, I suppose it was. Looks grand, doesn't it?"

"Ever hear of a roller?"

"There's a roller there someplace. I ended up using a brush because of all that close work around the window and the stations of the cross."

"You'll be too old to run for Pope by the time you finish, at the rate you're going."

"Well, what are you going to do about it?"

"Yeah, yeah, I'll come over and help you. But why not get a whole crew in? Tomorrow's Saturday. Make a little party out of it. Pizza, treats. Bribe some of the church crowd. Can't you see Marguerite over here in a pair of overalls and a cap?"

"Why don't you run over and see if Mike's there. He'd love to organize them all."

Did Burke, in the predicament he was in, feel he could not call upon his colleagues to help him fix up their church? "Sure. I'll check."

I crossed to the rectory, where O'Flaherty greeted me with a big smile. He walked with me to the church. The idea was put to the gregarious priest and he took it up with enthusiasm. "I'll get on the blower right away," he promised.

"And I'll be the pizza man," I offered. "Just let me know how many will be here, Mike, and I'll order them. Some sweets and drinks as well. I can run out and get some more rollers and brushes this evening."

When we entered the church, Burke was at the wall making small, painstaking brush strokes, wiping the excess off with his hand, and painting again. I jerked my head in his direction. "See what I mean, Mike?"

He got it. "You could use some help, Brennan, my lad. And keep in mind that I bought the paint for the church, not for you to bathe in. You're a sight."

Above us, the two young people were playing a duet on the pipe organ. "This goes down much better with music, I have to say," Brennan told us. "I'll move my stereo in here for the duration."

O'Flaherty went off to make his calls and Brennan stood looking after him.

"The oul' divil! Do you know what he's been doing?"

"What?"

"He's been chatting up my sister."

"The one in Ireland?"

"Right. Maire. And the old sneak never told me about it."

"Well, they're both over the age of consent! And he can hardly be compromising her virtue. Or she, his. She's over three thousand miles away. Seriously, though, how do you know this?"

"I walked into his room when they were having a row. He was on the phone, speaking quite heatedly. 'No, Maire, please don't do it! Well, I'm telling you you'll live to regret it!' He caught sight of me then, said he had to go, and hung up. He was a bit flustered. Then he came up with a cover story: 'Maire McLanahan, the poor soul. Don't even ask,' he said."

"How do you know it wasn't this McLanahan?"

"Because way back he made a remark about not knowing any other Irish women named after the Blessed Mother, and wasn't that a shame."

"Well, you set them up yourself, Brennan, that night she called during the poker game."

"No, it was before that."

"Oh. I had the impression that was the first time they spoke."

"So did I, but then I remembered Mrs. Kelly tormenting me about phone bills to Ireland shortly after I moved here. Maire must have called when I was out; maybe she ended up with O'Flaherty, he liked the sound of her and called her again. Who knows?"

"Call Maire and ask her."

"No, I'm not going to do that! I've given out to her enough times when she tried to ask *me* those questions."

The organ stopped and Lexie said she had to go. I heard my son clear his throat and invite her for some of his mother's lasagna, which she had been in the process of making when he left. I extended the invitation to Brennan but he was keen on his work, so we left him to paint his walls, his clothing, and every exposed inch of his flesh.

We were met at the door by Normie, who demanded to know why she had not been asked to paint. Then she fell silent and stared at Lexie. For once, she appeared to be shy.

"Maura!" I called out.

"What?"

"We have company."

"Oh? Who?" She came out to see, looking for all the world like a contented homemaker. She removed an apron (an apron!) as she came towards us. A new era of domesticity?

Tommy said: "Mum, this is Lexie. My mother, Maura MacNeil."

"Nice to meet you, Mrs. MacNeil." My wife looked from our son to the lovely young girl. Then she broke into a big, warm smile and said she was delighted to meet Lexie. Her delight grew as the evening wore on, because the young musician showed signs of a sly sense of humour MacNeil could appreciate. Maura was on her best behaviour during the meal. We all were. After the meal, Normie produced a pair of eyeglasses she had sworn were lost, and put them on. They looked remarkably like Lexie's. Everyone, it seemed, had fallen in love.

The next morning, when I arrived at St. Bernadette's with a supply of brushes and rollers, the worker bees were getting their orders from the queen. Sister Marguerite Dunne was not quite in overalls, but she was wearing something other than a business suit, covered by a smock. I recognized Erin Christie and Tyler MacDonald from the youth centre, with another guy and girl of college age. Brennan was at it again with his brush. Marguerite relieved me of one of my rollers and pointedly presented it to Burke; he accepted it without rancour. The nun directed her charges to various spots in the church and oversaw their first strokes. Father O'Flaherty burst in, beaming with pleasure at all the activity. He didn't look to me like a man fretting over a lover's tiff. Maybe long distance had a calming effect. My son had promised to join us in the afternoon, as had my wife. Normie would be spending the afternoon with a pal. Lexie was hoping to come over after a preliminary practice with her new choir. A stereo system had been set up and the space was filled with exquisite Renaissance polyphony.

I looked around at what was, in effect, much of the cast of Brennan's murder trial. If there had been any awkwardness when they all got together, I had missed it. They appeared to be quite happy in their labours. Marguerite marched over to me.

"You're providing the pizzas as usual, Mr. Collins?"

"I know my place, Sister, and the pizzas will be here in time for lunch, with enough left over for supper. I'll go get the soft drinks. I have them in a cooler." She nodded, as if this were the natural order of things, then took up a roller and set upon her segment of the church wall.

Everyone painted and gabbed till the pizzas were delivered. Tyler was bold enough to switch the soundtrack from the Renaissance to something closer to rock and roll. We fell upon the pizzas and sat around on the canvas drop sheets as if it were party time. Brennan was in a light-hearted mood and told an amusing tale about himself, his father, and his brothers deciding to surprise his mother by painting the interior walls of their house when Mrs. Burke had taken his sisters up to Boston for a girls' weekend out of town. Not surprisingly, the plan went off the rails: hideous colours, horrendous paint job, great blobs of oil paint all over the place, squabbles, tears, desperate measures to repair the damage before the missus got home. He did a perfect impersonation of his Irish father in high dudgeon as the crisis deepened. Everyone was laughing in sympathy, even Marguerite.

The church door opened; the sun blazed in and was immediately blotted out by the form of Eileen Darragh. Like Marguerite, she was dressed in a smock. I assumed Burke had not seen Eileen since I told him what everyone else already knew: her feelings for him were such that they could only be aired in somebody else's confession box. Someone the age of O'Flaherty perhaps. Or maybe not. Eileen smiled at everyone, but did not let her eyes rest on Father Burke. And one would never have known from his demeanour that he had heard anything embarrassing or unwelcome about her.

He rose from where he had been sitting on the floor. "Hello, Eileen."

"Hello, Father. Hi everybody. I was hoping you'd have it all done and I could walk in, congratulate you all, and get right down to the pizza and pop."

"Your timing was pretty cagey. Help yourself," Marguerite declared. "But don't regard it as anything but fuel for the afternoon's work."

We ate, then resumed painting. An hour or so later, Marguerite gave a sharp, nun-like clap of her hands and everyone turned in her direction. She called the workers together at the back of the church. Some people had painted as high as they could, standing on pews and anything else that would hold them. It was time to divide up responsibility, to get at the upper areas of the walls and pillars.

We heard someone coming in and everybody turned to the door. It was Maura, dressed in a blue sweatshirt that depicted the Sistine

Chapel as a paint-by-number. Brennan gave her a big smile, reached over and did something with a paintbrush, then grabbed her and held her close. Eileen glowered at my wife as she struggled playfully to escape the arms that held her like a vise. Burke pushed her away and was gratified to see that he had left a number of paint smudges on the front of her shirt. Then she turned slightly and I saw two nearly perfect cream-coloured handprints on the back.

Mike O'Flaherty said: "And him telling us he can't paint at all. Like many a great artist before him, all he needed was the inspiration of a beautiful woman."

"You'd better not be thinking Rubens there, Father," Maura admonished O'Flaherty.

"All right. You." Marguerite pointed a commanding finger at Maura. "Over there with Eileen. She needs somebody to help her around those windows. I want two people up on ladders for the tops of the walls. I'll give you the key, Tyler; bring the ladders over from the centre. Everyone else, back to work. And you, Michelangelo," she said to Burke, "you're going up there." She pointed to the scaffolding "Where you're going to be looking at God, and nobody else. I don't want to see any more grubby handprints on the women in this sacred place."

"Yes, Sister," Burke answered, in perfect obedience.

"Before he gets up on that," I interjected, "who put the scaffolding together? You didn't assemble it yourself, did you, Brennan?"

"No, it was done by the fellows who delivered it. Why? You don't think I could lay a few boards on a rack?"

"I rest my case. All right. Go ahead."

"Ever the lawyer," my wife remarked.

I whispered to her. "Did he tell me he had once planned on becoming an architect?"

"So? He'd have made the blueprints for magnificent buildings. You've heard it said that architecture is frozen music. You just wouldn't let him near the nuts and bolts, or the paint."

Eileen and Maura moved to the front of the church, Eileen staring dolefully at the hands of her beloved, imprinted for all time on the garment of my wife. She did not suffer in silence, as I learned from Maura later in the afternoon, when Eileen went to the basement of the church to use the washroom. Maura came over to me. "I thought Eileen regarded Burke as the nearest thing to God Almighty."

I put down my roller and wiped my hands on my pants. "What happened? Did she say something less than worshipful?"

"She cast a scornful eye at the paint he put on my shirt and said: 'Well, at least he only went at you with his paintbrush. Not his crucifix.' Then she kind of blushed and looked ashamed, but went bravely on: 'Or those mysterious initials.' Surely she doesn't think he's guilty!"

"She knows he's guilty of one thing, putting his arms around you. You've seen what she's like around him."

"Oh, yeah. Could hardly miss it."

"He missed it. Whatever you do, don't mention it to him."

"Not bloody likely."

"So, you can figure out what gave rise to her rare descent into bitchiness. But no, I can't imagine that she really thinks he's guilty. I suspect in moments of frustration or jealousy she finds it gratifying to be less than charitable about him."

The work went on for a while longer, then I noticed that everyone was laying down tools. Michael O'Flaherty called to the man on the scaffold: "Aren't you forgetting something, Father Burke?"

"No."

"Ever hear of the four o'clock Saturday Mass?"

"Ah." He climbed down from the ceiling, more paint-splotched than ever. O'Flaherty bustled away to clean himself up, and we moved tarpaulins and debris out of the way as people began to turn up for Mass. We painters stayed on our drop sheets, so as not to smear paint on the pews. Most of the faithful complimented us on our work, though a couple of people coughed ostentatiously, presumably at the smell of the paint.

O'Flaherty entered the church in his vestments, and the Mass began. We participated from our quarantine area at the back. The priest in our midst gave the responses quietly, unlike an older man at the front of the church who shouted each response a beat ahead of everyone else. I remembered from my altar boy days that there was always one like that. Tom and Lexie arrived midway through, and sat together in one of the back pews. Lexie knew all the words and gestures by heart; I could see Tom making an effort to look as if he participated in the Eucharist every week. When the celebration was over, and the congregation had been cheered on its way by O'Flaherty, we brought out our pizzas and pop and ate our supper.

Maura whispered: "Even though he was stuck at the back of the church on a drop sheet, and everyone in the building knew why, you could see a change in him during the Mass. It was like peace descending on him. I hope it lasts." But it didn't: Maura herself unintentionally raised his hackles. Leaning over to Brennan, she asked him whether he had said his Latin Mass that morning before the work began.

"I'm in the long grass these days, MacNeil," came the curt reply. "So no, I haven't been saying Mass publicly in my new role as convicted murderer. I thought it might be unseemly. I say it by myself." Maura closed her eyes and shook her head, mortified at herself.

The painting went on well into the night. If anyone was thinking about the dark undercurrents of life at St. Bernadette's, it was not mentioned within my hearing.

But there were dark currents ahead.

Chapter 20

Confutatis maledictis, flammis acribus addictis,
voca me cum benedictis.
(When the accursed have been confounded
and given over to the bitter flames,
call me with the blessed.)
— *Requiem Mass*

I

I was in court all morning on the Tuesday after the paint job, and I found my mind drifting while the lawyer for one of the other defendants argued an arcane point of law before an unreceptive judge. I tuned out and reflected instead on the painting crew. I had been caught up in the spirit of the day and had not considered them in their role as witnesses. But surely one of them had information that could help us, if only I knew what to ask. They had testified at the Cudmore trial, and I had questioned them in connection with Leeza Rae and the dance. I'd also heard all their accounts of the Beethoven wig affair. Well, not all accounts . . . I realized I had never interviewed Erin Christie about the skit, even though she had played a big part in the show. And then there were the choir school children. I would look into it as soon as the court took its morning break.

I made a call from the courthouse. "Hello, Sister Marguerite?" I would not be able to speak to any of the students, especially about so weighty a matter, without her permission.

"This sounds like Mr. Collins."

"It is. Sister, I'd like your permission to talk to a few of the choir members, the little ones who took part in the variety show last Christmas." The silence on the other end was so prolonged I thought we had lost the connection. "Sister?"

She surprised me, though, and asked no questions. "Perhaps right at the end of their last class of the afternoon. It will take a couple of days to set up, catching the parents and all. I'll call you as soon as I have it organized."

"Thank you. I'll try to speak to Erin Christie then as well."

"That won't be possible, I'm afraid."

"Oh?"

"No. Erin went home to Ontario. We're not sure whether she'll be back."

"Very well. I'll wait to hear from you about the students. And Sister, it would be best if . . ."

"Do I strike you as a gossip?"

"No. I appreciate your help."

I made a mental note to call Burke and let him know about the interviews, though he probably wouldn't be thrilled to hear the children were being questioned. But then, he seemed to dismiss from consideration everyone I mentioned. Which reminded me: I had never followed up with Trevor Myers. What was it about that incident that set Burke off every time the subject came up? I had tried only once to reach Myers by phone at the Miller's Tale. Whoever took the call that day had sounded quite familiar with Trevor. I decided to drive out there when court wrapped up for the day.

II

After a quick change into a T-shirt and jeans, I took the Macdonald Bridge and followed the traffic eastward. The Miller's Tale was a once-respectable neighbourhood pub that had fallen victim to unchecked development all around it. Located on a main thoroughfare in the sprawling city of Dartmouth, it was surrounded by fast-food joints and X-rated video shops. There were a couple of beat-up muscle cars with tinted windows in the parking lot. The bar was dim, and nobody looked up when I walked in. A few morose drinkers sat at the bar; several pool tables were in operation. I ordered a beer and told the bartender I was looking for Trevor Myers.

"You're not looking very hard."

"I don't know him."

"So what do you want to see him for?"

"A mutual friend, who won't be able to join us for two years less a day, sent me to buy him a drink."

"Yeah, right." He raised his voice. "Trev, this guy wants to buy you a beer."

A young man in a black muscle shirt straightened up from the nearest pool table. "I never saw this guy before."

"So let's get acquainted. What are you drinking?"

"Alpine."

"An Alpine for him and a Keith's for me. We'll be over there." I nodded towards a table at the opposite end of the room.

Myers trailed after me. I had to resist the urge to turn and watch my back. He sat in the seat against the wall and looked at me with a bored expression. He was fairly tall, muscular, and would have been good-looking if not for the cheesy moustache, the long, straggly brown hair, and the greasy ball cap pulled over his forehead. His knuckles were tattooed. I inferred that his appearance had gone down-market since the days when he enjoyed the attentions of a young woman enrolled at one of Canada's premier liberal arts universities.

"Who the fuck are you and what do you want?"

I waited until our beer had been delivered and paid for, then got to the point: "I want to know about the fight you had up at Mount A in 1982, when the police got involved."

"I don't remember any fight."

"Sure you do. What was it about?"

"I been in lots of fights. And I don't even go looking for them. There's a lot of assholes in this world. What can you do?"

"The sooner you tell me the sooner I'll be out of your hair."

"I don't give a fuck what you do."

I sat and sipped my beer as if I had all the time in the world. "Why do you suppose this man came flying out of his car and attacked you?"

"What's it to you?"

"I'm interested."

"You a friend of this guy?"

"You might say that. Do you know the guy's name?"

"Why should I?"

"Just thought you might."

He drained his beer and seemed to come to a decision. "He's a psycho. He tried to fucking strangle me. Lifted me up by the throat with one hand and slammed me up against a tree."

"Why do you think he did that?"

"Because he's nuts, why else?"

"Did he say anything?"

"He was all bent out of shape about this chick, this girlfriend of mine."

"He knew this girl?"

"Oh, yeah. Or wanted to, real bad. He had the hots for her and I guess he didn't dig the fact she liked me better than him. Tough shit. Get your own piece of ass."

"You told him that?"

"I don't remember. Prob'ly."

"So then what?"

"So then he cracked me in the face and I pulled a knife on him."

"A knife?"

"Yeah, a knife. You deaf? I seen the look on his face and went right for his heart — it was either him or me."

"Did you stab him?"

"I drew some blood. More like scratches. Mostly just managed to tear his shirt into shreds. He tried to get the blade away from me. Made a bloody mess of his hands, but that didn't stop him. He managed to get it and he threw it away. After all, the prick had about fifty pounds on me." He turned and looked at the bartender and I signalled for another beer for Myers.

"Did the police know about the knife?"

"Do I look like a fucking moron?"

"I'll take that as a no. So he got the knife away from you. Then what?"

"Then he came at me with his fists. I'd like to see him try me now!"

A young lout with a shaven head and a goatee approached our table. "Hey man, Trev, you gonna —"

Myers whirled on him. "Fuck off! Can't you see I'm busy?"

The interloper backed off. "Okay, man, take it easy."

"You seem a little tense, Trevor," I suggested. "Have you seen this guy lately?"

"No."

"Did you take anything from him?"

"Huh?"

"The guy in the fight. Did you take anything?"

"Like what?"

"Like a neck chain."

"He had on some Jesus medal or some fucking thing. Thought I might get a few bucks for it."

"Could it have been a cross?"

"I don't fucking remember. Like, I wasn't going to wear it, man."

"This girlfriend you had. Did she like the way you talk?"

He smirked. "She liked me well enough. I didn't say 'fuck' in front of her. She didn't like it. The word, anyway."

"How did you meet her?"

"I was taking a couple courses at the college. Told her I wanted to be an engineer. She liked that. I gave her some bullshit about trying to better myself, so I'd be good enough for her! She fell for it. For a while anyhow. But I ended up dropping out. It was boring."

"How did the police find the guy who beat you up?"

"I took down the guy's licence number, like a good citizen. Or maybe it was because I thought I might get a couple guys and go find this asshole again and kick his head in. But turned out the car was a rental. He didn't stick around."

Neither did I. On the way back to Halifax, I tried to make sense of Myers. The altercation was a little more serious than I had imagined, but, otherwise, the story was pretty much what I expected. The only thing that struck me as curious was his utter lack of curiosity about my identity and that of his assailant. Could I seriously believe he didn't know who Burke was? I didn't figure him for a regular reader of the newspaper, but had he never seen the television news? Burke and I had both had more than our share of publicity. I grew weary thinking about trying to raise the subject with my client again, but I headed for the rectory nonetheless.

III

When I got there, I didn't know whether to be disappointed or relieved. Burke was not alone. I was pleased once again to see that, although his wings had been — understandably — clipped following his conviction, he still had priestly company once in a while. He was sitting in his room chatting with a priest a few years older than he was. I had seen him on occasion around the city, at sporting events, if memory served. He was introduced to me as Father Bernie Drohan. They invited me to sit and have a drink.

"We were just discussing the Vanier Cup," Father Drohan informed me. The national college football championship, which was coming up in a few weeks' time. "Next year, Brennan, you and I will go up to Toronto for it. Your troubles will be all behind you by then, and —"

He looked towards the open door. "Are you going to hammer nails with that, O'Flaherty?"

Father O'Flaherty had halted by the door. He was carrying a large Celtic cross, made of stone with the familiar circle through its cross-pieces. Drohan said: "If you're going to bear Our Lord's crucifix through these hallowed halls, Michael, show a bit more reverence, would you?"

O'Flaherty's face blushed a bright pink. "You're right as always, Bernard. I didn't even realize." He held the cross before him as if processing into the church for Mass. "Better?"

Father Drohan and I laughed. Brennan was staring at the cross as if he had never seen one before.

Mike explained: "I'm taking it down to Mrs. Kelly. She wants one to show a relative but, of course, she didn't want to bring the woman up here. She might see us peeing or otherwise being less than holy, and lose her religion as a result." He trotted off.

Father Drohan shook his head. "Sweet guy. Mike showed me the ropes when I came here from Newfoundland."

"When was that?" I asked.

"Oh, back in the mid-sixties."

I turned to Burke. "Did you know Mike back then, Brennan? I've received mixed signals from him on the subject."

"No. I didn't even know he was here."

Drohan asked: "What years were you here at the first choir school, Brennan? I know I saw you around at some point in the past."

"From 1968 to 1970."

"Oh. Well, Mike may have been banished to the weeds by then, and he might not want you to know about it," the priest said uncomfortably. "But he was back in the game not long afterwards."

"Banished! What do you mean?" This I had to hear.

Father Drohan directed his reply to his fellow priest. "See, the thing was, Mike took part in an exorcism, which went way —"

"A *what?!*" Brennan barked.

Drohan cleared his throat. "An exorcism."

Burke stared at the other man, who busied himself with the ring of condensation his glass had left on the table. Round and round went his finger, then he added more water from the side of his glass.

Brennan found his voice: "You can't just do that sort of thing on your own. You have to get permission, don't you? Well, what would I know about it?" He got up and raised his glass. We all agreed to a refill. "When did this event take place?"

"Late sixties, or so I understand."

"Where was Archangel Michael stationed when he launched his operation against Lucifer?"

"Right here in Halifax."

"Here?" Burke slapped his hands on the table and glared at Drohan.

"What, in our house?" the older priest chided. "I suppose O'Flaherty would say the devil does his work wherever he sees fit. After the incident, Michael was transferred out of the city parish he'd been in, Holy Trinity, I believe it was. He was sent to some little village, I can't recall where, for a few years. Had to undergo some sort of re-education. Counselling maybe. He and old Rory Brosnan."

"Brosnan? I remember him," Burke said. "Great big fellow, rather wild-looking with a huge mane of fiery red hair. Talked as if he had just crossed over from County Kerry. I heard him say Mass in Irish one time."

"That's the man. He had done this kind of thing years before, in Ireland. A child way out in the country was supposedly possessed. Brosnan was the *primum mobile* of the Halifax episode. O'Flaherty was his acolyte."

"So tell us," I broke in, "what exactly happened?"

Bernard Drohan looked at the open door as if concerned, even after all these years, that the wrong ears might overhear. "It was a young child here on your turf, Brennan. St. Bernadette's, though back then it was an orphanage."

"Oh Christ, don't be telling me that," Burke muttered.

"I don't know whether you had anything to do with the place then."

"If anyone asks, no! But yes, I used to teach the kids music a couple of times a week. Helped out once in a while, if something needed to be done."

"Well, this one child —"

"Boy or girl?" I asked.

"Boy."

"Who?" Brennan demanded.

"Honestly, Brennan, I don't remember his name. Jamie? I don't know. Anyway, he was around twelve or thirteen, a bit of a handful but not uncontrollable. Not until this night back in 1967 or whenever it was. The kid went nuts —"

"A sounder diagnosis than the one made by Dr. O'Flaherty, I'm thinking," Burke butted in.

"Oh, well, it was Brosnan who saw the devil's hand at work, apparently."

"God!"

"Now, Brennan. Jesus of Nazareth cast out a few demons Himself," Drohan reminded him with a smile. He got up and quietly closed the door. "This kid attacked one of the other children when he was sleeping. Began hitting him, kicking, biting. Screaming obscenities at him, and babbling incoherently. The poor little boy in his bed didn't know what hit him. I'm assuming the sister in charge got the miscreant subdued for the night. But when they tried to deal with him next day, he went after the nun or the priest who was brought in to straighten him out. I don't know the sequence of events, but Rory Brosnan got involved. He brought O'Flaherty into it somehow and, well . . ."

"Well what?" Burke asked.

"They took the kid out to a camp or some other isolated spot."

"Wouldn't that look brilliant in a tabloid headline?"

"Nobody ever found out. Thank God. Anyway, out they went and began the ritual."

"What made them think this was possession as opposed to just bad behaviour or a psychiatric disorder?" I asked.

"I think it had something to do with the things the boy was saying. Mike spoke to me about it a few years ago. Long after he had done his penance and returned to the fold. I remember he was, by turns, sheepish about it and defiant. He said they went out there in their surplices, with a violet stole, holy water and copies of the *Rituale Romanum*, and started the procedure. Lots of prayers, signs of the cross, laying on of the stole. They kept him out there for two nights, maybe three. By the time they had finished, the interior of the building was virtually destroyed. There was a rumour afterwards that the priests whitewashed the walls to remove whatever was scrawled all over them during the uproar. O'Flaherty wouldn't answer when I asked him about the walls. But he did say that, with the benefit of hindsight, he believed he and Brosnan were right. That it was a case of diabolical possession. Whatever it was, the boy settled down at the end of the session. They took him to a medical doctor, and he was treated —"

"A little late in the day," Brennan observed.

"— for some cuts and bruises he suffered while thrashing about. He was given some kind of medication, I don't know what."

"Whatever became of the boy?" I asked.

"Don't know. He may have gone back to the orphanage. Or he may have been placed in a foster home. It's possible he was sent out of the city, or out of the province. He wasn't a local boy. Who knows?"

"Probably in a psychiatric hospital somewhere, to this day," Brennan commented tartly.

"Or prison," I added. "Father O'Flaherty seems like such a gentle old guy. I cannot imagine him in a situation like that."

"He was a gentle type of guy back then, too. This incident was rough on him, by the sound of it, mentally and physically. I think he took some punches from the kid; I suspect all three of them took some hits. But it was the verbal attacks that really had them spooked. 'He couldn't have known, he couldn't have known,' Michael kept saying. There was something they figured no human child of twelve could possibly have known. But he refused to tell me what it was."

"Where's Father Brosnan now?"

"He died not long afterwards. Maybe of old age, I don't know." Drohan pushed himself up from the table. "Hope you enjoyed your journey to the dark side, Montague. And you thought all priests talked about was the vintage of the communion wine. Sleep with your light on tonight!"

I left soon after. I slept well, and in darkness. But just before dawn, in a state between sleeping and waking, my mind was assailed by images of Brennan in white vestments splashed with red, looking on helplessly as a ghostly hand raised a Celtic cross and brought it down, over and over again, like a hammer, onto a figure dressed in black.

Chapter 21

O Sovereign, O Judge, O Father, always hidden yet always present,
I worshipped You in time of success, and bless You in these dark days.
I go where Your law commands, free of all human regret.
— Massenet et al., "O Souverain, O Juge, O Père," *Le Cid*

I

With the cold light of day, I was able to shake off the disturbing images of the otherworldly tale I had heard the night before. But, obviously, questions remained. And they dogged me all morning as I got ready for a session in court on a personal injury case. Who was the boy at the centre of the exorcism drama? Father Drohan had suggested the name Jamie; it was not too much of a stretch to wonder if the name had been Jason. Or if Jason was a name made up by Jamie. Just how violent was the encounter between the boy and the two priests? Were these the "Fighting Irish," or had that been directed at Burke? But the exorcism had nothing to do with Burke and everything to do with O'Flaherty. A sweet, gentle man caught up in a turbulent event that he believed was "beyond human ken," to use a phrase I had heard from him once. Just what effect had it had on him? Of course, it was Burke's sign that was carved on the victims' bodies. Or had Jason heard the story of a priest at St. Bernadette's who had the sign of the cross burned into him, and thought it was his old nemesis O'Flaherty? And didn't Drohan say the sign of the cross was part of the ritual? My speculations were getting me nowhere. I put my mind to my other clients.

The day after that, Thursday, I was about to book off early to meet some cronies at the Midtown Tavern when I got a phone call from Sister Dunne. With everything else going on I had nearly forgotten that I'd asked her to set me up with the children at the choir school. Did I want to come over and talk to them now? No, I wanted to go out and have a tall, cool ale. But I thanked her and headed to St. Bernadette's.

When the interviews were done, I raced across the street to see Brennan. I was met by Mrs. Kelly, with a face on her that said: "We regret to announce."

"No, I'm afraid you just missed Father, Mr. Collins. He's gone out to dinner."

"Do you know where?"

"No." She pursed her thin lips in disapproval. "He just laughed and said he had 'a date' and he scampered off."

My next stop was Dresden Row, where my children were happy to see me but my wife was in a rush. Getting ready to go out. And she was looking quite delectable in a black dress I had never seen before. Somebody was going to be led into temptation tonight.

"You're all dressed up," I remarked.

"Yes, occasionally I still make an effort."

"For favoured company."

"Exactly."

"Where are you going?"

"Dinner."

Just then our ears were assailed by the loud beep of a car horn. "Not very gallant," I remarked, "sitting outside and honking the horn."

"You're expecting gallantry? Consider the source. Goodnight, kids!" she called out. "Tom, make sure Normie doesn't get into the Halloween candy. Well, are you going to tag along with us, Collins?"

She swept out, her bag and coat draped over her arm. I followed. No sooner did she clear the doorway, in her uncommon finery, than she was greeted with a wolf whistle from the direction of the street. Unbelievable. Just who did he think he . . . Oh. Maura's best pals, Liz and Fanny, had their heads hanging out the car windows. Liz had a 1954 Chevy Bel Air, pale yellow with white trim, and I missed the occasional rides I used to have in it. Maura turned to me impatiently: "Get in, if you're coming. We're all anxious to get the feed bag on."

"No, I'm not coming. Too much to do tonight. I have to find Brennan."

"I was speaking to him earlier. He said he was taking somebody, a street kid, over to Hope Cottage."

His dinner date. Hope Cottage was a small, early-1800s house on Brunswick Street, where homeless men could get a meal. "I'll call over there then."

"All right. I'm off." She turned and climbed into the back seat of the car, and the women peeled away.

I went back inside and called Hope Cottage, but Brennan had left. I finally connected with him at the rectory. When I arrived, he was standing by the window of his room, gazing out, with a glass of orange juice in his hand. He was wearing a T-shirt MacNeil would kill for. It showed a 1950s housewife seen through a magnificent stained glass window. She was going at the window with a cleaning cloth and a jar of "stain remover." She had managed to get down to plain, clean glass in one spot and was wearing an expression of grim satisfaction.

Brennan looked as relaxed as I had seen him in a long, long time. That was about to change.

"Sit down, Brennan." I then relived for him the interviews I had conducted at St. Bernadette's Choir School.

II

I had brought the children into an empty classroom one by one. Most of the kids had an anecdote about the choir, or Janeece, or last year's variety show. But nobody remembered the wig being removed from Burke's head until I got to the twelfth choir member, Ben Foley, a tall boy with curly brown hair, a freckled nose, and very light blue eyes.

"Father O'Flaherty near broke my arm! He was trying to pull my robe off after the skit. The stupid robe was too small for me and he pulled the sleeve of my shirt at the same time as the robe, and he jerked my arm up. I yelped, and Miss Darragh said: 'Don't be so rough, Daddy-O' or something like that. And everybody laughed."

I hardly dared to breathe. The entire case against Brennan Burke could stand or fall on what this boy said. "Let's go through that once more, Ben. Father O'Flaherty was trying to get your robe off, and he pulled your arm."

"Yeah."

"And that's when Ms. Darragh said: 'Don't be so rough, Daddy-O'?"

"Right. She turned and looked when I yelled. Father felt bad about yanking my arm. He didn't mean to hurt me. I felt like a baby for crying out." He looked down and busied himself rubbing an imaginary stain from his thumb.

"Ben, what was Ms. Darragh doing just before she turned? Can you remember?"

The boy shrugged. "I don't know. Just getting the costumes together, I guess. She looked like she was in a hurry. It was funny. She tore that Mozart wig off of Father Burke's head and practically lifted him right out of the chair with it." The little fellow grinned at the memory. I didn't move a muscle lest I interrupt the story Ben was telling. "Burke was rubbing his hair but you know how cool he is, like he forgets there's anyone else in the room. You could throw a bucket of water on his head if he was reading something, and he wouldn't look up. He didn't even turn around or say anything to her. Just kept reading some paper he had on the desk in front of him."

III

"It's her, Brennan." Burke was staring at me in disbelief. "It was Eileen who took the wig from your head and pulled your hair. Thanks to my inept questioning before, she didn't have to admit it because I told her the story you told me, that Father O'Flaherty had done it. Which you assumed was the case. And Mike didn't remember one way or the other. Because the incident meant nothing to him. But it meant everything to her, and she lied to me about it."

"But why would she do this? Weren't you just telling me the other day that she's carrying a torch for me?"

291

"Oh, you can be sure there's a motive. It's her."

"But what about this?" He pointed to the spot above his heart where God had marked him with the sign of the cross.

"That's been a stumbling block for us all along, but there has to be an explanation. We have to confront her. Together. This is not a situation somebody walks into alone. As outlandish as it seems, the woman is a killer."

Brennan sighed. "How could I not have noticed this in someone I see every day?"

"What was she like when you first arrived here? Last year I mean."

"It had been twenty years since I'd been here. I didn't even remember at first that I had met her." I closed my eyes. She sure as hell remembered him. "I don't recall how she was when I arrived last year. I was introduced to everyone, but I can't picture the scene at all. Except for the penetrating gaze of Marguerite. And Mike got off on the subject of the old country the instant we met. Eileen? I don't remember." He looked uncharacteristically abashed.

"You loomed large in her young life, Brennan, at least for a short time. When all this started I was in Eileen's office, and she was showing me pictures of the children at St. Bernadette's when it was an orphanage. There was a story about you, and you came off looking good. I thought at that point you were pals."

The priest shrugged. "Stories in which I'm the good guy are in short supply these days."

I got up abruptly, no longer able to bear the suspense. "Let's go. We'll see if we can catch her in the office. I'd suggest you change out of that shirt and into something a little less entertaining. We're not going to have any fun tonight." He changed into a grey T-shirt that was too small, grabbed his leather jacket and keys, and we bounded down the stairs, nearly knocking poor Mrs. Kelly off her feet.

We ran across to the youth centre and I took hold of his sleeve before he could ascend the stairs two at a time and get to his destination. "We have to play this carefully, Brennan. I know I said 'confront' her, but I did not mean we burst in and shake it out of her. Nice and easy till we know what we're up against."

We entered the building quietly, but Eileen was nowhere to be seen. And why should she still be working, well after dinner time?

"All right, Brennan. Where is Eileen Darragh when she's not at the office? I don't think I've ever pictured her in another location." He shook his head. "Do we rifle her desk drawers to find her address?" Brennan shrugged. I looked at the photographs on the wall, the children at the orphanage. "There's the picture Eileen showed me. She was eight. I think that was the year the proposed adoption fell through. Remember, I mentioned it to you."

Brennan examined the picture, then looked away.

"Do you remember her when she was that age?"

He shook his head, then turned his attention to the photo. "Who's this lad? There's something familiar about him."

I looked over his shoulder. "Georgie someone. What did Eileen tell me? I remember fantasizing about calling him as a witness . . . Of course! You saved his life. I had visions of him being a success and coming to testify on your behalf. Don't you find it touching that, after twenty years of criminal law, I could still have a first year law student's fantasy of things coming to a glorious climax in the courtroom?"

"I have that same fantasy, Monty. Same courtroom, same glory finish. But you're right, I remember this kid. An annoying little gobshite. I nearly drowned pulling him out of an undertow. I haven't thought of that in years. Not even when I came back here. Guess I didn't take the time to look at the photo display. Should have done. For a number of reasons." He looked at me. "Eileen was on that beach trip, was she?"

"Yes, she was. And she had an endearing little story about you. I remember it now. Some complicated feelings on her part where you're concerned, Brennan. You and another priest took the children out to the beach. That kid, Georgie, nearly ruined it by drowning before the party was over. As if that weren't enough, he threw up in the bus on the way home. Eileen's shoe ended up in the mess and you advised her to tell the nuns she had lost it so she could get a new pair."

"I did?"

"Yes. And you offered to sit with her and hear her confession. You were going to give her absolution, in advance, for the lie to the nuns. Eileen treasured that story about you. Attention from the — dare I put words in her mouth? — handsome young priest on a day away from the orphanage."

Brennan had dropped down onto the visitor's chair. He put his elbows on his knees and held his head in his hands. "I'm remembering that now. Sitting on the beach, stretching my toes in the sand, watching the kids make sandcastles. It was so bloody hot. All I wanted to do was dive in and swim. But I had to keep watch over the kids. If something happened, I didn't think the old fellow — I can't remember the name of the priest now — would make much of a lifeguard. Good thing, as it turned out."

I put a hand up to silence him. I was back with Eileen in the same room, hearing her voice, seeing the animation in her face as she spoke of that day in 1968. I heard what she heard, saw what she saw. Then I yanked open the top drawer of her desk and started a frantic search. "Monty! What's got into you?"

"Turn the room upside down if you have to. Just find her address!" I motioned to him impatiently. We both started grabbing papers at random.

"This looks like a tax form. Ms. Eileen Darragh, 1798c Robie Street."

"Right, the frat house. Let's move." I shoved everything into the drawer, slammed it, and bolted from the room, Brennan at my heels. "We'll take my car."

We pulled out of St. Bernadette's parking lot and roared up Morris Street to the west, waited impatiently at a red light where Morris becomes University Avenue, continued to Robie, and turned north.

"What did you think of, Monty?"

"Your sunburned back. It must have been painful."

"Yeah, must have been. But I'm over it now."

"No, you're not. When Eileen told me the story, I pictured you and the older priest sitting on the beach in your black summer shirts. Eileen said something about priests' short-sleeved shirts, and something funny the older man was wearing."

"Yes, I seem to recall the kids giggling about something he had on. A hat?"

I drove for a few minutes in silence. "A tie, that was it, with a funny picture on it. But I don't think she said anything about what you were wearing. Not till she mentioned your sunburn." I looked at Brennan in the passenger seat. "You sat out there bare-chested long enough to get a burn. 'Some boy jumped on Father Burke's sunburned back and he looked as if he wanted to screech.' That's what Eileen told me. You see what I'm saying?"

He nodded, looking miserable. "I was sunbathing long enough for Eileen to get a very good look at the cross above my heart."

"We've got her."

"This doesn't feel like a glory finish, Monty."

"It won't. Not tonight."

IV

Eileen's flat was in a badly maintained three-storey house on the corner of Robie and Yew streets. I parked at the back of the house where there was a deck and a series of fire escape stairs to the top. By the time I had yanked on the emergency brake, Burke was out of the car. I called to him to wait, but he paid me no mind. Just as I opened my door, an old sedan pulled in behind me and the driver blasted the horn. When I turned my head, I saw a curtain move in the basement apartment. So much for the element of surprise. Several young men emerged from the old car and the driver said to me, courteously enough: "You can't park here. But you'll be all right on the street." By the time I moved the car and got to the basement door, Burke had gone in.

I peered through the lace curtain in the door window. There was no sign of Brennan or Eileen. The door was unlocked and it opened directly onto a small vestibule, leading into the kitchen. There on the kitchen floor was Eileen, flat on her back with Brennan on top of her, kneeling on her legs, his hands holding hers together on her belly. Both were trying to catch their breath. I could not see the expression on his face; her expression was one of sheer terror. I was not sure whether they were aware of my presence. There was blood streaming down the left side of Brennan's forehead. A big, heavy flashlight lay on the floor beside them.

The kitchen was dark and shabby, everything in ugly shades of avocado green, gold, and brown, from the torn linoleum floor to the appliances and cupboard doors. I could see part of the living room, a gold-and-brown patterned shag carpet and a flowered chesterfield.

Eileen saw me and I thought I detected a look of relief. "Get off me," she ordered Burke.

"Are you going to attack me again if I do?" he asked. She struggled without replying. He relaxed his grip on her hands, then eased himself up and backed away. She lay for a moment, massaging her wrists, then stood. She moved to the doorway between the kitchen and the living room and leaned against it, looking from Brennan to me. She wore a pair of light blue pants with an elastic waist, a drip-dry blouse of pale pink, and an old white cardigan. She had fuzzy pink slippers on her feet.

Brennan looked into her eyes, and said softly: "Rachel." Eileen propelled herself from the doorway and lunged at him, hands going for his throat. He was ready for her. He caught her right arm and wrenched it behind her back, twisting her around in the process. Her left arm flailed harmlessly. He pushed her, not roughly, so that her head was against one of the cupboards. I moved to her side.

"Shall we call the police, or do you want to talk to us?" I asked, but she made no reply. "Can we let you go, or do we have to hold you like this all night till we hear what you have to say? You decide."

"Let me go if you want me to talk." Brennan slowly released her. She walked into the living room without giving us another glance and sat in a garish arm chair that almost matched the chesterfield.

"What happened?" I whispered to Brennan. "Why did you rush ahead without me? I know she heard us in the parking lot."

"She was waiting for me. I knocked and the door was open. I walked in and she launched herself at me with that flashlight in her hand. I don't know what she was aiming for but I ducked and she got me here." He touched his hairline. "I landed on my arse on the floor, but I managed to pin her down. Strong woman!"

"It could have been a lot worse for you. Have you forgotten she's killed two people?"

We headed for the living room, where Eileen sat, glaring with malevolence at Brennan's approach.

"You're an intelligent man, Burke," she began. "But you didn't figure this out, did you? And why should you? You were hardly aware of my existence. And yet, in a way, I am your creature. If it hadn't been for you, twenty-two years ago, I would be a different woman today. And two other women would still be alive. Undeservedly so."

I began the questioning. "What happened twenty-two years ago, Eileen?"

"I told you what happened. But I suppose it was not significant enough to register."

"You told me about the adoption that fell through. And that was a tragedy for you, I know. But what does that have to do with Brennan?"

"Ask *him*." He stared at her without comprehension. "Doesn't remember. Big surprise. Why would it stand out in his mind, the fact that he ruined my chance to be adopted by the Kernaghans?"

"Did he even know about your hopes for the Kernaghans?"

"He knew, but he didn't fucking care. He didn't give me a thought. A little girl named Natalie came to St. Bernadette's that year. She was five, delicate and adorable, with curly hair and great big, dark eyes. The Kernaghans came for a visit. I was in the parlour, preening myself and waiting, trying not to bite my fingernails. Burke was with the Kernaghans when they came in and he said something like: 'You know Eileen. And oh, let me go find Natalie. She came to us last month.' I knew Natalie's parents had been killed in some kind of tragedy. She didn't come from a trashy background like the rest of us. The Kernaghans must have thought: 'Natalie's so young, not as much damage to show up later. And we can't leave her here to waste away.' Who knows? I did hear one conversation about adoption shortly after that. A conversation between Burke and one of the sisters. I heard him say: "Eileen? Oh, she'll be fine. Now I need everybody over at choir early tomorrow.' That was it. He just tossed me off. And her! Sister. She knew better, but she went along, didn't she?"

Her eyes blazed hatred at Burke. Her face was mottled; her hair hung in lank strands and clung to her cheeks; her hands were bunched in tight fists on the arms of her chair as she leaned towards him. Facing her, silent, Brennan was the picture of desolation.

"How did you do it, Eileen?" I gambled that, with her secret exposed, she might take advantage of Burke's undivided attention to rub our noses in it as much as she could. "It's not only Father Burke you managed to fool. The police department, the prosecutor's office, and a jury of twelve were all taken in. How did you manage it?"

She saw through me but didn't care. This was her moment and she was going to live it to the fullest.

"I wanted to help that c — . . . Leeza Rae." Eileen could kill Leeza with her bare hands but could not bring herself to use the c-word against another woman. "I got her the job at the centre. I tried to help her fit in and make plans for her future. But she began to confide in me about that monstrous boyfriend of hers. He had raped a teenage girl. She spent half her days at work trying to arrange trips to Dorchester to see him. I nearly tipped my hand to you the first time we talked. I said something about no woman being able to side with a rapist. I had to be careful after that." No, you didn't, I thought. I had missed it, as I had missed so much else. "Anyway, I was visiting the law school one day."

I remembered questioning the librarian about the vandal who had gone along on the career day trip; didn't she tell me Eileen had her head stuck in a book?

"Fate presented me with a copy of the decision of the Court of Appeal in the rape case. Leeza had collaborated with the boys while they raped and humiliated that little girl. You know how I feel about people who betray children. And betrayal was on my mind a lot last winter, after *he* arrived on the scene." She jerked her head in Burke's direction. "When he showed up at St. Bernie's, it all came back to me. I couldn't keep it buried."

Eileen stopped for breath, then went on with an eerie calm. "Leeza Rae did not deserve to go on living. One can't expect any better from the males — at least they served some time in prison, though it should have been life. But that's always the way, isn't it, Collins?

"I had to remove her from the human race, so no other young girl would ever suffer the same treatment from her and whatever male was directing her life in the future. So, how could I eliminate her, and get away with it? I had no idea where to get my hands on a gun, and if I did, the police might be able to trace it. A skull fracture would have to do. I would strike her in the head until all brain function ceased. I knew it would be messy. I ordered two plain plastic raincoats from a mail order place out west. One for me, one for her.

"It seemed only fitting that Burke should get credit for the murder. After all, if it hadn't been for him, I would not have been here to do the deed at all. I already knew one useful thing about him: that little scar on his chest. I could not take my eyes off it that day I saw him at the beach. He was the first man I had ever seen half naked, because you'll remember I never had a father. A crucifix inscribed on his skin! I thought he was a messenger from God.

"If a person commits a violent crime against another, we're told, he always leaves a trace of himself behind. So I had to deposit some kind of evidence from *him* —" she looked at Brennan as if he were vermin "— on the body. The chances of close physical contact between him and me were about zero." Brennan squirmed. "So I would have to be clever. There was a variety show in the works, and I came up with the generous idea of including the choir, and him, in a last-minute addition to the show. How could I get some of his hair? Put a wig on his head! I considered borrowing a clerical jacket and collar and playing the role of Father Burke myself, so I could get threads from the jacket. But that would be too obvious. So I let Erin do the honours, in her own black jacket."

I took a chance that a question here and there about her methods would not be unwelcome. This would be my only opportunity to question her. "How did you know Father Burke would not take the wig off when the skit was over?"

"Oh, I didn't," Eileen replied. She moved forward in her seat. "At first I just hoped a couple of hairs would stick to the netting of the wig. But I wanted to be sure, so I put a few small dabs of glue in it just before I passed it to Erin to hand to him. Then, when he didn't take it off right away after the skit, I decided to step in. Some of the children were starting to take their robes off. Burke had been looking for a copy of the program, so I put one on a desk, and he sat down. I got behind him and pulled the wig off, making sure I got a good grip on his hair." She seemed lost in memory, then continued: "I could scarcely believe my luck when you, Collins, came in to ask about the wig. Oh, you had me worried for a minute there, but then you told me Father O'Flaherty had removed the wig. Burke hadn't turned around, so he thought it was Mike. At the time, Mike was botching the job of pulling a robe off one of the kids, so I took the opportunity to use his name: 'Take it easy there, Father O'Flaherty' or whatever I said. It was at that moment I knew I was going to kill Leeza, and nobody was going to trace it back to me." Eileen sounded elated. "Two months went by before I got my chance." Eileen jumped up. Brennan and I tensed. But she turned away from us. "This is where it happened." She pointed to a simple wooden chair in front of a table, on which rested a dusty plant and a small plate of soda crackers smeared with margarine. "I made plans to meet Leeza after the Valentine's dance and drive her here. The pretext was that I had found a way she could get a regular ride up to Dorchester to see the rapist. I put a little address book on that table and told her the guy who would drive her was listed under T. Then I went into my room and put on my black raincoat and hood, so I wouldn't get anything on my clothes and there would be no traces of my clothing on her. I told her I had just bought the coat. Did she think it looked all right? I asked if she had found the guy's phone number, which she hadn't of course; it didn't exist.

"When she bent over the book again, I was ready. I pulled out my weapon. I wonder if Father O'Flaherty ever noticed that one of his stone crosses is missing, one the size of a small hatchet. You won't find it here. I should buy him a new one for Christmas! Sign Burke's name to the card."

"A Celtic cross!" I burst out. So she had made a slip that day we were painting the church. What had she said to Maura? "At least he didn't go at you with his crucifix." Poor Mike O'Flaherty.

"I pulled it out from under the raincoat. And I brought it down on her stupid, worthless little head. Over and over till I knew she couldn't survive. Carved my signature and yours, Father, into her skin, and waited till she breathed her last."

Eileen had her back to us. We didn't say a word, and she resumed her narrative, her voice now overly loud. "Do you hear that?" She pointed to the ceiling, and I realized a stereo had been thumping and pounding the whole time we had been in the basement apartment. She returned to her seat. "It's always like that. Frat boys. That's what I have to live with, every night. Can't afford anything better. It was like that the night I brought Leeza here. I knew I could count on the stereo. Nobody heard a thing. Then I pretended to stagger to my car, propping Leeza up with my arm around her. We looked like two more drunks reeling from the frat house. I had her in the other raincoat by that time. I didn't want any blood in my car. She had been in the car on the way over, so I vacuumed it the next afternoon at a car wash in Dartmouth. But the police never examined it. Anyway, that night I drove along the service road at the top of the peninsula, till I got to a good spot under the bridge. When I thought the coast was clear, I dumped her out. Once she was gone, I started shaking. I drove home, cleaned the apartment, had a shower, and hosed down my raincoat.

"Tanya Cudmore," Eileen announced in a voice that was all business. "Same thing pretty much. My pretext for her was something about financial assistance through St. Bernadette's for bereaved families. Good thing I set it up on the phone. I wouldn't have been able to keep a straight face in person. Bereaved, ha! 'What kind of financial assistance, Ms. Darragh?' How about this: not living long enough to have to pay another month's rent, you worthless child killer! I warned Tanya not to tell anyone about the offer because other relatives, greedy ones like the child's bereaved mother, for instance, might want the same. She fell for it and came for the secret rendezvous. I said: 'Excuse me, Tanya. I have to try on this raincoat. I only have one more day to return it if it doesn't fit. The papers for the assistance program are there on the table. Is the light okay there?' Whack, and whack again. One less wicked stepmother in the world. She got the initials and the crucifix too. Credit where credit is due. Of course, I only had one raincoat left so I had to hose it down to get any traces of my clothes off it. It was still wet when I put it on her. Another two drunks stagger out of the frat house in the wee hours. Same routine with the body drop. Same cleanup. Same lack of suspicion directed my way. And how could it be otherwise? They couldn't pin the Rae murder on you, but there was no room for doubt when it was Janeece's stepmother."

Brennan sat there, miserable, shaking his head. Then the telephone shrilled, and all three of us jumped. Eileen got up and answered it. "Oh, hi, Marguerite. No, no trouble. Dinner is long over. I have some friends in this evening." Brennan and I exchanged glances. "Uh-huh. Both folders are on your desk. You're welcome. See you tomorrow." Click. I tried to maintain a neutral expression. Eileen turned to us.

"Imagine you two being here. How does it compare with the place you lived in in Rome, *Father?* Even the mouldings were made of marble, I heard you tell someone. Well, no mouldings here, marble or otherwise. Not what you're used to either, eh, Collins? Somebody told me you have two houses. It's not the home I had hoped for, to say the least. But here I am."

Eileen walked to the end of the living room and turned: "Come into my room. I have something to show you." She caught us exchanging glances, and gave a harsh laugh. "Don't worry. Not *that.* And, it's not booby-trapped. After all, I wasn't expecting you."

She opened the door and preceded us in. She flicked on a low wattage lamp on her bedside table, and sat down on the narrow bed, with its white chenille bedspread. "Have a look around. Is this the room of a self-confident woman, or what? Confident the police would never suspect me. And confident that nobody, but nobody, would ever be joining me in my bedchamber. Guess I should have been the one to make a vow of celibacy, eh Brennan?" He stood in the doorway, unmoving.

On her bedroom wall was a large photo of a weeping woman, the text of Matthew 2:18 printed beside it: Rachel weeping for her children. On the opposite wall was a poster showing a baby's foot, with an inscription from William Blake: "The angel that presided o'er my birth said: 'Little creature, formed of joy and mirth, go, love without the help of anything on earth.'"

"So, who figured out the code for Matthew 2:18? I didn't think it would be that difficult. The letters are useful in another way, too. Both killers got to sign on. I, Brennan. I, Rachel." She turned and looked at Burke. "I think I got that cross just about where it is on you." She rose, went towards him, and put her hand on the hem of his T-shirt as if to pull it up, but he grasped her hand and held it still.

For a moment I thought he was going to throw her across the room. Instead he wrapped his arms around the woman and held her close. "Eileen, if your quarrel was with me, why did you take it out on those two women?" He spoke quietly, keeping her in his embrace. "Why didn't you try to kill me, if you hate me this much?"

Eileen began to tremble, and to weep. No one spoke. If Burke had not been holding her, I suspect she would have collapsed. After two or three wordless minutes, she began to speak in a broken voice. "I couldn't kill a priest. You have the power to change bread and wine into the real presence of Christ. And you have been marked by God. How do you think it feels to be betrayed by someone marked by God with His sign? When I heard . . . when I heard that you weren't wearing a cross around your neck when that image appeared, it was all I could do to keep from screaming out loud in the courtroom. What had I done? I knew I had done the right thing to eliminate those two people, to protect other children from them. To send them to hell. But was I wrong about you? If you were God's instrument, chosen to do His work, then who was I to question the decisions you made, even about me? But no." She wrenched herself away from Burke, sat on the edge of her bed, and fixed him with a look of utmost condemnation. Her voice grew harsh again. "What you did to me could not be called a decision, could it? You didn't give me a thought. You were so offhand about it, the day you cancelled my life. 'Eileen? Oh, she'll be fine.' Fine? Without parents, without a family, without love? Do I look fine to you, *Father?*"

Brennan slid down the doorframe till he was sitting on the floor, elbows on knees, head in hands. "I don't know what I can possibly say to you, Eileen."

"But the worst . . ." she broke in as if he had not spoken ". . . the worst moment of all was when I heard in court . . ." She turned her ravaged face to me. "You saw me that night when the jury went out. You thought I was falling apart about *him* going to jail. And in a way, you were right. The reason I lost control that night," she said, turning to Brennan, "was that I had heard you say in court that you were the father of a child."

Brennan opened his mouth, but he was either unable or unwilling to speak. I sat in the corner of the room running the numbers through my head. He had entered the seminary in 1962, and his child was born in 1963. Twenty-seven years ago. Surely Eileen could not be . . . It was 1968 when Burke arrived in Halifax, and later that year he "betrayed" Eileen by introducing a more lovable child to the Kernaghans. Didn't Eileen say she was eight years old at the time? That would make her thirty; she looked older, but a hard life will do that. Had the orphanage photos been dated, or had she supplied the dates when describing

303

them? But surely, she could not possibly think —

"You were the father of a child, who was given up for adoption. You said 'he or she.' Where was your child put up for adoption?" she challenged Burke. His face gave nothing away.

"You don't know, is that it?" she persisted. "Is your child here in Nova Scotia, Father Burke?" His face was white and he stared at her, speechless. I felt lost. What was going on? I knew of Sandra's connections with this province, her summers in Chester, her friendship with the Strattons. Was it possible the child had been placed here?

"Because if it was a baby girl, and she was here, that changes everything, doesn't it?" Eileen said, nodding in accord with her own internal logic. Her face was streaked with tears, her voice a mere whisper. "I knew I could not bear it. I would not be able to go on, if Natalie, the little girl placed with the Kernaghans, was your daughter."

Things had taken a turn I had not anticipated, and it was clear from Brennan's expression that his reaction was the same. Eileen continued: "Because if little Natalie was your child, then . . . then what you did was perfectly right, and it was not a betrayal of me. You would naturally have to take care of your own child first. What father would not? And if that was the case, then I had been wrong about you all my life. And I had committed two murders in your name when you were blameless." Tears streamed down her face. "I was ready to take my own life that night."

Brennan sat, pale and motionless, gazing at Eileen in silence. My mind went back to the night we had come upon her in the youth centre, when she wept so despondently. Of all the ways I might have interpreted the scene, I could not have come up with this.

Eileen dragged the sleeve of her sweater across her eyes, and spoke in a brisk, no-nonsense voice. "I told myself it couldn't be true. The age was right, but there was no way *his* child would be in such dire straits that she'd wind up at St. Bernadette's, with or without him on the scene. No doubt she, or he, would have been a beautiful, bright, talented little child. Not St. Bernadette's material. So I was determined to put the idea out of my head. Natalie Kernaghan has done very well for herself, by the way. She has her medical degree, is married and expecting her first child." Eileen made a point of looking around at her sordid surroundings, the frat boys hooting and stomping above our heads.

"Meanwhile I have to fear for my life, with all these drunken louts in the building. One night I woke up and found two of them in my kitchen, looking through the cupboards. I had to get a deadbolt after that. At my own expense."

A thought occurred to me then. "Did you break in to the arch-diocesan office?"

"I didn't break in! But I did spend part of New Year's Day there."

"Reading files."

"Reading *his* file, and scattering others to cover my tracks. Not because I expected to find anything useful for my plan. I already had everything I needed. It sounds so stupid now, but I wanted to see if he had written any letters, or if there was anything about his time here before." If there was any reference to her, is what she meant. "I knew where the secretary kept her keys and I copied one. I got in but somebody came so I had to run."

"Why did you remove Father O'Flaherty's file?"

"I didn't even see Mike's file. I don't think it was there."

He had removed it himself, I realized. He didn't want anyone reading about the exorcism or his exile afterwards. I wondered when he had spirited it away.

Brennan looked at me, and Eileen caught the glance. Her head swivelled from one of us to the other. "You're my lawyer!" It was nearly a scream. "He's my priest, my confessor! This conversation is secret. You can't use it!"

"It doesn't work that way, Eileen. You know what has to happen." I got up. "I'm going to the phone. Stay where you are and don't make things any worse." Brennan leaned forward, tense, ready to subdue her. But she didn't move. I dialed the number of duty counsel for Legal Aid. "You're going to have a lawyer and the police are going to be here. Talk to the lawyer, not the cops." She did not even glance at me as I spoke.

V

After the arrest, Brennan and I drove away.

"Where to?" I asked him.

"I'm too wound up to go home. Drive to the park."

We sat in the car, in the lot between Point Pleasant Park and the container terminal. We watched a heavy surf crash in from the ocean against the breakwater. Lights winked at us across the dark water. Uncharacteristically, Brennan talked at length about his reaction to Eileen's revelations, how his careless introduction of Natalie, almost offhand and quickly forgotten by him, was so unforgivable, in Eileen's eyes and now in his. I tried to offer comfort by reminding him that the decision was made by the Kernaghans, not by him, and that he could not be held responsible for the way Eileen lashed out at two young women twenty-two years later. But he wasn't listening. I knew it was a rare occasion when he gave voice to his innermost thoughts, and we would be back to the old self-contained Brennan before long. If it could do him some good, I would let him talk.

Eventually, he wound down and was quiet for a few minutes. All we heard was the sound of the breakers. Then he tried to laugh. "What wouldn't I give to see the face on Marguerite Dunne when she hears this."

"No reason you shouldn't see her. I had not considered anything beyond this moment, to tell you the truth. Isn't it better if Marguerite hears from us, rather than from the police or the news media, that the assistant director of St. Bernadette's Youth Centre is a double murderer?"

The choir school was in darkness when we went in. We found Marguerite's number and Brennan dialed. "Marguerite. Brennan Burke here. No, I'm not stocious drunk. And if I were, what makes you think it would be you I'd be calling? Yes, I do know it's after midnight." He looked at me and rolled his eyes. "Yes, my mother did bring me up right. Well, I've been accused of worse, as you know. Marguerite, shut the fuck up. This is urgent. Meet me at the centre. You won't want this to wait till morning." Click.

Brennan went into the hall when Marguerite arrived, combed, coiffed and dressed for the day. Was that a flicker of fear in her eyes?

If so, it was quickly masked. She stopped and stared.

"Brennan. You have blood on your hands."

"No," he said, shaking his head.

"Whose is it?"

Then he remembered and touched his head. The cut at his hair line was bleeding again. "It's just my own."

"Ah."

"I'll go clean up."

Burke disappeared into the nearest washroom and I heard water splashing. It was only then that I realized I was in the shadows, and that Marguerite thought she and Brennan were alone. "Sister," I said, stepping into the lighted hallway.

If she was startled, she didn't show it. "Are you catering this event, whatever it is?"

"I guess that will depend on how your appetite is later on."

"I see."

Brennan returned unbloodied and motioned with his head towards Marguerite's office. We followed her in and sat. She looked from one to the other of us from behind her desk.

"Well?"

Brennan leaned towards her. "The IBR carved into the victims' bodies. It stands for One, Two, Eighteen. Matthew."

She thought for a few moments, then: "Rachel, weeping for her children. Of course. Of course." She closed her eyes and seemed to be going over all the evidence she could recall. "It was a woman then." But she did not, or could not, make the connection between the killer and her own devoted deputy. "Weeping for her children, and striking out at you. A casualty of your Black Irish charms, I suppose, Brennan, coming back to haunt you?"

"A casualty of my black-hearted thoughtlessness. And it's very close to home. Otherwise, I wouldn't have called you here." Marguerite was very still. Her eyes locked on to Brennan's face. He finally said: "Eileen."

Neither of us took any pleasure in seeing Marguerite's face as the shock hit her full force.

Chapter 22

. . . there's someone who'll stand beside you.
Turn around, look at me.
And there's someone who'll love and guide you.
Turn around, look at me.
— Jerry Capehart, "Turn Around, Look at Me"

I

My client and I stood in the parking lot of St. Bernadette's, looking at the church. "I wonder if Marguerite had a moment of doubt about coming here tonight," Brennan mused. "Do you suppose it entered her head that I was the killer and she was next?"

"If she was afraid of you, she covered it well."

"She would. Well, everyone will know soon enough. I'm not a scary guy."

The words came to me then, from Moody Walker: "A real scary Irish guy." That encounter still haunted me. I grasped Burke's arm and spoke quietly: "Brennan, what was going on with that young girl up at Mount A, the one whose boyfriend you beat up?"

He sighed and looked into my eyes. "That was my daughter, Monty. That creature had hurt my little girl."

"Your *daughter!?*"

"My child, mine and my girlfriend in New York. My girlfriend Sandra." There was no point in telling him I knew Sandra. And hadn't

308

I heard something else just recently about the birth of the child? It would come to me. Burke continued: "I nearly passed out when Eileen asked if my child was here in Nova Scotia. This killer knows my little girl? Fortunately, for all of us, she does not."

"So it wasn't this little Natalie . . ."

"No. I don't even remember Natalie." He was silent for a few moments, then took up his story again: "I wasn't supposed to know where our baby had been placed for adoption. It was confidential. But I found out. The Catholic Church has a long reach! I'm sure Sandra has no idea where the child is or who the adoptive parents are; she didn't want to know. It was her decision to place the baby here. Maybe she thought it was a safer place to grow up. People aren't running around carrying guns here. I don't know. We weren't on speaking terms. But I had to know the baby was going to be all right. And she was. A beautiful family, the most loving parents you could ask for. I never went near them, or her. Just heard from time to time that the little one was doing fine. Till I was told that she had gone to Mount Allison on a music scholarship — of course! — and had fallen in with this ne'er-do-well of a boyfriend. I heard he had hit her and knocked her down a set of stairs. Then apologized, as they all do: 'It will never happen again.' Fuck that. It always happens again. I decided to make sure it didn't. Her parents probably knew nothing about it. You know what kids are like when they go off to college. They sure as hell don't fill the parents in on what they're up to. So I took it upon myself to do her father's dirty work for him, and leave the family in blissful ignorance. Problem solved. And I'd do it again."

I stood there, nodding. I knew the question was inane and probably inappropriate, but curiosity won out. "So, who does she look like?"

Far from being offended, Brennan seemed tickled to be asked. "I'd say Sandra's face, my colouring. Not as tall as Sandra. And too thin when I saw her. I did stop in to hear her play the violin here in Halifax before I went on my mission. And I had seen her perform once before. I was an anonymous smiling face in the audience. I'm sure her parents are very proud."

I smiled at him. "I'm sure they are."

"So you can see why I was so desperate to know whether that incident was going to come out in court. If it had turned out that this

Myers was involved in the killings, or if the fight was going to surface in court, I'd have pleaded guilty to the murders rather than drag her name into this. Nobody must ever know I've been watching out for her. She's the only one in this world I would protect by giving up my life." I stood staring at him. I knew he meant it.

It occurred to me then that the police might have unearthed this information, and that might explain why Karl Schenk had not used it on rebuttal. It would have corroborated the Crown's theory on motive, but it might also have engendered sympathy among the jurors. I would never know.

"Monty, I'm more grateful than I can ever say, for all you've done." He put his hand out and we shook. Then he pulled me towards him for a quick embrace. "Poker night Wednesday. Mass in the ancient tongue Saturday morning. Be there. I'm thinking of conscripting you as an altar boy. God knows, you look the part. So start brushing up on your Latin." Unfazed by what must have been a look of astonishment on my face, he continued: "You've done your job, for me. Now I'll do mine, for you." He started away, then turned. "Oh, and you'd better start bringing your own little daughter to Mass, so she can put a name to what she already knows."

II

Over the next few days a frenzy of publicity erupted. My client was exonerated, and the entire legal apparatus went into gear again, this time for somebody else. Brennan and I turned down requests for interviews and, as we had from the beginning, we referred all reporters' calls to Rowan Stratton.

Brennan had missed his chance to be guest conductor of the Halifax Symphony and the Recordare Chorus in Mozart's *Coronation Mass*; there was not enough time for him to prepare. But Rowan stopped by my office one day to tell me Brennan would have a spot in the program after all. The symphony's conductor had graciously offered to put the *Kyrie in D Minor* back in the program and have Brennan conduct that little segment. He was happy to accept, and he had embarked on a hectic rehearsal schedule with the performers.

I was pleased to hear it. "That should do him the world of good, take his mind off what he's been through."

"Most certainly. He is talking about scheduling a choir school concert as well, a few months down the road. So he is on the mend." Rowan got up to leave, then paused. "I was speaking last night to an old, old friend of Brennan's, and more recently of yours, I dare say."

"Oh?"

"Sandra Worthington called to express her relief at the way things had turned out. Said she had never doubted him. Good of her, I thought. But of course she knew him well enough to know he wasn't a killer. I had no doubts myself, it goes without saying. How about you, Montague?" Rowan gave me a cynical look.

"I doubt everybody, Rowan. I'd be no good to you otherwise."

"Sandra tells me she's flying up here in a few weeks' time. Not here exactly. She's renting a car and going to the old place in Chester. I got the impression the property may be about to change hands. When her grandparents died, it passed to their son, Sandra's uncle. Not sure what the story is now. Sylvia and I will drive out there to see her. Sandra asked me to pass along her congratulations, by the way, for the work you did on the case. So, there you have it."

Chester is only forty minutes from Halifax. I would make a point of getting the dates of her visit from Rowan. I thought about Sandra. I had taken a shine to her in New York, when she had filled me in on her history with Burke, and we had shared some laughs over a bottle of wine. Just then I recalled what I had been trying to remember when Brennan spoke of protecting his daughter. With all the drama that had unfolded in the murder case, I had never followed up on the information Sister Dunne had given me, about the maternity nurse who was present when Sandra and Brennan's child was born.

I called Marguerite, who still sounded shell-shocked over the unmasking of Eileen Darragh as the murderer, and I got the nurse's telephone number. It took a couple of tries, but later that afternoon I was on the phone with Mary Beth McConnell in Connecticut. I explained who I was and how I had obtained her number. I told her a bit about Brennan and the case, and how it had all turned out.

"Yes, I remember that poor girl. She came down with eclampsia. Hypertension, convulsions. She was so sick, and so unhappy. It was heartbreaking. I was the nurse in charge. We were keeping a close eye on her."

"Did anyone come to see her at all?"

"Her parents, of course, and her grandparents, I believe. So concerned. They spent as much time with her as they could during visiting hours. The poor little thing was so ill, I don't think she even knew they were there. And the young lad, the priest." I could tell from the nurse's voice that she was smiling. "He was new to his job, like me. Very nervous. He wasn't supposed to be there." That's putting it mildly, I thought. He was a seminarian.

"He asked me if he could come in and sit with her quietly in the nighttime. I didn't know what his connection was. At first I thought he was her brother or something. But why be so hush-hush? I had my suspicions, but I kept them to myself. What's the difference? He was so kind to her, even though she had no awareness of his presence. I remember looking in and he was wiping her face with a cool cloth, talking to her all the while. He was with her for . . . I think it was the two nights of her illness . . . always the same, there in his soutane, black hair falling over his forehead, holding her hand, talking quietly.

"And when the baby was born. Well! It was all I could do to keep him out of the delivery room. I mean men, fathers, go into the delivery room all the time now. As you probably know. But then? Fathers waited outside, and paced. Not that anyone ever said he was the . . . Well anyway, he was a nervous wreck, and the delivery was a long one. She was, of course, in bad shape afterwards. She had made arrangements beforehand about the adoption, and never wavered about that. I don't know whether she would even remember holding her baby. But he would."

"He held the baby?"

"Oh yes. He asked me if he could bless her . . . I think the baby was a girl. Maybe he wanted to baptize her. So I left the baby in the room with him and the mother that evening. Procedures are in place these days, God knows. But I was newly in charge, and he and I were both on the same side of the Tiber. That was much more of a bond then than it would be now. I knew he meant well. One of the other girls said she saw him walking back and forth in the room rocking the infant, talking and singing to her. I went in when it was time to take the baby to the nursery. The young fellow kissed the baby's forehead, kissed the mother, and walked out. I never saw him again."

"And she never knew he was there."

"She never knew."

III

I had a lot of work to clear away. I was determined to take some time off, to unwind from the pressures of the past months, and to enjoy the company of my kids. I managed to get out of the office and stay out for an entire week late in November. Winter had come early, and there was enough snow for a couple of days of tobogganing on Citadel Hill with Normie, Tom, and Lexie. I began to recover from the stress and exhaustion of the trial, and Maura and I were able to conduct ourselves with civility.

And then it was the eighth of December, a Saturday. Brennan's concert was scheduled for that night. The Strattons were planning to drive to Chester early in the afternoon to have a brief visit with Sandra before returning to the city for the performance. So I planned my visit for the morning. I took the old Number 3 highway and drove with the ocean on my left until I reached the turnoff to the small town of Chester. Large wooden houses with enormous sea-facing windows lined the narrow streets. I made my way past the Chester Yacht Club and across the causeway to the peninsula, where the Strattons had their cottage. The presence of a rental car tipped me off when I reached the Worthington place, a grey-shingled summer house with a veranda. And there was Sandra, all bundled up, returning from a morning walk. I got out and watched her approach. I could smell snow in the air.

"Monty!" She came over and gave me a kiss and a hug. Her cheek was pink and cold. She stood back and assessed me. "You look a little more, shall we say, bluesy than you did last time I saw you."

"Old and haggard, you mean? I've been through the wringer over the last few months, and I'm sure it shows. But a visit with you will perk me up. Rowan told me you were here. What brings you to Chester at this time of year?"

"I have to decide whether to buy this place or let the family know it can go up for sale. Come inside. I've got a fire on."

The cottage had a large living room with a stone fireplace and a crackling fire. Everything in the room was the colour of the seashore: the floor was the shade of sand, the walls were shell white, the furniture and other objects in the room were sea green or blue.

"Coffee or cocoa?"

"What are you having?"

"Cocoa."

"Make it a double."

While she waited for the milk to heat up, we chatted about New York, what was coming up at the Met, what her children were doing. When we were sipping our steaming cocoa, Sandra said: "You didn't drive out here to tell me war stories about the murder trial, I hope."

"No, I've already had all the attention I need for that episode. And a waiting room full of new criminal clients. No. I drove out here to see you." She smiled and waited in silence. "Though there is something I want to tell you."

"About *him,* I presume."

"Sandra, I probably shouldn't meddle in this. Even though you wouldn't believe the way he's meddled in my life, but that's a story for another day. Sometime we'll sit down over a few drinks and I'll tell you about the morning he showed up at my place unannounced, in clerical dress, and found me flaked out with a woman I'd brought home."

"Really!" She looked at me keenly. "I'm going to take you up on that; I intend to find out a lot more about this decadent life you seem to be leading. So, I suppose Bren got a leg up over this woman, to use his own words, as soon as your back was turned."

"No, no, he didn't. But all that can wait. As I said, I probably should leave this alone. In fact, those are the words I generally live by: let it be. One of the many things about me that my wife dislikes."

"That, and the other women you flake out with?"

"She doesn't sit at home nights, mourning my absence."

I became absorbed in swirling the hot, sweet liquid around in my mug. Then I faced her. "About Brennan. I know he's not perfect —" This brought forth an un-Worthington-like guffaw from Sandra, but

I soldiered on. "He's not perfect, but he's a better man than you think he is. In one way at least."

"Right. He's not a serial killer. *Ergo,* he's the man of my dreams." I hesitated and she said: "All right. Rehabilitate him in my eyes. Go ahead."

I put my cup on the table and leaned forward. "He was with you in the hospital for two nights when you were ill; he was there when the baby was born. He loved you very much. Both of you."

Sandra was completely still, her cup forgotten in her hand. She stared into my eyes. Then I could tell she was no longer looking at me but at a scene that had played itself out a quarter of a century before. Several minutes went by before she asked me in a low, nearly hostile voice: "How do you know this? Is this something he told you?"

"No. I heard it from the nurse who was on duty in the hospital at the time. Brennan doesn't know I found this out. It's not the kind of thing he would reveal. He was there, Sandra. He abandoned you after that, I know. He was called to the priesthood. You and I can't possibly understand that. But he was there watching over you, sitting with you, stroking your forehead, talking to you. He was there for the child's birth. He held the baby and sang to her. Then he kissed the baby, kissed you, and walked out."

I could see Sandra struggling to keep her face from betraying her emotions. She and Brennan were cut from the same cloth in that respect, I thought. She said, in not much more than a whisper: "You know, from time to time, something would come into my mind, something I thought Brennan had said. Something about a baby. Then I would realize he could not have said it. I attributed it to someone else, or to wishful thinking on my part. These may have been things he said to me then, when I was in such a fever."

She fell silent again, and gazed out the window towards the ocean, my presence forgotten.

Chapter 23

So I'll drink today, love, I'll sing to you, love,
in pauper's glory my time I'll bide.
No home or ties, love, a restless rover,
if I can't have you by my side.
— Jimmy Rankin, "Fare Thee Well Love"

I

The Rebecca Cohn Auditorium was filled nearly to capacity on Saturday night. I had parked the car at the house on Dresden Row, and I waited for Maura and Tommy Douglas to get ready. Lexie Robinson arrived just after I did, her magnificent golden hair shining over her black coat and dress. We settled Normie with a babysitter and walked to the Dalhousie Arts Centre, where the Cohn is located. The concert was to begin with a few arias and choral numbers from Mozart's operas, followed by a couple of short orchestral works. After intermission, Brennan would conduct the orchestra and chorus in the *Kyrie*.

Brennan emerged from backstage just before the concert began, and sat in front of Maura, who was to my right. I expected to see him in black tie, but he was wearing the Roman collar. He turned and greeted Tom and his new love: "Evening, Mr. Douglas. Ms. Robinson." They both smiled and Tommy asked Father Burke whether he was nervous. "Nerves of steel, my son, nerves of steel. Tempered in the forge of your dad's court room." I had a momentary vision of Burke on the witness stand, being eviscerated by the Crown prosecutor, as all the salacious details of his past were exposed to the merciless light of day. I resolutely put it from my mind.

Brennan reached over and took Maura's hand in his. "Any requests, sweetheart?"

She favoured him with a rare and beaming smile: "'Mack the Knife'?"

"After the show. There's a dinner party at the Faculty Club. You come, we'll dance." Brennan leaned over to me. "What did I tell you, Monty? I'm just a choirboy."

And then it was showtime. Whenever I looked at him during the first half of the concert, his hands were in restrained but constant motion as if he were directing the music.

He disappeared backstage at intermission. Maura and I chatted with the Strattons and other people we knew until it was time to resume our seats. I happened to be looking around as the lights went down, and that is when I saw her. She had not been in the audience for the first part of the show. Sandra Worthington sat in the middle of the auditorium and looked straight ahead. There were snowflakes on her coat and in her hair. She did not see me staring at her. She did not know I saw the quick intake of breath, the hand going up to her mouth, when she caught her first glimpse of the man who had been her lover more than twenty-five years before, a man now dressed in the immaculate black and white of a cultic priesthood, with lines at the corner of his eyes and strands of silver in his black hair. Her unblinking eyes were riveted to the stage. I turned to watch Brennan as he acknowledged the applause. He stood with his military bearing, and bowed his head to the audience, his face as usual giving nothing away, then took his place before the choir and orchestra at the left of the stage, so we saw him in three-quarter profile. He raised his arms to begin.

He had told me the opening chords of the *Kyrie in D Minor* would terrify me into submission to the Almighty, and I knew what he meant with the orchestra's first massive, threatening chord. The dark and foreboding music was taken up by the chorus, and the plea for mercy unfolded with sombre dignity. The music would be especially meaningful, I suspected, to a man who must have prayed ceaselessly to his God for mercy, as he faced the very real possibility of life in prison for murder. What I had seen in Brennan with his children's choir, I saw again. His face, transfigured by the music, registered every nuance of Mozart's divine composition. Nothing else existed for him; the audience was forgotten. When the last note sounded, the audience's reaction was immediate and heartfelt, the applause loud and prolonged. This time, as he acknowledged the applause, extending his hand to the chorus and the orchestra, he flashed a smile that reached his eyes and made him a new man. He had lived through the immeasurable stress of a harrowing year and had come out on the other side, doing what he most loved to do. Graciously, he turned and made a little bow in my direction. He was about to leave the stage, the applause still washing over him, when he froze and stared stupefied into the audience.

Eventually, he returned to his seat in front of us, but kept stealing glances to the middle of the auditorium for the duration of the concert. I did not dare turn to see if the glances were returned. When the music was over and the audience was filing out, dozens of people came up to compliment him on his part in the concert. He thanked them warmly but it was clear he was distracted, his eyes searching the crowd for that one face he had never expected to see. Then, when she finally appeared in front of him, all he could do was stare at her without speaking.

Sandra put out her hand and he took it in his. "Nothing to say, Brennan?"

"Be careful what you wish for," came a tart voice as a woman brushed past them. Marguerite Dunne, on her way out.

"The music was wonderful," Sandra said to him. He nodded. "You're looking very distinguished, Brennan."

That's when I could see the beginnings of a smile on his face. "Didn't I look distinguished way back when?" They stood, taking each other's measure. "And you, a woman of shining loveliness then and no less now."

"I'm going way out on a limb here, but it's not half bad to see you, Brennan."

He put a hand to his chest. "Be still, my heart!"

"Hi, Father!" The little voice came from somewhere below shoulder level. I recognized a brother and sister from the choir school. "We won't have to do that spooky *Kyrie,* will we? I mean I liked it and you did a good job and stuff, but . . ." The boy turned beet red.

"Ian, if you say it's off the program, it's off." He ruffled the little guy's hair.

Then Father O'Flaherty popped up, with a young priest I had never seen. Maura came over after seeing Tommy and Lexie off for the evening. When I looked around again, Sandra was gone. Brennan noticed this a moment after I did. He scanned the crowd to find her, but she had vanished. He turned to me. "Monty. Did you see the one I was just talking to here? About this high, short hair, lovely face, did you see her?" I realized he had no idea I knew who she was.

"Yes, I did, but I don't see her now." Why did she bolt like that?

"Excuse me," Brennan said to the person speaking in his ear, and he made for the exit.

"Are you going over for the party?" Maura asked me.

"Wouldn't miss it."

"Where is Brennan off to?" she asked, craning her neck.

I shrugged, and we started for the Faculty Club, a short walk away on the Dalhousie campus. A light snow was falling over the stately neoclassical stone buildings. The wind was starting to pick up. Father O'Flaherty was outside the auditorium, in a bright blue parka, with a gaudy, badly knitted scarf wrapped around his neck. I asked him if he was coming to the party.

"Monty, I cannot, as much as I regret to say so. I have a hospital visit I can't in good conscience put off any longer. Isn't it grand to see Brennan recovering from his ordeal?"

"Yes, it is."

"Thanks to you, Monty. Though I suppose . . . how should I put this? It must have been expensive for Brennan."

"You're right, Mike. I cut our fees as much as I could. I never understood how a priest could have that much money saved up but he assured me —"

"Oh, he'd have been coddin' you; he wouldn't have money like that. He had a line of credit, so I think he borrowed the money. You know his sister Maire was determined to pay for his defence. The two of them own a lovely piece of land outside Dublin. Apparently he's been willing to part with it for years, to help her out financially, but she always refused. She loves the place. Yet she was willing to give it up for her brother. She wanted to put it up for sale without telling him and forge his signature to sell his interest in it. Maire and I had sharp words about it over the phone! I urged her not to sell."

"That's what your calls to her were about? Brennan thought you were carrying on a long-distance love affair!"

We left him on the sidewalk, gobsmacked.

Maura and I entered the Faculty Club and ascended to the Great Hall, with its huge multi-paned windows, hanging tartans, and chandeliers. There were tables throughout the hall, many already taken. A buffet was being set up at one end of the room, and I took note of the bar at the other end. There was a small stage with microphones, a piano, and guitar. The Strattons waved us to their table. "Where's the good Father?" Rowan asked. Did the Strattons know Sandra had come from Chester to see the performance? Just then Brennan strode in, his black clerical shirt open at the neck, the white collar gone.

"Evening, fans. No, don't get up," he said, then immediately turned to whisper in my ear: "The one I asked you about?"

"Yes?"

"Ever see her again?" I said I had not, and he gave a short sigh of frustration. Then he put his game face on and offered to get us a round of drinks.

"Make it a double," Maura demanded and Brennan went to the bar.

When he came back, he turned to my wife. "Got your dancing boots on, MacNeil?" She allowed as how she did. He swigged down his drink in two gulps and went for a second. A young man was playing ragtime on the piano.

I was thinking about Sandra's disappearance. If she had made the effort to see Brennan after all those years, why would she leave after exchanging only a few words with him? Was his new life so foreign to her that she felt they had nothing to say? I caught Rowan's eye and gathered that he too had been aware of Sandra's presence. I went around to his side of the table.

"What do you think?" I whispered. "Has she bolted?"

"Unlikely," Rowan replied. "Good manners, if nothing else, will ensure that she sees the evening through, now that she's made her appearance. Why not take a look outside? She may not know where we've all got to." I nodded, left the hall, and bounded down the steps. I was headed for the exit when Sandra came through the door in a rush of fresh, cool air.

"There you are, Monty! I had to run off to move my car after the performance. I'd left it in a no parking zone." She smiled at me and I put my arms around her.

"It's great to see you, Sandy. Let's go in."

"Is he here?"

"Yes, with the Strattons and my wife."

"You didn't tell me much about this wife of yours," Sandra remarked.

"Well, as I told you, we're . . ." I paused theatrically ". . . *estranged.*"

She put her hand on my arm and said in a British accent: "I do hope it won't be . . . awkward."

"It's been awkward for more years than I can remember."

Sandra and I pushed open the door and went into the big room. Brennan had a drink in his hand and was sharing a laugh with Maura. He looked at the door, and did a double take. Rowan, Sylvia and Maura all looked at the same time. I saw Sylvia lean over and speak to Maura, obviously filling her in. Brennan put his glass down and made a beeline for us.

"You two know each other?" he demanded, the penetrating dark eyes moving from Sandra to me. We nodded. "You've been holding out on me, Collins."

"You held out on me all year when I was trying to defend your honour, Burke."

"So, you've met before. Where?"

"New York," I answered.

"*What?* When was this?" He did not look pleased.

"Brennan. I was not going to get anything out of you. I had to know whatever the police were going to dig up in your background."

"You were probing into my life? Questioning Sandra?" The arms were crossed over the chest, the voice clipped. "I can't believe I'm hearing this."

"And I can't believe you're questioning his methods, Brennan," Sandra said, "given the outcome."

"Was this the time you and I were down there?" he asked. I nodded. "So you were with my . . . with Sandra, then you went out with me, and you never saw fit to mention it?"

"How would that have gone over, Brennan? Clearly, from what we've heard tonight, it would not have been well received."

"Why not? We could all have been together," he protested.

"Brennan," Sandra retorted, "use your head. We've been living on the island of Manhattan all our adult lives. We never got together in all that time. You forgot I was alive, till I showed up to watch you on stage tonight."

"I have never, ever forgotten you were alive, Sandra. I'm just curious about how much young Collins could cram into a three-day trip. He was a busy lad in New York."

"What did we do during Monty's visit, Brennan? We talked about you, but not only about you. We ate, drank, and had lots of laughs."

"Did you now."

"And Monty composed a piece of music for me that would put you, with your considerable talents, to shame."

"Is that so?"

"It is so. Shall we, Monty?"

"Shall we what?" Maura joined us in the middle of the room.

I made the introductions. "Sandra Worthington, Maura MacNeil. Sandra is visiting from New York." I knew Maura had heard all about Sandra from Sylvia Stratton. If she hadn't, her swift glance at Burke and then at Sandra would have told her all she needed to know. I said: "Sandra and I would like to share our song with you. Be sure to remind us."

"You and Sandra have a favourite song already?" my wife quipped. "I've never known you to move that fast, Collins. But there was a bit of a line-up at the bar, so I've been out of touch for a while."

"It's a long story and it didn't start here," I answered, with one of those "tell you later" looks with which long-married people, however unfriendly, are able to promise revelations at a more convenient time. We all went to our table and sat.

"Now Sandra," Maura demanded, turning to her new acquaintance, "fill us in on what you do in New York."

Sandra spoke of the school where she was headmistress. Brennan said she must be a brilliant teacher because she tutored him so well in high school math that he had aced his calculus exams in his first year in university.

"Anyone could have tutored him. All you had to do was sit him down at a table and make him open the book. Instead of the debauchery he engaged in every night. Amazing how the numbers clicked into place after that. Just had to keep him at it."

"Keep at it?" He leaned back in his chair and looked down his nose at her. "It wasn't always me who leaped up from the work table, suggesting a little R and R whenever your parents went out on one of their very frequent social engagements."

"I don't *leap* up from tables, Brennan, even, *especially*, in response to smouldering glances from black-eyed Irish reprobates. You must have me mixed up with one of your many other conquests."

"Not a chance. I see you've had your ears pierced since I saw you last," Burke said with a smile.

"That way I can keep my jewels on for the entire evening," she said with deceptive sweetness. I caught her eye. "Should I?" she asked me.

"Go ahead. I'll collect my royalties later."

She leaned towards Burke and sang:

> Woke up this morning, got yo' earring in my mouth.
> Said, woke up this morning, woman, got yo' earring in my mouth.
> You don't give me nothing else, babe, I take yo' diamonds and go south.

He looked nonplussed for a beat or two, then burst into laughter and spewed whiskey all over Maura's shirt. Maura, dabbing at the liquor dribbling down her front, looked delighted with the song.

Gratified by her little coup, Sandra tuned him out and gabbed with the Strattons about people and places they knew. She managed to give the impression that she had forgotten Burke's existence. Unfazed, he sat smiling at her. She and the Strattons discussed the future of the house in Chester. Rowan got up for another round of drinks and Burke asked for straight orange juice. He was sitting back lazily in his chair but his eyes were alert the whole time, rarely leaving Sandra's face. But then she stole a glance at her watch and announced: "I have to be going."

Brennan lurched forward in his seat. "Going? Where are you going?"

"Home," she answered.

"What? Home where?"

"Needs a geography tutor," she said to the table at large.

"You're going to New York? Now?" Disappointment battled with disbelief.

"Well, not directly. I'm flying out early in the morning, and I have to get back to Chester first, then . . ."

"You're going to drive to Chester at this time of night? You can't do that. It's snowing!"

"Brennan, how much have you had to drink?"

"Not enough."

"We're from New York, remember? It snows in New York."

"How much driving do you do in New York, in the snow? She follows a line of cabs from East Fifty-Ninth Street, Bloomingdale's," he said to us in explanation, "to the East Seventies and calls that driving. That's a far cry from motoring out into the country, to Chester, in the middle of the night in a fucking blizzard. Why not stay in Halifax?"

"You can stay at our place, darling," Sylvia offered.

"Thanks, Sylvia, but my bags are out at the cottage. I didn't know I'd be staying in the city so late . . ."

"All right. I'll drive you," Brennan announced.

"No you won't," Sandra shot back.

"Why not?"

"I'm not going out in the country, as you put it." She looked around at the rest of us. "There is land and there is water for Brennan. Water is the ocean, which he approves of and enjoys. Land consists of great soaring monuments to man's creativity. Again, he approves. He thinks any place with a population density of less than thirty thousand people per square mile is primeval forest, teeming with voracious animals and bugs and gun-toting, cross-eyed, inbred hunters. Go ahead, ask him."

"How do you know what I think?" he protested.

"People don't change," she intoned in the manner of a wise old woman.

"I defy you to name anyone who has changed more than I have!" he exclaimed.

"Anyway, Brennan, I'm not driving anywhere with you. You're drinking; you're probably over the limit."

"How many drinks did I have? Sandra, you're giving out to me as if I'm legless here."

"Brennan." Maura cut in, and only then did it strike me how odd it was to have an argument going full tilt without her in the middle of it. "Do you ever wonder what it would be like if you were married? Exactly like this. You two sound as if you've been married for centuries." He and Sandra looked accusingly at one another for several long seconds, then burst into laughter. I saw Rowan and Sylvia exchange glances.

Sandra reached over and touched Brennan's hand. "Do something for me, Bren, before I go. Sing for me."

"What would you like to hear?"

"Something Celtic."

"Make it something sorrowful while you're at it," Maura added, "since we just met Sandra and she's leaving us so *soon* when we would all be glad to help her make arrangements to *stay*. Something heart-scalding, as Brennan puts it."

Brennan looked at Maura. "I'll sing something so sad, it will tear the heart right out of you, throw it on the floor, pour scalding water all over it, and turf it out the door where it will be torn apart and eaten by jackals."

"Does this mean you're auditioning for my blues band?" I asked.

"These are the finer feelings I'm singing about, Collins. Nothing your little garage band could ever hope to express, musically or emotionally."

He went to the stage and checked the mike, picked up an acoustic guitar and adjusted its tuning, then sat down. "This is an Eric Bogle song, 'The Leaving of Nancy.'"

I thought someone had told me Brennan didn't play any instruments but he was doing a creditable pick and strum on the guitar.

Well, it wasn't the first time I had had to rethink what I knew of him, and it wouldn't be the last. After the first few lines, Sandra lowered her head onto her hand, her eyes downcast. The evocative words and melody, and the beautiful voice, combined for an effect close to what Brennan said it would be.

> My suitcase is lifted and stowed on the train,
> And a thousand regrets whirl around in my brain.
> And the ache in my heart, it's a black sea of pain.
> I'm leaving my Nancy-o.
> And you stand there so calmly, so lovely to see,
> But the grip of your hand is an unspoken plea.
> You're not fooling yourself and you're not fooling me.
> Goodbye my Nancy-o.

When the song was done he returned to the table, sat, folded his arms across his chest and regarded Sandra with hooded, dark eyes. She did not look up. Nobody had anything to say. Brennan rose, went to the bar for a shot of whiskey and downed it. Someone put recorded music on and we listened for a few minutes. Finally, Sandra stood and announced that she had to go. She said goodbye to us all and we asked her to stay in touch, meaning it.

Brennan got up with her. "One dance, and then you go. And be careful on that highway." We all looked on as they waltzed to the Rankins' gorgeous lament, "Fare Thee Well Love." They danced the way they argued, as if they'd been at it for a lifetime. When the music stopped, Sandra put her face up to his, kissed him on the cheek, and turned to leave. He pulled her back and wrapped his arms around her, covered her mouth with his, and kissed her passionately for several long minutes. Then she pulled away, turned and walked out the door. He stood there so long it seemed he had forgotten where he was. But then he came back to us, doing his level best to look as if nothing had happened.

Brennan, Maura, and I walked home in the gently falling snow. There wasn't a breeze.

Brennan looked up. "All right. So it's not a blizzard." Neither of us took the opportunity to needle him about it.

We stopped at the house on Dresden Row. It was plain that there was a whole world of conversation Maura wanted to explore but she was no fool; there were times when the best course of action was to say absolutely nothing about the subject on everybody's mind. She told Brennan she'd see him soon; she told me I should stay rather than drive and risk arrest; then she turned and went into the house.

Brennan and I started walking in the direction of St. Bernadette's; without any conscious thought, we kept going down Morris to Water Street and turned right. The cool air was invigorating and the light snow enchanting. "A walk in the snow has great significance in the culture of this country, you know," I told him.

"Prime Minister Pierre Trudeau," Brennan answered. Catching my look of surprise, he said: "I've always been a fan."

"Yes, I can see that you would be. He went for his walk in the snow and made his decision to retire from politics."

"And you're thinking I have some kind of decision to make?" he asked, and stopped to light up a smoke.

"Do you?" I stopped and waited.

"My decisions were made a long time ago, Monty." He inhaled deeply, blew out the smoke and resumed walking.

"So, what now?"

"Now that I've just been face to face with the woman I've loved all my life? What can I do?"

"Get O'Flaherty to don his wedding vestments?" I ventured.

"It's a temptation that's always out there, to chuck it all and get married. But as much as I would enjoy having a woman in my life, I know I would never be happy, or at least not for long, if I abandoned the priesthood. That would not be good for me or for the unfortunate bride. Whether I'm a good priest, or an obedient one, well, that's always an open question. There's the other unedifying option. Continue being a priest of the Church, with a mistress tucked away on the side."

"I know a little hideaway that may be coming on the market in Chester."

He shot me a look, then went on. "Wouldn't that be an enticing life to offer a woman. Sit by the phone and wait for those occasions when my testosterone levels are higher than my aspirations to a life of the spirit. The other choice is that I try to keep behaving myself, at least to the extent that I've been able to up to now. This whole presumptuous conversation, of course, ignores a key fact that was obvious to us all tonight. The woman we're alluding to couldn't wait to see the back of me."

"I don't think we can assume that, Brennan." He gave me a carefully neutral glance. "The fact that she had to leave tonight had nothing to do with you. She has an early flight, and her bags are in Chester."

"Still, she could have —"

"She could have stayed in Chester and not come to the city at all. But she came to see you. What more do you have to know? At least it gives you something to work with."

"The fact that she came to see me was likely nothing more than a friendly gesture."

I knew, but was not about to say, that Sandra had discovered something about him she had never suspected, that he had been at her side when she gave birth to their child. I knew this went a long way in softening her attitude towards him.

"Did you mean that, when you said you've loved her all your life?" I asked him.

"Why wouldn't I?"

"It's been more than twenty-five years, for one thing."

"What, you're thinking I'm fickle, along with all my other character flaws?" He looked amused.

"Well, things tend to fade over time. And you must have met other women who captured your attention. You haven't exactly lived in a cloister."

"It's no secret, *now,* that I've had the occasional involvement I shouldn't have had. But no serious threats to my vocation, or to my memories of Sandra." He brought the cigarette to his mouth and inhaled deeply. "Well, with one potential exception. Oh Christ. Sandra was right: I've had too much to drink."

"I've seen you worse and you didn't let a stray word escape your lips."

"Made weak by my affection."

"Marc Antony."

"I'll try to be more like Augustus." He pitched his cigarette to the snow-covered sidewalk and ground out it with his heel. "I'd better get home and sleep it all off."

I stood there thinking over his words. Who was the possible exception, or was it potential exception? Potentiality, actuality. Obviously, I had not yet recovered from the tensions of the past year, if I was wondering just how loaded the word "potential" was in the mind of one steeped in the metaphysics of St. Thomas Aquinas.

But Brennan had taken my arm and turned me in the direction of our respective houses. He said: "We were speaking of Sandra. And whether or not I might renew my acquaintance with her. Perhaps Father Burke and his attorney will pop in to see her when they go to New York. And take it from there."

"New York? What are you talking about?"

"You've just solved a murder case, Montague. So I'll give you a bit of time to relax before I present you with the next problem."

"Oh God, Brennan. Are you going to age me another ten years? What is it this time?"

"There's a very intriguing document I want you to look at. I think there's more to it than meets the eye. And the answer may lie in New York."

OBIT

a mystery

ANNE EMERY

Author of *Sign of the Cross*

March 3, 1991

The white-robed priest, murder charges now behind him, lifted his arms, and the building was filled with the music of the spheres. Candlelight illuminated the small Gothic church of Saint Bernadette's and flickered against the magnificent stained glass of its windows. My little daughter sat at my side, enthralled with the beauty and the sound. On my other side was my son and his beloved, herself a budding choir director; they too were enraptured. At the end of the row sat the mother of my children, the wife who no longer shared my home. Lost in the music. Lost to me.

We were transported back in time from the Renaissance to the medieval as we heard the famous Gregorian *Pater Noster,* the Our Father. It is said that Mozart, when asked which piece of music he would like to have composed, named this setting of the *Pater Noster.* At times like this, when the music seemed to shimmer between light and sound, between the earthly and the ineffable, I could almost understand how a priest could turn away from the pleasures of the flesh and marry his spirit with the divine. This particular priest had stumbled the odd time, as I well knew. As everyone knew, after the trial. But he had picked himself up, brushed the dust from his robes and carried on. The glory of this night, the first student concert he had put on since coming to the Saint Bernadette's Choir School as music director a year and half ago, would buoy him through the next two days until it was time to leave for New York, for a rendezvous with his former lover, and a probe into the enigmatic past of his redoubtable father. If we had been able to foretell the events of the coming weeks, perhaps we would have remained in the sanctuary, contemplating the infinite and ordering in.

*   *   *

March 4, 1991

"My old fellow aged ten years when he read this, Monty. See what you make of it."

The choirmaster was in my Halifax law office when I arrived the

1

Monday morning after the concert. In civilian clothes Brennan Burke had the appearance of a military man, one regularly chosen for clandestine, lethal operations. With his hooded black eyes, silver-threaded black hair and austere facial expression, he was a formidable presence. He spoke in a clipped voice reminiscent of Ireland, where he had lived until the age of ten. That is when his family had fled the old country for New York, for reasons that had never been explained. The priest had come to Halifax eighteen months ago, in the fall of 1989, to establish the choir school at Saint Bernadette's. It had been quite a time. He and I had met when he was charged with two counts of first degree murder in the deaths of two young women. I am happy to say I successfully defended him against the charges, and found the real killer, who is now serving a life sentence in prison. All in a day's work for Montague Collins, Barrister, Solicitor and sole criminal lawyer in the corporate law firm of Stratton Sommers.

The priest pulled a piece of paper from the inside pocket of his black leather jacket and slapped it on my desk, and I directed my attention to whatever it was that had taken ten years off the life of Declan Burke. It was an obituary from the *New York Times* dated December 4, 1990. Three months ago.

"My brother Patrick sent it to me. He was visiting our parents. The old fellow was trying to fix something under the sink, and my mother was doing her customary scan of the death notices. 'Declan!' she calls out. 'Do you know a Cathal Murphy? Came over here from Dublin around the same time we did.'

"My father comes in to the living room and takes a look at the obit. The way Patrick tells it, Declan turned white and grew old in the time it took to read it over. 'Da, what is it?' Patrick asks, and tries to get him into a chair. 'Your face has gone the colour of your hair.'

"All Pat gets by way of an answer is: 'I straightened up too fast. You'd be white too if you had your mug parked under a sink all afternoon, then had to stand to attention for another dead Murphy.' And he stalks from the room."

I put up my hand to silence Brennan so I could read the clipping.

CATHAL MURPHY, 73, of Sunnyside, Queens, and formerly of Dublin, Republic of Ireland. He immigrated to the US in 1950 after working in Ireland as a Businessman. What is less well known is that he put in many long and arduous hours doing Volunteer work as well. Here in the US, Cathal quickly made a name for himself in the export business. His loyalty to his Uncle was never in question. He is survived by his devoted wife Maria, and his sons Tom, Brendan, Stanley and Armand. Predeceased by his brother Benedict and stepson Stephen. Those of us who had the privilege of knowing Cathal knew a man who enjoyed a good time, who was never shy about sharing a song or a drink. And if you said no, Cathal would share it with you anyway! He'll be sorely missed. When the members of a generation pass away, the family is often left with little more than its memories; the telling details are locked away in a trunk and never get out of the attic. A better way — Cathal's way — was to celebrate and live the past as if it formed part of the present, as indeed it does. He was fond of saying "nothing ever goes away." You're right, Cathal. Your spirit lives on in our hearts. We'll all be there to see you off, Cathal, dressed to the nines and raising a pint of Lameki Jocuzasem in your honor! Funeral arrangements will be announced when finalized.

Brennan resumed speaking the second my eyes looked up from the clipping. "How often would you say 'Republic of' in something like this?"

"Let me stop you for a second. What is it that has everyone upset? Is this someone your father knew? Someone he had a history with?"

Burke jabbed the paper with his forefinger. "What Patrick thinks, and I'm following him there myself, is that our father read this as —" he cleared his throat "— as an indictment of his own life. And an announcement of his death."

"What?" I exclaimed.

"Volunteer," he said then. "It's capitalized."

"So's 'Businessman.' You should see what gets capitalized here in the office. Lawyer, Adjuster, Report . . ."

He ignored me. "The Irish Volunteers. *Óglaigh na hÉireann*, the IRA. That much is clear. All the more so when the word 'Uncle' is added. My father's father and his uncles were known to have played a role in the 1916 uprising. 'He is survived by his devoted wife Maria.' Maria, a name that could be Spanish like my mother's name, Teresa. As you know, she had a Spanish father, Irish mother. A possibility. We're told he was also survived by his sons Tom, Brendan, Stanley and Armand." He looked at me. "Those four names. Does anything strike you about them?"

"No. Aside from the fact they are all men's names, and one of them sounds like yours — but isn't — I don't see a pattern. They're not even all Irish."

"Right, but Tommy, Bren —" He paused. I waited. "Guns, Collins."

"Brennan, for Christ's sake! This just doesn't sound like you. I can imagine your reaction if someone else came up with this, this —"

"Fantasy, you're thinking. I know, but Patrick and I both think there's something here and he's not a fey kind of man either. And we weren't stocious drunk when we spoke about this on the phone. So bear with me. Tommy gun, Bren gun, Sten gun, Armalite rifle."

"Brennan," I began and put up my hand to fend off an interruption. "Surely it has occurred to you that you may be reading something into this, something that is not really there."

"It has occurred to me. I've dismissed that notion. It's here, I know it." He paused to take out a pack of cigarettes from his jacket pocket. I had given up telling him that Stratton Sommers was a smoke-free office; he found the ashtray I kept for him, lit up a smoke, and returned to his train of thought. "Predeceased by his brother Benedict and by his stepson Stephen. Now, disregard those two names for a moment. I admit they throw me off, because my father did not have a brother who died, and he certainly does not have a stepson."

I shook my head, moved the paper closer with my finger and skimmed the obituary again. "I'm more interested in the pint of 'Lameki Jocuzasem.' What in the hell is that?"

"No idea. Doesn't sound like a local brew, does it? Let's stop by the Midtown Tavern and ask one of the waiters."

"Let's not. I'd like to be able to show my face in there again some day. And the day after that."

What I did not say was that I would like to enjoy the upcoming New York trip my family and I had planned with Brennan Burke. He had been asked to officiate at the wedding of his niece, Katie, and he decided to extend his visit for a few weeks. I hoped his distraction over the death notice would be short-lived. Brennan certainly needed a break, after the year he'd just had. And I could use a rest as well. My holiday was to start the very next day. I had leapt at the chance of a month in New York when a complicated products liability suit had been settled on the courthouse steps, affording me the gift of several weeks with no obligations. I was determined to take advantage of the free time. My wife, Professor Maura MacNeil, had strong-armed someone into taking over her classes at Dalhousie Law School for three weeks, so we could give our kids a trip to New York City.

I mentioned my wife; I should have said "estranged wife." But I'm not one to give up easily. I saw the vacation as an opportunity to put an end to years of squabbling and living in separate houses. After all, if I could oversee the settlement of years of squabbling and costly litigation between the consumers, suppliers and manufacturers of defective concrete, which had caused the foundations of two hundred new houses to sink and crumble, how difficult would it be to charm my own wife back into my loving embrace?